SECRETS

BOOK 2 OF THE JONATHAN SCANLAN SERIES

SECRETS

BARRY
SOLLOWAY

Library of Congress Control Number: 2025919437
Paperback ISBN: 979-8-9930967-04
Digital Book ISBN: 979-8-9930967-1-1

Pinted in the USA

For Amanda and Kate

CHAPTER 1

Jonathan Scanlan rarely strayed from his morning routine. After shaving and showering, he settled in with coffee, juice, and the *San Francisco Chronicle*. Jonathan found the newspaper's unrepentantly liberal bias mildly off-putting, but for local news and the current happenings of his beloved 49ers, Warriors, Giants, and University of California teams, it was the only game in town.

Today's paper offered scant news of interest; the unending squabble among the city's supervisors, the inability of the police to halt the auto break-in problem, and whether sugar-heavy soft drinks should be banned occupied the front page. Jonathan skipped to the Sporting Green section and was reading an article evaluating the quality of the last year's 49er draft picks when an incoming call broke his concentration. A glance at the screen showed the call was from his close friend, Cal Hulse.

Jonathan knew Cal was a night person and was surprised his friend was up this early in the morning. "Morning, Cal. What's up?"

Hulse laughed. "You mean other than me. I pulled an all-nighter finishing a project for INA. I'm about to sack out, but how about catching a drink later?"

"Sure, Waterbar?"

"Too many tourists this time of year. How about Palomino at eight o'clock?"

"You're on."

Jonathan and Cal were a study in contrasts. Jonathan was tall and athletic, while Cal was a man of medium height, plump, and one who believed jogging to be a masochistic experience. They met at the University of California, Berkeley, where both were on full-ride scholarships, Jonathan for golf and Cal academic. In many ways an odd couple, but best friends through college and beyond.

When Jonathan's attempts to qualify as a PGA touring pro failed, he returned to the university for his Master's and PhD, which led to his teaching position at San Francisco State University.

Cal Hulse turned his unique programming and problem-solving talents into becoming one of the computer industry's most sought-after consultants.

Jonathan spent two hours grading papers for his contemporary American literature class. For a period of several months, he had been placed on paid leave when he was being investigated as a person of interest by the FBI over what the media called the *Culprit Murders*. While Jonathan had been cleared of any involvement in the killings, his fellow faculty members still viewed him with suspicion. Several, including the head of his department, campaigned to have Jonathan fired, and only the threat of a lawsuit allowed for his reinstatement. It also did not help that Jonathan was a conservative in a sea of progressives.

As Jonathan drove across the city to the state college, he acknowledged to himself that he was drifting from day to day without much direction. The enthusiasm he had felt when first presenting his course had faded with the acceptance that the vast majority of his students couldn't care less about Hemingway, Steinbeck, and Faulkner.

Jonathan arrived at Palomino to find Cal, dressed in his typical 49er sweatshirt and baggy Dockers, seated on one of the outdoor cushioned sofas, sipping a pale- colored drink in a sugar-rimmed martini glass. Jonathan pointed to the drink. "What is that?"

"It's called a French Seventy-Five."

"You're sure it's legal for a man to order one of those things?"

Hulse smiled. The waitress didn't even blink."

"Careful, they're going to be pulling your man card."

Cal shrugged and looked across the small table at his friend. "You seem to be running a little low."

Jonathan took a sip from his newly arrived beer. "Just bored. I'm teaching a bunch of kids who have no interest in literature, and I've been trying to write, but nothing is coming out. It doesn't help that my colleagues at State look at me and see a far-Right nutjob that was probably involved somehow in the murders."

"What about Carmen?" Carmen Costello had been the FBI agent given the task of keeping Jonathan under surveillance when he was considered a person of interest. As the investigation progressed, Carmen's involvement evolved, as did her relationship with Jonathan.

Jonathan glanced away before returning to his friend's gaze. "Our off-the-book efforts helped her career... but not our relationship. She's now assigned to the LA office. We're not seeing much of each other."

Cal thought for a moment. He hated to see his friend going through a hard time and tried to think of a way to perk him up. "You said nothing's working on the writing front?"

When Jonathan nodded, a thought came to Cal. "You're trying to write fiction because of the comments by that critic at the *New York Times*, right?"

Jonathan agreed but had no idea where his friend was going.

"Why not go back to nonfiction? It worked very well for you with *Culprits*."

Jonathan smiled and shook his head. "We both know the only reason the book did well was because it was used as a guide for the murders. Its success had nothing to do with my literary prowess."

Cal became more animated, waving his arms as he made his point. "Don't sell yourself short, Jon. And don't lose sight of the fact that you now have a name."

"Okay, but what would I write about? I started a book about

political correctness in the country, but I quit when I realized it was dull as dirt."

"Why not write about how we solved the *Culprit* murders?"

Jonathan pushed back in his seat and stared at his friend. "If I did that, you would be in jail, Carmen would be fired and our friends at Lockheed would probably lose their security clearances."

Cal waved away Jonathan's comment. "Change the names. Don't mention Carmen's involvement. She helped, but she really wasn't how we figured it out."

Jonathan sat forward in his chair, his features showing both his interest and his skepticism. "The FBI really wouldn't want the full story to come out."

Cal laughed. "So what? They can't stop you, and if they tried, think of the publicity that would bring. They never told the public what really happened. They took credit and basically covered it up."

Jonathan was lost in thought for several minutes. When he surfaced, he smiled at Cal. "It wouldn't be hard to write."

Cal ordered another drink and turned to Jonathan. "Think the Warriors can go all the way again?"

CHAPTER 2

Jonathan immersed himself in the project. The book followed the timeline of the events, starting with the series of murders. He found the book almost wrote itself. Most of his writing efforts were spent trying to allow the reader to understand the characters as they entered the story. In three months, he had a rough draft ready for the skilled hands of his editor.

He considered contacting a new literary agent, but loyalty prevailed. Jonathan really did not like Harvey Ballow, but he had been the only agent willing to represent his earlier book, *Culprits of the American Culture*.

Jonathan cringed when Ballow's Boston Brahman voice answered the phone. Jonathan could picture the man wearing an ascot. "Harvey Jonathan Scanlan. I have a new book getting ready to go."

There was an awkward pause on the line. While the agent certainly made serious money on *Culprits*, he never believed the book's commercial success had anything to do with Jonathan's writing skills. "Can I ask what the book is about?"

"Of course, it's about the *Culprit* murders."

Ballow was silent for a moment. When he responded, there was a heavy layer of skepticism in his voice. "Why would you write about the killings? It was the FBI who solved the crimes."

"No, Harvey. It was my friends and I who figured out who was behind the murders."

"I don't understand." Jonathan could hear a heavy level of skepticism in the agent's voice.

Jonathan sighed. He never enjoyed dealing with the man. Bellow had an inflated sense of self-importance. "I'll send you a copy of the draft. The edit should be completed in about two weeks. Let me know if you'll represent the book; if you don't, I'll shop around for another agent."

Jonathan had done little more than eat, sleep, teach his course, and write for months. Normally, his life included exercise and a reasonably active social life. With the completion of the book, he realized he had gained weight and fallen out of shape. After a moment's hesitation, Jonathan changed into shorts, a T-shirt, and running shoes. When he jogged downhill from his apartment toward the Marina Green, his lack of conditioning quickly became apparent. Jonathan was wheezing like a broken-down school bus by the time he reached Lombard.

Harvey Ballow called Jonathan two weeks later. The message on his machine was far from enthusiastic. "Ballow here. I have a publisher willing to put out the book. They're talking about a minimal print run and no advance."

Jonathan returned the call and smiled as he recorded his reply. "Thank you, Harvey. Please be informed that you are no longer my agent."

He looked at his watch. It was still working hours on the East Coast. While a minimal marketing effort had been exerted to promote *Culprits,* Jonathan had gone to a number of book signings and, as a result, had met several other authors and a few literary agents. He had been impressed by one of the agents, a woman named Mary Downs.

A woman's voice greeted Jonathan after the second ring. "Downs Literary Agency."

"May I please speak with Mary Downs?"

"This is Mary."

"I don't know if you remember me. Jonathan Scanlan, we met at a book signing in Denver."

"Of course, I remember you. Congratulations on your book. I saw it made the best-seller list."

Jonathan was tempted to mention that *Culprits's* success had little to do with his talent as a writer but let the thought pass. "Thank you. Mary, I have a new book that's just finished being edited. Would you be interested in representing it?"

There was a pause on the line. "Don't you have an agent?"

"I did, Harvey Ballow, but he's no longer my agent."

"What is the new book about?" Jonathan could not tell if the agent was positive or negative about Jonathan as a new client.

"I don't know if you followed what the press labeled the *Culprit Murders,* but the FBI considered me to be a person of interest for quite a while. The book is about the crimes and how my friends and I figured out who was behind the killings."

Mary was again silent for a moment. "You and your friends solved the crimes?" Jonathan could hear the doubt in her voice.

"Yes, we did."

"Send me the book. I'll be back to you in about ten days."

Two days later, Jonathan arrived early for his class at State and was about to pour himself a cup of coffee in the cafeteria when Emily Martin, the dean's assistant, approached him.

"Mr. Scanlan, Dean Belknap wants to see you."

"Morning, Emily. Can it wait? I only have a few minutes before my class."

Jonathan could tell from the assistant's expression that she was extremely uncomfortable. "He said he had to see you now."

Jonathan shook his head, replaced his empty cup, and followed the woman out of the cafeteria and down the hall to Dean Robert Belknap's office. With Jonathan delivered, Ms. Martin scurried away. Jonathan's relationship with the dean was one of mutual dislike. Belknap was an ardent progressive and believed anyone to the right of center to be a fool or mentally challenged. He also had fought Jonathan's reinstatement when Jonathan was cleared by the FBI. The man still believed his contemporary English literature professor had played a role in the *Culprit* killings.

When Jonathan entered the dean's office, he stood inside the doorway, waiting to be acknowledged. The heavy-set, balding man continued to read from a file on his desk. After several minutes, he looked up over his wire-rimmed glasses and waved Jonathan toward one of the visitor's chairs. From his expression, Jonathan assumed Belknap had just swallowed something extremely bitter.

"Mr. Scanlan, it has been brought to my attention that you have been behaving inappropriately toward one of your female students."

The statement rendered Jonathan momentarily speechless. After staring at the man across the desk, he felt the anger rising within him. "Who is saying I've been acting inappropriately?"

"I'm not going to divulge the person's name."

Jonathan stared into the dean's watery blue eyes. "This is all bullshit."

Jonathan could see the color rising in Dean Belknap's cheeks. "How dare you question me."

"How dare you abuse your authority. I have a class to teach." Jonathan stood and moved toward the door.

"I can suspend you." Belknap was so agitated that Jonathan wondered if he might have a stroke, a thought he considered with mixed feelings.

Jonathan turned back toward the dean. "And I can sue your ass off." Feeling somewhat better, Jonathan walked out of the office and made his way to his classroom.

CHAPTER 3

Jonathan waited for the other shoe to drop, perhaps a disciplinary hearing or a notice that he was again suspended, but none occurred. He occasionally gave thought to quitting his teaching position, but each time the idea was quickly dismissed. While *Culprits* had been extremely successful, Jonathan was unsure how much he could depend upon income from his literary career. While his teaching salary was unimpressive, it did pay the rent.

He arrived home after a particularly uninspiring day at State and noticed the message light was on his phone. He picked up to find a requested call back from Mary Downs, hopefully his new agent.

Mary picked up on the second ring. "Jonathan, I have good news. We have an offer to publish *The Culprit Murders* at Dell.

"That's fantastic. What size is the print run?"

"Thirty thousand. I know, we'd like a bigger run, but they did agree to spend a decent amount on promotion."

Jonathan had been hoping the success achieved by *Culprits of the American Culture* would translate to a larger print run for the current book, but he did not want to rain on Mary's parade. "Great news."

"If the book sells, I'm sure there'll be a second printing."

Following publication, Jonathan's book was greeted with lukewarm interest. Dell spent a modest amount of promotional money on *The*

Culprit Murders at the time of the initial launch, which created the smallest of ripples in the literary community.

Mary Downs lined up a series of book signings. The out-of-town events were scheduled during San Francisco State's Easter break. Jonathan had hoped the success of his first book would propel him into the 'well-known author' category. It appeared *The Culprit Murders* would not be riding on the earlier book's coattails.

Jonathan's first book signing was at Book Passages in Corte Madera, just north of San Francisco in Marin County. The bookstore had an extensive mailing list and actively promoted authors and their products. While the signing was reasonably well attended, Jonathan found himself bored to tears. He signed and sold thirty books and hoped he did not have to show up at a thousand signings to meet the print run.

When Jonathan returned home, he went to his desk and rummaged through the collection of debris. Languishing under a pile of forgettable notes and other things that should have been thrown away years ago, he found the card. Nicholas Abendroth, the literary critic from the *New York Times*, who had interviewed Jonathan when *Culprits* became a hot property. The interview and book review had been generally complimentary, with a few negative comments to appease the paper's left-of-center readership.

It was too late to contact the critic in New York, so Jonathan placed the card near his phone as a reminder to call first thing in the morning. He went to bed wondering if Abendroth would even take his call.

Jonathan woke early, hurried through his morning routine, and dialed the number on Abendroth's card. Not surprisingly, the call was answered by one of the critic's assistants. "Nicholas Abendroth's office."

"Mr. Abendroth, please."

"May I ask your name and what this is regarding?" Jonathan moaned silently, the gatekeeper.

"Jonathan Scanlan. Nicholas interviewed me several months ago."

"And the reason you wish to speak with Mr. Abendroth?"

Jonathan mentally shrugged; he might as well tell the truth. "I have a new book out and I'll be doing a signing in New York next week. I was hoping to get together with Nicholas." Hoping that using the critic's first name might help.

"May I have your number? I'll give Mr. Abendroth the message."

Jonathan gave the critic's office his cell number and, as he prepared for his upcoming classes, he wondered what the odds would be for a return phone call, perhaps one in ten?"

Nicholas Abendroth ran through his phone messages as he prepared to leave the office. The vast majority were from aspiring authors begging for a review. He had the power to make or break an unknown author, a power he accepted but never abused. He stopped when he came to the message from Jonathan. Abendroth sat back in his chair and recalled their meeting in San Francisco. The thing that impressed him was the unabashed honesty with which Scanlan had stated that the commercial success of his book had little if anything to do with his writing skills. In a sea filled with oversized egos and writers with unrealistic opinions of their talent, Scanlan was a rarity.

Abendroth picked up the phone.

Jonathan had finished his second class and was walking to his car when his cell chirped. A glance at the screen told him it was coming from New York. "Hello, Jonathan Scanlan here."

"Good afternoon, Jonathan, Nicholas Abendroth."

Jonathan was sure his heart skipped a few beats. "Hi, Mr. Abendroth, how have you been?"

"Just fine, Jonathan. Your message says you have a new book out and that you're coming to the Big Apple."

"Yes, I have a signing at Barnes and Noble on May fourth."

"What's the book about?"

"I'm afraid I'm going to disappoint you. You said I should try fiction. Well, I tried and nothing came out, so I went back to nonfiction. The book tells the story of the *Culprit* murders."

"I know the killings were in the same sequence as they appeared in your book, but why would you have enough material to write a book about it?"

"Because my friends and I uncovered the person behind the murders."

There was a significant pause. "Really?"

"Yes, Nicholas, really. I'll send you a copy. I obviously hope you like it."

"I look forward to receiving it. Talk to you later."

No commitment to write a review, but way further down the path then Jonathan had considered possible.

———

Jonathan did not subscribe to the *New York Times,* so, with fingers crossed, he went online every day to see if his book had been reviewed. Three days before he was scheduled to leave for his New York signing *The Culprit Murders* appeared in Nicholas Abendroth's section. The review complimented Jonathan's writing talent and said that it was a good read. The review hedged when stating that it was an accurate description of what actually happened.

Abendroth's review had the desired effect. Sales jumped. The entertainment section of local newspapers featured the book, mostly unfavorably, as it did not sit well with their Left-leaning belief system, but buzz was buzz. It would be an exaggeration to say it was the hot topic around the water cooler, but the thirty thousand print run appeared safely in view.

More free publicity arrived when William Palacin, the director of the FBI, issued a statement saying the book was highly inaccurate. When asked to explain what really happened and how the book was inaccurate, the director claimed that national security interests were at stake and he could not, therefore, provide additional information. This triggered the BS meter for those following the matter and enhanced the book's credibility.

Jonathan was packing for his trip to New York when he received a call. "Mr. Scanlan?"

"Speaking."

"I'm a program manager at Fox. Would you be willing to come to New York and to be a guest on the *Hannity Show*?"

Jonathan was momentarily stunned. "I'd love to be on the show. When did you have in mind?"

"We have you tentatively scheduled for April twenty-third."

"Any chance to move it up? I'm coming to New York this week to do a book signing on April sixteenth."

There was silence on the line for a moment. "Okay, I think I can squeeze you in on Friday the eighteenth. I'll call you back with the details."

As soon as his conversation with the program manager ended, Jonathan called Cal Hulse. Knowing his friend never picked up, he waited for voicemail to kick in. "Cal, call me. I'm treating for dinner."

———

If the attendance at the New York book signing was any indication of overall book sales, things were definitely on the right track. The event had been scheduled for two hours, but to satisfy the line of book buyers, Jonathan was pinned at his table for over four hours.

Fox had offered to pay for Jonathan's hotel. He had originally reserved a room at the Marriott near Times Square. With Fox picking up the tab, he canceled the Marriott and reserved a room at the Waldorf Astoria. He wondered if Fox would be picking up room service.

Jonathan arrived at the studio an hour early with nerves as tight as a piano wire. A woman named Lisa greeted him and led him to a side room where another woman applied a light brush of makeup. It quickly became apparent that one of Lisa's duties was to calm the guests when they arrived in an agitated state. By the time Jonathan was led into the area being filmed, he had regained the power of speech. He could feel himself sweating as he sat at the desk across from the host.

Hannity could sense Jonathan's tension. He offered his

professional smile and extended his hand. He also hoped that the interview would not be a disaster.

"We'd like to welcome Professor Jonathan Scanlan, the author of *The Culprit Murders*."

"Thank you for having me on."

"What motivated you to write the story behind the series of killings?"

Jonathan offered a weak smile. "As you probably know, the killings followed the sequence in which the public figures appeared in my book, *Culprits of the American Culture*. Without any leads, the FBI considered me to be a person of interest. I was under surveillance twenty-four hours a day, and I was suspended from my teaching job at San Francisco State University. I also became one of the killer's targets."

"Your new book appears to have created a good deal of controversy. The other day, the director of the FBI claimed that what you wrote was inaccurate."

Jonathan shook his head. "The FBI was embarrassed. They were getting nowhere. The director claimed he could not discuss what really happened because of national security interests. There were no national security interests involved. The book describes how my friends and I figured out who was behind the murders."

"I was going to ask you about your friends. Can you tell us who they are? In the book, you state that the names used are fictitious."

"Five of my friends helped to clear my name and solve the crimes. They don't wish to be identified."

"Well, it's a really good read. What's next for Professor Scanlan?"

"Back to teaching and, I guess, trying to write another book."

"Thank you so much for coming on the show."

"It was my pleasure."

Jonathan was barely aware of the cab ride back to his hotel, so lost in thought as he evaluated his appearance on the show. Overall, he mentally gave himself a B minus.

CHAPTER 4

Jonathan arrived home to find a dozen messages on his phone. The most significant was from Mary Downs, telling him Dell was running a second printing of his book. A few messages were from friends congratulating him on his Hannity interview, and one was from Cal telling him their poker game was set for Wednesday. Jonathan smiled at the thought of getting together with his friends.

Jonathan arrived at Cal's condominium on Pacific Avenue well before the other players. The spacious two-bedroom unit was heavily decorated with sports paraphernalia. Signed Joe Montana and Steve Young jerseys were flanked by two from Jerry Rice, one from his glory days with the Niners and one when he played for the Raiders. Football helmets and signed baseballs rested on stands alongside framed programs signed by Palmer, Player, Nicklaus, and Tiger. As Cal laid out snacks for the players, Jonathan wandered through the condo. A large flat screen was featuring highlights from the prior year's playoff games. Jonathan wondered if Cal ever tuned to anything but ESPN.

"Anything new?" Jonathan waved at the collection.

Cal shook his head. "Not yet. I have an offer out for one of the balls Madison Bumgarner pitched to win the series."

"How much does something like that cost?"

Hulse smiled. "If you have to ask, you can't afford it."

Unlike his friend, Jonathan had no interest in sports collectibles. Trophies from his days as a high school baseball player and as the most talented golfer on the University of California's golf team collected dust in his bedroom closet. Cal, on the other hand, was consumed by his collection, sports trivia, and complex computer programming. As a freelance rock star problem solver for many of the country's tech companies, Hulse had more than enough income to feed his collection.

Cal had just finished laying out an unhealthy array of chips and dips when Greg Stokes arrived. Greg was a nationally recognized research biologist employed by Genentech. He and Cal launched into a discussion over a recently published paper that predicted behavior characteristics based on human protein analysis. Carlos Hermosillo, the lead physicist heading a research project at Stanford, was next to join the group. Alan Thielen and Harold Kurtovich were the last to arrive. Alan and Harold worked at Lockheed on advanced weapon design. Jonathan sat in Cal's favorite chair as he observed the group. As the only member of the poker gang possessing a relatively normal level of intelligence, he was amused and somewhat intimidated by the sheer brilliance contained in the group. The poker players had originally been put together as a collection of Cal's friends, but through the *Culprits's* experience, Jonathan now felt close to each of the men.

Hulse was dressed in his usual baggy shorts and a well-worn sweatshirt, while the others appeared to have shopped at a thrift shop before leaving home. Stripes and plaids were well represented, unfortunately, on the same individuals. Another characteristic common to the group was their abysmal ability to play poker. Harry Kurtovich was unreasonably committed to a probability theory that did not appear to apply to poker, while Alan became highly agitated when he was dealt a decent hand. Greg would either fold too soon or try to run a bluff without any chance of pulling it off. Carlos utilized an incomprehensively complex decision theory in his game, and Cal remained in losing hands too long. While the stakes were nickel, dime, and quarter Jonathan was virtually guaranteed to walk away with most of the money.

A great deal of the discussion around the table focused on Jonathan's appearance on Hannity's show. They all wanted to know every detail of his brief interview.

The game was always called at ten o'clock. As the players were cashing in what was left of their chips, Cal turned to Jonathan. "Can you hang out for a bit? Something I want to talk to you about."

Jonathan simply nodded.

Cal went into the kitchen and retrieved two cold ones. "Spending any of your royalties?"

"I bought a set of the new Callaways."

Hulse laughed. "Most people that come into a pile of money start spending it as fast as it comes in. Travel, expensive toys, maybe a new home. At least you're using my investment guy rather than having it sit in your checking account."

Jonathan shrugged. "I don't really need anything."

"Why don't you buy a condo in the city rather than pay your landlord rent every month?"

Jonathan considered his friend's advice. "I guess I never gave it any thought. Don't you have to be a grown-up to own a home?"

Cal smiled. "No, and you don't have to pass a test. Actually, given what happened in the housing bubble, maybe they should have one. There's a great realtor I know. Why don't I give her a call?"

Jonathan began shaking his head. The last thing he wanted was to be hounded by an aggressive realtor. "Let me think about it. I'll let you know if I want to consider it."

Jonathan loved where he lived. His apartment on Green was one block from one of the most active areas of the city. One of the disadvantages of Cow Hollow's popularity was the difficulty involved in finding street parking. It took three circles through the neighborhood before he was able to find an available space. He made a mental note to himself to use a piece of his newfound wealth to rent a garage. Jonathan's mind was elsewhere as he approached the entrance to his building, forcing him to stop abruptly as a man blocked his passage.

"Evening, Jon."

It took a moment for Jonathan to recognize his brother. "What—what do you want?"

"Is that any way to greet a brother?" Not asked as a question. Jonathan could see the arrogant expression on his younger brother's face in the muted streetlight. The animosity between the siblings had been long-lasting and, at times, violent.

"What do you want, Rick?"

"You haven't been answering my calls."

"Didn't you get the hint? I don't want anything to do with you." Jonathan stepped back, anticipating the wild swing that often initiated the family meetings; instead his brother seemed to relax.

Rick offered an insincere smile. "Come on, bro. Let's forget all that. Say, with all the money you made off your book, how come you still live in this dump?" He waved vaguely toward the six-unit Victorian building behind him.

"I like it here. Get out of the way, I'm going in."

Rick hesitated, then stepped back. "I have a problem, Jon. I need your help."

"You always have a problem, Rick. Tell your story to someone else." Jonathan moved past his brother toward the building's entrance.

"Jon, these are bad guys." The arrogant attitude was gone, replaced with a note of pleading.

"Not my problem."

Jonathan stopped and turned back to his brother when Rick said, "Actually, it's also your problem."

"What are you talking about?"

"Look, I had a plan to make a lot of money, but things didn't turn out too well. I borrowed from these guys."

A lifetime of seeing his brother always take the easy road, the quick path to the big bucks that never materialized, flashed through

Jonathan's mind. The borrowings from their parents that were never repaid. "Tough shit, Rick. I'm going to bed."

"Jon, I just said it's our problem." Some of the stiffness came back in Rick's voice.

Jonathan waited for the rest to come out. "They know you're my brother. They know you have enough money to bail me out."

As Jonathan put his key in the front door, Rick called out. "These are bad guys, Jon. They're not going to go away."

Jonathan found sleep elusive. The exchange with his brother played through his mind, calling back their last meeting. Three years earlier, Jonathan found out that Rick had obtained access to their parents' retirement account and had relieved it of nearly a hundred thousand dollars. The ensuing confrontation had left Jonathan with bruised ribs and Rick with a broken jaw. He had not spoken to his brother since.

After another depressing day at State, Jonathan began circling the neighborhood in search of a parking space. While he was willing to pay an unreasonable amount for a garage in the area, none seemed to be available. As a result, it had taken twenty minutes before he could jump on a space being vacated. Jonathan walked toward his apartment with his mind a mile away and failed to notice a huge man stepping out of the shadows to block his path. The man was at least two inches taller than Jonathan and outweighed him by seventy pounds, all of which appeared to be solid muscle. Jonathan did not believe the man was with the Jehovah's Witnesses.

"Mr. Scanlan?" The man's tone was neither threatening nor friendly.

When Jonathan did not answer, the man showed him a copy of *Culprits of the American Culture* with Jonathan's picture on the back cover. Jonathan noticed that at least the man had purchased the hard bound copy. He also was confident that if things went downhill, he could easily outrun the big man.

"What can I do for you?"

"I've been sent to collect the amount your brother owes my employer." The man spoke in a neutral, businesslike voice.

"I already told Rick that I wasn't going to bail him out." As Jonathan spoke, he edged away slightly, giving him a little more room if running became the viable option.

"I understand you could cover the debt without it really impacting you financially."

Jonathan shook his head. "Not going to happen. So, what happens next? You do your leg-breaking thing?"

The man laughed. "I consider what I do more in the motivational arena."

Jonathan looked at the man for a moment. "Look, why don't we go down to Starbucks. Buy you a coffee?"

The offer surprised the man. This was not how his collection activity usually went. "Sure."

The two men walked in silence to the coffee house on Union and Laguna. When they approached the counter to order, Jonathan's new companion ordered a venti latte. The place was only half full, and they were able to find seating away from the other patrons.

Jonathan watched the man sip his drink. "So, like I asked, what happens next?"

The man shrugged. "I'll tell the powers that be that working you over won't get us our money and would probably put me in jail. So, you're not going to pay, and your brother doesn't have any money. We'll probably just write it off. I imagine your brother will get roughed up as an object lesson. We'll keep track of him, and if he ever has any money, we'll be there. I take it, you and your brother aren't close. By the way, we don't break legs. Do you know how difficult it is to break a leg?"

"Ah… no. And no, Rick and I aren't close."

The man across from Jonathan nodded. "By the way, I thought your book was great. Would you autograph my copy?"

The man smiled at Jonathan's expression. "You can be a thug and still appreciate a good book."

Jonathan took the book and opened the cover. "Who should I thank for buying *Culprits*?

"Myron Rossi. I guess we haven't been formally introduced as they say." Myron reached across the small table and shook Jonathan's hand. Jonathan's hand was like a child's as it was engulfed by Myron's. Thankfully, the big man exerted very little pressure.

The two men walked back to Jonathan's apartment and Myron's car in a comfortable silence. Before getting into his rental, Myron again shook Jonathan's hand and gave him a business card. "Who knows? Someday you might need someone like me."

Later, Jonathan looked at the card. Myron's title appeared as a motivational specialist

The following afternoon, Jonathan was changing into his running gear when his cell rang. He picked up when he saw it was Mary Downs. "Afternoon, Mary."

"Just wanted to give you a quick update on your book. It's selling well, and they're thinking of doing another print run. It isn't in best-seller territory, but it's not too far off. Have you given any thought to having an audio version produced?"

"I guess I never considered it."

"Let me put some numbers together and we'll see how they look. I have a great guy to do the work if we want to go that route."

Jonathan was smiling as he was leaving his apartment. Everything is going so well; how could anything go wrong?

CHAPTER 5

A cold wind was blowing in from the west when Jonathan parked in the faculty parking lot. He swore he could taste the salt from the nearby ocean as he turned up the collar of his coat and walked quickly into his building. He was checking his inbox for messages when Emily Martin approached.

Keeping her eyes directed toward her shoes, she whispered so faintly that Jonathan had to ask her to repeat what she had said.

"You're wanted at a meeting in the conference room next to President Woods's office." With the message delivered, Ms. Martin turned and walked away at just below a jogging pace.

Knowing from experience it was not going to be an awards ceremony, Jonathan walked over to the administrative building. When he entered the conference room, he was not surprised to see familiar faces. Irene Woods sat at the head of the table, flanked by Dean Robert Belknap and Virginia Tindall, the head of Human Resources. A man of middle age, wearing an expensive suit, sat next to Tindall. Jonathan did not bother to acknowledge the group as he took a seat several spaces away from the foursome.

Irene Woods was the first to speak. "Professor Scanlan, a serious accusation has been brought to our attention. One of our students has accused you of inappropriate sexual behavior."

Jonathan could see his department head trying to hold back a smile. "I have no idea what you're talking about."

"We have zero tolerance for these matters."

"Who made this accusation?"

"Our policies do not allow us to release that information."

Jonathan could feel the anger building. "I deny the charge."

The college president ignored Jonathan's response. "On the advice of our legal counsel, you are suspended until a hearing can resolve the matter." She nodded her head toward the man in the expensive suit.

Jonathan tried to control his voice. "President Woods, we've been down this road before, and if you recall, it didn't end well for the school. I'm sure Dean Balknap had a hand in this. Last time I decided not to take legal action. If you pursue this phony charge, you, Dean Balknap, and the college won't be so lucky this time."

"How dare you threaten us." Irene Woods's voice rose, and her body tensed.

"It isn't a threat, it's a promise."

"Your suspension will be without pay. Turn over your ID and parking pass, clear out your desk, and leave the campus."

Jonathan stood and walked out of the room. He could hear the buzz of conversations behind him as he closed the door. After he packed up his personal items, he made his way to his Jeep and left the college, perhaps for the last time.

Once back at his apartment, he called Cal, leaving a message to call back, and that it was important. It was two hours before Cal's name appeared on Jonathan's telephone screen.

"Sorry for the delay, I was in the middle of a project and not able to check messages."

"No problem. Can I come over?"

"Sure, come on over."

Being midday, parking was readily available near Cal's condo. Cal buzzed Jonathan in and stood at the open door to his unit. Jonathan waited until they were settled into chairs in the living room before he described his meeting at State.

Cal was silent for several minutes before he spoke. "Is there any chance one of your students could have misinterpreted a comment you made?"

"None. No chance."

Cal scratched his jaw. "So, what do you think is going on?"

"I think Dean Belknap, the head of my department, is behind this."

"What do you want to do?"

Cal could see how angry Jonathan was. His friend's body was stiff with suppressed tension as he sat on the edge of his chair. "I'm tired of being a nice guy. Last time they suspended me, I didn't do anything when they lifted the suspension. This time, I want them to pay, particularly Belknap. This type of accusation could follow me for the rest of my life."

"I guess that means filing suit."

Jonathan nodded. "Right now, it's a he-said-she-said situation. What if we, meaning you, are able to figure out why this student is charging me with this?"

"Well, first we would need to find out the name of the student."

Jonathan smiled for the first time in the day. "I assume that would have to be in the university's computer."

Cal nodded. "Let's see what I can do."

––––––

Cal Hulse found the state college's firewall as flimsy as papier-mâché. He zeroed in on the Human Resource Department and quickly located the email correspondence between the department and Ronald Chernay, the attorney called in to deal with the harassment charge.

In the exchange of emails, he uncovered the name of the woman who had filed the claim, Heather Daniels. Out of curiosity, Cal accessed her academic record, which presented an uninspired academic achievement, basically a C average.

He called Jonathan and left a message telling his friend the name of the accuser.

Later, when Jonathan checked his messages, he sat back and tried to remember the woman who had charged him with sexual harassment. No image came to mind. He went to his files and searched for the woman's name. Heather Daniels was in his Tuesday, Thursday classes, but again he could not place the name with a face.

Jonathan knew he was going to need an attorney. He returned Cal's phone call, which of course went to voicemail, and asked his friend if there was anyone he could recommend. Two hours later, the two men were finally able to connect.

"I have a name, Marilyn Ullom. She's with a large firm, Dahir and Weinrott. I've never used her, but I'm told she's very good and very pricey."

"I don't see that I have a choice." Cal could hear the resignation in Jonathan's voice.

"I know." Cal tried to think of something to lift his friend's mood but came up dry.

"Cal, I've been thinking. If Belknap is behind this, wouldn't he have to pay this young woman to get her to do this?"

"I think I can see where you're going, the old follow the money game plan."

"Can you dig around a little?" Cal sensed a slight lift in Jonathan's attitude.

"I'm on it. It's going to take a little while, so don't expect anything for a few days."

After the conversation ended, Jonathan googled Marilyn Ullom. He really did not enjoy dealing with lawyers, but as he told Cal, he really did not have a choice.

His call was answered by a woman with a cultured English accent. "Dahir and Weinrott. Can I help you?"

"I would like to speak with Marilyn Ullom, please."

"Can I ask what this is concerning?"

Jonathan always found the gatekeeper routine annoying. "I'm interested in becoming a client."

There was a pause before the call was transferred. A strong, no nonsense woman's voice came on the line. "This is Marilyn Ullom."

"Good morning, I'm Jonathan Scanlan. I teach contemporary American literature at San Francisco State, or I should say I was teaching the course until earlier this week. I've been suspended. I've been charged with sexual harassment by one of my students."

"All right, Mr. Scanlan, why don't we set up an appointment. Can you come to our office on Thursday at nine o'clock a.m.?"

"Fine, I'll see you then."

———

The days moved slowly as Jonathan waited for his appointment with the attorney. When Thursday arrived, he woke early and took a Lift to the law office.

The law office of Dahir and Weinrott was everything he had visualized: paneled walls, leather chairs, English prints, and a receptionist from *Downton Abbey*.

When Jonathan gave his name, the well-groomed receptionist smiled and told him Ms. Ullom would be out shortly. Shortly turned out to be thirty minutes. Jonathan scanned the available reading material but found nothing of interest.

When Marilyn Ullom made her appearance, there was no apology for the wait. She was a large woman in her fifties, hair beginning to gray, and had a somewhat formal countenance. Jonathan's initial impression was not leaning toward the positive. He had the impression that the lawyer valued her time and, if Jonathan was inconvenienced, that was his problem. She led him to a small conference room down a well-carpeted hallway. Once they were seated, Ms. Ullom laid a notepad and pen on the table and offered a courtesy smile.

"You said on the phone that you've been suspended from your teaching job at San Francisco State. I believe you said you've been accused of sexual harassment. Is that correct?"

"Yes, I teach a course on contemporary American literature."

"How long have you been teaching at State?"

"About three and a half years."

"Is this the first time you've had a problem at the school?"

Jonathan paused before replying. "No, I was suspended six months ago."

Jonathan could see Ullom's reaction, which was not positive. "Sexual harassment again?"

The meeting was not going in the direction Jonathan had planned. "No, I wrote a book titled *Culprits of the American Culture*. I don't know if you followed the FBI investigation, but the people being murdered in what the press called *The Culprit Murders* were being killed in the same sequence that they appeared in my book. Initially, I was considered a person of interest because my book was the only connection to the crimes. The school suspended me until I was cleared."

Marilyn Ullom's expression was less than understanding. "I do remember what appeared in the press. You said you were cleared?"

"Yes, and reinstated at State."

"Do you know who is accusing you of sexual harassment?"

Jonathan knew the accuser was Heather Daniels, but he only knew her name through Cal's hacking efforts. "No, they refused to tell me the person's name."

The attorney's attitude showed little empathy. "And you want us to defend you against this charge?"

"Yes, but that's not all. A man named Robert Belknap is the dean of my department and, therefore my boss. He pushed for my permanent termination when I was previously suspended, and I believe he manufactured the current charge. I want to sue him and the school."

"Do you have any evidence that this man is behind this?"

Jonathan could hear the heavy layer of skepticism in the lawyer's voice. "Not at this time. But the charge is bogus."

"Well, we'll be happy to represent you. We will need a substantial retainer; I think eighty thousand dollars should be adequate."

Jonathan sat back in his chair and studied the attorney. "Tell me, do you think we can be successful in proving the charges are false and receive a substantial settlement from the university?"

The woman seemed somewhat put off, as if Jonathan had just asked her what feminine products she used. "Of course, we don't know enough about the case to have an opinion. Often, these matters come down to a he-said-she-said situation. The current political environment does not help."

When Jonathan looked over the table at the woman, he did not see a strong advocate. He stood up and turned to the attorney. "You know, I don't think this is a good fit. If there is a cost for this preliminary meeting, please send me an invoice."

Marilyn Ullom sat at the table, her expression somewhere between confusion and anger as Jonathan left the room.

Marilyn Ullom had not worked out, but there were more lawyers in the Bay Area than fish in the bay. He was not worried about securing the services of a lawyer; he just wanted one who believed in his innocence. Jonathan thought back to people he had known at college. To his knowledge, none of the classmates in his area of study went on to law school. He did remember a young man who had been on the tennis team telling him that he planned to go to law school at Boalt. Jonathan strained to remember the man's name.

When nothing came to the surface, he dialed Cal. He left a message asking for a callback.

It was early evening when his friend returned the call. "What's up?"

"Well, it didn't work out with Marilyn Ullom, so I'm still trying to line up an attorney. There was a guy at Cal who was on the tennis team. He was a nice guy, and he was planning ongoing on to law school, but I can't remember his name."

There was a pause as Hulse did a deep dive into his memory. "I think the man you're trying to remember is Jessie Roberts. I liked Jessie, but shouldn't you be going with a big firm? I doubt Jessie is with one of the white shoe firms."

"I'd like to work with someone I trust, but Jessie may not work out. For all I know, he may not have passed the bar, or he could be practicing something obscure like patent law."

When he was off the line, Jonathan googled Jessie Roberts. His search brought him to Jessie Roberts's website. As far as Jonathan could tell, his former classmate had no specialty and would handle anything that came his way.

Jonathan made a note of Jessie Roberts's phone number, placed it on his desk, and planned to call the office first thing in the morning.

The woman who answered the law office phone seemed pleasant and courteous. She asked for Jonathan's name and number and promised to return his call as soon as Jessie was out of a meeting.

It was a short wait before Jonathan's phone rang. "Jonathan, it's been quite a while. I always thought you'd be on the tour."

"I tried to qualify but couldn't make the cut."

"I'm not a big reader, but I know the book you wrote was a big success."

"Thanks, I have a legal problem and wanted to see if you could help me."

When Jessie responded, the light-hearted banter was replaced with a neutral, businesslike tone. "I'd like to help. What is the problem?"

"I teach contemporary American literature at San Francisco State, and I've been accused of sexual harassment."

"What steps has the school taken?"

"I've been suspended without pay. They say they're doing an internal investigation."

"Who is the accuser?"

"They won't say."

"I assume you deny the charges."

"Absolutely. The head of my department and I hate each other. I believe he trumped this up."

There was a long pause as the attorney absorbed Jonathan's statement. "So, what is the outcome you want, reinstatement, damages?"

"Both. I don't know if I want to continue teaching there, but I don't want to go out this way."

Jonathan could hear Jessie sigh. "Okay, let's get together."

"Do you need a retainer?"

"We can talk about that when we get together. What's your schedule like tomorrow?"

Jonathan laughed. "Well, since I'm unemployed, I'm pretty free."

"How about eleven at my office? Do you know where it is?"

"I have it off your website."

CHAPTER 6

Jessie Roberts's office was on Delores in the Mission. The Mission District is an eclectic blend of cultures. At one time, the area was predominantly Latino, low-income, and had a reasonably high crime rate. As housing costs accelerated in the city, the multicolored Victorian homes attracted a more white, affluent population. While drug dealing was still a common pastime in places like Delores Park, the young, hip millennials kept the bars and restaurants busy.

Robert's law firm was located in a two-story Victorian, half a block from the Mission Delores Academy. Jonathan was able to find a parking space a few buildings down from the office.

The lawyer's office occupied the first floor of the building. A young, attractive woman seated at a desk greeted Jonathan with a friendly smile.

"I'm here to see Jessie."

"Of course, Mr. Scanlan."

"Jonathan, please."

The woman stood up and waved for Jonathan to follow her through a waiting area and into what Jonathan assumed had once been a parlor. Jonathan recognized his friend from college as the man who stood to greet him. A few more pounds, thinning hair, but the same upbeat smile.

After they shook hands, Jessie motioned Jonathan toward a comfortable visitor's chair. "By the way, you just met my wife, Lyn."

Jonathan returned Jessie's smile. "She seems really nice; you're a lucky man."

Roberts nodded. "Yes, I am. So, tell me more about your situation at SF State."

For the next forty minutes, Jonathan described his difficulties at the college and his opinion regarding the role he believed Dean Robert Belknap may have played in the harassment charge. The lawyer took notes and asked a few questions.

When Jonathan finished his tale, Jessie put down his pen and pushed back in his chair. He took a moment before he spoke, and the smile had disappeared. "What we appear to have is a classic he-said-she-said situation. Your dean may be behind the whole thing, but that may be difficult to prove."

"We may have a little more to go on than that." When Roberts waited, Jonathan leaned forward in his chair. "We learned that the young woman bringing the charge is named Heather Daniels. We're looking into her finances to see if she recently came into any money."

Roberts looked at his friend. "You hired a private investigator?"

"Something like that."

Jonathan could see the lawyer's growing discomfort. "If I'm going to represent you, I need to know what's happening."

Jonathan smiled as he tried to lead Roberts away from his source. "A friend happened to have a few tidbits of information. Nothing big. How long have you been in practice here?"

Roberts realized Jonathan was evading his question but decided not to push it at this time. "About five years. When I graduated from Boalt, I worked for a big firm and hated it. I decided to go off on my own, and we're happy here.

"What do you need as a retainer?"

The attorney thought for a moment. How about fifteen thousand, if we need more down the road, I'll let you know."

Jonathan took out a checkbook, and ten minutes later, he was in his Jeep heading home.

Jonathan's afternoon was interrupted by a call from Cal. The message was cryptic. "Call me, it's important."

When Jonathan returned Cal's call, his friend suggested they meet at his place as quickly as possible. It was early enough to have street parking still available. Hulse motioned Jonathan into one of the chairs at his cluttered kitchen table. Cal was staring at the screen of his laptop.

"I've had enough open time to look into the woman accusing you of harassment. Heather Daniels banks at the Bank of America near Ocean Avenue. Her checking account shows regular monthly deposits, which I believe come from her parents. Her checks are for what you'd expect, rent, credit card payment, again, pretty normal stuff."

Jonathan was growing restless; there had to be more to the story for his friend to send for him.

"And now..." Cal paused for dramatic effect. "The news. Fifteen thousand was deposited into her account three weeks ago."

Jonathan shot up in his chair. "Can you tell where the money came from?"

His friend shook his head. "It was a cash deposit."

Jonathan sat back. "So, she was paid to create the claim, but we don't know who paid her."

Cal smiled. "We don't know yet, but we have a pretty good idea where to look."

"Can you get into Belknap's accounts?"

"Have faith, my friend. It's going to take some time, but we'll get to the bottom of this dirty little scheme."

Jonathan stared at Cal. "Is it that easy to hack into the systems used by these banks?"

Hulse shook his head as his fingers played across his keyboard. "No, it isn't that easy. The average hacker wouldn't be able to get through their firewalls, but I'm not the average hacker. I've written a portion of the software they're using."

"How long do you think it will take?"

"Go home, I'll call you when I have more."

———

Jonathan reached home as dusk was approaching the city. He paced in the small confines of his apartment as he waited for more information from Cal. His concentration was interrupted by someone buzzing his doorbell. Without thinking, he pushed the control, releasing the lock at the building's entrance.

Moments later, there was a forceful knock on his unit's door. Jonathan opened it to find two men in suits that he had never seen before standing outside. The larger man presented his credentials.

"Jonathan Scanlan?"

When Jonathan nodded at the larger man produced a set of handcuffs. "Detective George Vogal and Detective Marc Shelton, San Francisco police. We're here to place you under arrest."

Jonathan was momentarily speechless. The two detectives pushed their way into his apartment, spun him around and cuffed his hands behind his back. One of the men pulled out a card and read Jonathan his rights. When asked, he agreed that he understood his rights.

"This is crazy. What am I being charged with?"

Shelton shrugged. "You'll find out when we get to central booking. The district attorney's office issued the arrest warrant."

Realizing nothing could be gained by questioning the two policemen, Jonathan remained silent as they led him from the building and into a waiting unmarked sedan. Neither of the detectives tried to engage him in conversation. When they reached central booking, Jonathan was uncuffed, photographed, fingerprinted, and told to turn over any personal items. He was relieved of his belt before being led to a cell occupied by several men, none of which seemed to be pillars of the community. The stench of sweat and fear was palpable.

Several hours after he was placed in the cell, one of the guards motioned him forward, unlocked the cell door, and led Jonathan down a hallway to an interrogation room. He was again cuffed and secured to a metal ring on the table. Jonathan had seen scenes in the movies and on television depicting his situation, but he could not imagine why he was being arrested.

After a wait long enough to make Jonathan feel uncomfortable, a middle-aged woman walked into the room, slapped a file on the table and stood staring at Jonathan. She was somewhere in her forties, heavy bodied, graying hair and a hard face devoid of humor.

"I'm Ruth Gupta. I'm with the district attorney's office."

Jonathan stared at the woman in silence. When her introduction elicited no response, she continued. "Do you know why you're here?"

"No."

"You've been charged with criminal counts of sexual harassment, and further, threatening the woman who brought the charge."

"This is bullshit, and I want a lawyer." Jonathan felt the heat rising within his body as he fought to control himself.

"You listen to me. We have overwhelming evidence concerning these charges. I know you have no criminal history. If you agree to plead guilty to the charges we can offer a reduced sentence."

"No, you listen to me. I want my lawyer."

This was not going the way Ruth Gupta had envisioned. The man did not seem intimidated; if anything, he seemed angry. The assistant district attorney had expected a quick kill. The man pleads guilty, he receives a suspended sentence, and the expense and uncertainty of a trial are avoided. The woman sighed as she looked across the table at Jonathan.

"Have it your way. The guard outside will take you to a telephone for your one phone call. Perhaps after spending some quality time with your cellmate, you'll have a change of heart."

When Gupta left the room, she spoke to the waiting guard, who then unlocked Jonathan's handcuffs and escorted Jonathan to a wall-mounted phone. Jonathan wanted to call Jessie Roberts, but could not remember the lawyer's number. Instead, he called Cal and left a message.

After exchanging his clothes for an orange jumpsuit, he was led to a two-prisoner cell. His cellmate was asleep on one of the bunk beds. Without waking his new companion, Jonathan lay down on the vacant bed and stared at the ceiling. It was going to be a long night.

It was after ten the following morning when Jonathan was led to a conference room where Jessie Roberts was waiting. Neither man spoke until the guard left the room.

Jessie smiled across the table. "How's public enemy number one doing?"

Jonathan failed to return the smile. The evening in the cell had not diminished his anger. "When can I get out of here?"

Roberts shrugged. "There will be a preliminary hearing this afternoon where the charges against you will be read. You'll be asked how you plead, and the judge will grant bail. We'll post bail and you should be able to be released at that time."

"You don't expect there to be complications?"

Jessie shook his head. "No, but the way this is being handled isn't normal. This comes down to a he-said-she-said situation. When a charge like this is made, the person charged is asked to show up with his or her attorney, charges are made, bail is set, and the charged person goes home. Cops don't drag the guy to jail in handcuffs. There's a lot of overkill here."

"They say I threatened the woman accusing me of harassment."

"Any truth to the claim?"

"None." Jonathan thought about Jessie's comments for a moment. "We need to look into what connection there might be between Robert Belknap and the DA's office, but right how I need to get out of here."

The first thing Jonathan did when he finally reached home was strip off his clothes and stand in the shower until the hot water ran out. The long shower did nothing to quell the man's anger. Later he sat in his small living room and considered his next action. He dialed Cal and left a message for a call back.

Hulse called back as Jonathan realized he had not eaten since lunch the previous day.

"When did you get home?" Cal's voice was subdued.

"Just about an hour ago. Have you turned up anything more on the payment to the woman?"

"Fifteen thousand was withdrawn from your favorite dean's

checking account two days before Heather Daniels deposited the same amount in her account. He pulled the money out of his line of credit."

Cal could hear a sigh of relief from his friend. "They'll claim it's a coincidence, but a jury will have trouble buying that story. What about communications? Could Belknap be stupid enough to put their little arrangement in an email?"

"I've gotten into the email system at State. There's no question that Belknap is campaigning for your ouster, but nothing on that system between Belknap and the girl. I haven't taken a look at the server he has at home. That's my next project."

"I don't know how to thank you." Jonathan could not disguise his emotions.

Hulse cut him off. "That's what friends are for. We're not all the way there, but we now have a good head start."

Sleep was elusive as Jonathan knew where his life would be if his best friend was not one of the most talented computer wizards in the world. He kept telling himself that all this would pass, eventually he would get through this.

In the morning, he felt groggy as he sat in his breakfast nook with his orange juice, coffee and *Chronicle*. He scanned through the paper until his eye caught his name mentioned in the local news section.

The article described Jonathan's arrest on charges of sexual harassment and for making threats to his accuser, who was not named. While nothing in the piece was factually incorrect, the average reader would assume Jonathan was guilty as sin.

Bile rose in his throat and, for a moment, he thought he was going to throw up. His discomfort was quickly dissipated by raw anger. This insignificant little man was doing everything in his power to destroy Jonathan, and the establishment was helping him along.

He wanted to call Cal and push him for more information that would ruin Belknap, but he knew his friend was a night person and it was too early to call.

CHAPTER 7

Jonathan sat across the desk from his attorney. Jessie Roberts noticed that his client was remarkably relaxed, a stark contrast from his demeanor on their last visit. Jonathan's trial date had been set at ninety days out.

"Are you sure you don't want to accept the plea deal. I understand they'll drop the threat charge, and you won't do any time. They'll go for time served."

Jonathan smiled and leaned forward in his chair. "That's not where we're going."

Roberts looked at his client. Something was going on, and he had no idea what it was.

"I want you to file suit against Robert Balknap and the university."

"On what grounds?"

"That this whole thing is a frame. The charges are bogus, and the entire process was designed to ruin me."

"How do you know this?"

"Trust me. I guess we have to come up with an amount. It has to be enough to shake them up. How about twenty million?"

Roberts stared at his college friend, thinking the man was crazy. "Jonathan, this doesn't make any sense. What are you basing all this on?"

Jonathan ignored his attorney. "As soon as you file suit, you need to obtain bank records on Balknap and Heather Daniels. And oh, when you receive frantic calls from Balknap and the school's attorneys, tell them the amount is not negotiable. By the way, throw in that we want to be reimbursed for reasonable attorney's fees."

"If this is a bluff, we could come out of this looking ridiculous."

"It's not a bluff."

"Do you know something, or could this come back and bite me in the ass?"

Jonathan noted his attorney did not say bite us in the ass. "Yes, I know something." That said, Jonathan stood and left the office.

As Jonathan predicted, the first wave of phone calls came in hours after the suit was filed, and papers were served. The initial calls were threatening counter suits and potential ethical challenges over filing a frivolous lawsuit. When Roberts responded by simply telling them he would see them in court, there was a lull in the screaming and yelling.

Two days later, he received a call from Balknap's attorney suggesting a meeting to see if these matters could be resolved in a professional manner. Following Jonathan's instructions, Jessie refused the meeting. By this time, Roberts was feeling much better about the sanity of his client.

The most serious battle waged by Balknap's attorney was trying to keep the dean's financial records out of play. While the defense fought hard to protect the bank records, the judge ruled them admissible.

Ronald Cheronay, representing the university, argued that the school should be excluded from the lawsuit. Unfortunately for the school, when the university suspended Jonathan without pay, they sealed themselves into the legal proceedings.

A week before the trial date, Jessie Roberts received a call from Judge Adam Pinney's clerk. The judge wanted to set up a pretrial meeting later in the week. When Roberts relayed the request to Jonathan, his client's initial reaction was negative.

"I thought I was clear on the subject. I don't want to meet with their lawyers."

"Jonathan, this isn't coming from Balknap or the school's lawyers;

it's coming from the judge. The last thing you want to do before a trial is piss off the judge."

After a brief period of grumbling, Jonathan agreed.

Jonathan had no idea what to expect at the pretrial meeting. The meeting was being held in the judge's chambers, and, as soon as Jonathan and Roberts arrived, they were ushered into a relatively small wood-paneled room. They could hear laughter as they entered the chambers. Apparently, Ronald Cheronay had just finished telling an amusing story.

Jonathan's first thought was, "Am I going up against a collection of the judges' old friends?"

Everyone stood up to shake hands. Jonathan recognized Balknap and Cheronay, both dressed in conservative business suits. A woman standing next to the dean was introduced as Sharon Mansky, Balknap's attorney. She was a middle-aged, somewhat overweight woman in a pantsuit. The judge, dressed more casually than the others, was a tall thin man with a full stock of snow-white hair. His somewhat sharp features saved him from being handsome.

Once past introductions, Judge Pinney described the decorum he expected to see in his courtroom. He said he demanded punctuality and would not tolerate disruptions. Jonathan felt like he was back in grammar school.

The judge turned to Jessie Roberts. "Is there any chance this could be settled out of court?"

Roberts turned to Jonathan, who simply shook his head.

Penney stood, smiled at his small audience, and said, "Very well, I'll see you in court."

As they left the building, Jonathan glanced at his attorney. "What's the story about the judge? Is he close to Cheronay?"

Jessie shrugged. "I've never appeared before Pinney, so I don't know. The word is that he's fair. Keep in mind he squashed their pretrial motions."

As Jonathan walked to his car, he hoped his attorney was right.

———

Jonathan met Jessie early on the morning of the first day of the trial. They sat together in a booth at a diner two blocks from the courthouse. Jonathan looked at his college friend. "I don't get it. They did discovery, they know what we know. We can tie Belknap to the payment. They claim I threatened the woman by email, but we can prove it was not sent from my server. Why don't they just give up?"

Roberts leaned back in the booth. "Two reasons; one, every hour their lawyers work on the case they're billing their client hundreds of dollars. Two; you didn't give them a chance to settle by refusing to meet with them."

Jonathan thought for a moment. "I can agree to a settlement, but only under my terms."

Jonathan spent the next ten minutes describing the terms he could agree to. Roberts sat back and looked across the table at his client. "I don't know that they'll go for that. Typically, you would have to sign an agreement not to disclose the terms of the settlement."

"This isn't your typical deal, and I have an idea that might make it work."

Jessie was on his cell phone talking to Cheronay and Mansky before they left the table.

Judge Pinney agreed to allow all parties to use his chambers with the understanding if an agreement could not be reached before the scheduled time of the trial, the trial would proceed.

When everyone was seated, Jonathan glanced around the room. "I will agree to a settlement, but only under my conditions. The university must make a public statement acknowledging that they made a mistake, no sexual harassment or threat occurred, and Dean Balknap must be fired."

This brought both Balknap and his attorney to their feet. As they shouted their objections and, in Dean Balknap's case, several creative insults, Jonathan waited for them to lose steam. He also noted Cheronay had not joined the shout fest.

Cheronay was the first to speak when there was a lull. "What about the money?"

"I'll reduce my demand to ten million and would agree to keep the money part of the deal confidential."

Jonathan could see the wheels turning in Cheronay's mind. "Make it five million and we have a deal."

Robert Balknap screamed at Cheronay, "You can't do this."

Ronald Cheronay waved the dean away. "Shut up, Balknap. You're the reason we're here. We go to court and lose, which we will, you'd be out in a heartbeat."

Jonathan smiled at the university's lawyer. "No, it's ten million. You weren't taken to jail in handcuffs."

Cheronay returned the smile. "Had to try, ten million it is."

Cheronay and Jonathan shook hands, and the gathering broke up with decidedly different opinions regarding the settlement.

Jonathan, Roberts, and Cheronay informed Judge Pinney's clerk that a settlement had been reached and the trial could be canceled.

CHAPTER 8

Jonathan was smiling as he loaded his golf clubs into the back of the Jeep. A college friend had called and invited him to play a round at the Sharon Heights Country Club. While Jonathan no longer possessed the talent that had made him a top-rated amateur, he still loved the game.

Highway 280 is one of the most attractive roadways in the country, once past the turnoff for the airport, and Jonathan was enjoying the drive. The weather was perfect for golf, clear blue skies and only a light breeze.

Jonathan's friend, James Glasman, had lined up two club members to make up the foursome. The group had enjoyed each other's company. The three club members were in awe as they watched Jonathan par hole after hole. While he was content with his game, Jonathan knew that ten years ago, he would have been collecting birdies.

It was late in the afternoon when Jonathan picked up a call from his friend. "Jon, are you free to go out to dinner?" Jonathan caught a note of weariness in Cal's voice.

"Sure, what do you have in mind?"

"Something casual."

"How about Gordon Biersch?"

"Perfect, seven-thirty?"

"Why don't we take Uber? Parking down there is a bitch. I'll order a ride and come by your place at about seven-fifteen."

Jonathan was so engrossed in a new book by Daniel Silva that, when he looked at his watch, he realized he was running late. Fortunately, the Uber driver was only minutes away, allowing Jonathan to reach Cal's condo on time.

Jonathan could not fail to notice his friend's subdued attitude as Cal slipped into the car. He knew Cal was working on a complex project and hoped things were not going badly. He decided to wait and let his friend tell him what was bothering him when he was ready.

They were seated at the bar with drinks on the way when Cal turned to Jonathan. "Thanks for coming out tonight."

Jonathan smiled. "Not a problem. You seem a little off; problems with your project?"

"No, it's coming along. I've been on this for about four days, virtually nonstop. I felt like I was having an ice cream brain freeze and needed to take a break."

"Any time." Jonathan knew Cal could not discuss the details of his assignments. In addition to the confidentiality agreement, Jonathan knew he would not understand anything about the project. Jonathan was still struggling with his smartphone.

"It also doesn't help that the CEO is constantly demanding updates. Every time he calls it breaks my concentration."

"Can't you tell him to back off?"

Cal laughed. "They believe when they hire you, they own you."

"So... not a nice guy?"

"If I only worked for nice guys in Silicon Valley, I'd be on food stamps."

Jonathan nodded. "Hey, anytime you need a little R and R, I'm available."

Until they called it an early evening, they debated which Warrior team was the best, with Durant or post-Durant.

Jonathan was not a man given to introspection, but later that night, he thought about what he wanted to do with the rest of his life.

He could not see himself returning to his teaching assignment at State. What had been a difficult environment would now be toxic.

In his mind, the legal battle had all been about punishing Balknap and the administration for how he had been attacked. He now realized how wealthy he had become. While the money provided him with economic freedom, it also posed a question. Freedom to do what? Jonathan was less than optimistic that he could sustain a long-term writing career, regardless of the success of his two books. He had read stories about the idle rich, jetting off to southern France and other exotic locales, but he could not possibly see himself in that role.

Jonathan had finished his run along the Marina and was about to take a shower when his phone chirped. He did not recognize the incoming number and was about to let it go to voicemail. Changing his mind, he answered, planning to hang up if a long pause indicated an incoming sales pitch.

"Hello."

"Mr. Scanlan, my name is Tom Scheer. I work for a government agency, and I'm hoping you can help me."

"I don't understand. What government agency?"

"I'd rather not go into this over the phone. Can we meet?"

Jonathan paused, trying to decide whether this man's request was real and even if it was, did he want to get involved? Curiosity won. "Are you familiar with the city?"

"Not really."

"There's a Starbucks on Union near Laguna. Can you be there in two hours?"

"Sure, I'll grab a cab."

Jonathan had no idea where this was going, but it had piqued his interest.

Jonathan arrived fifteen minutes early, ordered coffee, and took a table with a view of the entrance. He guessed from the man's voice that he was fairly young. He also thought he heard a faint Midwest accent.

Several men in the twenty to thirty age range entered the coffee shop, but none looked around as if meeting someone. At 2:20, Jonathan was thinking that the man on the phone looked more and more like a no-show. He decided to give it another ten minutes when a slender, blond-haired young man walked into the shop and stood by the entrance, glancing at the seated customers. When his eyes focused on Jonathan, he headed for his table.

"Jonathan Scanlan?"

Jonathan stood and offered his hand. "How did you know what I looked like?"

The man offered a tentative smile. "Your picture is on the back of your book."

"Would you like to order something?"

"Sure, can I get you anything?"

"No, I'm fine."

Jonathan studied the man as he waited in line to place his order. He guessed Tom Scheer to be in his late twenties. While the young man appeared to be pleasant, Jonathan sensed a somewhat nerdy feel. Scheer was dressed casually, short-sleeve polo shirt, tan pants, and loafers. Nothing beyond Target's price range.

When Scheer was settled across the table with his latte, Jonathan smiled. "Okay, Tom. Why did you want to get together with me?"

"I read your book. About how you solved the murders."

Jonathan stared at the young man. "That's great, but again, why did you want to meet?"

"All right, I work for the government, the federal government. I'm involved in processing contracts."

Jonathan nodded, unsure where this was going and thinking about excusing himself and leaving.

"I believe money is being siphoned off."

"You're saying someone is stealing money?"

"A great deal of money."

"Why don't you notify one of the government agencies that investigates things like that? Maybe the FBI?"

Scheer shook his head. "I have no idea who is doing this. Whoever is doing this is very clever."

"What department or agency do you work for?"

"The Department of Defense."

Jonathan leaned back in his chair, clearly not following what Scheer was saying. "The Department of Defense?"

Jonathan paused for a moment. "All right, but I still don't know why you're coming to me rather than going to the FBI."

Scheer's face flushed. He stared at the table for a moment. "I did contact the FBI."

"And?"

"And they blew me off. They said they'd look into it, but I could tell they didn't take me seriously. They believe I'm a disgruntled employee."

Jonathan was silent for a moment as he considered everything the young man had said. "You know I'm not the best person to analyze government contracts."

"In your book, you say that you had a brilliant team to help figure out what happened."

Jonathan smiled. "You have to understand. These were my friends helping me clear my name. I'd been suspended from my job, and the FBI was looking at me because of my book, *Culprits of the American Culture.* I have no idea if they would be interested in trying to find out who is misusing government funds."

Tom sank back in his chair, his features clearly showing his disappointment. "I don't know where else to go."

Jonathan felt sympathy for Scheer. He reached across the table and touched the young man's shoulder. "Look. No promises, but I'll give it some thought. Is there anything you can give me that backs up what you're saying?"

Jonathan's comment acted like a lifeline thrown to a drowning man. Tom Scheer gave a weak smile as he handed Jonathan a thumb drive.

————

Jonathan had placed Tom Scheer's thumb drive on his desk next to his computer. He was ambivalent about pursuing the man's claims, and he had neither the talent nor interest in studying government contracts. His prior experience with the FBI had not been confidence-building, other than with Carmen, but he assumed they would not have dismissed Scheer's claims if they had been credible. After glancing at the thumb drive, he picked up Baldacci's latest book, settled in a comfortable chair, and began to read.

The next morning, Jonathan was sipping his morning coffee as he skimmed through the *Chronicle*. He had little if any interest in local or national politics, and with the national election coming up in a few months, those stories dominated the news. He was passing over the local news and ready to pick up the sports section when a brief article caught his eye. A man had been the victim of a hit and run as he was walking across the Embarcadero. Witnesses claimed the man was crossing with the light and that the car that hit him had been speeding through the intersection. The man's identification was being withheld pending notification of his family.

After finishing the sports section, Jonathan put the paper down and stared out his kitchen window. While he had lost his enthusiasm for teaching, it had filled his day. As he thought about it, until now he had never been idle. After college and golf, there had been teaching. Even while suspended, he and his friends had worked diligently to clear his name, and then there had been writing.

It seemed odd that now, with no financial worries, he was adrift. Jonathan sighed, turned to his computer, and began playing solitaire. He was into his third game when his cell phone began chirping. He glanced at the screen, but the caller was not identified. Jonathan considered not picking up, but curiosity won out.

The caller's voice had the heavy tone of officialdom. "Is this Jonathan Scanlan?"

When Jonathan acknowledged, the caller continued. "This is Detective Wright of the San Francisco police department." Jonathan's stomach tightened, given his recent experience with law enforcement. "Are you familiar with a man named Thomas Scheer?"

Jonathan paused for a moment. "Yes, I met the man."

"Mr. Scanlan, I'm with homicide. Mr. Scheer was killed yesterday. He had your name and telephone number in his possession."

When Jonathan did not respond, Wright asked, "What was your relationship to Mr. Scheer?"

"We didn't have a relationship. He called me and asked to meet with me. We went down to Starbucks on Union. Can I ask how he was killed?"

Wright paused before answering. "It was a hit and run. Why did he want to meet with you?"

Jonathan thought for a moment. He knew Scheer had contacted the FBI about his belief that there was a problem at the Department of Defense. "He wanted me to look into what he thought was a problem where he worked."

It was the detective's turn to pause before his next question. "Why did he come to you?"

"From what he said, he went to the FBI, and he didn't think they took his concerns seriously."

"But again, why did he come to you?" Jonathan could hear the edge in the detective's voice.

"Scheer had read a book I had written and thought I might help him."

"So, did you agree to help him?"

"No, detective, I did not."

There was a long pause before Detective Wright said, "All right, Mr. Scanlan. I'll get back to you if we have more questions."

After Jonathan hung up, he sat and thought about Tom Scheer, who had seemed to be an earnest, decent young man. He had intentionally not mentioned the thumb drive to the detective. He now stared at the device on his desk.

After a few moments, Jonathan called Cal and left a message to return the call as soon as possible. He inserted the device into his computer and viewed the information as it appeared. The initial data that came up were copies of contracts. As he scrolled forward, pages and pages of financial information related to the contracts appeared.

Jonathan found the legalese of the contracts incomprehensible and the financial data beyond his ability to fathom. He knew he was not the person who could analyze Tom Scheer's information.

It was late in the afternoon when Cal returned the call. " Hi Jon, what's up?"

"Do you know anyone who would be really good at analyzing government contracts?"

"Give me a moment."

Jonathan waited as Cal searched his memory bank. "Not really. Alan and Harold's work involve government contracts, but that's not part of their jobs. I doubt they even see the actual contracts. So why the interest in government contracts?"

Jonathan explained his meeting with Tom Scheer and Scheer's belief that there was a problem at Defense and his request that Jonathan and his friends help him verify his claim.

He heard Cal chuckle. "Come on, Jon. This really isn't our thing."

"I know it isn't, but did you read in the paper yesterday about the guy who was killed by a hit and run when he was crossing the Embarcadero?"

"No, I missed it."

"Scheer was the guy."

Cal was quiet for several moments. When he spoke, his voice was subdued. "It could be a coincidence."

"Hell of a coincidence. He gave me a thumb drive with copies of contract information that he thought was off."

"Why didn't he just go to the FBI or whoever handles this kind of thing?"

"He said he did, and they blew him off. Thought he was some type of disgruntled employee."

"Maybe he was."

"Maybe, but his being killed is, like I said, a hell of a coincidence. Look, I thought he was a nice guy trying to do the right thing."

"So, what are you thinking about doing?"

"Looking into it. If his claims were real, there's a good chance that he was murdered to shut him up."

"As I said before, not really our thing."

"You don't think the Pacific Avenue Irregulars would be interested?" Alan Thielen was a great fan of Sir Arthur Conan Doyle and had named the team. The name is derived from the street urchins, known as the Baker Street Irregulars, who assisted Sherlock Holmes.

"I don't know Jon. The guys were primarily motivated to help you clear your name."

"Why don't we get them together and see if they would want to be involved? If they aren't, I'll drop the thing." Jonathan did not want to tell Cal that, besides seeking justice for Tom Scheer, he was searching for something meaningful to fill his days.

After a long pause, "All right. I'll make the calls." Jonathan could hear the skepticism in Cal's voice.

————

There was an aura of confusion as the poker group gathered at Cal's condominium. Neither Cal nor Jonathan had briefed any of the men, other than to request the meeting. When the last man was seated in the living room, Jonathan stood and glanced at his friends before speaking.

"Thank you all for coming. Let me explain why we asked you to be here. A few days ago, a young man named Tom Scheer called me and asked to meet with me. When we met, he told me he worked for the Department of Defense, and he believed a great deal of money was being illegally siphoned off from his department. When I suggested that he contact the FBI, he told me he had done so and they had dismissed his claim. He gave me a thumb drive that contains copies of government contracts. Of course, I'm not capable of analyzing the contract information. The following day, Scheer was murdered by a hit and run driver in the city. I've talked to Cal, and the question is, do we want to get involved?"

A moment of silence passed as the group absorbed the

implications of Jonathan's question. Greg Stokes was the first to speak. "Why did he come to you?"

"He had read *Culprits* and hoped we would pursue it. We were his last option when the FBI didn't take him seriously."

Alan Thielen raised his hand. "Maybe the FBI looked at the data and determined there was no substance to his claims."

"Maybe, but his being murdered is a hell of a coincidence."

There was a good deal of cross-talk as the group discussed the pros and cons of looking into the situation. Carlos Hermosillo spoke up. "I'm having a problem seeing this as our thing. Besides that, none of us have expertise in reviewing what I am sure are complex contracts."

A mummer of assent gave Jonathan the belief that his proposal was going nowhere.

Harold Kurtovich could sense Jonathan's disappointment. He agreed with his friends that ferreting out government corruption was not something the group wanted to do, but he decided to throw Jonathan a bone. "Jon, I have a friend at Lockheed who works in procurement. She's quite an expert at creating and reviewing contracts. I can ask her if she would be willing to look over the stuff you have."

Jonathan offered a weak smile. That would be great. I'd be willing to pay her for her time."

Three days later, Jonathan's phone chirped. Harold's name appeared on the screen. Jonathan picked up, resigned to be disappointed.

"Jon, I talked to Cory Bishop, the woman who works in contracts here, and she's interested in reviewing your information."

Jonathan was surprised and had to take a moment to collect his thoughts. "That's great. Did she mention what she would like to be paid?"

"No. You'll have to work that out with Cory. She would have to do this outside of work hours. Let me give you her cell number."

Jonathan wrote down the woman's number and thanked Harold.

Heading Harold's comment, Jonathan decided not to call Cory Bishop at work. He glanced frequently at his watch as the day seemed to drag on forever. He waited until well after 6:00, assuming Cory would have finished her day at Lockheed and would have made her way home.

A woman's voice answered on the first ring. "Cory Bishop?"

"Yes, who is this?"

"Jonathan Scanlan. I believe you talked to Harold Kurtovish today."

"Yes, I did. I'd like to help you with your project."

Jonathan was not sure he would refer to what he was doing as a project but let it pass. "When can we get together?"

"How about tonight? I was planning on being home all evening."

"Would you prefer to meet somewhere, like a local Starbucks?"

"Why don't you just come to my place? I'm in San Carlos." Jonathan wrote down her address.

"Okay. I'm coming down from the city, so it will take me a little time."

"No problem."

Jonathan grabbed the thumb drive and left his apartment. He had not been able to tell Cory Bishop's age from her voice. He pictured her in his mind as a very bright, nerdy, middle-aged woman.

His GPS led him to a large condominium structure two blocks west of El Camino Real. The building appeared to be fairly new and, while not in the Cal Hulse category, quite nice.

He was buzzed in and took the elevator to the fourth floor. His knock was answered almost immediately. The woman who opened the door was strikingly beautiful. Cory Bishop was in her early thirties, nearly six feet tall, and possessed the classic features of a model. The oversized sweatshirt and jeans could not mask her figure.

Jonathan was briefly stunned, a reaction that seemed to amuse Ms. Bishop. The woman smiled and motioned Jonathan into her unit. "Please come in, Mr. Scanlan."

"Jonathan, please."

Cory Bishop's home was spacious and tastefully decorated. The furnishings were comfortable-looking and, Jonathan assumed, fairly expensive. Oriental carpets added color to the room. Jonathan noticed framed vintage movie posters on the walls.

"You're into the old classic movies, I see."

"I am, love Turner Classics."

"I agree. They don't make them like they used to."

"Can I see the contract information?"

"Of course." Jonathan handed Cory the thumb drive.

"Why don't you sit down and make yourself comfortable while I see what we have. Would you care for something to drink while I boot this up on my computer? I just made a fresh pot of coffee."

"That would be great."

"Sugar or milk?"

"Black would be fine."

When Jonathan settled into one of the overstuffed chairs with his coffee, Cory Bishop disappeared into one of the rooms off the living room. He wondered how long it would take for her to review the voluminous amount of data on the device.

Surprisingly, she returned to the living room in less than half an hour. "A lot of information. It's going to take me a good deal of time to analyze it all."

"I understand. I certainly want to compensate you for your time."

Cory curled up on a small sofa across from Jonathan. "I don't want to be paid."

Jonathan was obviously confused. "I don't understand."

"Jonathan, I've read both your books and, besides being great reads, I'm incredibly impressed by how you and your friends figured out who was behind the murders. If, after studying the stuff on the thumb drive, we determine nothing illegal is happening, no harm, no foul. If, on the other hand, we uncover massive fraud, I want in."

"What do you mean, you want in?"

"I would want to be involved as part of your little team to pursue the investigation."

Jonathan sat in silence for several minutes as he thought about Cory's proposal. He shook his head as he responded. " I don't know, Cory. As you said, there are others involved. Let me talk it over with the team. I'll let you know in a couple of days."

Jonathan had mixed feelings about including Cory Bishop as he drove back to the city.

As Cory lay in bed her thoughts kept turning to Jonathan. She felt a level of attraction that she had not experienced for some time. The majority of the men she had known spent a great deal of time projecting their self-importance. Jonathan was a college professor and a successful author, but he displayed none of that type of arrogance. She found him interesting.

CHAPTER 9

The next morning, Jonathan left a message for Cal, knowing his friend would not check in until later in the day. He put on shorts and running shoes and headed down toward the Marina Green. He hoped a run would clear his mind. He was not sure why he was conflicted about including Cory Bishop in the investigation, should fraud be found.

Jonathan was watching the local news when Cal returned his call. "Sorry to be so late getting back to you. I was working on a project and lost track of time."

"Not a problem." Jonathan described his meeting with Cory and her desire to be involved if she uncovered fraud.

"I don't see the problem, Jon. The odds are high that she won't find anything, and, even if she did, why not let her in?"

"I don't know. I told her I'd talk it over with the group and get back to her."

"Jon, this isn't a democracy. You and I can decide. Was it her personality? Would she be difficult to work with?"

"No, she was fine. You know Harold didn't mention that she is knock down gorgeous."

"And that's a problem?"

Jonathan had to laugh. "No, it's just not what I expected."

After a few moments of thought, Jonathan called Cory and left a message that she was in.

It was six days later when Jonathan's phone chirped. When he glanced at the screen, he saw it was Cory. "Hi Cory. How is it going?"

"Well, it's going. I've broken down the information pretty well, but I need some help."

"Sure, what type of help?"

"In *Culprits* you mention that one of your team is a computer genius."

Jonathan had no idea where this was going. "That's right."

"I think we need to bring him in."

"Okay. Let me give him a call and find out when he's available. What's your schedule like?"

"Any evening during the week, or any time on the weekend."

"I'll call you back and let you know."

"Fine. If he's in the city, I can come up."

"Yes, he's in the city. I'll call him now."

Jonathan called Cal and left a message."

Several hours later, Cal returned the call. "So, did Bishop find anything?"

"I don't know. She wants to get together with you. She's willing to come up here and is pretty open on when. When do you want to meet?"

Cal thought for a moment. "How about Wednesday, about six-thirty at my place?"

"Sounds good." Jonathan called Cory and gave her the time and Cal's name and address."

Jonathan left his apartment early, knowing how difficult it would be to secure a parking place near Cal's condo in Pacific Heights. He scored a space only a block from Cal's building. Jonathan zipped up his jacket against the summer fog that had rolled into the city.

Jonathan and Cal glanced at their watches as 6:30 came and went. It was past 7:00 when the condo's buzzer announced someone at the entrance. A few minutes later Cory Bishop appeared at the unit's front door.

She was shivering. "God it's cold. I didn't think I needed to wear winter clothes to come to the city."

Jonathan smiled. "Summer in the city."

"I'm sorry I'm late. I had to drive around forever. The space I found is about four blocks away."

Cal hustled into a bedroom and came back with a blanket. "Here, wrap this around yourself."

When everyone was finally settled in the living room with mugs of coffee, Jonathan turned to Cory: "I should have warned you about parking and the fog. I'm sorry."

Cory smiled. "I should have known about the summer fog. I don't get up to the city often, and I just wasn't thinking."

Cal watched the exchange between Cory and his friend before addressing the woman. "Were you able to find anything out of line?"

Cory shook her head. "No, but I have reached a conclusion. We won't be finding fraud in the major contracts. Maybe a little overpricing, but not fraud. The department is their major source of revenue, and the risk would not be worth the reward. If there is something going on, it would be with the smaller guys."

Neither Cal nor Jonathan spoke for moments. Finally, Cal looked at Cory. "So, where does that leave us?"

"It leaves us with you."

Both men clearly had no idea what Cory was saying. "I understand you're an incredibly talented IT expert. You need to look into the smaller contractors. How long have they been in business? Do they have the infrastructure to perform the described work? Any shady backgrounds with the principals? That sort of thing."

From his expression, it was apparent Cal had not seen this coming and was not thrilled with the task. "I'm not sure I have the time that would require."

Cory shrugged, pulled papers from her purse, and handed them to Cal. "That's up to you. This is a list of the companies."

A chill engulfed the room that had nothing to do with San

Francisco's summer fog. Jonathan stood up and moved next to Cory. "We'll check it out. I'm parked nearby. Why don't I give you a ride to your car?"

"That would be great." She gave Cal a cold look as she made her way to the door."

When they reached Jonathan's car he glanced at his watch and turned to Cory. "I don't imagine you had time to catch dinner."

Cory hesitated, then shook her head. "No."

"Let me buy you dinner before you head home. We can go down to Union."

"That's very kind of you, but it's not necessary."

"It may not be necessary, but it's something I want to do. I appreciate the time and effort you've put into our little investigation."

She smiled as she slid into Jonathan's Jeep. "Okay."

Jonathan drove down to Green Street and used a remote to open a garage door. "So, this is where you live?"

"No, I was just able to rent this garage. I live two blocks away."

Jonathan grabbed a fleece jacket from the back seat and handed it to Cory. "The restaurant's about two blocks away."

Jonathan led Cory to Perry's, one of the most popular restaurants in the Marina. As usual, the place was packed.

Cory looked around and said to Jonathan. "It's so busy. Do you think we can get a table?"

Jonathan smiled and approached the hostess at her station. "Hi Amy, any chance for a table?"

The attractive young woman returned Jonathan's smile. "Give me five minutes, Jon."

After the brief wait, Amy led them to a vacant table. Cory noticed the hostess was paying scant attention to her and a great deal of attention to her companion. She felt annoyed, and a pang of jealousy. She knew her reaction was unreasonable and a bit confusing.

When they were settled in at their table, Cory realized Jonathan had not noticed that the hostess had been brazenly hitting on him. For a moment, she wondered if Jonathan was gay, but none of her gaydar senses were going off. Cory found Jonathan's obliviousness both puzzling and endearing.

When the waiter appeared, Jonathan ordered a beer and Cory a chardonnay. Cory smiled as she studied the menu. I'm surprised we were able to get a table so quickly. The place is packed."

Jonathan returned her smile. "I guess you could say I'm somewhat of a regular here." Cory thought the hostess's interest in Jonathan was more likely the reason for their good fortune.

Dinner progressed in pleasant conversation, mainly Cory questioning Jonathan on his experiences in what was described as the *Culprit's* affair. At one point, Cory pressed Jonathan on whether Cal would be researching the list of government contractors that she had provided.

"He'll do it, Cory. Cal doesn't like surprises, and he didn't see this one coming."

"Are you sure?"

"I promise you he'll do it." Jonathan was not sure how much pressure he would need to apply to his friend, but he was confident he could make it happen.

After dinner, Jonathan drove Cory to her car. Cory was about to open her door when, on an impulse, she turned and kissed Jonathan. Both Jonathan and Cory were stunned for a moment. Cory quickly slid out of the Jeep. Before she closed the door, she turned back to Jonathan. "I hope you call me."

With that, she seemed somewhat flustered as she trotted to her car.

———

Jonathan sat at his small kitchen table and stared out the window. Cory's impulsive action at the end of their evening dominated his thoughts. He had been attracted to her at first sight, but believed she was completely out of his league. Remembering his promise to Cory, he picked up his phone and dialed Cal. As expected, his call went to voicemail.

Several hours later, Cal returned the call. "Hey Jon, what's up?"

"Not much. Have you had a chance to look at the list Cory gave you?"

"Not really. I've been working on another project."

"Could you do me a favor and spend some time on the companies on the list?"

There was a long pause before Cal responded. "I really don't have the time right now."

"Please Cal. I made her a promise." Cal could hear the pleading tone in Jonathan's' request.

Cal was about to mention that he had made no such promise, but he did not. "Jon, is there something going on between you and Cory?"

Jonathan knew his friend was both smart and perceptive. He sighed and glanced out the window before responding. "Yeah, I think so."

Cal took his time before answering. "Okay. I'll start on it tomorrow."

Jonathan waited a day before calling Cory. The term uptight came to mind as he dialed the number.

She answered on the first ring. "Hi Cory. I was calling to see if you'd like to get together this weekend."

"I'd love to."

"Dinner Saturday night?"

"Great. But rather than going out why, don't you come over here, and I'll put something together."

"I'll bring some wine. What time?"

"How about six o'clock?"

"Six works for me."

"Any news from Cal?"

"He's working on it, but it will take a little more time."

The week seemed to fly by as Jonathan looked forward to his dinner with Cory with nervous anticipation. As he dressed for the evening, he glanced at his closet. He possessed none of the expensive clothing that he imagined men who had dated Cory would have worn.

He finally shrugged and went with his basics, tan Dockers, and a polo shirt.

Earlier that day he had visited a local liquor store. Jonathan had limited knowledge of wines, but he knew Cory had ordered chardonnay at Perry's. He asked the clerk for a recommendation and settled on a bottle from Frank Family.

When he arrived at Cory's condo, Jonathan was greeted with a smile and a warm hug. Cory was dressed casually: jeans and a loose-fitting light blue pullover.

When Jonathan handed Cory the bottle of wine, Cory gushed, "Frank Family, my favorite."

"Let me pour you a glass, and you can relax while I finish up in the kitchen."

Jonathan wandered around Cory's living room. He studied several framed family photos that he had not noticed on his earlier visit. The pictures showed a remarkably attractive family. Cory's mother was an extremely attractive woman, and her father was a very handsome man. Even the family dog, a Labrador, was great-looking.

When Cory joined him, Jonathan pointed to the picture. "Really a beautiful family. Where do they live?"

"Just outside Denver."

"What's for dinner?"

"Veal. It's a new recipe I'm trying out."

"Smells great."

They made their way to a small dining room table. Caesar salads had already been served. Jonathan complimented Cory on the dressing. The next dish was veal served with small potatoes. As Jonathan tasted the main course, he realized it was almost inedible. The meat was overcooked to the consistency of shoe leather, and the potatoes were virtually uncooked. When he looked over at Cory, she was apparently enjoying her dinner. Jonathan smiled as he realized this perfect woman had a flaw. She could not cook.

It was a struggle, but Jonathan was able to force down his dinner. When they had finished, Cory turned on her television and called up her saved shows. She turned to Jonathan. *"The Treasure of Sierra Madre?"*

"Perfect. I love Bogart."

On the drive home Jonathan thought the evening had, with the exception of dinner, been perfect. He simply had to find a way to keep Cory out of the kitchen.

———

Jonathan was restless as he waited for Cal to complete his analysis. He burned off energy by daily runs and time at the gym he had recently joined. Six days had passed before Jonathan's cell chirped.

"Okay, Jon. I've finished looking at the contractors."

"Find anything?" Jonathan was not sure which way he was hoping the analysis would turn.

"It's complicated. Let's get together."

"All right, but I think Cory should be in on it."

"Give her a call and let me know. I'm fine with this evening or tomorrow after six."

A quick call to Cory lined up a meeting at Cal's the following night. Jonathan could not define the reason for his anxiety. If Cal's conclusion was that there was no evidence of fraud, that was it. Their little project was over. He did not believe such an outcome would affect his budding relationship with Cory, but if there was evidence of fraud, they could document what they found and turn it over to the authorities. While he accepted those possible outcomes, his gut instinct was telling him that things were not going to be that simple.

As usual, Jonathan arrived at Cal's condo early. His friend seemed unusually subdued. When Jonathan pressed him for a hint about what he had found, Cal shook his head and told him to wait for Cory.

When Cory arrived, Cal motioned them to chairs in his living room. Cory and Jonathan stared silently at him, waiting for the great reveal.

"Sorry for the drama. What I found isn't going to make you very happy. In the case of two of the contractors I found things that are questionable, but not conclusive."

"What were the things that were questionable?" This came from Cory, who was setting so close to the edge of her seat Jonathan thought she might slip off.

"The questionable item at Consolidated is the CEO. Justin Tanner arrived three years ago with some baggage. He had been the COO at Allied. The word is that he was asked to leave Allied. I couldn't find out why. The other contractor was Independence. They're a fairly new company. They are a privately owned corporation, and I was unable to discover where the startup money came from."

Neither Cory nor Jonathan spoke for a moment. Finally, Jonathan broke the silence. "So, where do we go from here?"

Cal shook his head. "That's the question."

"Do you think there would be any value to bringing together the Pacific Avenue Irregulars?"

Cal shrugged. "I don't know. Let's take a day to think about it."

As they were leaving Cal's condo, Jonathan turned to Cory. "Did you drive up or use Uber?"

"I used Uber. Parking around here is terrible."

"I'll give you a ride home."

"Jonathan, that's silly. I'll call Uber. Let's get together on the weekend."

"Great. I'll give you a call."

When Jonathan returned home, he sat on one of his kitchen chairs and stared into space. His thoughts were jumbled. How badly did he really wish to pursue the potential misuse of government funds? Was this about Tom Scheer or his own need to be doing something relevant? Thrown into the cerebral mix was his budding relationship with Cory. Like any normal heterosexual male, he was strongly attracted to the woman, but was it more than just physical attraction? Jonathan decided to let his relationship with Cory simply play out. He knew he did not have the luxury of procrastinating with the investigation of possible fraud.

The following day Cal sent Jonathan a text with Matthew Tankel's contact information. The man was now CFO of a regional health care organization located in Burbank, California. Tankel had previously been the CFO at Consolidated. Jonathan immediately called Cory.

"Hi, ready to make a road trip?"

"Sure, when and where?"

"Matthew Tankel was CFO at Consolidated and now works at a health care company in Burbank. Do you want to wait for the weekend?"

"Yeah, I better. I'm in the middle of reviewing a complicated contract at work."

CHAPTER 10

Jonathan spent Friday night at Cory's, thankfully with a Chinese takeout dinner. After watching another Bogart movie, Cory took Jonathan's hand and led him to her bedroom. They initially began slowly undressing, but in moments, the pace accelerated. Their lovemaking became almost frantic, as if each felt an indescribable urgency.

Cory had been adamant about driving to Burbank rather than flying. Jonathan had no idea why this made sense, but finally agreed. It took the entire day to make the trip. They checked into a Ramada Inn for the evening and enjoyed dinner at a nearby Italian restaurant. The following morning, they made their way to Matthew Tankel's home using the GPS on Jonathan's phone.

Tankel lived in a modest, somewhat Mediterranean, two-story home on a quiet, tree-lined street. They pulled to a stop and glanced at the house for a moment. Jonathan turned to Cory. "Why don't you do the questioning. He's probably not going to want to cooperate, and it will be harder for him to blow off a beautiful woman."

"I appreciate the compliment, but I'm not sure what to say."

"How about you're a freelance reporter doing a story about Consolidated?"

"And, why are you with me?"

"I'm just a friend living in the area and offered to pick you up at the airport and drive you here."

Cory gave him a look of total skepticism, but opened her door and stepped out of the car. They walked together up the flagstone walkway until they reached Mr. Tankel's front door. Jonathan pushed the doorbell, then stepped back behind Cory.

The man who opened the door was in his midfifties, relatively short, and more than relatively overweight. Cory smiled and asked, "Mr. Tankel?"

Matthew Tankel's expression was wary as he eyed his visitors through wire-rimmed glasses. "Yes."

"My name is Cory Bishop. I'm writing an article regarding Consolidated Corporation and I was hoping you, as their prior Chief Financial Officer, could give me some insight into the organization. I'm sorry that I didn't call you, but I did not have your home number."

Tankel made no move to invite Jonathan and Cory into his home. "I'm sorry, but I don't see how I can help you."

As he began to close the door, Cory stepped closer to the man. "I'm not looking for any confidential information. Perhaps you could share your insight on the personalities of the management team. I'm interested in their outside interests, community activities, things like that." As Cory spoke, she stepped even closer to Tankel and offered an alluring smile.

Tankel's eyes strayed to Cory's chest. "Well, I'm not sure how much information I can give you. Shouldn't this be something you should be asking the people at Consolidated?"

Cory laughed, "I have talked with a few of the management team, but quite frankly, they seemed very guarded and uptight. I thought you, no longer with the company, might be more open."

Tankel again gazed at Cory's remarkable physique. "Well, why don't you come in. I can spare you a little time."

Tankel led them to his family room where Jonathan and Cory sat on a sofa with Matthew Tankel facing them in an overstuffed chair. The room was comfortable, but Jonathan thought, as colorless as the man they were talking to. Cory pulled a notepad and pen from her oversized purse. She began asking innocuous questions about members of the Consolidated management team. As Tankel responded, she pretended to scribble down his answers.

"What can you tell me about Justin Tanner?"

Tankel paused and stared at Cory. "Really nothing. I was let go when Tanner came in."

Cory smiled at the man. "I understand he had been let go at Allied."

"So?"

"Do you have any idea why he was removed as COO at Allied?"

Jonathan could see Tankel stiffen and thought the interview was probably over. Tankel shook his head. "No idea."

"No hard feelings when you were let go?"

Tankel's face flushed. "No. When a new CEO comes in, he or she, often brings along some of their people. I was given a generous severance package, so no hard feelings." He glanced at his watch. "I'm sorry, but I have to cut this off. I'm meeting a friend."

Tankel stood up and waited for Cory to put away her notepad. He led them to the entrance and opened the door.

"Well, thank you for taking the time to talk to me." Cory continued smiling as she was ushered out of the house.

As they walked back to their Jeep, Cory said, "I'm getting a cramp in my face from having to keep smiling at that dull little man."

Jonathan laughed. "You were great. Let's head back to the hotel."

"We really didn't learn anything."

"Not really, but it was worth a try."

They decided to break up their drive back to Bay Area with an overnight stop in Carmel.

———

Two days after Jonathan and Cory returned from Burbank, Jonathan received a call from Cal. "Hi Jon, I have a contact at Lockheed and was able to get some info on Justin Tanner. It's industry gossip, but probably accurate. Word is Tanner is a hound dog and had affairs with a number of his female staff. Lawsuits were threatened, and the board cut him loose."

"Thanks, I guess we can cross Consolidated off the list."

"How are you going to check out Independence?'

"I don't know. I'm sure we'd be stonewalled if we took a direct approach."

"I'm sure you're right."

"I haven't come up with any disgruntled ex-employees."

"They're a fairly new player, so probably not much turnover." Jonathan could see their little investigation going nowhere.

Jonathan thought for a moment. "Can you get a list of their main suppliers?"

"It'll take a little digging, but yeah, I don't see a problem."

"Let me know when you have something. Dinner tonight?"

"Sure, let's do Mexican."

"I'll line it up and give you a call."

Jonathan had just finished a run along the Marina Green when his cell chirped. He answered when he saw the call was from Cal. "Hi, were you able to find anything?"

"I'm sending you a list of several companies that supply Independence. Check your email."

As soon as he made it home, Jonathan went to his computer and glanced at his emails. He made a quick call to his friend. "Great Cal, thanks. I'll let you know our game plan as soon as I have one."

The list provided the company names, headquarter locations, and the names of the chief executive officers. Jonathan called Cory as he studied the list.

When Jonathan relayed what Cal had dug up, she asked, "So, how do we approach them?"

"I don't know." Jonathan thought for a moment. "Maybe use a variation of the same scam we used on Tankel. How about saying we're researching fraud and abuse in government contractors as a basis for my next book? Hell, I'm a successful nonfiction author."

Cory paused as she thought about it. "That might work, but we would need to study up on this before we contact any of these companies or we would sound like idiots."

"There has to be public information on this."

"When we get off the line, I'll google it and order any studies that could help us."

On the weekend. Jonathan and Cory huddled in her condo, reading copies of congressional committee findings on fraud and abuse among contractors under contract to various federal agencies. While Cory breezed through the material, Jonathan's mind went numb after the first half hour.

"Jesus, this stuff is drier than reading a phone book."

Cory looked up, "Really? I find it fascinating."

"Different strokes for different folks, I guess."

"Tell you what, I'll make notes of points you will need to know while you order takeout."

Jonathan jumped on it. This was a winner on two fronts. First, he escaped a task he found incomprehensible, and second, he could enjoy a dinner at Cory's that would be edible.

After dinner Jonathan studied Cory's notes, trying to memorize the salient points. While he found the task difficult, he knew he had to sound credible when he talked to people at the contractors.

"So, who do we talk to first?"

Cory answered immediately. "The one in Boston."

"Why that one?"

"I've never been to Boston."

Jonathan gave a surprised look at Cory and was about to criticize her choice. Then he thought, why not? At this stage, one supplier was as good as another. "Okay, I'll make the reservations."

Cory took some vacation time, of which she had accrued a great deal, and Jonathan lined up the air and hotel reservations.

Three days later, Jonathan and Cory arrived at the San Francisco airport an hour and a half early, cleared TSA, and ordered breakfast at the Lark Creek Grill. When they were seated, Jonathan noticed that Cory seemed agitated.

"What's wrong?"

Cory shrugged her shoulders and tried to smile. "I'm a little nervous about flying. I'll be all right."

"Look, you don't have to do this. I can meet with these people alone."

Cory shook her head. "No, I'm coming. I said I'll be all right." A slight edge to her voice made Jonathan back off.

When they left the restaurant and made their way to their gate, Cory's posture was incredibly stiff. Jonathan wanted to help but had no idea what he could do.

Once seated in business class, Cory remained silent, staring straight ahead. Her body was rigid for the entire six-hour flight. When Jonathan suggested a Bloody Mary, Cory shook her head without replying. It was one of the longest six hours of Jonathan's life.

Cory did not relax until the plane touched down at Logan.

They grabbed a cab but barely talked on the short ride to their hotel. Cory was surprised when the taxi pulled up at the Ritz Hotel. "The Ritz?"

Jonathan smiled as he said, "Nothing's too good for my girl."

"I'm sorry about my problem."

Jonathan took her hand and gave it a light squeeze. "The flight must have been exhausting for you. Cory smiled and patted his hand. "It was. I'm really tired, can we just order room service?"

"Absolutely."

Cory had trouble keeping her eyes open as they finished dinner. Jonathan smiled and suggested that she turn in early. She nodded and headed to the bedroom. Cory fell into a deep sleep moments after her head hit the pillow.

Jonathan watched a movie with the sound low.

———

The morning found Cory fully recovered. After a quick breakfast, Jonathan and Cory took a cab to their appointment at Encore, an electronic guidance system supplier to Independence. Jonathan was dressed for the meeting, wearing a blue blazer, a white shirt with a pale blue tie, and gray slacks. Cory wore what she normally wore to work at Lockheed, a white blouse, tan skirt, and jacket, and low-heeled shoes.

The cab dropped them off at a large two-story building in an industrial park on the northeast edge of Boston. The structure was pure vanilla in architectural style. Other than the company's name on the front of the building, it did not differ from any of the other structures in the park.

Once inside, however, it definitely varied from its neighbors. Security was on overkill. They identified themselves and told the man at the security desk that they had an appointment with a woman named Marci Guerrero. A phone call was made, and they were handed visitor passes and told to place them around their necks. Cory's bag was examined, and they had to pass through a metal detector. A uniformed guard escorted them to Ms. Guerrero's office.

Jonathan noted that all the security personnel were armed. Marci Guerrero's office was medium-sized and furnished with modern, autonomous furniture. Her desk was bare except for her computer and phone. Jonathan guessed the woman to be in her midfifties. Marci Guerrero was of medium height, stout, and was wearing a conservative pantsuit. She stood and greeted her visitors with a smile and an inquisitive expression.

"Welcome to Encore, Mr. Scanlan. You said when you called that you are writing a book about fraud in the defense industry. I have no idea how I can help you." While she appeared friendly, she had a distracting voice that sounded like a chipmunk.

"Yes, I am. At this stage, I'm simply gathering information."

Guerrero motioned Jonathan and Cory to the two visitor chairs in front of her desk. "After you called, I googled you, and I'm aware that you are a successful author, but again, I have no idea how I can be of help."

"Perhaps not. By the way, this is my assistant, Cory Bishop. I understand Independence is one of your largest clients."

Jonathan noted a tenseness in the woman's body at the mention of Independence. "Yes, Independence is one of our customers."

"As one of your largest clients, I assume you're knowledgeable regarding their financial condition."

"I'm not going to be discussing that type of information regarding any of our clients." Jonathan watched as Ms. Guerrero's face became flushed.

"I only asking because there is very little, if any, public information available."

"We have an excellent relationship with Independence."

"I'm sure you do. I understand Encore invested a good deal of capital to manufacture the electronic guidance systems for Independence. I would assume your company would want to be confident in your client's financial situation."

Marci Guerrero abruptly stood up. "Mr. Scanlan, this meeting is over." She picked up her phone, dialed an extension, and asked security to escort her guests out of the building.

Cory turned to Jonathan as they waited for their Uber ride. "That was a waste of time."

"She seemed overly defensive."

"Well, you did come on a little strong."

Jonathan simply shrugged. "Since this is your first visit to Boston, let's check out some of the sights."

The balance of the day was spent touring the city, starting with the historic *USS Constitution* in the harbor. As they walked around Boston, Jonathan kept trying to think of what he could do to help Cory for the flight home.

When they returned to the hotel, Jonathan excused himself, telling Cory he had to run an errand and that he would be back in about an hour. Cory gave him a curious expression but just nodded. He grabbed one of the taxis stationed in front of the Ritz and told the driver to take him to the nearest pharmacy. After a short ride he asked the driver to wait. Jonathan stood in line and waited while the pharmacist took care of a woman.

When the pharmacist was free, Jonathan stepped forward. "My friend has a severe fear of flying and we're about to fly back to San Francisco. Can you recommend something that would help her? We don't have time to get a prescription from a doctor, so it would have to be something over the counter."

The man led Jonathan to an aisle and pointed to a small package. "This may help. RediCalm by Nutreance, it will cause drowsiness, but it's the best I can do without a prescription."

Jonathan thanked the man, paid for the product and returned to the Ritz. When he opened the door to their room, he found Cory watching the local news.

"So, what was your secret mission?"

He handed her the RediCalm bottle. "This may help on the flight home."

Cory glanced at the small bottle of pills, jumped out of her chair and embraced Jonathan. Tears welled from her eyes as she smiled at Jonathan. "Oh, Jonathan, I love you."

Jonathan was momentarily stunned as he held her. He kissed her as he searched for an adequate response. Finding none, he steered Cory to the room's king size bed.

CHAPTER 11

Cory took the RediCalm tablets shortly before boarding their plane at Logan. Jonathan noticed that she seemed remarkably calm compared to her behavior at SFO. He wondered if it was the medication working or her belief that the tablets would solve her problem.

Cory dozed off shortly after takeoff to Jonathan's great relief, allowing him to relax and watch a ridiculous action movie. He nudged her awake as the plane was landing. She remained somewhat groggy as they deplaned and made their way to her condo. Jonathan helped her into bed, retrieved his Jeep, and drove to his apartment.

Once home, Jonathan looked at the list of companies that supplied products or services to Independence. No individual supplier stood out. One, Hayden Software, supplied software to Independence and was located in Palo Alto. He went online and googled the company. They were just under ten years old, appeared to specialize in software for defense contractors, and appeared quite profitable.

Jonathan called the company and arranged a meeting in two days. That accomplished, he sent Cory an email, letting her know about the pending meeting.

The next day, Cory called Jonathan. "Okay, remind me. What does this company do?"

"The name is Hayden Software, named after the company's founder. I'm not sure, but they must create the software for the guidance systems."

"I assume we'll use the same story as the one we gave Encore."

Jonathan nodded as he replied, "Yes, it worked to get us in the door at Encore."

"Hopefully, we can get more information this time."

"Agreed. Why don't I come down to your place tomorrow night, and we can drive down to Palo Alto from there?"

"Great, I'll fix something for dinner."

Jonathan grimaced at the thought, but could not think of a believable excuse. "I'll be there about six."

Luckily, dinner consisted of a salad, previously frozen ravioli, and ice cream for dessert.

The meeting had been set for 10:00, allowing Jonathan and Cory to avoid the morning commute traffic. Hayden Software occupied a medium-sized, glass-fronted building not too far from Hewlett Packard's old headquarters facility.

When they arrived, they were greeted at the reception desk, provided with visitor passes, and escorted to the office of the controller. While security was apparent, it was nothing like at Encore. Norman Dempsey stood, walked away from his desk, and offered his hand. Dempsey was a tall, thin man somewhere in his midforties. Jonathan thought the man's trim physique might be that of a long-distance runner or bicyclist.

Dempsey was smiling as they shook hands. "Welcome to Hayden. Please take a seat. Can I get you anything, water or coffee?"

Jonathan and Cory declined the offer but were encouraged by the man's attitude. Stacks of folders occupied a portion of the controller's desk alongside several family photos.

"So, Mr. Scanlan, I understand you're writing a book about corruption within government contractors. I'm not sure how I can help you, but I'm happy to answer any questions you may have."

"Thank you, and please call me Jonathan. At this stage, I'm simply in the process of gathering information."

"Well, I can assure you that everything is on the up and up at Hayden. I'm sure you're aware that companies like ours are closely monitored by the federal government."

"I'm sure you are and we're not here about Hayden Software. We understand Independence is one of your clients."

Jonathan's statement caused a puzzled expression to appear. "Yes, Independence is a client. Are you suggesting something is going on at Independence that shouldn't be?"

"No. Our problem with Independence is basically a lack of information. Do you have any information on their finances?"

Dempsey shrugged and shook his head. "Not really. They are a privately held corporation. All I can say is their credit rating is excellent. Payments are always made on time, and we've had no disputes with the company. I don't know what else to say. Just like us, the government monitors them closely."

"They're fairly new on the scene. The capital investment required to establish that kind of operation had to be considerable. Do you know the source of their startup capital?"

Dempsey again shrugged and took a moment to adjust his wire-rimmed glasses. "No. To my knowledge the question never came up."

Jonathan sat back in his chair. It was obvious no more information on Independence was going to be forthcoming. "Well, thank you for your time, Mr. Dempsey." Jonathan and Cory stood and shook hands with the controller.

"Let me escort you."

When they were walking back to Jonathan's Jeep, Cory turned to him: "Not a lot there."

"No, but it's interesting. Would you be doing a significant amount of business with a company that provides no financial information?"

Cory thought for a moment. "No, I wouldn't. So, what do we do next?"

"I'm not sure. Maybe visit other suppliers." Not a lot of confidence in Jonathan's voice.

CHAPTER 12

John Owen, the CEO at Independence, lifted the phone, noting from its screen a familiar name. "Morning, Norman."

"Morning, John. I just had an interesting visitor. Are you familiar with an author named Jonathan Scanlan?"

"No. Why was he an interesting visitor?"

"He's written a couple of nonfiction bestsellers. He claims to be doing research for a book on corruption within the defense contractor community."

There was a pause before Owen replied. "Okay."

"Basically, he wanted information about Independence."

"What did you tell him?"

"Nothing. I told him Independence was privately held and there was nothing I could give him."

"How did he respond?"

"He pressed me. Asked me how we could be doing business with a company and not know anything about their finances."

"And you said?"

"That Independence had a great credit rating; paid its bills on time, and we have no disputes with you."

John Owen thanked Dempsey, ended the call, and sat back in his chair, considering what he had just heard.

———

After Jonathan had dropped Cory off at her condominium, he drove back to his apartment. The first thing he did was call Cal, leaving a message to return his call when he could. Jonathan was watching the evening news when his cell chirped.

"Hi Jon, how's the investigation going?"

"Not that well. I have some real questions about Independence, but no answers. Does it seem odd to you that their suppliers either won't talk about the company or claim they know nothing about where the startup money came from or anything else about their finances?"

Cal thought for a moment. "It does sound odd."

"Any chance you could dig up that type of information?"

"By dig up, you mean hack."

"I was trying not to be crude about it."

Jonathan could hear his friend chuckling. "I'll look into it."

Cal got back to Jonathan two days later. "I think the firewalls at Independence are more secure than those at the CIA."

"So, no luck?"

"Not much. I wasn't able to find out the source of their startup money, but they do have deep pockets."

"Anything on the management team?"

"The CEO is John Owen, and the CFO is Blake Dunne, and here it gets interesting. Normally, chief executive backgrounds are all over the place. Owen is fifty-four and graduated from Yale. Dunne is forty-five and went to the University of Chicago. That's about it."

"Unlike you, I don't have any experience dealing with corporate executives, but that strikes me as beyond unusual."

"It is. Chief executives tend to have oversized egos. They like the limelight. I've never seen anything like this."

Jonathan paused as he considered Cal's comments. "You know, it fits with the lack of information on Independence."

"I agree. I'll keep digging, but that's where we are now."

Jonathan had earlier gone to the Independence website, which had also provided almost no useful information. He discounted any form of direct approach, which would be tantamount to waving a red flag and saying we're investigating you.

He thought for a moment and called Cal back. "They must have banking relationships, and they would have to provide financial information to them. Any chance you could come up with information through them?"

"I probably could if I knew who they banked with."

"They're based in Austin, Texas. I imagine they would use one of the larger banks in the state."

"Let me see what I can come up with."

Three days later, Cal called Johathan, suggesting a meeting. Jonathan agreed to get together Saturday evening. He then contacted Cory, who agreed to come up to the city.

They sat around Cal's dining room table, anxiously waiting for information from their host. Cal looked up from his notes and shook his head. "Something is definitely wrong at Independence. They bank with Bank of America, but only for their payroll and checking accounts. As far as I can determine, they have no line of credit or any other form of debt. I was able to obtain a copy of their incorporation papers. They were incorporated in Delaware, but set up operations in Austin."

"You said something is wrong. I'm not seeing it."

"They're a private corporation and under contract with the Department of Defense, so I can understand a high level of security, but this is over the top. They shun publicity, no information is available on the management team, they appear to have no debt, and their firewall is the best I've ever seen."

Jonathan studied his friend. "Unusual but not criminal."

"No, but it's like they don't want anyone to know anything about their business. There's something else." Cal glanced at Jonathan and Cory. "They may have detected my efforts to get in their system."

Cal saw the immediate concerns on Jonathan and Cory's faces. He held up his hand. "There's no way they can trace it back to me. They would only know someone was trying to hack them. I imagine, as a defense contractor, quite a few organizations have made attempts to get into their system."

Cal saw Jonathan and Cory relax slightly. Cal did not say anything, but he hoped his efforts would not be linked to Jonathan and Cory's recent visits to Hayden and Encore.

———

Owen put down his phone. His head of IT had just informed him of an unsuccessful attempt to hack their system. He paused and thought about his earlier conversation with Norman Demsey. A consequence? Possibly.

Owen went online and googled Jonathan Scanlan. The website described Jonathan's degrees from Cal, his teaching career at San Francisco State and the success of his two books. Owen studied Jonathan's photo for a few moments. He then went to his private Amazon account and ordered *Culprits of the American Culture* and *The Culprit Murders*.

John Owen was not a reader and only skimmed through *Culprits of the American Culture* when the books arrived. He did study *The Culprit Murders* in great detail, making notes as he went through the book. He made a few calls, trying to learn more about the author's personal life. When he finished, he called a number, using a recently purchased burner phone.

When a familiar voice answered, he said, "We have to meet."

"Where and when?'

"Long Metropolitan Park at seven o'clock tonight. There are benches by the northeast entrance."

Owen arrived early, picked the bench furthest from the park entrance and settled in. A tall, thin man, somewhere in his midthirties, walked into the park and glanced around the area before joining Owen.

"We appear to have a problem."

The tall man did not reply, waiting for Owen to continue. "An author named Jonathan Scanlan has been making inquiries at our subcontractors. We also detected an attempt to hack our systems. The attempt was unsuccessful. I believe it was related to Scanlan."

"You want the author to disappear?"

"The problem is more complicated than that. Scanlan is not alone. A woman named Cory Bishop was with him when he visited Encore and Hayden. In one of his books, he mentions a computer friend, I believe that would be a man named Cal Hulse."

"Where are these people located?"

"Hulse and Scanlan are in San Francisco. I don't know the location of the woman."

"One person wouldn't be a problem. Three, all related, would be."

Owen nodded. He handed the tall man an envelope. "Here's what I have on Scanlan and Hulse and some travel money. You need to get to San Francisco and follow them, learn their habits. Let's wait and see if we have to take extreme measures. Call me when you know more about the involvement of this woman, Cory Bishop."

The tall man pocketed the envelope, rose from the bench, and left the park. John Owen sat for a few more moments, thinking about what may have to be done.

CHAPTER 13

Jonathan was at a standstill in the investigation, a situation he found extremely uncomfortable. He thought, when all else fails, eat and drink. He called Cal and left a message, hoping his friend was free for dinner.

It was late afternoon when Cal returned the call. "Sure, Jon. Where do you want to go?"

"How about Boulevard? My treat."

"Pricey."

"We're worth it. Parking is impossible down there. I'll make reservations for six-thirty and pick you up in an Uber.

"Sounds like a plan."

With drinks in hand, Cal turned to his friend, "You know, I've had a change of heart over our current little project."

"How's that?"

"Well, as you know, I initially felt looking for government corruption just wasn't our thing. I have to say that looking into Independence has me intrigued. It's like a puzzle that I want us to solve."

Jonathan smiled and lifted his glass. "Glad to have you on board."

"It bugs me that I couldn't get into their system. I've never had that happen before."

"So, you're going to keep trying?"

"You bet your ass I am."

The conversation shifted to the 49er's efforts to land a new defensive coordinator and what the team should do at the upcoming draft. Neither man noticed a tall, thin man seated at the bar.

Jonathan was frustrated as he sat in his apartment watching the evening news. He wanted to be working on the investigation, but had no idea how to proceed, other than through Cal's efforts. He also gave thought to his relationship with Cory. A woman he had only known for a less than two months has said she was in love with him. Things seemed to be happening too fast. On the other hand, he could not envision ever finding a woman that was as intelligent, beautiful, and sexy as Cory Bishop. He could not visualize his life without Cory, but did that mean he was in love?

———

The thin man sat in his hotel room and called John Owen. Owen picked up on the second ring. "It's me."

"Any news?"

"Scanlan and Hulse had dinner together this evening. I wasn't close enough to hear what they talked about, but I was able to find out a little info on Hulse. He's apparently a really big-time high-tech computer consultant."

"So, our hacker?"

"Probably."

There was a pause as Owen thought about Cal Hulse. "I'm wondering, if we took out Hulse, would that stop their little project?"

It was the thin man's turn to pause. "Well, so far, he hasn't been able to penetrate your system. If I got rid of Hulse, Scanlan would not sit still. He'd raise hell, probably go to the FBI, and that could be a problem."

"Anything on the woman that had been with Scanlan at Encore and Hayden?"

"Nothing yet, I'm working on it."

"Lots to think about. Keep me posted."

———

Jonathan put on shorts, a T-shirt, and running shoes, made his way out of his apartment, and began jogging down toward the Marina Green. The day was clear and sunny with a slight breeze coming off the bay. He began running down Octavia and paused before crossing Union, checking to make sure there were no cars coming his way. He noticed a silver Ford Escape that had stopped to let him get across the street. The man at the wheel seemed vaguely familiar, but he could not come up with where he had seen him.

He was nearly home, walking now to catch his breath, when he saw what looked like the same man driving past his apartment. His mind went back to the days when he had been a person of interest and under twenty-four-hour surveillance by the FBI. He told himself that he was being paranoid but could not shake his lingering concern.

Jonathan had made reservations for dinner at Spasso in San Carlos. After cleaning up and paying a few bills, he left for his date with Cory. He glanced around as he walked to his new garage but saw no sign of the Ford Escape.

Traffic was slow on the 101, Jonathan having caught the tail end of the commuters heading home. He arrived at Cory's condo a little later than expected, but still with plenty of time to make their reservation. Spasso turned out to be an upscale, attractive restaurant. Jonathan and Cory chatted about the upcoming national election. Fortunately, they were politically kindred spirits.

On the short drive back to Cory's condo, they failed to notice the beige Toyota Camry that followed them home. The thin man parked with a view of Cory's fourth-floor windows and did not leave until the unit's lights were turned off.

He called John Owen as he drove back to the city. "The Cory Bishop woman is Scanlan's girlfriend. He's at her place for the night."

"We have to assume she's participating in their investigation."

"Safe to say."

"The biggest threat is Hulse getting into our system. Apparently, he's the best around."

The thin man did not bother to comment. Finally, Owen said, "You're right, if we take out Hulse, Scanlan will not go quietly into the night, but it may be necessary. I have to think about it."

"Let me know. I'll stay in the area until I hear from you."

CHAPTER 14

Cal drove down 101 for a meeting in Foster City. He anticipated another difficult project but knew that was why they were willing to pay him the big bucks. With his mind focused on the upcoming meeting, he took no notice of the Camry that had followed him from his condominium on Pacific.

The beige rental had remained several car lengths behind Cal's Lexus. The Camry peeled away when Cal turned into his client's parking lot. The thin man had no interest in spending hours sitting in his car, only to then follow the man home.

His appraisal of the area around Cal's home had not been encouraging. He would stand out like a red flag if he sat in his car for an extended period of time. He also could not see a workable spot for a long-range shot. Another complication was Cal Hulse's lack of a consistent behavior pattern. The man did not go to work and come home on a consistent schedule like most working people. He left and returned on an erratic basis.

He also noted that the building appeared to have excellent security. Cameras covered the street and entrance. If he were told to hit Cal Hulse, the task would not be an easy one.

On the other hand, Scanlan would not be a problem. He ran by himself on a semi-regular basis, and his building's security was a joke.

Unfortunately, killing Jonathan Scallan would not eliminate the threat of the system being hacked.

He decided there was little to be gained by continuing to follow and surveil the two men, or, for that matter, Cory Bishop. *Wicked* was appearing in the city, so he decided to take a night off and treat himself to the theater.

———

Cal concluded a direct assault on Independence's internal system was not going to be successful. After a great deal of thought he concluded that Independence's suppliers had to have some degree of access to the company's system. If he could get into one of their systems, see how they interacted with Independence, he might exploit the connection.

He thought about what Jonathan and Cory had told him about their visits to Encore and Hayden. Encore appeared to be overly security conscious. That did not necessarily extend to their cybersecurity, but it might. He decided to begin probing Hayden's systems.

Cal smiled as he noted Hayden was using Oracle, an excellent software system, but one that he had worked on for the company. Disguising his IP address was as challenging as attempting to penetrate the system. There would be little mercy if he were caught hacking a United States defense contractor. Cal did not wish to spend the rest of his life in an unpleasant federal penitentiary. It took several days, but a diligent and talented investigator, trying to trace the source of the penetration, would conclude that it had originated in China. Who would be surprised?

Satisfied, Cal used a backdoor to penetrate Hayden's system. He probed until he found the link between the Hayden and Independence systems. The link gave him limited access to a portion of the Independence IT system, and he was finding it difficult to expand his search.

As he took a break, he checked his messages. Jonathan had called several hours earlier, asking if he was free for dinner.

Call returned the call. "Sure, I could use a break."

"How about the Slanted Door?

"Sure."

"I'll make a reservation and come by and pick you up at seven-thirty."

————

John Owen was about to call it a day. He was clearing his desk when his office phone rang. "Michael Aochi, we've detected a penetration of our system."

"How bad?"

"Nothing sensitive was taken so far but that could change."

"Do you have the source?"

"It appears to have come from China."

"Do everything you can to block it, and I mean everything." Owen was breathing heavily as he ended the call. He muttered, China my ass. He sat back down in his chair and fought to control his breathing. He picked up his private phone and made the call.

The thin man picked up after the first ring. "Yes?"

"It's Hulse, he's gotten into our system. Take him out." His hand was shaking as he considered the implications.

CHAPTER 15

They arrived at the Ferry Building via Uber. Entered the restaurant and were immediately guided to a table. Jonathan turned to Cal as they studied the menu. "Are you familiar with Vietnamese food?"

"No. I assume it's somewhat like Chinese."

"Somewhat, but also somewhat different. Remember, the French were there quite a while."

Cal put down his menu. "You order."

After a predinner cocktail, Jonathan ordered Pho, Bun neu Cua, and Bun Do Hue and beer. Cal's expression was one of surprise. "How did you know what to order?"

Jonathan smiled at his friend. "I dated a Vietnamese girl for a little while when we were at Cal."

When they were served, Cal looked up from the table, "Well, this is really good."

"Glad you liked it. Any progress with Independence?"

"I'm in. I got into Hayden's system and used it to penetrate Independence's system. I haven't been able to get anything interesting, but I'm close."

"That's great. Keep me posted. When I get home, I'll give Cory a call."

"How serious is it with Cory?"

Jonathan looked away for a moment, clearly uncomfortable with the question. "I don't know Cal. I'm taking this day by day."

Seeing Jonathan's reaction, Cal changed the subject to the April NFL draft and the needs of the 49ers. After dinner, Jonathan called to arrange an Uber pickup. It was cold outside, and the two men huddled in the building's entry as they waited for their ride. They stepped out when a gray Toyota with an Uber light on the dash arrived.

Before they reached the car, Jonathan noticed a tall, thin man approaching with something in his hand. Jonathan realized it was a gun. He grabbed Cal and dragged him around to the front of the vehicle, putting it between them and the thin man.

Cal was yelling, asking Jonathan what he was doing when Jonathan pulled Cal to the ground. The man fired three quick shots. The shooter, still twenty yards away, tried to move out into the street for a clear shot. Cal and Jonathan scooted to the passenger side of the vehicle as the man fired two more shots, one hitting the Uber driver.

The Embarcadero was crowded with locals and tourists entering and leaving the Ferry Building, and others walking along the sidewalk. Everyone was panicking, screaming, and either diving for cover or running away.

The shooter, realizing time was running out, turned and ran.

Jonathan and Cal remained crouched behind the Uber vehicle for several minutes before standing. They could hear approaching sirens. Jonathan glanced at his friend and noticed Cal was shaking. He put his arm around Cal and tried to comfort the man.

The first black and white screeched to a halt beside the Uber, and two uniforms jumped out of the vehicle with weapons drawn. They swung their heads, surveilling the area, before focusing on Jonathan and Cal. They shouted at them, demanding they raise their hands over their heads. Jonathan immediately did so, but Cal simply stood still, shaking and staring at the ground.

The younger of the two officers pointed his gun at Cal and shouted, "Raise your hands or we'll shoot."

Jonathan yelled back at the man, "He's in shock, you idiot."

The older officer told his partner to back off and stepped forward. His gun remained out as he told Jonathan to stand still. As he glanced around at the bullet holes in the Uber vehicle, he began to realize Jonathan and Cal were the victims, not the shooter.

He holstered his weapon and told his partner to do the same. The younger officer hesitated until his partner glared at him. He glanced at Cal before addressing Jonathan. "What the hell happened?"

"My friend and I just had dinner at the Slanted Door. When we came out to meet our Uber driver a man, coming toward us, began shooting. I think the driver got hit."

The officer immediately rushed to the driver's side of the car, opened the door, and checked the Uber driver. The man had been shot in the side of his head and was clearly dead.

He spoke into his com set as he walked back to Jonathan and Cal.

"Can I lower my arms?"

The man nodded and asked for identification. Jonathan glanced at the younger officer, who apparently had not bought the concept that Jonathan and Cal were victims. Jonathan pulled out his wallet slowly, removed his driver's license, and handed it to the uniform in front of him.

"Can you call for an ambulance? My friend is in bad shape."

"Who is your friend?"

"Cal Hulse. He's a computer guy. We both live in the city."

The uniform looked at Jonathan's driver's license. "At the same address?"

"No, Cal lives on Pacific Avenue."

"Detectives are on the way."

"Okay, but get Cal to a hospital."

The officer did not reply but told his partner to tape off the area.

Twenty minutes later, a black sedan parked on the edge of the crime scene, and two men stepped out and walked over to the Uber. The older uniform took them aside and told them what he knew. The lead detective stood and looked at Jonathan and Cal for a full minute before addressing Jonathan.

"Detectives Leo Simon and Leroy Johnson, and you are?"

"Jonathan Scanlan, and this is my friend Cal Hulse."

"Can't Mr. Hulse answer?"

"He's in shock. You need to get him medical attention."

"We'll see." Detective Simon was a big man, in his midfifties with thinning brown hair, broad shoulders, and somewhat overweight. His partner, Leroy Johnson, was a Black man who was rail thin and of average height.

"We'll see is not good enough. If Cal doesn't get medical attention and his condition worsens, the city isn't going to like what happens next."

"You a lawyer?"

"No, but you're going to need one if you don't take care of him."

Detective Simon's face reddened, and he was about to snap back, until he thought about it. It was clear Cal was in no condition to make a statement. He nodded and called for an ambulance.

"So, tell us what happened."

"We had dinner at the Slanted Door and called Uber for a ride home. As we approached the car, I saw a man coming toward us with a gun. I pulled Cal behind the car, and the man began shooting at us. After a few shots, he took off running in that direction." Jonathan pointed to the south.

Detective Johnson was taking notes. His partner was studying Jonathan as he spoke. When Jonathan paused, he asked, "What did the man look like?"

"Caucasian, tall, probably about six-three, thin, and I'd guess about forty."

"If we showed you mug shots, do you think you could identify him?"

"Probably."

"Why was he trying to kill you and Mr. Hulse?"

Jonathan was not about to tell them about their investigation of Independence and Cal's illegal hacking. "I have no idea."

Simon and Johnson clearly did not buy this. Detective Simon stepped close to Jonathan, invading his space. "Come on. We're not in the mood for bullshit. Jealous husband? Some type of drug deal gone bad?"

Jonathan was pissed and about to respond when the ambulance arrived. Instead, he turned and led Cal toward the vehicle.

"Mr. Scanlan, we're not through with you." Detective Simon grabbed Jonathan's arm to detain him. Jonathan shook off the detective's arm and continued to lead Cal to the ambulance. He waited while the emergency personnel loaded Cal into the back of the vehicle before turning back to the two detectives.

"I assume you will want a formal statement. I would think you should be marshaling the troops to look for the man I described."

Detective Simon was fuming as he turned away and called it in. His partner seemed more stoic and, if anything, curious as he watched Jonathan.

The crime scene had become extremely busy and crowded with a dozen uniforms, another set of detectives, and a crime scene team. The press crowded outside the yellow tape, cameras running and questions being shouted. Jonathan and the police ignored them.

At a point, Detective Johnson tapped Jonathan on the shoulder and pointed to the car the two detectives had arrived in. Jonathan was seated in the back and driven to police headquarters on 3rd Street. Neither Jonathan nor the detectives spoke during the ride.

Once in the building, Jonathan was led to an interrogation room and left alone for a brief period of time. Finally, the two detectives, an older black man and a middle-aged woman, joined him at the table.

The older man shook Jonathan's hand and introduced himself as Chief of Detectives Lincoln Fenton and the woman as Judith Lavin.

Fenton sat down and studied Jonathan for a moment before speaking. "I was briefed by the detectives at the scene and had time to google you and Mr. Hulse before you came in. Why is someone trying to kill you or your friend? Do you know who the man is that shot at you?"

"I have no idea and no I don't know the man that shot at us."

"You'll have to do better than that."

"No, I don't."

The room was silent for a moment. "Was Mr. Hulse the target?"

"You'll have to ask Cal when he's able to give a statement."

"A man was killed. It's a crime to hold back information in an investigation."

"Am I free to go or do I need a lawyer?"

Chief of Detectives Lincoln Fenton paused several beats before he nodded. "We're going to ask you to work with our people to identify the man you saw. Yes, you can leave, but we're not finished talking to you."

––––––––

When Jonathan reached home, he called around and found that Cal was at San Francisco General. He was dreading his next call. Cory answered on the second ring.

"Cory, Cal and I are all right, but a man shot at us earlier this evening."

He could hear her gasp before she said, "Oh my god."

"We had dinner at the Ferry Building and were about to get in an Uber we had called for when a man with a gun moved toward us and started shooting. He killed the Uber driver, but didn't hit us. I'm sure it's going to be on the news. Cal went into shock. They took him to SF General.

"I'm coming up."

"Don't do that. I'm going to pack a bag and leave my apartment. I believe Cal was the main target, but we have to assume they know where we live. You were with me when we went to Encore and Hayden, so they probably know about you. Is there somewhere you can go for a day or two?"

Cory paused as she thought for a moment. "There's a woman at Lockheed that's a friend. I'm sure I could stay with her."

"That would work. I'll get Cal out of the hospital as soon as I can and we need to figure out what we're going to do."

"I'm scared."

"So am I, but we'll get through this. I'll call you in the morning."

"Do you think I should go to work?"

"Yes, be careful, but as I said, I believe they're mainly after Cal."

"I love you."

Jonathan knew he had to respond. "I love you too." Jonathan quickly packed. Before leaving the apartment, he went to his miscellaneous drawer, rummaged through the things he should have thrown out years ago, until he found Myron Rossi's business card.

After picking up his Jeep, Jonathan stopped at his bank's ATM and withdrew up to his limit. He then drove to the Chelsea Inn on Lombard. He called the motel from the parking lot and was told rooms were available. When he approached the counter in the lobby, he wondered how awkward this was going to be.

The man at the counter smiled as Jonathan walked toward him. "Hi, I'd like a room."

"Certainly, do you have a reservation?"

"No, is that a problem?"

"Not at all. How long will you be staying with us?"

"I'm not sure, at least two nights."

"Fine. Can you give me your credit card?"

"I'd prefer to pay cash for two nights."

The man stepped back and stared at Jonathan. "You don't have a credit card?"

"I do, but I don't want to use it. My soon-to-be ex-wife is trying to serve divorce papers on me, and I'm trying to disappear for a few days."

"This is highly irregular."

"What would be the cost for two nights?"

"With tax, one hundred and eighty."

"How about I give you three hundred."

The man hesitated for a moment. "I think that would work. What name should I put on the registration?"

"Lincoln Fenton."

Jonathan placed three hundred on the counter. The clerk handed him a paper sleeve with the electronic keys inside. "Room two fourteen. Have a good sleep, Mr. Fenton."

When he reached his room, he called the hospital to check how Cal was doing and when he might be released. Apparently, Cal was doing well, and he was expected to be released the following day.

Jonathan's second call was to Myron Rossi, the motivational specialist. "Myron, it's Jonathan Scanlan."

"Hi, how's everything going?"

"Not too well. Have you ever done protection work?"

"Protection work?"

"You know, keeping someone from getting shot."

There was a pause before Myron replied. "Yeah, I have."

"I want to hire you. A man tried to shoot me and a friend I was with earlier this evening."

"Since we're talking, I assume he was unsuccessful."

"Yes, but he did kill the Uber driver who was picking us up."

"How soon do you want me up there?"

"As soon as you can get here."

"I'll be there tomorrow evening. I'll be driving so it'll take me about eight hours."

"Why don't you fly?"

"I couldn't fly with some of the stuff I'll be bringing."

"Call me when you're getting close, and I'll tell you where I'll be. I'm not staying at my apartment."

Jonathan lay in bed, staring at the ceiling and trying to decide what to do next.

CHAPTER 16

After a fitful sleep, Jonathan rose early, showered, and went downstairs for the motel's complimentary coffee and juice. He found a copy of the morning *Chronicle* and stared at a picture of Cal and himself on the front page. The article was vague on specifics but at least described Cal and himself as victims.

The morning was spent at police headquarters, first reviewing mug shots, second working with a sketch artist, and third, signing a formal statement. The man's face was not among the mug shots, but he thought the sketch artist pretty well nailed it.

Jonathan's next stop was San Francisco General Hospital. He was directed to the second floor, and finally to Cal. His friend was fully dressed, prowling the small space he shared with another patient.

"Jesus, Jon, get me out of here."

"What did they tell you?"

"The doctor has to release me. I've signed a boatload of papers, and they have all my insurance information."

Jonathan sat on one of the visitor's chairs and glanced at his watch. He tried to calm his agitated friend. "Take it easy, Cal. You'll be out of here soon." His words had little effect as Cal continued to pace.

The patient in the other bed seemed amused by the situation. "Hey, take it easy. At least you're getting out today."

Cal was about to snap back at the man, but instead just shook his head. An hour later, a short man in a white coat came into the room and smiled. "You're free to go, Mr. Hulse. An orderly will escort you."

When Cal started to move toward the door, the doctor put up his hand. "You have to leave in a wheelchair. Hospital policy."

Cal was about to argue when Jonathan stood and turned to the doctor. "That's fine, doctor. Can you arrange for that to happen?"

The doctor stepped out of the room, and moments later, a young man, dressed in white, pushed a wheelchair into the entry. Cal reluctantly sat in the chair and was pushed through the hospital to the main entrance. Cal stood, and Jonathan led him to his Jeep.

"Thanks, Jon. Sorry if I'm being a bit of an asshole. I just want to go home."

"Not going to happen."

Cal twisted in his seat and nearly shouted, "What?"

"Come on Cal, you're a smart guy. A man, who I believe is a pro, just tried to kill us. He has to know where you live. We're not going be staying at our normal places. I'm at a motel on Lombard. Cory is staying at a friend's place."

Cal relaxed and thought the situation through. "I need my stuff. My computer and some of my files."

"We'll get someone to pick up whatever you need. Maybe we can rent someplace: a VRBO-type place."

Cal rubbed his forehead in thought. "I can line something up through that realtor I mentioned to you."

"Can it be done without using our names? I don't want anyone to be able to trace us."

"I'll explain the situation to Jean. I'm sure she can make it happen."

"We also need cash. I have to assume they can trace us through our credit card usage. I used an ATM, but that doesn't give us much."

"I'll need my checkbook."

"We can have that picked up when our guy gets your other stuff. I'll have him do the same at my place."

"What guy?"

"You'll meet him tonight. He's coming up from LA."

"Is this someone we can trust?"

"I hope so. I hired him."

Cal pulled out his phone and called his realtor. When he finished the call, he turned to Jonathan. She'll call back in a bit. She said lining up a place won't be a problem. You heard me tell her we need three bedrooms and someplace in or near the city."

Cal looked down at his feet and was silent for several moments. When he spoke, his voice was hushed. "I would be dead if you hadn't dragged me around that car."

Jonathan smiled at his friend. I didn't think, I just reacted."

Neither spoke for a while as Jonathan drove through the city. Cal glanced at Jonathan. "You said you hired this man. How much did you agree to pay him?"

"A thousand a day."

Cal looked startled. "Holy shit, that's three hundred-sixty thousand a year."

Jonathan laughed at his friend. "He won't be with us for a year. Probably a matter of weeks, and what is it worth to protect us?"

Cal glanced out the Jeep's window before nodding his head. "Okay, I'll split the cost with you. You think he can do that, protect us?"

"I certainly hope so."

"Where are we meeting him?"

"I lined up three rooms at the place I'm staying on Lombard."

"You didn't use our names, I hope."

"No. The rooms are all under the name Lincoln Fenton; he's the San Francisco chief of detectives."

This brought the first smile of the day to Cal Hulse.

When they reached the Chelsea Inn, Jonathan led Cal to his room and gave him his electronic key. "You have the room next door."

"I wouldn't want to live here, but not bad."

"We're only here until your realtor finds us a place."

Jonathan called Myron and gave him the address of the motel. "He's about two hours away."

He then called Cory and brought her up to speed. When she

offered to come up and stay with him, he declined. Telling her to wait until the realtor lined up their new place.

Cal was still in Jonathan's room when there was a knock on the door. When Cal opened it, he stepped back and stared up at one of the largest men he had ever encountered. In a deep voice, the man said, "Hi, I'm Myron."

Cal was startled for a moment until Jonathan said, "Come on in, Myron. Myron this is Cal."

Myron offered his hand, and after a moment, Cal shook it."

Jonathan stepped forward. "You have the room two down. Here's the key. We're only here until Cal's realtor lines up a VRBO-type place. Why don't you put your things in your room and then come back. We'll go over what we need you to do."

Myron nodded and carried his bags down the hallway. Cal turned to his friend and in a low voice said, "I'm glad we're not paying him by the pound."

"Why don't you make a list over everything you'll need from your condo. I'll be doing the same."

Both men were working on their lists when Myron returned. Jonathan's bed made a slight groaning noise when Myron sat down. Jonathan described what they were doing with their investigation of Independence and the shooting at the Ferry Building.

"Since then, we've basically disappeared. We're not registered here under our names, and we're using burner phones from now on." He handed Myron one of the phones. "There's another member of our little team, her name's Cory Bishop, and she'll be joining us when we move to our new place. Tomorrow, we need you to go to my apartment and Cal's condo and pack up the things on our lists. I have to assume our places are being watched."

Myron listened without comment. Finally, he asked: "Are there places you have to be in the next few days?"

"I don't have any place I have to be. What about you, Cal?"

"There's a meeting I have to attend in four days in Foster City."

"Where's Foster City?"

"On the peninsula, below the airport."

"Cory works at Lockheed in Sunnyvale. That's a little further south of Foster City. She's staying with a friend. They may know where she works and try to follow her when she leaves. We'll have to figure that one out."

Myron looked at the lists Jonathan and Cal had been working on. "Do you want me to pick up your stuff tonight?"

"No. You've had a long drive. Get some rest and you can do that tomorrow. We need a little more time on our lists."

Myron nodded, stood, and left the room.

The tall, thin man sat in his hotel room and thought about his situation. He had screwed up, and John Owen did not tolerate people who screwed up, and in his opinion, Owen was unstable. Owen had demanded immediate action, and he had reacted, making his move without serious planning.

He did not worry about the police. There had been no cameras outside the Ferry Building, and he was not in their databases. He did worry about Owen. While not probable, it was possible his employer would want him to permanently disappear. He was not in a forgiving business. It was also true that Scanlan, Hulse, and probably Bishop would not be going about their normal business.

His anxiety heightened as he glanced at his phone. He considered leaving the country. He had been well paid for his services over the years, and he had not spent his money foolishly. He had documents that supported several false identities. He had been born Leo Zesiger, but he barely remembered that name and had not used it for over twenty years. Even Owen did not know the name.

Reluctantly, he picked up his phone and called Owen.

John Owen's voice was calm, but not friendly. "Things did not go well."

"No, they did not."

"Do you know where they are?"

"Not at the moment but they have to surface."

"How sure are you?"

"Quite sure. They're amateurs."

Owen was silent for several moments. The man who had once been Leo Zesiger was wondering if the connection had been lost when Owen spoke. "All right, stay where you are. We have tools to trace them. At some point, one of them will probably use their credit card or be in their car that has GPS. I'll let you know as soon as we have a fix on them."

"All right, I'll wait to hear from you."

As soon as he was off the phone, the man packed his bags and left the hotel. He turned in his rental, then rented a car at a different agency, using one of his other identities. Using that same identity, he checked into a new hotel. His one exposure was his phone. He could not get rid of it, leaving Owen with no ability to contact him. He turned it off and removed the SIM card, knowing it would be some time before Owen would have useful information. He also knew that when he reactivated it, Owen could track his location.

When he thought about his phone, he realized he could use it to set a trap if he believed Owen was sending someone to take him out. He had to give that more thought.

CHAPTER 17

Cal's realtor called the following morning. She'd lined up a place, but needed a name for the rental and, of course, cash for the deposit and rent. After a quick conversation with Jonathan, he gave her Myron Rossi's name and promised to drop off a check later in the day. The rental was in the town of Los Gatos, just west of San Jose. Cal and Jonathan knocked on Myron's door, and when he opened it, they gave him keys to their homes, the addresses, and lists of what they needed. He was also given the code for Cal's condominium's entrance.

Cal and Johathan hung out at the motel until Myron returned. Cal wanted to pick up his Lexus, but Jonathan reminded him that it could be tracked through its GPS. They would be using Jonathan's older Jeep, which was GPS-less, and Myron's rental, since no one knew he was involved.

Jonathan drove Cal to the realtor's office, where he provided her with a check and received keys to the rental. Myron was given the address, which he programmed into his GPS. Jonathan followed Myron's Ford out of the city, down 280, and eventually to Los Gatos.

The rental was a two-story contemporary, light yellow in color with green shutters. A small garden with a mixture of peony, roses and azaleas bloomed in an array of colors. The home's downstairs was comfortably furnished with a leather sofa facing a big screen and overstuffed chairs bracketed by end tables. A small dining room allowed seating for six. The kitchen was modern, featuring stainless steel appliances. The master bedroom was downstairs with a connecting bath. Two bedrooms upstairs shared a bath.

When Jonathan saw the arrangement, he said, "Is it all right if Cory and I share the master?"

Myron nodded. Cal shrugged as he was busy setting up his computer equipment. "Myron, I talked to Cory. We need you to pick her up after work and take her to her friend's home so she can collect her things. She's off at five-thirty. She'll be leaving her car at Lockheed. Please make sure you're not followed. Take my Jeep. I'm worried about the GPS thing. I talked to her and gave her your description" He gave the big man Lockheed's address and the keys to his Jeep.

"How long will it take me to get there from here?"

"It's not all that far, but it will be commuter time, so allow an hour."

After he had unpacked, Jonathan sat on the sofa and turned on Fox News.

———

The thin man realized Jonathan Scanlan and Cal Hulse had gone to ground. When he phoned Lockheed and asked for Cory Bishop, the call went through. He hung up before she answered the call. He glanced at his watch, 2:30, leaving plenty of time to drive down to Sunnyvale and follow Bishop.

He considered Cory Bishop a minor player in Scanlan and Hulse's project, but an excellent vehicle to lead him to the two men. When he arrived at the Lockheed facility, he found the parking lot divided between employee and visitor sections.

He parked in the visitor's area with a clear view on the building's main entrance. He knew he could easily recognize the woman and that she would probably be leaving somewhere between 5:00 and 6:00. A security vehicle cruised the lot periodically, and when it approached, he slid down in his seat.

As he watched, a number of people entered and left the building. At 5:30, they began to pour out, heading for the employee parking area. None were a stunningly beautiful blonde women. It was nearly 6:00 when an older silver Jeep made its way through the lot's visitors' area to the building's entrance. Cory Bishop stepped out and slid into the Jeep.

The thin man started his car and followed as the Jeep drove out of the parking lot and onto the street. Cory was glancing nervously at Myron. Jonathan had warned her that Myron was big, but he had not described the man as huge.

"Myron, I appreciate you picking me up, but why?"

"Jonathan knew your car had GPS, and he thought it could allow the bad guys to track you to where we're staying."

"Oh…" She wondered if Jonathan was being a little paranoid but then thought about the Ferry Building. "Okay, if we're going to my friend's house, we need to get on 101 north."

"We're going to take a little detour before we do that."

"Why?"

"I have to be sure we're not being followed."

Cory looked out at the mass of cars. "How can you tell?"

"We have a few tricks." He turned north off Enterprise Way, drove two blocks and then east toward El Camino Real. "We have a tail. Don't turn around. We don't want him to know we spotted him."

"How did you see him?"

"Only one car followed us on the two turns I made, but just to be sure we'll see what he does when I turn north on the next street."

A few minutes later: "Yeah, he's on us. I want to go north on a street with a lot of signals."

"You're close to El Camino. You'll come to it in two or three blocks."

When they came to it, Myron turned north toward Mountain View. The following car, a black sedan, tucked in two cars behind Myron. Myron slowed as he approached the next intersection. When the signal turned yellow, he powered through the intersection. The car behind him had to stop, blocking the black sedan.

"Okay, he's out of the picture. Let's get off this street for a few minutes." He turned into a strip mall, drove to the rear loading docks, and stopped. He waited ten minutes before turning around and returning to El Camino Real. "All right, tell me how to get to your friend's place."

Myron and Cory picked up her things at a Mediterranean-style two-story on a quiet tree-lined street. When they were back in the Jeep heading south on 280, Myron turned to Cory. "Beautiful home."

Cory nodded, clearly agitated. "I don't see how I can go to work if this person is going to follow us every day."

Myron remained silent, as he had no answer.

When they reached the rental in Los Gatos, Cory grabbed her bag and, head down, strode into the house. When Jonathan rose to hug her, she dropped her suitcase on the floor and faced Jonathan and Cal.

"This isn't working. We were followed when we left Lockheed. They obviously know when I leave. Look, I don't want to quit my job, but they can do this every day. Myron lost the car that was on us, but sooner or later we won't lose them."

Nobody spoke for a very long minute. Cal asked, "Could you do your work remotely?"

Cory frowned as she gave his question her attention. "It's something I've never done, but I imagine I could. I'd have to talk to my supervisor."

Jonathan said, "This isn't forever. I don't know exactly how long it'll take to wrap this up, but it should be soon."

Cory dropped into a chair and tried to think it through. "I'll talk to Carl tomorrow. If I explain that I'm dealing with a temporary problem, I'm pretty sure he'll approve it. Tomorrow I can collect the files I'll need and transfer the contracts I'm working on into my laptop."

Myron looked at Cory. "Is there any way you can enter and leave without going through the main entrance?"

"I have to go through security at the main entrance when I go in, but I can leave through a different exit, like the loading docks."

Myron glanced around the room. "What if I drop you off really early, like at six o'clock? I don't believe they'll be set up that early."

"We can do that. Some people come in early to work out at the gym."

Myron smiled: "We'll do that tomorrow."

Cory nodded and relaxed. "Sorry I was so uptight. This is all new for me. You know, I could use a glass of wine."

When Cory left the room to put her things away, Myron took Jonathan aside. "She's really nice."

Jonathan nodded, wondering where Myron was going. "You know, when I told you I had done quite a bit of protection work, it was true, but it was always protecting bad guys from other bad guys. I've never protected good guys from bad guys. It's really a good feeling."

Jonathan smiled and patted Myron on his very large shoulder.

————

The thin man prided himself on his inner control. He never panicked, regardless of how tense or threatening the circumstances. The problem was, he did not know what the current circumstances were. He knew he could not trust John Owen. Did Owen consider him a liability after the fresco on the Embarcadero?

It had been five days since the Ferry Building. If Owen had set up a hit, that would be enough time to do so. He decided to conduct a test. Later that night he drove his rental to one of the city's downtown self-park garages. He parked on the third floor in one of the far corners of the garage. The facility primarily catered to workers from the nearby office buildings, and after 9:00 in the evening, it was nearly empty. He placed the SIM card back in his phone, turned it on and placed it on the passenger seat.

He left the car and moved into the shadows of one of the pillars about twenty yards away. He screwed a silencer to the end of his pistol and settled in to wait. He knew tracking his phone and isolating his location would take time, as would moving someone to the garage.

He had a great tolerance when it came to waiting. He sat down on the garage floor with his back against the wall. He thought about what he should do if Owen had sent someone to take him out. He could disappear. He had the financial resources and experience. The problem was, Owen and Independence had more resources and a long and unforgiving memory. Perhaps such thoughts were unnecessary, and no one was coming.

It was closing in on 3:00 when he heard a sound. He stood, listened, and peered around the support pillar. Two men in dark clothing were approaching from the garage's stairwell. They moved slowly toward his rental. When they were forty yards away, he could see their weapons.

As they closed on the car, they divided, one toward and driver's side and the other the passenger side. The thin man stepped away from the shadows and shot the man on the driver's side in the back of his head. The other man spun around, but before he could raise his pistol, the bullet from the thin man's pistol hit his forehead.

The thin man thought, "Well, I have my answer."

He opened the rental's trunk, which he had earlier lined with a drop cloth, and shoved the two bodies inside. He did not bother to check for identification, knowing none would be found.

He drove out of the garage and across the city. He found an industrial area off Cesar Chavez, now deserted, parked, and pulled the bodies from the trunk. He dragged them away from the street and into an empty parking lot. The drop cloth went into a dumpster three blocks away, and the cell phone was dismantled and thrown out the car window.

His evening's work done, he drove to his hotel and went to bed.

CHAPTER 18

The following morning, Myron drove Cory to Lockheed using Jonathan's Jeep. Later, Cal, never an early riser, caffeinated up and continued to scurry through Independence's computer system. Jonathan, with no task at hand, went for a run.

When Myron returned, he went to his room and spent the morning cleaning his weapons. On the way to a morning shower, Cal glanced into Myron's bedroom and gasped at the array of semi-automatic pistols and rifles spread out on Myron's bed.

"My god, Myron. You think you'll need all that?"

Myron smiled. "I hope not."

Cal, who had never fired a pistol, rifle, or shotgun in his life, shook his head as he headed to his shower.

When Jonathan returned and cleaned up, he paced the home's small downstairs in frustration. He knew everything hinged on Cal finding something they could use, but sitting on the sideline was maddening.

Cory immediately noticed Jonathan's discomfort the moment she and Myron walked in the door.

Jonathan glanced away from the television. "Did anyone try to follow you?"

Myron shook his head. "No, I was careful, but no one was there today."

Cory sat down next to Jonathan and took his hand. "I can tell you're upset. What is it?"

"You have your work, and Cal's doing his computer thing. I feel I should be doing something."

"I understand." She thought for a moment. "I know this isn't an answer, but why don't we go out tonight and have a nice dinner?"

Jonathan smiled, reached over, and hugged her. "Sure, they don't know where we are." He turned to Cal and Myron. "Let's go to a nice place for dinner."

Cal looked up from his laptop. "I don't want to stop right now. Just bring me back something."

Myron, sensing that Cory would prefer to be alone with Jonathan, shook his head. "You go ahead; I have some calls to make."

After a quick internet search, Jonathan made reservations at Teleferic Barcelona.

"We're on for seven-thirty."

Los Gatos was a fairly small town, and the restaurant on University Avenue was a short drive. They had to wait for a table, which led them to the bar. Jonathan ordered a beer while Cory opted for a Spanish version of a chardonnay.

Cory smiled and looked at Jonathan. "You never told me how you and Cal became close friends."

"We met at Cal. I was there on a golf scholarship, hoping to be able to turn pro, and Cal was on an academic full ride. Cal has always been into sports. Not as a participant, but as a fan. He took an interest in the school's golf program. If I remember right, he came to a function after we beat Stanford. We just hit it off."

"But you became a professor, and not a golf pro."

"Couldn't make the cut."

"Lucky me. If you were on the tour, I would never have met you." She had just planted a kiss when the girl at the desk arrived to tell them their table was ready.

They chatted throughout dinner, Jonathan telling her how he had met Myron, and Cory about her earlier life. Jonathan visibly relaxed, the day's frustration at least temporarily pushed aside. No doubt, the bottle of excellent wine helped. Before they left, they remembered to order a takeout for Cal.

As they walked back to the Jeep, Jonathan felt an intense closeness to Cory. He had been attracted to her from the time they first met, but now there was much more.

Although the evening was still young, they passed through the living room, pausing only long enough to hand Cal his dinner, before proceeding to their bedroom.

————

When he had received no phone call the prior night, John Owen had no doubt what had happened. The question was, what would his man do? He assumed the man would try to disappear, and finding him would be a challenge. He knew the man, whom he had always referred to as Johnson, was smart and experienced.

Disappearing was not as easy as one might think. Owen had enormous resources that he would apply. The man knew too much. He sat back in his executive chair and thought about his immediate plans. Jonathan Scanlan and Cal Hulse represented the most immediate threat.

With the tall, thin man calling himself Johnson gone, Owen had contacted his principals and had been put in touch with a man they referred to as the handler. He picked up his private phone and made a call to a man he had never met. He told the handler that Scanlan and Hulse must be eliminated at all costs. If they were in a building with a thousand other people, blow up the building. Put everyone you have on this."

The listener made no comment. "Do you understand me?"

"Yes, but this could become very messy."

"It could, but we have no other choice."

The line went dead, which the CEO understood as acceptance.

———

The days at the Los Gatos home passed with an unchanging routine. Cal was married to his computer. Cory worked on her Lockheed contracts, and Jonathan alternated between running and golf. Myron seemed content to read and to take long walks.

Cal surfaced and reminded the group that he had to attend a meeting in Foster City the next day. Myron simply nodded. Jonathan asked, "What time is your meeting?"

"One o'clock."

"All right, Myron will drive you there and pick you up." He turned to the big man. "Take the Jeep. If they spot your rental, they may be able to trace it and access the GPS."

The following morning broke clear and sunny. When it was time, Myron placed a daypack on the floor on the Jeep's passenger side and a duffel bag behind the front seats. When Cal slipped into the SUV, his feet landed on the daypack.

"What's in the bag?"

"Insurance."

Following Cal's directions, Myron took the 280 north to 92, then a short ride down to the 101. Myron dropped Cal off at the main entrance. "How long is the meeting?"

"It varies, somewhere between three and four hours." Cal stepped out of the vehicle with his laptop and briefcase.

As Myron pulled away, he noted armed security by the entrance.

John Owen had thoroughly researched Cal Hulse, and one of the products of that research was a list of Hulse's clients. He had instructed the handler to place surveillance at the headquarters of each of those clients. The man at the Foster City facility dialed the only number on his burner phone.

"I think the man we're looking for just arrived."

"What do you mean, you think you saw him?"

"Look, I'm a hundred yards away from the entrance and I only saw him for a few seconds."

"What type of car dropped him off?'

"An older silver Jeep."

The handler listened, then called two of the men who took care of his difficult problems. Cal Hulse was pretty much an average-looking guy. Caucasian, average height, and that's about it. It could be Hulse, or it could be someone else. Thinking about Owen's instructions, and that they had earlier used an old silver Jeep, He told his two men to kill the man who was probably Hulse.

Myron wasted two hours at a Starbucks, reading a Clancy novel and nursing a latte. He glanced at his watch, left the coffee shop, and drove back to the software company. He parked the Jeep with a clear view of the building's entrance and settled in.

Cars were sporadically entering and leaving the large parking lot. Without exception, the drivers of the arriving cars and trucks left their vehicles and walked into the building. Just before 3:00, the exception occurred. A large sedan parked, and no one stepped out of the car. Myron thought it likely the driver, like himself, was waiting to pick someone up. He noted that, again like himself, the sedan had parked with a clear view of the entrance.

Jonathan's Jeep was about forty yards from the sedan. Out of caution, Myron pulled the duffel bag from behind his seat, unzipped it, and removed a .223 semiautomatic rifle with a folding stock. He unfolded the stock and placed the gun on the passenger seat. He was also carrying a 9mm Glock.

After nearly an hour wait, Myron saw Cal at the building's entrance. He was about to start the Jeep when he looked over at the black sedan and saw two men step out of the vehicle. Both were holding handguns.

Myron grabbed the rifle and jumped out of the Jeep. Before he could bring up his gun, one of the men fired his pistol. Myron saw one of the security guards go down. Myron's first shot hit the shooter in the back, dropping him instantly. The shooter's partner spun around to face Myron. Myron's second shot hit the man's forehead.

Cal had scurried back into the building and Myron had no interest in talking to the police, who would be arriving in minutes. He quickly moved back into the Jeep and drove out of the parking lot.

When he arrived back in Los Gatos, Myron calmly related the afternoon's events. Cory and Jonathan stared at the man in dumbstruck silence. Myron might have been describing a trip to the supermarket.

Jonathan gathered his wits enough to ask, "Is Cal all right?"

"He's fine. He dove back into the building before they could hit him. One of the security guards was hit."

"You left before the police arrived?"

Myron nodded. "The police and I have, as they say, a failure to communicate."

Jonathan thought for a moment. "They must know Cal is making progress. They're taking big risks to shut us down."

Cory kept staring at the big man. He was totally unfazed after just killing two men. The thought frightened her but also gave her greater confidence that Myron could and would protect them.

She turned to Jonathan. "What happens to Cal?"

"He'll be questioned by the police. They'll want to know why he's been targeted and who is after him. Assuming he plays dumb, they'll threaten him, but eventually they'll have to release him."

"Is what we're doing worth it?"

"At this stage, it doesn't matter. We can't send them an email saying 'we quit'. They're not going to go away. The only way to stop this is to expose whatever the hell they're doing."

Later, when he was alone, a wave of guilt washed over Jonathan like a tsunami. His friends were being targeted because he wanted to pursue a meaningful project. Cal and Cory could easily be killed because of his selfish interests. He also knew what he had said to Cory was true. If they stopped investigating Independence, the threat would not go away. The only thing that would stop the threat was to uncover Independence's secrets.

———

Cal was visibly shaken as police swarmed the crime scene. He knew what had happened, but his mind was having a problem accepting that a second attempt had been made on his life. The first officers to arrive found it difficult to get any coherent answers from him. Frustrated, they backed off, leaving that task to the soon-to-arrive detectives.

By the time the Foster City detectives arrived, Cal had pulled himself together. He watched as emergency workers tended to the security guard. They treated the man and quickly placed him on a gurney and into an ambulance.

The lead detective, who identified himself as Ralph McCarthy, took Cal aside and asked him why people were trying to kill him.

"I don't know."

"Come on. We know about what happened at the Ferry Building. Who's after you and why? And who's the good Samaritan that shot the shooters?"

"I told you, I don't know."

"Tell you what... let's go down to headquarters and take a statement. Maybe we can come up with a better answer."

Cal was led to one of the unmarked cars, placed in the back seat, and driven to the Foster City police headquarters on East Hillsdale Boulevard. No one spoke during the short trip. Once inside, he was led to an interrogation room. Cal was asked if he would like water, and when he nodded yes, he was given a cold bottle.

Ralph McCarthy and two other plainclothes officers sat in silence for a few minutes before McCarthy began the process. "You have to know who's after you."

"I do not."

"Why do you think someone wants you dead, and who shot the guys trying to kill you?"

"I have no idea. I'm a computer guy. I'm a consultant to several of the high-tech firms and, in my work, I deal with sensitive information. Beyond that, I don't have a clue."

Everyone in the room knew Cal was lying. They just did not know what they could do about it. He was, after all, the victim here. "Look, we're here to help. We can protect you."

"Can I leave?"

"You were a witness to a crime. If you don't cooperate, we can hold you as a material witness."

"I wish to call my lawyer."

The men in the room made no effort to hide their frustration. After another half hour of unproductive questioning, they had Cal give a statement of what he had seen and released him.

Cal called Jonathan on his burner before he left the building. "Jon, I've just been released. I'm afraid either the police or the people after us might try to follow me."

Jonathan took a moment to consider the situation. "Wait a minute, I need to go online." After a few minutes, he picked up his phone. "All right, take Uber to the Hillsdale Shopping Center in San Mateo. It appears to be a fairly large operation. Myron will pick you up at the exit on the east side. Don't wait outside. He'll call you when he's in position."

Call hung up and arranged to be picked up.

Two men sat in a car parked on Hillsdale across the street from the police headquarters. When Cal emerged from the building and got into an Uber, they pulled away from the curb and followed. They considered ramming the mid-sized Ford and killing Hulse and the driver, but were hesitant given the amount of traffic on the street.

They decided to wait and make their move when the driver stopped to drop off Hulse. Their plan was not working out well when the Ford turned into a large and crowded parking lot for a shopping mall. Cal Hulse left his ride and moved quickly into the mall's main entrance.

As soon as the driver reached the mall's entrance, the man in the passenger seat jumped out and ran into the structure. His partner found a parking space some distance from the entrance. He considered following his partner, but decided to wait in the car, so they could take off quickly after his companion killed Hulse.

Neither Cal nor the Uber driver had spotted the tail, but, playing the odds, Cal assumed it could have happened. He moved as quickly as he could to separate himself from the entrance. He went into Macy's, found the men's department, grabbed a pair of pants, and found the changing rooms. Before he ducked in, he viewed as much of the store's floor as he could see. A dark-complexioned man of medium height was moving quickly through the store, glancing in every direction.

Cal went into the changing room, closed the door, and sat down, breathing heavily. He knew if the man thought of the changing rooms, he was dead. He dialed Jonathan.

"I'm at the shopping center. I'm at the men's department at Macy's, and I'm pretty sure I was followed. There's a man running around the store, and I don't think he's looking for a lost child."

"Are you safe?"

"Sort of, I'm hiding in one of the changing rooms."

"Smart move."

"Smart if he doesn't come looking in the changing rooms."

Jonathan paused for a moment. "Unlikely. He probably has no idea which store you're in, and it's doubtful he'll think of the changing rooms. Think about how much attention he'd raise if he started busting into the rooms with people trying on clothes."

"Your mouth to God's ears."

"How about a little change of plans. Rather than Myron picking you up at the east exit, I'll tell him to park, find you at Macy's, and escort you out of the mall?"

"The guy might try to kill both of us."

"Unless the guy's suicidal, he isn't going to do that. First, odds are Myron would kill him, and second, the place must have hundreds of cameras."

"Okay, have Myron call me when he's in the men's department."

The wait was a little over forty-five minutes, but to Cal, it felt like an eternity. When Myron called, Cal stepped out of the changing room. The big man was standing next to a display of sweaters. He motioned for Cal to join him as he led the way out of the store.

They left the mall through an exit on the east side of the mall and crossed the parking lot to Myron's rental. Myron asked Cal to slump down in his seat as he drove out of the parking area. Several cars were backed up, waiting at the signal leading to Hillsdale Boulevard. When the signal changed, Myron turned left and then, at the first opportunity, turned right. He relaxed when no other cars followed.

"We're clear."

Cal sat up and offered a weak smile. "Thanks for coming."

"Hey, that's my job."

After a few more jogs, just to be sure, Myron got on the 101 heading to Los Gatos.

CHAPTER 19

John Owen went into a violent rage. His face was flushed as he paced the floor of his corner office. He swore at the absurd outcome. Cal Hulse had again escaped unharmed. The man was the furthest thing from a skilled opponent. He was a goddamned nerd, a thirty-something programmer.

Owen also knew the people he reported to were losing patience. Hulse simply had to be stopped. That said, in the rational portion of his mind, he realized time was running out. He'd send an army after the man if he only knew where Hulse was hiding.

He fought to control himself. There was one course of action that he had earlier considered and discarded. While it would stop Hulse, it contained its own set of risks. Owen returned to the chair behind his desk and stared into space as he considered the implications. Everything could be lost if the plan backfired.

One of Owen's roles, in addition to managing Independence, was to develop and maintain cordial relationships with key personnel in the Department of Defense and with members of Congress. He and his company were not significant enough to shmooze with the most senior officials, but he spent a great deal of time with those one and two layers down.

Senator Alice Monley of the great state of Road Island was one such person. Through campaign contributions and personal visits, Owen had invested a great deal of time and money courting Senator Monley, who did not chair, but was a member of the Defense Intelligence Committee.

It also helped that Senator Monley was not the sharpest knife in the drawer. Her father had been the governor of Road Island and the undisputed head of the state's Democratic Party. When the opening occurred, Alice was pushed to the head of the line.

"Alice, how are you?"

"I'm just fine, John. And you?"

"Well, I do have a problem, and I could use your advice."

"What is it? I'll do anything I can to help."

"Independence has been hacked. I was about to notify the FBI. Is there some other agency that would be more appropriate?"

"Oh my god, this is terrible. You should notify the FBI, but I'll also make a few calls. I have excellent contacts at the Defense Intelligence Agency. We have to stop this immediately."

"I appreciate your help. I'll call the local FBI office right away. I'm going to be in DC next week. Would you be free for dinner one night?"

"Of course. Keep me posted on this."

Owen sat back in his chair and thought about how he would frame his next conversation. He needed to stop Hulse, but how to implicate the man? The company had no direct evidence to give the FBI investigators. They would, of course, want to know why he thought it was Hulse. He could tell them that Hulse was working with Scanlan, who was nosing around the company, but that sounded lame even to his own ears. He had to keep the Hulse involvement vague, sort of like a rumor. The game plan came to him. First, a call to the FBI on the successful hack. Second, a little later, an anonymous call naming Hulse as the hacker. The second call would be placed from somewhere far away from Austin, and to a different FBI office. Not a perfect plan, but it should work. Even if Hulse was not arrested, he would have to stop his activities, flush him out, and then eliminate him.

Owen made the call to the local FBI office. His call was

immediately bumped up to the senior special agent in charge, a man named Arron Verducci. The man listened as Owen explained the attack on Independence's systems and the sensitive work they did for the Department of Defense.

"We'll be at your office within the hour."

John Owen sat back, pleased with the bureau's response. He called the head of his IT department and told him to be prepared for the upcoming meeting.

When the agents from the bureau arrived, they were immediately escorted to John Owen's office. Verducci was a tall, broad-shouldered man of about fifty. His once, no doubt, trim figure had slipped somewhat, but his serious expression and intelligent eyes provided assurance that he was highly competent.

He provided a firm handshake as he introduced the two other agents. "This is Special Agent Tara Schell and Special Agent William Foley. We've notified DC regarding the situation, as we know it. We're a relatively small office. Personnel with the technical skills we'll need will be here tomorrow."

Owen introduced his head of IT, Drake Henderson. After a group handshake, Owen suggested they move down the hallway to a conference room. When they were seated, Verducci asked, "Can you assess the damage that's been done?"

Henderson shook his head. "Not at this time. Nothing appears to have been removed or changed, but we don't know what information is now in the hands of the hacker."

"Have you attempted to trace the source of the attack?"

"We've tried, but so far, no luck. Perhaps your people have more resources and can figure that out."

After a half hour of unproductive back and forth it was obvious the technical questions would have to wait for the incoming bureau technicians.

As he escorted the three FBI agents from the building, Owen was pleased with the first phase of his plan.

When he returned to his office he placed a call on his special phone. The man that answered simply said, "Yes?"

"In two days have someone place a call to the Los Angeles FBI office from somewhere on the West Coast. Obviously, using an untraceable phone. All they need to say is, Cal Hulse, living in San Francisco, is the person that hacked Independence. Are we clear?"

"Yes." And the call ended.

CHAPTER 20

C al was badly shaken. He looked around the room at his friends. "I received a call from my investment guy. Apparently, the FBI tracked him down through my tax filings. He said they're looking for me, in a serious way."

The room was silent for a moment. Jonathan was the first to speak. "It's Independence. They tried to kill you and, when that didn't work out, they sicced the bureau on you. Can they connect you to the hack?"

Cal was offended. "Please, Jon. No way."

"All right, so what do we do?"

"I'll scrub everything connected to Independence from my devices. The information will be saved in the cloud and unreachable by anyone but me."

Cory looked around the room. "Can't we just stay here?"

Cal shook his head. "They'll find us. They have unlimited resources. It would just be a matter of time."

Jonathan nodded. "Okay, we go back to our normal lives. Myron, you head back to LA. Cal, find the nastiest criminal defense lawyer west of the Mississippi. When they start questioning you, you say nothing."

Cory's voice betrayed her nervousness. "If we go back home, go to work, and all. Won't we then be open targets?"

That brought the room back to silence. Jonathan paced as he spoke. "Cal will be under twenty-four/seven surveillance. They're not stupid enough to try something with the bureau right there." He turned to Cory. "I don't believe they'll go after you. That would be another red flag, and they wouldn't be gaining anything. I don't know if the bureau will be looking at me."

No one seemed happy with the new turn of events.

Jonathan tried to force a smile. "How about we all think about it. Maybe one of us can come up with a better idea. We can decide what we're going to do tomorrow."

Myron took Jonathan aside. "I'd like to stay here, rather than go home. I want to be close if things turn nasty. You guys don't have to keep paying me."

Jonathan was visibly touched. "You can stay if you want, and forget about the no-pay idea."

After a few phone calls, Cal lined up Constantine Weiland, an attorney with offices in the city and a reputation as a world-class ball-buster. He agreed to meet with her the following morning

Jonathan assumed that if the bureau would be keeping Cal under heavy surveillance. The only reason he and Cory had been targets was to use them to get to Cal. Now that Cal would be settled in at his condominium, there was no reason for Independence to go after them.

He smiled as he looked at Cory. "Pack up, we're going home."

———

Cal appeared promptly at Constantine Weiland's office on California Street at eleven. He was ushered immediately into the woman's corner office. When asked, he declined coffee or water as he settled into a comfortable visitor's chair.

He began to stand when the woman appeared, only to be waved down. Weiland was a small woman at just over five feet, of medium build and with short cut graying hair. She possessed sharp features and intense brown eyes.

Weiland moved to her chair behind her glass toped desk, stared at Cal for a moment, before addressing her prospective new client. "So, tell me what's happening."

"I'm a computer guy. I work under contract for several of the tech firms."

"Stop. I know who you are and what you do. Google tells all. What I want to know is why you're here."

"I understand the FBI is looking for me."

"Why?"

"I haven't met with them, so I don't really know. I'd like you to represent me when I do meet with them."

"Is there an arrest warrant?"

"Not that I'm aware of."

Weiland glanced out her window with a view of the downtown for a moment. "Why don't you just meet with them and then determine if you need a lawyer?"

"I have no confidence that I'll be treated fairly."

This brought a thin smile to the woman's face. "You're probably right. So, what do you want to do?"

"Have your office contact the local FBI office and arrange a meeting."

"When do you want this to happen?"

"If you agree to represent me, today."

"All right, I'll give you some papers to sign. We need a retainer. Let's say initially twenty thousand. That could go up big-time, depending on what happens at the meeting and after."

Cal took out a check book, wrote out a check and handed it to his new attorney.

One hour after Constantine Weiland's call to the San Francisco office, a team of six people appeared in Weiland's lobby. They were led to one of the firm's conference rooms.

A large, heavy-set man in his late fifties stepped forward. Cal thought the man had somewhat of a military bearing. "Richard

Hollingshead, I'm the Senior Special Agent in Charge of the San Francisco office." He produced his credentials with somewhat of a flourish. "The people accompanying me are all special agents from our office. And you are?" Waving in Cal's direction.

"Cal Hulse."

"Fine, Mr. Hulse. Please come with us."

Constantine Weiland stepped forward, blocking Hollingshead's way as he moved toward Cal. "No."

Hollingshead jerked his head toward the much smaller attorney. "What do you mean, no?"

"Are you placing Mr. Hulse under arrest?"

"Not at this time."

"Then he's not going anywhere." Weiland was familiar with this typical law enforcement tactic. They wanted the advantage of controlling the environment and the intimidation that accompanies it.

Hollingshead glared at Weiland, his rising anger apparent. "Please get out of the way. Cain, Siguuenza, bring Mr. Hulse. Counselor, you can meet with your client at our office."

"You touch my client, and I'll have you brought up on charges. Mr. Hulse has agreed to meet with you, not to be dragged out of this office."

The Senior Special Agent in Charge looked like he was about to physically shove Weiland aside when a Special Agent stepped in, placed a hand on Hollingshead's arm and said, "A word, Richard."

Hollingshead shook off Cain's hand, but stepped back. Cain spoke quietly into the senior agent's ear. "We push this, and Weiland will tell him to remain silent. Let's see what he's willing to tell us."

On a scale of one to ten, Hollingshead was pissed at fourteen, but he knew Cain was right. After a moment to gain control he said, "All right, we'll talk to Mr. Hulse here."

While the tension in the room was there, everyone took seats around the table. Seeing that Hollingshead was still struggling, Cain took the lead. "I'm Special Agent Gregory Cain. We've had some difficulty locating you, Mr. Hulse. Cal you tell us where you've been?"

Weiland interjected. "I don't see how that's relevant to your investigation, Agent Cain. My client will not be answering that question."

Cain paused for a moment. "Fine. Mr. Hulse, did you hack the IT systems at Independence?"

"No."

"We are aware that there have been two attempts on your life. Who is making those attempts and why?"

"I don't know."

"That's hard to believe. By the way, the security guard who was shot is going to make it."

Weiland stepping in, "Do you have evidence that my client was involved in this hacking incident, or that he knows who attacked him?" When no one spoke, she said, "I think we're through here."

"We want access to your computer and cell phone."

Constantine Weiland waved her hand at Agent Cain. "Not without a warrant, and you have shown no evidence that could support such a request."

Hollingshead surfaced. "Mr. Hulse, are you aware of the penalty for lying to a federal agent?"

Weiland shook her head. "Don't answer. Are you through trying to intimidate my client?"

Hollingshead stood and leaned across the table and shouted, "Independence is a defense contractor producing sensitive and highly classified products. I'll be happy to see your client spend the rest of his life in a federal prison."

"Special agent in charge, unless you're going to arrest my client, leave my office."

Hollingshead, his face flushed with anger, hovered over the table for another minute before straightening and marching out of the room, followed by his colleagues.

Weiland and Cal remained seated after the door slammed shut. A sheen of sweat glistened on Cal's forehead as he turned to his attorney. "Thank you, You're worth every penny of the retainer."

Weiland smiled. "I hate bullies. Call me if they contact you again."

Cal called Jonathan from the building's lobby. "The feds just left. I have to tell you, my attorney stopped them cold."

"I guarantee they'll have you under surveillance."

"You don't think the bad guys will come after me?"

"Like I said before, these guys aren't stupid. They won't make a move while the FBI is hovering around, but be careful. Don't expose yourself."

Call called for an Uber ride, when it arrived and they were on their way, Cal kept nervously glancing behind, trying to see if they were being followed. He did not relax until he was safely in his building.

CHAPTER 21

John Owen made his way to the IT center on the second floor. The relatively small offices were crowded to capacity. His staff, the technicians from the FBI and several agents from the Austin field office filled the facility.

Owen tapped one of the agents on the shoulder and motioned for him to step out into the hallway. "Any progress in tracing the source of the hack?"

"Not yet. Whoever got into your system was very careful and very good. Every time we think we've traced the IP address, we find it to be a false lead."

Owen wanted to scream but simply nodded. "Do you believe you'll get there?"

The agent shrugged. "I frankly don't know. Our guys are really good, but so are the people behind the attack."

When Owen returned to his office, he pulled out the upper drawer of his desk, shook out two Xanax pills and swallowed them dry. When he looked down his hand was shaking. He knew that if he could not stop Hulse, he was a dead man.

He thought about fleeing the country, just disappearing. He was single, had no children, and he had enough resources to last the rest of his life. As he considered the idea, he knew he could not pull it off. He would need false identification papers and had no idea how to obtain them. He also knew that, while he was smart, the people that would come after him would also be smart.

Hulse would be on guard and watched by the FBI. It would be extremely difficult to get to him. What would Hulse do if his best friend were grabbed? Something to think about. Would Hulse back off? Not likely, and what about Scanlan? Would he just forget about being abducted? Again, not likely. The only answer he could come up with was to kill Hulse.

Owen called the man that had been assigned to follow Hulse. "Where is he?"

"Back at his condo on Pacific Avenue."

"I assume the feds are watching him."

"Yeah, two in a Suburban outside his building."

"Does his unit face the street or the other side of the building?"

"I don't know."

"Find out."

An idea had come to Owen. A bit outrageous, but maybe doable, if Hulse's condo was on the north side of the structure.

Carmen Costello badged her way into the FBI field office on Wilshire Boulevard in Los Angeles after a pleasant, leisurely weekend spent with Adam Walsh. Carmen found the man to be charming and attractive, but also increasingly possessive. She was thinking the relationship may be reaching its expiration date. Her thoughts were interrupted by her chirping cell phone. She glanced at the screen. The call was from Suzanne Kroeber, her immediate supervisor, and her closest friend at the bureau.

"Hi, Suzanne, I just got through the door."

"Get yourself a cup of coffee and join me."

"Be right there."

One perk at the office, they had excellent coffee. Carmen grabbed the cup off her desk and walked over to the machine. Two minutes later she was knocking on her boss's door. Carmen was smiling as she settled into one of the visitor's chairs.

Special Agent Suzanne Kroeber took a sip of her own coffee and returned Carmen's smile. "Good weekend?"

"It was fine. Didn't do much."

"Didn't do much with Adam?" Smiling as she asked the question.

"Yeah, we got together, but I'm not sure it's going to work out."

Suzanne frowned and leaned across the desk. "Really? I thought everything was great."

"It was until it wasn't. He's becoming more and more possessive."

"I'm sorry. I thought this might be the right one."

"So did I, at first, but enough about me. You wanted to see me about something.?"

"Yes, before you came down here, I believe you spent quite a bit of time surveilling Jonathan Scanlan." Carmen was not sure where this was going. She simply nodded agreement.

"I understand Scanlan's best friend is Cal Hulse. Did you get to know him?"

Carmen shook her head. "I know who the man is, but I had no contact with him." Carmen was hoping her friend and boss could not read the lie from her expression.

"Yes, of course. Hulse is considered a person of interest in the case of a defense contractor that was hacked."

Carmen was genuinely surprised. "Really?"

"Yes. You know, the San Francisco field office is pretty small. The Senior Special Agent in Charge, Richard Hollinshead, asked if we could help out and send you up.

Carmen's first thought was, oh shit, I don't need this. Jonathan could not be happy with how she handled the relationship once she moved south. She also knew she was in no position to tell Suzanne Kroeber, no. "Sure, whatever the bureau wants. When do they want me there?"

"Yesterday. I know you'll have to take care of a few things here. Do you think you can go up there on Wednesday?"

"I can make that work."

"Great. I'll call Hollingshead and tell him your coming."

Carmen's thoughts were jumbled as she walking to her desk. This is going to be one weird reunion.

———

Carmen caught the ten o'clock United flight from LAX to SFO. After picking up a rental and weaving her was into the city, she did not arrive at the Federal Building at 90 7th street until after the lunch hour. She badged her way to the area that had once been her office.

The woman at the front desk smiled. "Welcome back, Carmen."

"Hi, Sally. Is Richard in?"

"Yes, he's waiting for you."

Carmen made her way to Richard Hollingshead's inner office. She knocked before opening the senior agent's door. Hollingshead stood and crossed the office to greet her. Rather than shaking her hand, Hollingshead embraced her, which made Carmen quite uncomfortable.

"Glad to have you back, even if it's only temporary."

Carmen pulled back and stood awkwardly, waiting for Hollingshead to motion her toward one of the visitor's chairs. After a pause, he returned to his chair and waved Carmen to the chairs in front of his desk.

Carmen was never a fan of the man who had been her supervisor. Large ego, minimal talent, and too much interest in her in a very personal way. Hollingshead was one of the reasons she jumped at the opening at the Los Angeles office.

"I've been told Mr. Hulse is a person of interest in the hacking of some defense contractor. What would you like me to do?"

Hollingshead cleared his throat. "Yes, the contractor is Independence, headquartered in Austin. They believe Hulse is involved."

"Do they have proof?"

Hollingshead took a moment before responding. "Nothing tangible. Hulse denies any involvement and has lawyered up."

"If there's nothing tangible, why are they pointing at Hulse?"

"I'm not sure. His friend, Jonathan Scanlan, was nosing around a couple of Independence's subcontractors, saying he was doing research for a book on fraud and abuse in the defense industry."

"Well, Jonathan Scanlan is a successful author."

Carmen could tell; this was not the response Hollingshead was looking for. "That's true, but Scanlan seemed to be focusing on Independence shortly before the hacking, and Hulse is a highly skilled computer guy."

Carmen was finding the focus on Cal Hulse thin on substance. "So, again, what do you want me to do?"

"We have Hulse well covered. My belief is, if Hulse is behind the hacks, Scanlan is involved. I want you to do exactly what you were doing when we had Scanlan under surveillance before."

Carmen had to stifle a laugh. She thought, I doubt you want me to do everything I did with Jonathan. Instead, she nodded, stood, and left Hollingshead's office.

Sally pointed to a vacant desk and asked, "What will you need?"

Carmen thought for a minute. "Right now, the only things I can think of are a decent set of binoculars and a camera with a long-distance lens."

"Coming right up." Sally disappeared for a few moments. When she came back, she handed Carmen a camera and a heavy set of binoculars. "Let me know if you think of anything else."

Carmen left the Federal Building and drove across town to the Cow Hollow area. She parked on Green three houses down from Jonathan's apartment and stared at the building. She knew Cal and Jonathan were not some kind of spies, stealing secrets from a defense contractor. It did not make sense. Her mind wandered back to her time with Jonathan, first conducting surveillance, and later working with Cal, Jonathan, and the Pacific Avenue Irregulars to clear Jonathan's name. She also thought about those intimate times with the man. Would she want to return to those times? It bothered her that she did not have a clear answer.

Carmen's vigil was rewarded after about an hour, when Jonathan stepped out of the building and began jogging down Green Street. Carmen slouched down in her seat as he approached her car. She had no interest in following the man, knowing he would be headed down to the Marina Green. When he was out of sight, she left the car and walked down to Union, used the restroom at Starbucks, and purchased coffee and a scone. Unless he had changed his pattern, Carmen knew he would be gone for somewhere near an hour.

She relaxed at the coffee shop for half an hour before returning to her rental. Carmen again ducked down when Jonathan returned. She decided to continue watching Jonathan's apartment until she was sure he was home for the night.

Evening was approaching when Jonathan again left his building and began walking down Green. He was dressed casually, perhaps going out to dinner. Carmen waited until he was almost a block away before starting her car and following him. Jonathan was almost two blocks away when he entered a garage. Carmen pulled to the curb and waited. The man backed his Jeep out of the structure and began driving away.

Carmen followed, keeping back far enough not to be noticed. The ride took them to the 101 and eventually to the exit for San Carlos. Jonathan parked on the street next to a large residential building that appeared to be condominiums. Carmen parked half a block away and wrote down the building's address. It was not long before Jonathan emerged, accompanied by a strikingly beautiful woman.

Jonathan was holding the woman's hand as they moved toward the Jeep. There was no question in Carmen's mind that this relationship was personal, not professional. She followed the Jeep down to El Camino Real and to an Italian restaurant. As Carmen sat in her car her emotions ranged from jealousy to anger, which she knew was irrational. She had basically broken up with Jonathan when she stopped taking his calls, and she had been seeing Adam. Of course, Jonathan had every right and reason to find someone else.

Later, she followed the couple back to the condominium building, and after a long wait, she knew Jonathan would not be leaving. Carmen was upset as she drove back to the city and was at a loss about why she was feeling the way she was.

Later that night, in her hotel room, she tried to be rational and put aside Jonathan's current relationship. She knew Jonathan and Cal were rational, good people. Perhaps they were looking at Independence for good reasons.

Carmen's problem, which she had faced once before, was to hold the line and simply surveil Jonathan, or find out what they were really doing. She tossed and turned for most of the night.

CHAPTER 22

Carmen was lying in bed in her hotel room, staring at the ceiling. Beyond her mixed feelings regarding Jonathan's love life, she thought the surveillance task she had been assigned was a ridiculous waste of time. It would not take long for Jonathan to spot her, and then what? She had little regard for Hollingshead's abilities. Following Jonathan around was not going to be a productive activity.

The more she thought about it, the more she was convinced a more direct approach was necessary. Carmen reached over to the small table beside the bed and set her alarm for six. While she knew what she was going to do in the morning, that clarity did not prevent a restless sleep.

Carmen arrived at Jonathan's apartment early and settled in to wait for his return from San Carlos. Several hours later, she saw him walking up Green from his garage. She slid out of her car as he approached his building.

"Morning, Jonathan."

Jonathan spun around and stared at Carmen. He could not have been more surprised if she had used a cattle prod. "Carmen?"

"Yep."

"What... what are you doing here?"

"My job. Can we go inside and talk?"

The totally confused man opened his building's front door and followed Carmen inside. Neither spoke as they made their way to the second floor. Jonathan unlocked his unit's door and motioned for Carmen to follow him inside.

"Coffee?"

"Yes, thanks."

As Jonathan busied himself with his coffee maker, Carmen glanced around the apartment. Nothing had changed. She was curious why a successful author preferred to live in a small inexpensive one-bedroom apartment.

Once coffee was served, Jonathan, now in better control, sat down and asked, "You said, your job. Care to elaborate?"

"The bureau believes Cal may be up to something regarding a company named Independence. Since you're his wingman, they assigned me to watch you."

"Just like old times."

"Sort of, except this time instead of you, Cal is the person of interest."

Jonathan sat in silence for a moment. Eventually, he said, I don't see how I can help you."

"Can't or won't?"

"Both. Why are you here, and what are you trying to accomplish?"

"You don't trust me?"

Jonathan stood and stared out the window toward the bay. "I have no idea where you're coming from."

Carmen stared at the floor for a moment. "Look, Jonathan, I don't believe you and Cal are trying to steal defense secrets from this company. I do believe you're investigating Independence for some reason."

Jonathan was conflicted. He wanted to trust Carmen, but if he was wrong, the risk was too high. He decided to give a little, just a little.

"A young man named Thomas Scheer came to me. He worked for the Department of Defense and believed there was fraud and abuse coming from one or more defense contractors. He wanted me to help him."

"Why come to you and not the FBI?"

"He went to the FBI, and they blew him off. He had read my books and came to me as a last chance. The next day, he was murdered, run over when he was crossing the Embarcadero. I didn't think this smelled right. We began looking at defense contractors. Independence was one of those contractors. Independence stood out because there is virtually no information available about the company."

"So, you think someone at Independence had Thomas Scheer killed?"

"I don't know, but his being killed after he was raising the alarm seemed an odd coincidence."

"Are you saying Cal hacked Independence?"

"No, I am saying that when we began looking at Independence, there were two attempts to kill Cal. I happened to be there for one of them. Don't you think that rings any bells?"

"It does. The principals at Independence contacted the bureau, saying they'd been hacked. Later, an anonymous source claimed Cal was the hacker. The bureau doesn't seem to be tying the attempts to Independence."

Jonathan laughed. "Have they lowered the bar at the bureau? I thought they were supposed to be the best."

Carmen raised her arms in a defensive posture. "Jonathan, I'm not saying that's what I think."

"Well, I guess you can follow me around until they tell you to stop."

Carmen said nothing for several minutes. "Okay, Jonathan. Thank you for seeing me." She stood and walked out of the apartment.

———

Owen called the man on his private phone. "Can you provide a shoulder-held grenade launcher and someone who knows how to use it?"

There was a pause before the man replied. "Yes. Why would you want this?"

"To go after Hulse. But before I can do that, I need more information."

"Shootings happen every day. Using that type of weapon would bring in all types of heat, like Homeland Security."

"I know, but we have to stop him." As Owen said this, he realized the man had hung up.

CHAPTER 23

Carmen was not surprised by Jonathan's reaction. Her move to the Los Angeles field office and, later, not returning his calls pretty much signaled that the relationship was dead. Not exactly a way to build trust.

She was surprised that Jonathan had provided as much information as he had. In addition to the man's death on the Embarcadero, something about Independence had made them investigate the company. Despite Jonathan's denial, she knew Cal had hacked into the defense contractor's systems.

As she walked back to her car, Carmen considered doing her own digging into the company. It would not hurt her career to find misdeeds at Independence. She had no intention to inform Senior Special Agent in Charge Richard Hollingshead of her visit with Jonathan or her pending examination of the contractor.

———

A short, muscular black man in his thirties met John Owen at a Starbucks on Airport Boulevard in Austin. It was late, and there were only two other customers in the coffee shop. No names were shared, nor hands shaken.

Each man studied the other for a moment before Owen spoke. "You have the equipment I requested?"

The man nodded in agreement. "And I understand you know how to use it."

"Yes."

Owen handed the man an envelope. "This is the information you'll need and the funds that have been agreed to."

The man opened the envelope and studied its contents. "San Francisco?"

"Yes, is that a problem?"

"No, but it will take me some time to get there, I'll be driving."

"Driving?"

"I can't very well bring my equipment, as you call it, on an airplane."

"Of course. If you do this at his home, It's absolutely necessary that he's in his condominium."

"I understand." That said, the man stood and walked out of the building.

John Owen left the coffee shop extremely satisfied that his problem was about to be eliminated.

The man, currently using the name Robert Curtis Allen, returned to the Residence Inn, where he was currently staying, packed his bags, and headed to San Francisco. He hovered near the speed limit, not wanting to be stopped for speeding, resulting it three and a half fairly boring days. He turned up the radio and listened to '70s rock to stay awake.

He had never been to San Francisco and used the car's GPS to navigate to his hotel. Tired of three and a half days of fast food, he asked the concierge for a recommendation and ended up eating a pound of medium rare tenderloin, mashed potatoes and drinking two glasses of a decent cab. Feeling somewhat overstuffed, he returned to his hotel, went to bed and fell into a dreamless sleep.

The following day he picked up a coffee to go, retrieved his late model Audi and again, following the GPS prompts, drove across the city to Cal Hulse's condominium on Pacific Avenue. He cruised the block once, not wanting to linger as he had been told the FBI had Hulse under surveillance.

He took the first right, parked the car, and walked down the hill to Lombard. While Pacific Avenue was fairly quiet, traffic wise, Lombard Street was extremely busy.

Owen's idea was to use a grenade launcher to fire into Cal's condo. The man took only a moment to conclude the plan had a variety of problems. He would have to gain access to the building on Lombard directly below Hulse's condominium, and position himself on the roof. Pacific Heights was a hilly part of the city, which gave the residents facing north magnificent views of the bay and Marin County. The drop-off from Pacific Avenue to Lombard Street was significant. This meant, even on the roof of the Lombard Street building, he would be firing uphill at an extreme angle.

He studied the situation for several minutes before returning to his car and driving back to his hotel. He had no desire to talk to Owen, who he did not consider a reasonable man. Instead, he called his handler.

The man answered on the first ring. He explained the logistic problems to the man.

"So, it can't be done?"

"If I could get on the roof of the building, which is a big if, the probability that I could hit the target's north facing window is about twenty-five percent."

He did not verbalize his thoughts, but the handler was thinking, *this is the problem when amateurs like Owen create the plan.* After a moment he said, "I'll get back to you."

Later that evening the handler called. "Stay in the city. I'm trying to find out when and where you can get to Hulse. Forget the grenade launcher."

"I thought the grenade launcher was a really bad idea."

"It was." And he was gone.

CHAPTER 24

M yron was bored and had the uncomfortable feeling that Cal was at risk and that he should be doing something about it. He had run out of reading material and was flipping channels, hoping to find something to catch his interest. Nothing did. He turned off the set and thought about Cal's current situation.

The FBI had released Cal but was certainly keeping him under surveillance. As long as he stayed in his condo, he was probably, but not certainly, safe. A person could enter the building, possibly faking a delivery, gain access Cal's unit, and kill him.

Myron called Cal, who did not answer, and left a message. He felt he could not leave it at that. Myron called Jonathan and expressed his concerns.

"I appreciate you wanting to protect Cal, but do you really think they would try something like that with the FBI watching him?"

"Yes, and the FBI isn't watching him, they're watching his building. Jonathan, I've been associating with really bad people for a long time. If the pressure is heavy enough, they'll make a move."

Jonathan thought about it for a moment. "What do you suggest?"

"I sneak him and his computers out of his place and bring him down here."

There was another pause as Jonathan rolled the idea around. "Have you talked to Cal?"

"I called and left a message. He hasn't called me back."

"Let me try to reach him. I'll call you after I talk to him."

It was over an hour when Jonathan called back. "He's not happy with the plan. I think he believes he's safe where he is."

"Thanks for trying, Jonathan." Myron did not believe Cal had an understanding of the risk he was taking. He collected some of the items he was going to need and left the house, heading for the city.

On the way, Myron stopped at a uniform store he had located on the internet and purchased what he was going to need. At another stop at a McDonalds, he went into the restroom and changed into his new clothes. Before leaving McDonalds, he went to the back of the building and retrieved an empty carton.

Myron parked half a block from Cal's building, in a space that allowed him to watch the entrance. The flaw in his plan was that virtually all delivery people arrived in a company truck or van. He thought he could see the FBI agents sitting in a dark colored sedan on the opposite side of the street.

It was all about timing. When a large UPS delivery truck pulled in front of the building, Myron hustled out of his rental with the empty box. He was able to use the UPS truck to block his line of sight from the agents. Myron was three feet behind the UPS driver who was buzzing one of the units. When the driver pushed open the door, Myron was right behind him.

The driver turned to the big man with a surprised look. Myron offered his most ingratiating smile. "Sorry to startle you. Package for Cal Hulse on the 203."

After a moment's hesitation, the driver shrugged and moved down the hall. Myron used the stairs to the second floor, walked down the hall to Cal's unit, and studied the lock. Using his picks, he heard the lock disengage in seconds. He opened the door and stepped inside.

He could hear keys being punched on a keyboard and followed the sound. Cal was hunched forward, working the keyboard and staring at the computer screen.

Myron pulled out his Glock, tapped Cal on the shoulder, and said, "Bang, bang, you're dead."

Cal whirled around, nearly falling off his chair and stared, first at the muzzle of the gun, then at Myron.

"What the fuck?"

Myron put his gun back in his pocket and looked at his shocked friend and employer. "Still think you're safe here?"

"God damn it Myron, I almost had a heart attack."

"If I had been an employee of Independence, you wouldn't have had a heart attack, you'd have a bullet in your head."

"You did this to prove I'd be better off going back to Los Gatos."

"You got me. Actually, I don't care if it's Los Gatos or somewhere else, as long as they don't know where you are."

"What about the feds?"

"You're not under arrest. You can go wherever you want."

Cal leaned forward with his elbows on his desk as he rubbed his forehead. He finally looked up at Myron. "All right, you made your point. How would I get out of here without the FBI following me?"

"I have an idea. Besides your garage here, do you have access to any other parking lot that's restricted?"

Cal thought for a moment. "I've done a lot of work for INA. Because I've been in and out of their facility so much, they put one of those sensors on my car, so the gate to their employee parking lot automatically opens."

"Perfect. If you entered through the building's main entrance, could you then exit through an exit on the side of the building near the visitor's parking area?'

Cal thought for a moment. "Yes, I could do that. You have to go in the main entrance because of security, but you can leave through any exit. I think it has to do with fire regulations. What are you thinking?"

"I'll leave here ahead of you by, let's say, a half hour. I drive down to this company and park in the visitor's lot near the side exit. You drive down, park in the employee area, go into the building and then out the exit we're talking about. The feds will be focused on your car. You jump in my car and we're out of there."

"Okay, I'll be waiting by the west side exit."

"Okay, give me the address of this company and pack up whatever you'll need in Los Gatos."

Twenty minutes later, Myron left the building carrying boxes with Cal's computer equipment and the personal items Cal would need for an extended stay.

Using the car's GPS, Myron followed the prompts to the INA facility, parked by the west side exit, and waited. Cal emerged about forty minutes later. And slid into Myron's car. Myron asked him to scoot down to avoid the FBI and any cameras. Within minutes, they were out of the lot and on their way to Los Gatos.

———

It took a while for the FBI to realize Cal Hulse was in the wind. It started with unanswered phone calls, followed by no one answering the condominium's door. They could not get a warrant, but pressure on the property manager worked. The agents took only minutes to determine Cal was gone.

Senior Agent in Charge Richard Hollingshead was beyond irate. After berating the agents that had been watching Cal, he demanded a BOLO be issued on the man. After a moment of silently raging, he called Carmen.

"Agent Costello?"

"Yes."

"Hollingshead. Cal Hulse has taken off. Would you have any idea where he might have gone?"

"None. I've been watching Jonathan Scanlan and Mr. Hulse hasn't gone there."

"All right. Keep watching Scanlan, he may lead us to Hulse."

Hollingshead hung up and considered the consequences of losing Hulse on his career. It would all depend on how the Independence thing ended. He believed he could shift the blame if it ended badly, and that took some of the edge off.

Carmen had no interest in following Jonathan. Instead, she began taking a hard look at Independence on her laptop.

CHAPTER 25

Cal looked up from his computer and tried to organize his thoughts. Independence appeared to be a successful defense contractor. The fact that it is privately held is an oddity, but not illegal. There was no question that the attacks in San Francisco and Foster City were the result of his assault on the company's systems, but why?

Calling the FBI was a normal reaction; sending people to kill him was not a normal reaction. Cal decided to begin digging into the backgrounds of the company's management team. When he was roaming through Independence's systems, Cal had printed out a list of upper management.

He began researching each member of that team. The list was quite short, as Cal's assumption was, a mid or lower-level employee would not have the contacts and resources to orchestrate the attacks. Four people were on the list: John Owen CEO, Ann Dean CFO Kent Sass VP Operations, and Drake Henderson IT Manager.

Cal was familiar with the basic roles each of these people would play in the business. However, as a computer guy, Cal had little to no knowledge of the details of each manager's role. He decided to call for help. He dialed up his poker-playing buddy and Pacific Avenue Irregular, Alan Thielen.

"Hey, Alan. Cal."

"Hi, what's up? A poker game?"

"No, I need a little business 101 help."

"Okay."

"At a typical defense contractor, would the CFO be tuned into the technical aspects of production?"

Alan laughed. "No way. The CFO is strictly a numbers person."

"What about the head of IT and the VP of operations?"

Alan thought for a moment. "The head of IT would be somewhat involved but limited. Everything today involves the computer, so they would be involved in any software utilized by the products. They wouldn't have anything do with production per se. Certainly, the head of operations would be involved."

"Anyone else you can think of?"

"The head of engineering and the person running research and development."

"Thanks, Alan. You've been a big help."

"Can you tell me what you're looking at?"

"Not now, but I'll fill you in later."

Cal paused for a moment and thought about what Alan had said. He went back to his personnel information. Grant Quantana was the head of R&D, and Luis Maher was the VP of Engineering. From what Alan had said, the only people with access to really sensitive information were the CEO, VP of operations, VP of research and development, the head of engineering, and maybe the head of IT.

While the company had a few quirks, Cory had found nothing in the contracts that pointed to fraud. Independence was well paid for its products, and the DOD seemed satisfied with the products and costs. Cal concluded that one executive at the company was selling top-secret technical information to one of America's enemies. When they discovered someone was poking around in Independence's computer systems, they narrowed it down to him and attempted to silence him.

Cal also concluded that the odds were long that this person was doing this for money. While payments could be made in ways that were difficult to detect, like offshore banks, the odds again said some of the money would be used to improve the individual's lifestyle.

Cal began digging into the finances of the people on his list.

———

Like Cal earlier, Carmen found information on Independence to be surprisingly scarce. The website was a generic waste of time. It did mention John Owen as the CEO. When Carman googled the man there was little of interest. Ivy league education, and before he was brought in as CEO, he had been the CEO at a regional supermarket chain. Carmen sat back and thought about that.

Most large companies bring in management from within their industry. Why was Owen selected? While Independence has been operating successfully, the decision to bring in someone to run it from outside the defense industry seemed unprecedented.

Carmen was part of what she called a girl's club. This was a loose-knit collection of friends of similar age working in mid-level positions in government agencies and private industry. Carmen picked up her phone and dialed Lori Bouton. Lori was an auditor at the IRS.

"Hi, Lori. Carmen Costello."

"Carmen, good to hear from you." Carmen smiled at Lori's typical upbeat personality.

"I'm involved in an investigation of a defense contractor named Independence. They're based in Austin and the CEO is a man named John Owen. Could you glance at his tax files and see if there's anything hinky?"

Lori did not answer for a long moment. "Look, Lori. I don't need to know any details, and I don't want you to get in trouble. I just need to know if I should be taking a hard look at this guy. Frankly, we have an old boys club here, and I'm trying to crack the glass ceiling." Carmen was hoping the old boys club line would sway her friend.

"You know I can't give you detailed information without going through proper channels."

"I know. I just want a hint that Owen is squeaky clean or of questionable virtue."

Lori laughed. "No details, but I'll take a peek."

"Thanks, I owe you one." Carmen relaxed and leaned back in her chair. She did not know if anything would come from the 'peek', but at least she felt she was moving.

————

Special Agent Gregory Cain called Carmen as she was leaving her hotel. "Morning, Carmen. Gregory Cain."

"Good morning, Gregory."

"Are you watching Scanlan?"

"I'm on my way to his apartment."

"I understand he goes for a run almost every day."

"Yes, usually in the early afternoon."

"Give me a call when he goes for his next run."

"Sure." Carmen wondered what that was about. Was Cain going to search Jonathan's apartment when he was out? Seemed unlikely. She would have known if a search warrant had been issued. From what she knew about Gregory Cain, he was too by the book to do an illegal search. She thought. This could get interesting.

In the early afternoon, Carmen watched Jonathan leave his building and begin jogging down Green Street. She called Cain and let him know.

"Why don't you take a break for a couple of hours. I'll come over and watch him for a bit."

"All right, I do need to do a little shopping." Stranger and stranger. Agent Cain was too senior to be doing surveillance. Carmen had no plans to go shopping. She moved her car away from Jonathan's apartment building, but close enough to be able to see the entrance.

Twenty minutes later, she watched the special agent park near the building, get out of his vehicle, and walk over to the front door, but instead of gaining entrance, Cain sat down on the front steps.

A half hour later, Jonathan walked up the street, cooling off from his run. He stopped when he saw the man sitting on his steps. "Can I help you?"

"I think you can." Cain pulled out his credentials. "Special Agent Gregory Cain."

Jonathan backed up. "I'm not talking to you without a lawyer."

"That's fine. Don't talk to me, just listen. Can we go inside?"

Jonathan stared at the man for a moment, finally moving past the agent and opening the front door. Neither spoke as Jonathan led the way to his apartment on the second floor. He went to the kitchen, took a bottle of water out of the refrigerator, and glanced at Cain, who nodded.

Jonathan handed Cain another bottle, drank half of his, before moving to his small living room and taking a seat on his sofa. Agent Cain settled into one of the chairs.

"I've spent some time looking into you and Cal Hulse. I know you're not bad guys. There's something going on at Independence that caught your interest. I also believe the attacks on you and Mr. Hulse are connected to you and Cal Hulse poking around the company."

Jonathan did not respond. Gregory Cain stood up and handed Jonathan his card. "Look, I know it's difficult to know who you can trust. Maybe at some point, you and Cal Hulse will figure out I'm not trying to jam you up. Thanks for your time."

Jonathan continued to sit and think about what Agent Cain had said. He was right about not knowing who to trust.

CHAPTER 26

Robert Curtis Allen turned down the volume on the hotel's television and answered his phone. He recognized the voice of the handler.

"Hulse has taken off, and we have no idea where he is. There's no question his friend, Jonathan Scanlan, knows where Hulse is hiding. We want you to grab Scanlan and force him tell you Hulse's location. Obviously, Scanlan would then be a liability."

"Where do I find this man?"

His handler provided Jonathan Scanlan's address. "Go online and look up Scanlan, so you'll know what he looks like. Scanlan was a college professor but is no longer teaching. He's probably home most of the time."

"I assume I'll be receiving additional compensation."

"Of course." And the call was disconnected.

After googling Jonathan Scanlan and studying his photo, the man left his hotel, programmed Jonathan's address into his GPS, and drove across town to Green Street. He drove past Jonathan's building slowly. It was midafternoon, and the street was quiet with parking readily available. He pulled into a space twenty yards from the entrance to Scanlan's building.

A little over an hour later, he watched Jonathan leave the building and begin jogging down the street. He waited until Jonathan had turned the corner before starting his car and following. He knew he could not keep pace with Scanlan without becoming obvious so he passed the man, drove down to Lombard, crossed with the signal, and then pulled over.

Grabbing Scanlan in public was not a winning plan. Too many people around and too many cameras. When Jonathan ran past, he pulled away from the curb and drove back to Jonathan's apartment. He sat for over an hour considering how to abduct the man. While simple on the surface, he could see a number of problems. He did not see a challenge, gaining entry into Scanlan's building, and then the man's apartment. Subduing the man could be difficult. Scanlan was fairly big and appeared to be athletic. The three-story building looked like it had six units. Shooting the man was out of the question. The noise, even with a silencer, would probably bring the police. If shot and not killed Scanlan would be making a great deal of noise, and if killed, the whole purpose would be lost. He would have to think about this.

When he was back in his hotel, he called his handler. "I'm not sure how to grab this guy."

"What's the problem?"

"First, he's a pretty big guy and in good shape. I don't know if I could take him alone. Second, from what I've seen, there are people around him all the time. There are six units in his building. Taking him there would probably create a good deal of noise, and someone would probably call the cops. Killing him would be easy, but that doesn't get you his friend's location."

His handler did not speak for a moment. "I can send you some muscle."

"That would help, but we have to isolate him."

"I understand. I'll get back to you. Stay on Scanlan, maybe we'll get lucky."

It was Saturday, and Jonathan was looking forward to spending the weekend with Cory. He had booked a room and a reservation for dinner at Auberge du Soleil in Napa. He picked her up at her condominium in San Carlos in the late morning. From there, they threaded their way back through the city and across the Golden Gate Bridge. He had only told Cory that they would be in Napa and going to a high-end restaurant for dinner and spending the night.

Cory had been to the valley for daytime wine tasting but had very limited knowledge of the resorts and better restaurants. She smiled as they turned into Auberge's parking lot. The valet car parker smiled at Jonathan's aging Jeep. Jonathan explained that they were checking in and wanted their bags delivered to their room. He asked the young man if he could keep the Jeep available, as they would be going out after checking in.

Cory smiled as the valet moved the Jeep to a space surrounded by a variety of luxury vehicles. While Jonathan was checking in, Cory wandered through the lobby and looked out the rear windows at the valley below.

The man had followed Jonathan to San Carlos and then north to Napa. When Jonathan drove into the entrance at Auberge, he drove past the resort without stopping. There was no way he could continue watching Scanlan at this facility without being seen. He decided to return to San Francisco and wait for a better opportunity and for the hired muscle to arrive.

Jonathan spent the day driving through the valley. They continued up the Silverado Trail and into Calistoga. On the way back on the 29, they stopped in St Helena and spent time walking along the main street. Jonathan had also made a point of stopping at Frank Family Vineyards to give Cory a case of chardonnay.

Later, at dinner at Auberge, Cory turned to Jonathan. "Jonathan, this is wonderful. I know you're a successful writer, but this is over the top. Let me chip in on the cost."

Jonathan smiled and shook his head. "Don't be silly, this is my treat."

"Jonathan, please."

Jonathan studied Cory for a moment. "Look, I don't like to talk about money, but I'm quite well off."

"From the sales of your books?"

"That's part of it, but you know I sued San Francisco State when they accused me of sexual harassment. It was a big settlement."

"Can I ask how big?"

"Ten million." Cory dropped her fork and stared at Jonathan.

When she was able to speak, Cory said, "You don't live like a millionaire."

Jonathan grinned. "I don't think that lifestyle suits me."

Cory paused for a moment. "I think you're right."

Later, in their suite, they watched *The Thin Man* on Turner Classics before making full use of the king-sized bed.

CHAPTER 27

Robert Allen was not an early riser. He was sound asleep when his cell went off at nine thirty. He glanced at the screen and saw the handler's number.

"The two men who will be assisting you will be arriving this afternoon. They'll come to your hotel."

"All right. Do you know if they're any good at surveillance?"

"I don't know. Why are you asking?"

"If they're competent, they could spell me watching Scanlan. If he sees me sitting in my car on his street more than once, he might be more careful."

His handler paused before replying. "These guys are muscle. I doubt they've done much surveillance."

"Okay, I'll figure that out when I meet them."

He spent the balance of the morning watching Jonathan's apartment. He decided it would be wise to stop using his car and switch to a rental. That accomplished, he returned to his hotel and waited for the two men to arrive. His hotel phone rang, and the desk clerk told him his guests were in the lobby.

The men were not hard to spot. Both were over six feet and appeared heavily muscled and liberally decorated with tattoos. He motioned for them to follow him as he left the lobby and walked to an isolated area on one side of the building.

One of the men stepped forward. "I'm Mickey, and this is Luis."

"Call me Robert. Will you be staying at this hotel?"

"No. Not in our budget. We'll find a cheaper place."

"What are you driving?"

"We were told to rent a van. It's parked in a lot a block away."

The smaller man nodded approval. "Good. You know what the job is?"

Mickey nodded. "We're going to grab some guy."

"Right, but we want to do it when no one else is around. Have you ever done surveillance?"

"Not really, but it can't be too hard."

"Does Luis speak?"

"Not very often."

"All right. Give me your cell number." Mickey gave him the number for his burner phone, and Robert gave him his. "Okay, find a place to stay. I'll be watching the man we want. I'll call you when I see an opportunity to grab him. When I do, plan to act fast."

Mickey nodded and the two big men walked away.

———

Jonathan had finished his run and was cooling down by walking up Green toward his apartment when he noticed a black man sitting in a car across the street. As he fumbled for his keys at the front door, he realized he had seen the man earlier, even though he thought the car was different.

Later that day, Jonathan stepped out of his apartment, crossed the small second-floor, landed, and peered out the window facing Green. The man was still there. He returned to his unit and called Cal.

Remarkably, his friend answered rather than letting the call go to voicemail. "Hey, Jon. What's up?"

"I have a guy watching my apartment building. Do you think it's the FBI?"

"Could be. You told me Carmen had been told to watch you. Maybe this guy is working with her."

"Carmen thought watching me was a waste of time."

"Well, now that I've taken off, they may think you'll lead them to me."

"Perhaps, but I have a funny feeling about this."

"Why don't I send Myron up to you, he's bored silly watching television and reading."

Jonathan thought about it. "Yeah, send him up here." Jonathan did not want Myron exposed to the bureau, but having the big man around felt like the right thing to do.

The man watching the apartment had figured out that Jonathan rented a garage a short distance from his building. He concluded that this would be the ideal place to jump him, preferably at night. He smiled as he dialed Mickey's number.

———

Carmen was not sure what she should be doing. While she did not see any value in keeping Jonathan under surveillance, that was what she had been ordered to do. Her examination of Independence had yielded nothing of substance. Reluctantly, she gathered the things she would need and drove to Jonathan's apartment.

After her conversation with Jonathan, she saw no need to be covert and parked directly across the street from his apartment building. Carmen had developed an interest in early American history, and as she sat in her Toyota Camry, she picked up where she left off on the book she was reading.

When Jonathan went down to his building's lobby to pick up his mail, he glanced out the window by the front door and saw Carmen sitting across the street. Further up the street, he could see the black man in his car.

Jonathan stepped back and thought. If they were both from the bureau, why would they not be in the same vehicle? There might be a logical explanation, but none came to mind.

———

Myron checked in at the Chelsea Inn, this time using his own name, before calling Jonathan. "Hi Jonathan, I just took a room at the Chelsea Inn. Do you want me to come up to your place?"

Jonathan thought for a moment. "There are two people in two cars watching my building. One is an FBI agent named Carmen Costello. I don't know who the other person is. They might question you if they see you here."

Myron paused. "Not something we want to have happen."

"No. Why don't you stay where you are for right now? I doubt they're going to continue watching my place all night. I'll keep you posted."

"I haven't had anything since breakfast. I'm going to get something to eat. I'll have my burner."

"Sounds good."

Myron went down to the lobby and talked to the clerk at the desk. Five minutes later, he walked in a bar named Westwood, ordered a beer and a plate of Tex-Mex bites. He thought about what he was doing. Jonathan, Cal, and Cory were good people who had become friends, and he was happy to be helping them. He did not relish the thought of returning to his prior work.

Jonathan checked the street periodically to see the status of his watchers. Carmen apparently believed Jonathan was in for the night and drove away at eight. The black man hung in for another hour. When they were both gone and no replacement appeared, he called Myron.

"The coast is clear, if you want to come up."

"Parking in the area is a bitch. I'll walk up in a few minutes."

Jonathan ordered Chinese to be delivered while he waited for Myron. Myron arrived before the takeout, and Jonathan buzzed the big man in. Once inside, he handed Myron a beer, grabbed one for himself, and joined Myron in his small living room.

Myron took a sip of his beer and asked Jonathan, "What do you make of all the surveillance?"

Jonathan shrugged. "I assume they're hoping I'll lead them to Cal."

Myron frowned and shook his head. "So, what happens then? They may want to know where he is, but then what? They can't arrest him."

Jonathan nodded. "You're right, but I'm sure they're not happy that he took off."

"I have an idea, and you're not going to like it."

Jonathan stared at the big man, waiting for the rest. "You said there were two cars, each with one person. You recognized the female FBI agent, but not the person in the other car."

"Right."

"We know the bad guys want to kill Cal. They've tried twice. They know, you know, where Cal is. Why wouldn't they want to grab you and force you to tell them where Cal is hiding?"

Jonathan absorbed this for a moment. "You think the black man in the other car is waiting to grab me?"

"Possibly. Look, I've spent the vast majority of my career working with bad guys. I know how they think. I may be wrong, but if I'm right, you're in a high-risk situation."

Jonathan thought for a moment. "You think Cory could also be at risk?"

"Maybe, if I were to guess, they think Cory is a peripheral player and may or may not know where Cal is hiding."

"So, what do you think we should do?"

"Act like you normally do. They're not going to take you during the day with a lot of people around. I know you run, work out. Don't change. If I'm right, they'll try to take you when you're isolated. I'll be hovering around, if it happens."

Jonathan had a restless sleep that night.

———

John Owen was frustrated and angry. He called the handler. "What's taking so long? Why haven't you snatched Scanlan?"

"It's not that easy."

"He's a goddamned college professor and writer. Why isn't it easy?" His voice rising with his emotions.

"For one thing, the FBI has him under surveillance."

This tempered Owen's animus somewhat. "Twenty-four-seven?"

"No. They're watching his place during the day. If he goes out, they follow him."

"Why can't your people take him at night?"

"He lives in a building with six units. Taking him, that way would be noisy with people calling the police."

"So, what's your plan?"

"He rented a garage two blocks from his apartment. We plan to jump him when he's getting or returning his Jeep."

"Why hasn't that already happened?"

"He hasn't used his Jeep since we've been on him."

Owen popped another Xanax as the call ended. For the past several days he was experiencing stomach cramps and thought about ulcers.

CHAPTER 28

Jonathan called Cal, and as usual, left a message on his voicemail. Later that day, his friend returned the call. "Hi Jon, still working on Independence."

"How's it going?"

"Slow. When they figured out that they'd been hacked, they installed a number of changes."

"Is that going to be a big problem?"

"A problem, but not an insurmountable one."

"Myron's here, and he thinks they might plan on grabbing me as a way to find out where you are."

Cal was silent for a moment. "You think he's right?"

"Could be. Carmen is watching me during the day, but there's also a black guy in a different car watching."

"Hey, that's not good. Maybe you should come back down here."

"I'm thinking about it."

"What about staying at Cory's place?"

"They have to know about her, and I don't want to put her in danger."

"Okay, I guess that makes sense."

"You have any idea how long it will take you to figure out what's going on at Independence?"

"Not really. Certainly, more than a day or two."

"All right. I'll let you know if Myron and I'll be coming down."

Jonathan spent the balance of the day paying bills, cleaning up around the apartment, and trying to come up with an idea for his next book. None of those efforts were satisfying or productive. That evening he called Cory.

Cory saw Jonathan's name on her phone's screen. "Hi, any news from Cal?"

"No. I just talked to him. Apparently, Independence made some changes to their system, and it's slowing him down. Let's get together on the weekend." Jonathan decided not to frighten her with Myron's idea.

"Would you rather come down here or have me come up to the city?"

Jonathan gave it a moment's thought, "I'll come down to San Carlos. I've been cooped up here and need to get out."

"Okay, there's a street fair in Santa Clara that might be fun."

"Great, I can use a little fun. Saturday, about ten o'clock?"

"Perfect."

Jonathan wondered if Carmen and the other watcher would be following him on the weekend. He called Myron and told him about his plans.

Myron paused before he spoke. "This could be interesting. The FBI woman follows you; the black guy follows her, and I bring up the rear."

"A regular caravan."

When Jonathan left his building, carrying an overnight bag on Saturday morning, Carman pulled away from the curb and drove down to his garage. She saw no reason not to be obvious. The black man stayed back until Jonathan was in his Jeep. He kept a one-block distance behind Carmen.

Myron turned onto Green from a side street and fell in behind the black man's Toyota. When Jonathan took the exit for San Carlos, Carmen knew where they were going. She again felt a flash of irrational jealousy.

When Jonathan parked in front of Cory's building, Carmen pulled to the curb three spaces behind the Jeep. The black man in the Toyota passed by and parked half a block down the street. Myron, amused by this cavalcade, parked near the corner of the street. He called Jonathan as he was stepping out of his Jeep with his overnight bag.

"Jonathan, Myron. I don't see you in any danger today. Assuming the black guy is from Independence, he's not going to do anything in broad daylight and with the FBI lady watching you. I'm going to bail out, unless you see it differently."

"No, you're right. I'll call you when I'm leaving tomorrow morning."

As Jonathan was walking toward the entrance, he gave Carmen a little wave.

Allen decided to continue following Scanlan, even though it made no sense to try to take him with the FBI woman hovering around. He called Micky as he sat in his car.

"Yes?"

"It's Robert. I'm watching the man we want, but it looks like he won't be back in the city until tomorrow. He parks his Jeep at a garage near his apartment on Green Street. Be ready to take him tomorrow." He did not bother waiting for a reply as he ended the call.

When Jonathan and Cory left her building, the now three-car procession drove down the 101 to the Santa Clara exit. Cory used the GPS in her phone to guide them to Central Park and the Art & Wine Festival.

It was a warm, cloudless day, and Jonathan had gone summer casual: shorts, polo shirt, and topsiders. Cory was wearing white shorts, a pale blue blouse, and sandals. They roamed through the booths displaying art and crafts. Jonathan purchased a watercolor of a scene that he thought looked like Sonoma County.

After a couple of glasses of wine for Cory and the same number of beers for Jonathan, they decided to call it a day. When they got back to Jonathan's Jeep he glanced around. Carmen's car was parked nearby, but there was no sign of the black man.

When they returned to Cory's condo, they watched a little television before turning in early.

Jonathan headed home after a late breakfast with Cory. He called Myron as he walked to his Jeep. Jonathan listened to some '60s and '70s rock as he made his way north toward the city. He could see a heavy blanket of fog to the west and wondered if the Marina would be spared.

———

Robert Allen sat in his Toyota across the street from Jonathan's garage. Micky and Luis were in their van parked nearby. The black man would have preferred to take Jonathan Scanlan at night, with fewer people around, but the pressure was building and the opportunities few. He knew he would have to torture Scanlan to obtain Cal Hulse's location and it was not something he was looking forward to. He had no problem killing people when ordered to do so, but he did not relish inflicting pain.

The plan was for Mickey and Luis to enter the garage once the Jeep was parked. They would grab and subdue Scanlan as he stepped out of the vehicle. One of them would move the van to the driveway and throw Scanlan inside. They would then follow the black man out of the city to an isolated area where he could work on the writer. Once he had the information, he would kill Scanlan, and the body would be dumped.

Jonathan was thinking about going for a run as he opened the garage door with his remote. He drove in and paused as he pulled his overnight bag and the watercolor from the back seat. A big man grabbed him and shoved him against the side of the Jeep when he stepped out of the vehicle. Another large man roughly pulled duct tape over his mouth and started to tape his hands behind his back.

Neither man noticed Myron, who had moved behind Mickey, spun the man around, and threw him against the garage wall. When Luis turned, Myron clubbed him with his Glock. Mickey was stunned but was able to get to his feet in time to be clubbed by Myron.

Jonathan tore the tape from his mouth and stared at the two unconscious men. Myron turned to Jonathan. "What do you want me to do with them?"

It took a few moments for Jonathan to understand what Myron was asking. "Do you think they could tell us who sent them?"

Myron shook his head. "No. They're just muscle. The black guy drove away when he saw me coming into the garage."

"We could call the police."

"That would involve me. No offense, but they're not going to believe you did this."

Jonathan was at a loss. Myron said, "I can put them in their van and drive it somewhere, say down to Lombard, and leave it."

Jonathan thought for a moment, then nodded. "Okay."

The van keys were still in the ignition. Myron carried each of the men to the vehicle and threw them in. Without another word. He climbed into the driver's seat, started the van, and drove away.

CHAPTER 29

When the handler called John Owen to let him know of the failed attempt, Owen was speechless. When he gained control, he wanted to scream at the handler but held back. Screaming at the man who directed hired killers would not be a wise move.

He ended the call and began pacing in the confines of his office. Cal Hulse had been thoroughly researched. The man was focused on two things: information technology and sports. Finding him through his computer skills had not proven productive. Hulse's fascination with sports and related collectibles was another matter. The information Owen had received noted that the majority of Hulse's collectibles related to the San Francisco Bay Area teams.

John Owen had no interest in sports and had no idea why a grown man would want to collect items related to the teams he followed. When he sat down and tried to think of something he could use as bait to draw out Hulse, nothing came to mind.

He went online googling San Francisco sports collectibles. He started with the Giants. Most of the items were not really collectibles: clothing and what he considered junk. The most valuable items were signed Willie Mays baseball cards. He saw nothing that might get Hulse interested.

He tried San Francisco sports collectibles, which named several auction houses: Lelands, Gokdin, and Heritage. Again, mostly baseball cards. Owen left the website and thought, "This isn't getting me anywhere."

He had another thought. What about primo tickets to a game being played by one of Hulse's teams, say front row seats for a Warrior game? Appealing idea, but how would he be able to get the tickets to Hulse without him sensing a trap? The guy was a genius. Have to think about that.

———

Myron and Jonathan went to Jonathan's apartment. It took only minutes for him to pack for an extended stay in Los Gatos. On his way out the door Jonathan checked his mailbox. He saw nothing of interest and dumped the junk mail.

Jonathan called Cory and told her about the attempted abduction.

"Oh my god, Jonathan. Are you all right?"

"I'm fine. Myron was there. The two guys that jumped me were really big, and Myron took them out without breaking a sweat."

"When you say, took them out..."

"No, no, he didn't kill them. I'm on my way back to Los Gatos. Do you want to come down?"

Cory thought about it. "Not right now. I'll come down on the weekend."

Myron followed Jonathan as he crossed the city and took 280 south. He watched his rearview mirror but was quite sure they were not being followed.

The return to the Los Gatos house was also a return to the earlier daily pattern. Cal hovered over his computer, Myron read and took long walks, and Jonathan did not do much. He alternated between working out at a local gym and running in the nearby hills. More as a distraction than anything else, Jonathan became the house cook. He surprised himself by finding the task enjoyable. To supplement his limited knowledge, Jonathan became a frequent visitor at the Beyond Text Bookstore on North Santa Cruz Avenue.

As he was preparing the evening meal of grilled skirt steak and cipollini onions, he thought about Cory and her culinary skills. Perhaps, if he expressed his desire to be the family cook, he could keep her out of the kitchen. He had to think of the best way to sell the idea without offending her.

———

When Carmen arrived at Jonathan's apartment, she sensed something was wrong. After hours of sitting in her car and watching the building, she slid out of her vehicle, walked to the Victorian building, and rang the bell for Jonathan's unit. When there was no response, she took out a pick, and within minutes, was inside, a skill not learned at the bureau's training classes. Carmen took the stairs to the second floor and knocked on the apartment door. There was no response. Could the people after Cal have gotten to Jonathan?

She used her lock picks on the flimsy lock and was quickly inside the unit. The apartment was empty and there was no sign of a struggle. Enough clothing and toiletries were missing for Carmen to know the man had taken off.

She thought about how she could report it to Richard Hollingshead. She could not tell him that she illegally broke into the apartment. If Jonathan had been in the unit and had not gone out, she could have spent days sitting in her car outside, but she had no basis for reporting him missing. She could ask for a trace on his cell phone, but she knew he was smart enough to be using a burner.

Carmen returned to her car and sat thinking about how she could report Jonathan missing without putting her career at risk. With no solution coming to mind, Carmen picked up her laptop and resumed digging into Independence.

Her investigation of Independence was interrupted by the chirping on her cell. A glance at the screen showed Lori Bouton's name. She answered the call, hoping for something helpful.

"Hi, Lori. Anything interesting on John Owen?"

"Sorry to disappoint. He makes a healthy salary, but that's about it. Nothing out of the ordinary."

"Well, had to give it a try. Thanks. I'm in the middle of something right now, but let's get together when I get loose."

After three days of sitting in front of Jonathan's empty apartment, Carmen decided she had to do something. She called her supervisor and told him something was wrong. Jonathan Scanlan had not left his building to go to the store, go running, or anything else.

Senior Agent in Charge, Richard Hollingshead, knew they had no grounds for a search warrant and was at a loss. Carmen suggested a welfare check to determine whether the man was all right. Hollingshead agreed, planning to take credit for the idea.

Carmen called Hollingshead's assistant, Sally. "Hi Sally, Carmen. Can you find out who manages the property at 924 Green Street in the city and give me the person's name and number?"

"Sure, I'll call you as soon as I have it."

A little over an hour later, Sally called with the property manager's name and number. Carmen made the call. "Hello, my name is Carmen Costello, and I'm an agent with the FBI. We're trying to reach Jonathan Scanlan, who is one of your tenants on Green Street. We need to do a welfare check to ensure he's all right. Can you meet me with keys to his apartment?"

Holly Rob's voice rose with her concern. "Is Mr. Scanlan in trouble?"

"Not at all. As I said, we can't seem to contact him, and we want to make sure he's all right."

"I'll be over right away."

Right away turned out to be forty minutes. Ms. Rob turned out to be a pleasant, if concerned, matronly fifty-year-old woman. She led Carmen up to Jonathan's apartment, fumbled nervously with the keys, and opened the door to his unit. A quick look around the apartment confirmed what Carmen already knew: Jonathan was gone. Carmen thanked the woman as they locked up the unit and left the building.

When Carmen arrived at the office, she immediately knocked on the door of the senior agent in charge's office. Hollingshead was behind his desk, and Agent Gregory Cain was in one of the visitor's chairs. Hollingshead motioned toward one of the vacant chairs.

"So, what happened?" The senior agent's voice did not sound supportive.

"Mr. Scanlan wasn't there. Some clothing and toiletries were gone."

Hollingshead pointed his finger at Carmen. "You were supposed to have him under surveillance. This is on you."

Carmen was pissed. "How many hours a day was I expected to sit outside his apartment?"

When Hollingshead did not respond, Carmen continued. "If you wanted twenty-four-seven, you needed to assign more than one agent."

Special Agent Cain spoke up. "I don't see any value in casting blame here. Scanlan has probably joined Hulse, wherever he is."

"Let's put out a BOLO on Scanlan." Hollingshead was also obviously pissed.

Cain looked at the senior agent, "What happens if someone, say local police, spot him? We have no grounds to arrest Scanlan or Hulse."

"We put them both on twenty-four-seven surveillance."

Carmen watched the exchange between the two men. She was gaining more and more respect for Agent Cain. She also realized he was quite an attractive man. She broke in when there was a pause in the conversation. "Since my role here was to provide surveillance on Mr. Scanlan, and now that he's gone, I might as well go back to LA."

Hollingshead seemed to be about to agree when Cain responded. "Why don't you wait a few more days in case Scanlan turns up?"

They both looked at the senior agent, who finally nodded. "Perhaps you can find something for Agent Costello to do."

That said, Carmen and Agent Cain stood up and left Hollingshead's office.

As they walked across the office, Carmen asked, "Any idea about what you want me to do?"

Gregory Cain looked at his watch and said, "Have dinner with me."

Carmen stopped in her tracks and looked at the man. "Are you hitting on me?"

Cain smiled. "Is it working?"

Carmen returned the smile. "We'll see."

"Look, I have another meeting I have to attend. Pick you up at your hotel at 7:00?"

Carmen smiled and nodded agreement. She watched Gregory Cain as he walked away. The agent was a little over six feet, somewhere in his midthirties, dark brown hair cut short, trim and athletic. He had the squared jaw, no-nonsense features of a cop. She liked the look.

Carmen had not brought anything dressy up from LA, so the best she could do was a tan skirt, white blouse and low heels. She was in the hotel lobby when Gregory walked in. "I have Uber outside. I thought it might be wise if we have something to drink."

"that's fine. Where are we going?"

"Gary Danko."

"I'm really under dressed then. I didn't bring Gary Danko type clothes when I flew up here."

"You look great."

Neither spoke on the short ride to the North Point Street restaurant. They were led to their table and immediately approached by their waiter. Carmen ordered a glass of chardonnay and Gregory a gin and tonic."

Gregory asked if Carmen had been to the restaurant before. "Only once, several years ago."

Carmen knew Gregory Cain when she was posted to the bureau's office in the city but had never directly worked with him or even had a social conversation with him. The dinner progressed at a leisurely pace, a lot of where you grew up and what college did you attend, type of chit chat.

Carmen visibly stiffened when Gregory asked what she thought about Scanlan. "I really don't know the man." She began wondering if this was the reason for the dinner.

Gregory noticed the change, "I know. I just thought you spent a lot of time watching him when he was a person of interest on what they called the *Culprit* killings."

Carmen relaxed slightly. "Well, it was determined that he had nothing to do with the murders. I read the book he wrote about it."

Gregory paused and studied Carmen for a moment. "I know the agency discounted his book, but I don't agree. I think the agency handled the investigation quite poorly."

It was Carmen's turn to put down her fork and stare at her dinner partner. "When you relieved me at Scanlan's apartment, did you talk to him?"

Another pause. "Yes, I did."

"And?"

"I tried to convince him to trust me, but he didn't tell me anything."

Carmen was not sure what to make of Gregory Cain's statement. She knew Gregory had not reported his encounter with Jonathan, as she would have heard. Carmen concluded that there was more to Gregory than first met the eye.

When they finished dinner, they took an Uber back to Carmen's hotel. Their evening ended with a hug. As he started back to the Uber for his ride home, he turned to Carmen, smiled and said, "I hope we can do this again."

Before she went to bed, Carmen spent time thinking about Gregory Cain.

CHAPTER 30

Jonathan and Cory had agreed they deserved another weekend getaway. Jonathan booked two nights at the Hazel Hill Montage Resort in Healdsburg. Cory was able to leave work early and when Jonathan arrived to pick her up, she was waiting outside with her roller suitcase. Even with an early start, traffic was heavy. Crossing the city on 19th Avenue was painfully slow, as was the 101 once they crossed the Golden Gate Bridge and began working their way through Marin County.

Cory had never been to Healdsburg and was impressed with the town as they drove through what had once been a farm-based community and was now home to high-end restaurants, tasting rooms and boutique shops. The resort was in the hills on the north edge of the town.

When they turned east off Healdsburg Boulevard, they wound their way past hillsides of dry grass and small oaks. Jonathan thought the area was beautiful, but perhaps a fire hazard.

When they crested one of the hills, they pulled into the area for arriving guests. Valet car parkers were beside the Jeep before Jonathan could turn off the ignition. They asked if Jonathan and Cory were checking in or just here for dinner.

Cory glanced around at the exotic cars parked in the area and smiled at the contrast with the well-used Jeep. Bags were carried into the reception area. While Jonathan had been to Healdsburg several times, this was his first visit to the resort.

Their room, which was referred to as a Queen Queen, was spacious and floor-to-ceiling windows offered views of the surrounding vineyards. Cory hugged Jonathan and said, "I could get used to this."

Jonathan grinned, glanced at his watch, and said, "Let's go down and have a drink. We have a little time before our dinner reservation."

Cory stayed with chardonnay and Jonathan beer, as they sat on the terrace enjoying the view. Cory turned to Jonathan with an expression of serious concern. "How long is it going to take for Cal to come up with something?"

Jonathan shook his head. "I don't know. He said this is the most difficult system he's ever tried to crack."

"I'm really worried. The longer it takes, the better chance these people have to get to us."

"It's a problem," Jonathan acknowledged. "Unfortunately, we don't have a second choice. Let's just try to enjoy ourselves this weekend."

Cory forced a smile. "Not too hard. This place is beautiful."

Dinner was superb. Jonathan was impressed with his veal dish and Cory her salmon. Jonathan glanced across the table. "You know, I've really gotten into cooking. It started out as just something to do, but I've found I'm really enjoying it."

Cory smiled. "Well, when things settle down and we're back to normality you can be the house chef."

Jonathan returned the smile, "Looking forward to it." And he really meant every word.

The weather was perfect and they spent the following day walking around the town. Cory thought the park-like town square was perfect. They had a light lunch in town before returning to the resort. They lounged around the pool in the afternoon, enjoying the warm weather and the poolside bar. Not that hungry, they opted for a light room service dinner.

They checked out after breakfast and began their journey home.

Jonathan turned off 101 at Navato for gas. Cory went inside to use the restroom while Jonathan filled the tank. As he stood by the Jeep, he noticed a vehicle that had pulled off the highway behind him but then parked at the curb below the gas station.

When Jonathan and Cory got back on 101, the gray sedan followed. Jonathan told Cory, "Don't turn around, but we're being followed."

She visibly stiffened. "Do you think it's the people who tried to abduct you?"

"No, I'm sure it's the police."

"Why would the police be following us?"

"Good question."

"What do you want to do?" He could tell; Cory was shaken.

"I'll take you home. After that, we'll have to think about that. I don't want to lead them to Cal."

When they reached Cory's condo, Jonathan parked the Jeep on the street and carried his overnight bag and Cory's roller into the building. Jonathan sat down on the sofa and motioned for Cory to join him.

"I have an idea. They're not looking at you. You drive your car out of the garage with me slouched down in the back. Take me down to Los Gatos and either stay with me there or come back here."

"I'll come back here."

"All right. I'll have Myron line up a rental for me, so I don't have to use my credit card."

Cory grinned. "Let's do it now."

They took the elevator down to the garage. Jonathan climbed into the back and lowered himself as far as he could. Cory wore a Giants baseball cap as she pulled out of the building. She glanced nervously at the gray sedan as she turned down toward the freeway. She breathed a sigh of relief when the sedan did not follow. When they were several blocks away, Cory pulled to the curb and Jonathan moved to the front seat.

The ride south to Los Gatos was uneventful. When they reached the house, Cory smiled at Jonathan when he asked if she wanted to come in. She shook her head. "I'm a little tired, so I'll just head back. It was a wonderful weekend."

Jonathan grabbed his bag, kissed her and stepped out of the car.

Jonathan stood and watched her drive away, thinking how deeply he felt for the woman. When he stepped into the house, Cal and Myron looked up with happy faces.

Myron was the first to speak. "God, we missed your cooking."

CHAPTER 31

The handler called Owen. "The FBI has put out a BOLO on both Hulse and Scanlan. Scanlan was spotted driving south on the 101 near a town called Santa Rosa. They followed his Jeep down to San Carlos, to his girlfriend's place, and they're still sitting outside her building."

Owen thought for a moment. "Have your man watch the place and follow Scanlan when he leaves."

The handler hung up.

The handler called the following day to report that Scanlan had not left the building and that his Jeep had not moved. When the same information was relayed the next day, Owen knew something was wrong.

"He must have spotted the tail. I don't believe Scanlan is still at the condo."

"You're probably right. What do you want us to do?"

"Grab the girlfriend. She has to know where Scanlan is, and he's probably with Hulse."

When the handler hung up, he thought about it for a minute before calling Robert Curtis Allen. While the man had failed to abduct Scanlan, he had been, in the past, quite reliable.

The handler told the black man what Owen wanted. There was a pause before the man asked, "Will the police be watching her place?"

"I don't know. They may have decided that Scanlan slipped away."

"Do you know where she works?"

"Lockheed in Sunnyvale. Will you need help?"

"I don't think so." The handler hung up.

The short black man had been about to leave the city and had been unsure of his status with the handler after the attempt on Scanlan. He was relieved to find he was still useful to the man. He called down and asked to have his car brought up from the garage. Fifteen minutes later he was driving through the city on the way to San Carlos.

He made one pass by Cory's building, looking for ongoing surveillance. He did spot Scanlan's Jeep, still parked on the street. Not seeing any police presence, he parked a half block away and settled in. The handler had provided information on the make, color and license number of Cory's car. It was a weekday, and the man assumed the woman was still at work.

At a little before 6:00 in the evening, a car matching the handler's description drove up the street and entered the building's garage. He was too far away to see the driver but was quite sure it was Cory Bishop. He began thinking about how to grab her with a minimum of risk.

The building appeared quite secure and, no doubt, had cameras. He did not know much about Lockheed Martin, but as a major defense contractor, he assumed they would probably have tight security. He was not about to have this be a suicide mission.

On the surface, abducting a single woman should not be a challenging task. Women go running, meet friends at bars and restaurants, go shopping, and often park their cars in somewhat isolated places. He had not spent very much time watching Cory Bishop, but, so far, he had not seen her expose herself in any of those ways.

———

Jonathan was lying in bed at the house in Los Gatos when he sat bolt upright. If the plan had been to grab him and force him to tell them where Cal was hiding, why would they not do the same thing to Cory?

He scrambled out of bed, threw on his clothes, and ran upstairs to Myron's room. The big man woke up when the bedroom door flew open. His instincts kicked in as he pulled his Glock from beneath his pillow. When he saw it was Jonathan, he lowered the gun.

Jonathan shouted at him. "Get up. We need to get to Cory."

"Why, what happened?"

"If we don't get there quickly, it's what's about to happen. Hurry and bring your hardware."

They were out the door in fifteen minutes. As they drove north, Jonathan explained why Cory was in danger. Myron nodded without saying a word.

Jonathan called Cory, who woke up confused. It took her a few minutes to absorb what Jonathan was saying.

When they arrived at Cory's condominium, they found her dressed in shorts and a sweatshirt and drinking a freshly brewed cup of coffee. She pointed at her coffee maker and the cups she had laid out.

Cory's face was tight with tension. "Do you really think I'm in danger?"

Jonathan took a chair opposite Cory and nodded, as Myron hovered behind him. "Think about it. They are desperate to get to Cal. They tried to take me and force me to tell them where he is. Now Cal and I are hiding and they have to know you know where we're staying."

"This is crazy."

"I agree. Did you notice anyone following you to or from work, or parked outside your building for long periods of time?

"No, but I wasn't really looking. There was that car earlier that you said was the police, but they're gone."

Jonathan glanced at his watch. "Let's try to get some sleep. We'll get you to work in the morning."

Cory led Myron to her guest room/home office. Myron was the only one able to fall asleep easily.

When Cory and Jonathan came out of the bedroom in the morning, they found Myron, fully dressed and holding a fresh cup of coffee. Cory patted the big man on his shoulder. "Thanks for making a fresh pot. I'm going to take a shower and dress for work."

Myron turned to Jonathan. "How do you want to play this?"

"We'll follow her to Lockheed and see if we have company."

Myron nodded and sat down to finish his coffee. When Cory was ready to leave, Jonathan told her his plan. "If there is someone watching, I don't want them to know I'm here. I'll go down to the garage with you. When you drive out, I'll slip out before the door closes. You drive away, but not too fast, and Myron will be waiting and pick me up. We'll follow you to work."

"All right."

"I'll call you at work before you leave, and we'll be there to follow you home."

They gave Myron a ten-minute head start before taking the elevator to the garage. Cory drove out slowly, and Jonathan walked out behind her. Myron let Cory get down the block before moving to the garage's entrance and picking up Jonathan.

"Did you see anything?"

Myron nodded. "A cream-colored Toyota pulled out when Cory left."

"Okay, we know where she's going, so we don't need to follow too closely. Did you see the driver?"

"Yeah, I think it was the black guy I saw at the garage."

Jonathan did not say anything for a moment. "Stay on top of him."

They drove behind the Toyota for a while. "If we take him, do you think he'd know who's doing this?"

"Maybe. Speaking from experience, a hired thug normally doesn't deal with the guy at the top."

Cory's drive to work continued without incident. The Toyota drove past the Lockheed facility when Cory turned into the employee parking lot. Jonathan glanced at Myron. "Let's stay on the Toyota and see where it goes."

They followed the Toyota as it made its way to the 101 and headed north toward San Francisco. Myron and Jonathan turned away when the Toyota pulled into the entrance to the Hyatt Regency on the Embarcadero.

Myron turned to Jonathan. "Is knowing where this guy is staying helpful?"

"It might be. Let's go back to Los Gatos. We can follow Cory home when she leaves work."

Myron nodded. "You were right, they're going after Cory to get to you and Cal."

Jonathan simply nodded.

————

The man registered at the hotel waited until he was in his room before calling his handler on his burner. The handler picked up on the second ring.

"Yes?"

"I followed the woman from her building to where she works. She didn't stop anywhere so there was no opportunity to take her."

"All right. Stay on her. At some point, she'll make a mistake." With that, the handler hung up.

The man spent several minutes fantasizing about what he would do to Cory Bishop after he got the information on Scanlan and Hulse, and before he killed her

Jonathan and Myron drove back to the house in Los Gatos, where Jonathan described the situation to Cal, who nodded. "Why not bring her down here?"

"As long as she's going to work, she's vulnerable, whether she's at her place or here."

Myron said, "I could take this guy out."

Cal dropped the pen he had been fiddling with. "By taking him out, do you mean kill him?"

Myron's voice was as calm as if he were ordering a ham sandwich at the deli. "Kill him or put him in the hospital."

Jonathan stepped in. "No, they would just send someone else."

Later, when Myron left to go to the store, Cal approached Jonathan as he was putting together lunch in the kitchen. "Jon, I have a problem with what Myron just said."

Jonathan looked up. "You mean about taking the guy out?"

Cal nodded.

"Look Cal. If Myron wasn't helping us, you'd probably be dead, and I'd be dead in my garage."

Cal turned away, his face flushed. "You're right. I guess I have a problem with the idea of killing someone."

"There's no question Myron is a dangerous man and he's also what we need right now."

―――――

Carmen sat at her desk in the bureau office, waiting for Gregory Cain to step out of a meeting. When she saw the agent leaving the meeting room and crossing the open office area, she stepped in his path.

"I need to talk to you about something." Cain thought, "Oh, oh, is this about the other night?"

"Sure, why don't we grab a cup of coffee?" *And let's not have this talk in the open office.*

With coffee obtained, Cain steered Carmen to a quiet corner of the break room. He noticed Carmen was holding a file.

"Rather than sitting here doing nothing, I've done some research on Independence."

Both startled and relieved, Gregory Cain leaned back in his chair and gave her an inquiring look.

"There's virtually no information available on them. I know they're a private corporation and not, therefore, subject to SEC regulations, but it goes beyond that."

"What do you mean?"

"They're highly secretive. There's almost no information about the CEO or the rest of the management team. I couldn't find out who's on the Board of Directors, or anything regarding their financial structure."

Agent Cain studied Carmen for a minute. "Granted, that's unusual, but, as you said, they're a private corporation and not required to make that information public."

"There's the anonymous phone call claiming Cal Hulse hacked into Independence's systems, and two attempts were made on Mr. Hulse's life. Coincidence?"

Gregory Cain leaned back in his chair and said nothing for a moment. "I don't know. We know Independence never used Mr. Hulse's services. It's hard to see the connection."

Carmen leaned across the table. "I think we should be looking at Independence rather than Mr. Hulse."

Agent Cain offered a weak smile. "Senior Agent Hollingshead isn't going to buy that."

"That's why I'm talking to you and not the senior agent. I'm not asking you to go rogue."

"You, apparently, are asking me to investigate an important defense contractor without the bureau's permission."

"At this time, I'm only asking you to keep an open mind."

Cain thought for a moment, then nodded. "Are you up for dinner?"

"Not tonight." Carmen smiled when she saw Gregory deflate. "Tomorrow would be fine."

———

John Owen was coming apart. He was popping anxiety pills like M&Ms. He tried to present a calmer, in-control image to his staff, but he knew they sensed something bad was on the horizon. One or two had put out feelers to other defense contractors, anticipating some type of financial disaster.

He wanted to call the handler daily but knew that was pointless. The man would call when he had something. How long could this woman go about her daily life before exposing herself to the handler's man?

He knew the Warriors had made the playoffs and was confident that the floor tickets would lure Hulse out of his hiding hole. The problem was, how could he get him the tickets without it signaling an obvious trap? As he paced in his office, an idea came to mind. Have the tickets appear to come from one of his clients.

All right, but how can the tickets get to Hulse when we don't know where he is? Didn't people pickup tickets at the stadium? Buying the tickets was no problem when you are willing to pay any price. What he needed was Hulse's email address to notify him that the tickets were at Chase Center.

If the handler's man had not obtained Hulse's location in the next few days, he decided he would be purchasing the tickets.

CHAPTER 32

The routine of the prior days continued. Cory would leave home and return after work with the Toyota following, and with Myron and Jonathan behind him. One day Cory stopped at a Safeway near her home and shopped for thirty minutes, but the parking lot and store was crowded and the man in the Toyota made no move.

Jonathan recognized that it was a race between Cal uncovering whatever Independence was hiding and their people getting to them. He had talked to Cory about doing the away-from-the-office plan, and she told him she believed she needed to be on site.

On the third day, Cal received an email from INA, complimenting him on his work and telling him that two floor tickets for the next Warriors home game were waiting for him at the arena.

When Jonathan and Myron returned from shopping, they met a man jumping around the living room.

"You can't believe what just happened," Cal shouted.

Myron wondered if Cal had just won the lottery. Jonathan had never seen his friend so animated and had no idea what was going on.

"I have courtside seats for the Warriors game on Sunday."

Jonathan thought about it. "How did this happen?"

"INA set it up. I can't believe it."

Jonathan was aware that Cal had solved a particularly difficult problem for the company. Everyone knew about Cal's obsession with the Bay Area teams, so maybe this was their form of a perk.

Jonathan grabbed Cal as he was still bouncing around the room. "Cal, how did you find out about this?"

"I got an email from INA telling me I could pick up the tickets at the stadium."

"Can someone locate you through your IP address when you get an email?"

Cal thought for a minute. "No. It can only be done if I send an email."

Jonathan relaxed. "Cal, has this ever happened to you before?"

Cal shook his head. "No, a few times a client has given me a bonus, but not something like this."

"Can you contact someone at INA to check if they were, in fact, the organization that sent you the email?"

Cal thought for a moment. "Normally, that wouldn't be a problem, but today is Saturday. There wouldn't be anyone there today."

Jonathan stared at his friend. "This could be a way for the bad guys to get at you."

"Jon, I'm going to go."

Jonathan did not like it, but could tell he was not going to be able to stop Cal. "You said seats. How many seats?"

"Two. I assumed you'd want to go with me."

"Normally, I'd jump at it, but I want you to go with Myron."

Cal gave Jonathan a blank stare. "Why? Myron's not a Warriors fan. I don't know if he even cares about sports."

"Cal, you're the brightest person I know. You're maybe the brightest person west of the Mississippi. We can't verify that the tickets came from INA. If it is a trap, having Myron along gives you some protection."

Cal reluctantly agreed.

The following day Cal and Myron left early for the city, knowing parking would take some time. The game was scheduled to start at 5:30 and Cal wanted to be in his seat well before game time. On the drive, Cal rattled on and on about how much Jimmy Butler had improved the team and how the Warriors experience could outweigh the Rockets' height advantage.

Myron tuned out his companion, his thinking focused on where the risks could come from in a sold-out 18,000-seat-capacity arena. He assumed security would be tight with bags being checked, and possibly they would be passing through a metal detector system. Of course, that issue cut two ways: if he could not bring in a gun, neither could the bad guys.

As expected, getting into the parking facility was a slow process. Myron hated to leave his handgun in the car but reluctantly did so. Another wait occurred when they joined the line at the will-call window. With tickets finally in hand, they passed through security and eventually found their seats on the arena floor.

While Cal was oblivious to any threat, Myron spent time glancing around the facility. He did not like the fact that half the people in the building were seated behind them, but knew there was nothing he could do about that. The more he thought about it, he believed nothing would happen inside the arena. Even if a shooter could somehow bring a weapon inside the building, he could never escape after the shooting. The danger, he concluded, would be when they left the facility.

Every time Curry hit a three, Cal would standup and do a little dance. The Warriors struggled on the boards but managed to maintain a narrow lead. The stadium hummed with the energy of eighteen thousand rabid fans. On the last shot, Curry put an exclamation mark on the win with a half-court three.

Cal's face was flushed as he sat and savored the win. "This has been amazing."

Myron, who had no interest in the game, smiled and said, "I'm glad you enjoyed it."

It took some time for them to shuffle out of the arena and to their car in the stadium parking area. Myron was hyper alert but saw nothing of concern. Once in the car, he retrieved his Glock from under the seat and placed it in the pocket of the driver's side door.

They crept out of the parking garage at a snail's pace. The streets were clogged with departing Warrior fans as they made their way south toward the 280. Myron kept glancing at his rearview mirror, but the amount of traffic made it impossible to spot anyone who might be following them.

Once on the freeway, things opened up. Myron slowed and moved to the right lane and watched as several cars followed. As the next exit approached, he accelerated and watched as the two cars that had been behind him took the exit. A black Mercedes, thirty yards back, stayed in the lane, and accelerated to keep pace with Myron's SUV.

Myron knew he could not outrun the Mercedes, and there was no way he was going to lead them to Los Gatos. Another problem was his lack of familiarity with the area. They were past the exit that would lead to the airport when Cal realized something was happening.

"We have company."

Cal started to turn around when Myron placed a hand on his shoulder. "Don't look. They may not know we've spotted them."

"What are we going to do?" Cal's anxiety level was starting to peak.

"I'm trying to figure that out. Look, you know this area, and I don't. Would one of the exits work for us?"

Cal's voice mirrored his fear. "What do you mean, work for us?"

"We have to do something. I can't outrun them in this car, and if there's a shootout, they'll have more firepower than I have. We need to go somewhere that's safe."

Cal fought to control his fear. After a few moments, he said, "Take the exit that says Woodside. At the bottom of the exit, turn right."

"Why Woodside?"

"You'll see."

The freeway sign for Woodside appeared about twenty minutes later. Myron took it, coasted down to the bottom of the sloped exit, and turned right on Woodside Road. When Myron glanced at his rearview mirror, he saw the Mercedes.

Myron and Cal drove uphill along the two-lane road until the road crested at a stop sign. Cal pointed at a market a short distance away on the left. "Turn into the market's parking lot."

As Myron turned into the lot, Cal pulled out his burner phone and dialed 911. When the call was answered, Cal said, "Listen, I'm Austin Simmons. I was on my way home when a black Mercedes began following me. I pulled into the Robert's Market parking lot in Woodside. They followed. I'm frightened. Come quickly."

The Mercedes had turned into the parking area, stopping about forty yards from Myron's car.

Myron was smiling as he stared at Cal. "Well done. How did you know about this place?"

"A couple of years ago, I was invited to a Christmas party at the home of one of the INA executives who lives down the road. Woodside is like the Beverly Hills of the Bay Area. I figured the response time would be good."

About five minutes later, a police car raced into the lot, hemming in the Mercedes. Two officers jumped out of their vehicle with guns drawn.

Cal patted Myron on the arm and said, "Time for us to leave."

Myron pulled out of the lot and retraced his way down the hill and onto the 280, heading to Los Gatos.

When they arrived, they were greeted by Jonathan and Cory. In a booming voice, Myron shouted, "Your boy here just saved our asses."

CHAPTER 33

The handler was not looking forward to the phone call he was about to make. John Owen picked up on the first ring.

"We were unable to take out Hulse after the game."

There was silence for a moment, then Owen screamed, "What do you mean you were unable to take him?"

The handler recognized that Owen was losing control. "Just what I said."

Fighting to control his anger, Owen said, "Explain."

"They picked up Hulse and his friend when they left the arena and followed them south on the 280. They took the Woodside exit and pulled into the parking area for a market. Within minutes, police arrived and took my three men into custody."

There was another long silence as John Owen absorbed what the handler just said. "What were the men charged with?"

"Felons in possession of firearms."

"Will they talk?" The handler could hear the fear in the CEO's voice.

"No. They may have to do a little time, but they know they'll be taken care of."

"Well, I'm out of ideas, and time isn't on our side."

"I tried to look into recent rentals in the South Bay Area, but the number was too large to help us."

"This is crazy. We can't find a college professor and a computer nerd."

The handler was about to say something but decided not to respond. When he finally spoke, in a calm voice, he said, "We have people covering all three residences. Sooner or later, one of them will have to return home to collect mail or to take care of other daily matters."

Owen hung up, sat down, and tried to organize his thoughts. Perhaps the handler and the people he directed were the problem. Their track record was not impressive. For a moment, he regretted no longer having the thin man available. In retrospect, the decision to send the Broussal brothers after him was emotional and illogical, but what was done was done. He mentally dismissed the thought and decided a discreet talk with the people in control might be called for. Hulse has to go.

When the call was over, the handler thought about John Owen. The man was veering out of control and that presented an unacceptable risk. Perhaps a tragic accident followed by a quick cremation was called for. The man was unmarried, without children, and appeared not to have even close friends. Not his decision, but a discussion with those in charge seemed necessary. That did not change the Cal Hulse problem.

———

Carmen sat at her desk and stared at the stack of activity reports that Hollingshead had asked her to summarize. She shook her head. This was not what she had signed up for when she joined the bureau.

She had been reluctant about returning to the San Francisco office and was not willing to sit around doing paperwork. She crossed the office and knocked on the senior agent in charge's door. When she heard a muffled, come in, she opened the door and entered the office.

Richard Hollingshead looked up from a report he had been reviewing. "Yes, Agent Costello?"

"Sir, I wish to return to the Los Angeles office."

"But this is still an ongoing investigation."

"I understand that, sir, but I'm not doing any investigating. I was sent here to provide surveillance on Jonathan Scanlan, and I can't do that since we have no idea where he is."

Hollingshead stared at the woman for a long moment without speaking. "It's only a matter of time before he surfaces."

"I can be on a plane and back up here in a matter of hours."

"I can order you to stay."

Carmen had been afraid that this was where her request would lead. She steeled herself and said, "Yes, you can, but I wasn't brought here to do clerical work. I'm a trained and experienced investigator. Give me something to investigate or allow me to return to LA, where I can do my job."

The senior agent glanced out his office window and considered the request. His last performance review had been critical of his leadership skills, and it would not help if this woman pressed the issue.

His annoyance was clear as he turned his attention back to Carmen. "Very well. I'll have Agent Cain assign you to an active investigation while we wait for Mr. Scanlan to show up." That said, he went back to reviewing the report on his desk.

Carmen returned to her desk, gathered up the activity reports, and walked over to Sally's desk. "Hi Sally, I won't be working on these reports."

Sally gave Carmen a weak smile. "That's fine; it's part of my job." She took the stack of reports and said, "You shouldn't have been told to do this."

Carmen glanced at her watch. "If anyone needs me, have them call my cell. I'm going to the police gun range near Skyline Boulevard."

As she drove to the range, she thought firing a couple of clips was the solution to working off her pissed off attitude. She also wondered if her reassignment would involve working with Gregory Cain.

———

Jonathan was bored, sitting around the house in Los Gatos. Cal was busy trying to break through the newly installed firewalls at Independence, and Cory was working offsite again. Myron was doing errands and escorting Cory when there was a mandatory meeting at Lockheed. There had been attempts to follow Myron and Cory on those trips, but Myron had been able to easily lose the tails. Jonathan felt his only contribution was preparing dinner. Afternoon runs and an occasional trip to the driving range were not cutting it.

He thought about a change of scenery, a short trip, but he did not want to travel by himself, and the only people he would want to be with were in the house in Los Gatos, doing their things. Also, traveling usually meant providing identification. He did not know if the Independence people could track credit cards, but certainly the FBI could.

The idea of returning to his apartment and his normal life was appealing, but that would mean exposing himself and putting his friends at risk. Not a viable option. Instead, he decided to take a drive up the coast, maybe as far as Pacifica, then come back south on the 280.

His Jeep was still parked in front of Cory's condominium, so he picked up the keys for one of the rentals and headed out the door. It was a postcard California day, warm, clear skies with a slight breeze.

He rolled the window down as he took Highway 17 over the hills to Santa Cruz. Once there, he turned north on Highway 1, also called the Coast Highway. Being in no rush and enjoying the ocean views, he stayed in the slow lane and drove at the limit. Half Moon Bay was coming up when Jonathan noticed he had less than a quarter tank. When he reached the small town, he turned off the highway and into a Shell station.

Jonathan pulled up to the pumps and went into the office, and gave the clerk forty dollars. When he went back to his car and began pumping, a highway patrol car drove into the station, stopping at the pumps across from Jonathan's rental.

The highway patrolman used a credit card and began filling up his tank. He glanced at Jonathan, then slid back in his car and got on the radio.

He identified himself and told the dispatcher, "I'm at a Shell station in Half Moon Bay, and I believe the subject of a BOLO is here. If I remember correctly, the man's name is Jonathan Scanlan."

The dispatcher patched the call through to the San Francisco FBI office, where it was forwarded to Senior Agent in Charge Richard Hollingshead. The officer, Thomas Ratto, explained where he was and that the man he thought was Scanlan was finishing pumping his gas and was about to leave. "Sir, what do you want me to do?"

"Apprehend him."

"Is he dangerous?"

Hollingshead paused for a moment. "No, I don't believe so. Hold him until federal agents arrive."

Officer Ratto, stepped out of his patrol car, pulled his weapon, and moved next to Jonathan who was about to start his car.

"Stop, hands out the window."

Jonathan was startled as he turned and looked at the service weapon pointed at his head. He shifted in his seat and threw both his arms out the open car window. "What's this about?"

"I don't know. I've been instructed to hold you until FBI agents arrive."

He opened the car door and told Jonathan to step out of the vehicle with his hands up. He turned Jonathan around, pulled his arms behind his back, and cuffed his wrists. He then patted Jonathan down, finding no weapons, and placed him in the back of his cruiser. Officer Ratto drove to the side of the station where the air and water pumps were located, lowered the car windows, and waited for the feds.

It took over an hour for the bureau to arrive. During the wait, neither Jonathan nor Officer Ratto spoke a word.

The two agents thanked Ratto, pulled Jonathan out of the patrol car, and into the back seat of their bureau car. One of the agents moved Jonathan's rental away from the pumps to a customer parking space, went into the office, and handed the car keys to the clerk. He told the frightened woman that a tow truck would be by to pick up the vehicle. The agent ignored the clerk's questions and walked back to the bureau car.

Jonathan knew, from prior experience, that the agents were not going to answer any of his questions, and so he remained silent.

They kept him cuffed when they arrived at the Federal Building and escorted Jonathan to an interview room, where the handcuffs were removed. As in his earlier arrest by the San Francisco police, they let him marinate for a considerable length of time.

Finally, two men and a woman entered the room. The older man spoke. "I'm Senior Agent in Charge Richard Hollingshead. This is Special Agent Gregory Cain and Agent Carmen Costello."

Jonathan looked at the senior agent in charge. Hollingshead was a big man, somewhat overweight, and probably nearing midfifties. From his facial appearance, he appeared to be a man who enjoyed his beverages and had dark eyes that showed a bureaucrat's lack of empathy.

Jonathan tried to avoid eye contact with Carmen. "Am I under arrest?"

Hollingshead remained standing, glaring down at the seated man. "That's about to be decided."

"Then I want a lawyer."

"You haven't been charged and, therefore, are not entitled to a lawyer."

"On what grounds are you holding me?"

The senior agent paused for a second. "As a material witness."

"A witness to what?"

"Don't play stupid games with me," Hollingshead shouted, his face flushed with anger.

"I don't play games with stupid people," Jonathan said in a calm, controlled voice.

Hollingshead lost it. In an uncontrollable rage, he hit Jonathan, knocking him out of his chair and onto the floor. Agent Cain grabbed his boss as he lunged at the dazed man. Carman stood frozen, not sure what to do.

The senior agent shook off Agent Cain, stared down at Jonathan, and said, "You're under arrest for attacking a federal agent."

Jonathan struggled to his feet; his face was starting to swell as he said, "If I'm under arrest, I want my phone call and my lawyer."

Two uniformed men grabbed him under his arms and led him down a hallway, where he was photographed, booked, and escorted to a cell. His day was not turning out well.

CHAPTER 34

J onathan had been in his cell for over an hour when Agent Cain had a guard unlock the cell door. He handed Jonathan a towel wrapped around a Ziplock bag of ice. He sat on the bed and studied Jonathan.

"Here to make friends?"

"No. Agent Costello and I don't share my boss's opinion of you and Mr. Hulse."

"When do I get to make my phone call?"

"I'll take you down the hall to make your call."

It was Jonathan's turn to study the man in his cell. Was this a good cop, bad cop play? Jonathan mentally shrugged and said, "Let's go."

Cain called for the guard to open the cell door and led Jonathan past the line of cells to a wall-mounted phone. Jonathan dialed Cal Hulse.

"Cal, I got picked up. The FBI has me in the city. Get me the attorney you used and get out of the house. They'll be able to locate it from my rental's GPS. Do it quickly."

Jonathan hung up and was led back to his cell.

Cal told Cory and Myron that they had to leave immediately. When Cory asked why, he said, "I'll explain in the car. Hurry."

Cory packed up her own things, then collected Jonathan's. Myron gathered his belongings quickly, then helped Cal pack up his computer and supporting hardware. They were out of the house in fifteen minutes. Myron was driving the new rental he had obtained from a different rental company. He had been worried that the people he and Cal almost met had the prior rental's license number.

As they drove out of Los Gatos, Cal told them what Jonathan had said. He then dialed Constantine Weiland's office.

After being screened by the lawyer's gatekeeper, Weiland picked up. "Mr. Hulse, please tell me you're not in trouble again."

"No, but my best friend is."

"Tell me more."

"My friend is Jonathan Scanlan. The FBI picked him up and they're holding him at the Federal Building in the city."

"What is he charged with?"

"I don't know, but whatever it is, is bogus. Look him up on the internet, he's a college professor and bestselling author."

"Those are great credentials; that doesn't make him innocent."

"He needs your help. I'm telling you he's innocent, but meet with him and decide for yourself. And hell, don't tell me all your clients are innocent."

"Touché. I'll meet with him, and if he agrees, I'll represent him."

The following morning, Constantine Weiland appeared at the FBI office in the Federal Building. She politely asked to see Jonathan Scanlan as she presented her credentials.

"Are you his lawyer?"

"He asked for me."

The receptionist asked one of the agents to accompany Ms. Walland to a room used for attorney/client meetings. She then called Agent Cain, explained what was happening, and asked if he could have someone take Scanlan to meet his attorney.

Weiland was seated, working on her phone, when Jonathan was led into the room. She had googled the man the prior evening and now studied her prospective new client. Her first impression was that Jonathan Scanlan was a very attractive man. Her second impression was that his face was black and blue and badly swollen.

She did not speak until the guard left the room. She motioned for Jonathan to sit down. "Mr. Hulse called me yesterday and asked me to represent you. Do you accept me as your lawyer?"

When Jonathan nodded, she slid a form and a pen across the table. Without bothering to read it, he signed his name.

"Have you been charged?"

"I think so."

"No one told you what the charges were?"

"An agent named Hollingshead claimed I attacked him."

"He's the head of the bureau here. So, did you attack him?"

"No. They were questioning me in an interrogation room. He became really irate, lost control, and hit me."

Constantine sat back and stared at her new client. "Are you telling me the truth?"

"I'm sure it's all on tape. Ask to see it."

She thought for a moment. "Why were you here in the first place?"

"When I asked the senior agent, he said I was a material witness. When I asked him what I was the witness to, he didn't say."

"Were their other people in the room? "

"Yes, agents Cain and Costello."

Constantine again sat back and thought. If what her client had said was true, the head of the San Francisco office and, therefore, the FBI, were in deep guano.

"All right, first things first. We need to get you out of here. I assume you can post bail."

"Yes."

"I'm pretty sure I can arrange a bail hearing this afternoon. I want to get ahold of the tape from the interrogation. I also want to talk to Hollingshead, Cain and Costello."

Jonathan was feeling optimistic as he was led back to his cell.

Constantine found out the name of the federal prosecutor that would be handling the Scanlan case and, after a light dose of browbeating, was able to arrange a bail hearing at 3:00 in the afternoon. She then went back to the bureau office and requested a meeting with Senior Agent in Charge Richard Hollingshead. She was told the senior agent was in meetings and would be tied up the rest of the day.

She was smiling at the receptionist when she said, "I was hoping to talk to Mr. Hollingshead before I meet with Harry Wixson at the *Chronicle*."

The receptionist paused for a beat before saying, "Let me see if he can squeeze you in."

After a muttered conversation on the phone, she looked up and smiled. "Senior Agent Hollingshead said he could give you fifteen minutes at ten-thirty."

Constantine glanced at her watch; it was only 9:10. "Fine, can I talk to agents Cain and Costello?"

The receptionist, Karen Boblitt, was not sure what to do. She was not a stupid woman and knew the Scanlan case was a problem. Unable to decide, she called Gregory Cain.

A few minutes later, Gregory Cain appeared at the reception desk. Constantine provided an artificial smile as she said, "Ah, the man from the Cal Hulse meeting."

Agent Cain provided an equally insincere smile as he said, "Yes, a meeting that's hard to forget."

"Can you spare a few minutes for a brief meeting?"

Gregory Cain smiled and shook his head. "I understand this relates to the Jonathan Scanlan case. Any meeting I have with you would have to include the prosecutor and, perhaps, legal counsel."

"Not even a little informal chat?"

"Afraid not. Good seeing you again." With that, Special Agent Cain turned and walked away.

With over an hour to kill, Constantine went down to the cafeteria on the second floor. She ordered a coffee and, against her better judgment, a blueberry muffin. She took a table away from the other customers, sipped her coffee, took a bit of her muffin, and called her office.

Constantine still had time before her meeting with the senior agent in charge but decided to go back to the bureau's office and wait in the visitors' area.

Agent Hollingshead called Gregory Cain and asked him to come to his office. When Cain arrived, Hollingshead motioned to one of his visitor's chairs.

"I'm meeting with Ms. Weiland in about thirty minutes. I expect you to support my statement that the Scanlan man attacked me."

Cain took a moment to reply. "But sir, he didn't attack you."

"He was about to."

"Sir, he was sitting in his chair when you hit him."

Cain could see the annoyance building in his boss's face. "I want you to support me." Hollingshead was now shouting.

"Sir, it's all been recorded."

"Recordings don't tell the complete story."

"Sir, if this goes to trial, which it will if we don't drop all charges against the man, I will have to testify. Sir, I'm not going to lie under oath."

"I expected more from you."

"The feeling's mutual." Agent Cain stood and walked out of the office, wondering if he still had a career.

Hollingshead felt as if the walls were closing in. He called Jason Sartorio's office. When the gatekeeper told him Sartorio was on another line, the senior agent screamed into the phone, "This is the head of the San Francisco FBI office, put him on."

A moment later, Sartorio picked up. "Jason Sartorio."

"This is Senior Special Agent in Charge Richard Hollingshead. Drop all charges against Jonathan Scanlan."

"But I understood the man attacked you."

"I'm recanting that statement. Drop the charges."

There was a long pause before Sartorio responded. "All right."

When he hung up, he was informed that Constantine Weiland was here for her meeting. Hollingshead rose, left his office and marched across the room to the visitor's area. He forced a smile on his somewhat flushed face.

"Constantine, sorry to keep you waiting. Please come in." He led her to his office, and once seated, asked if she would like coffee or water. When she declined, he asked how he could help her.

"I represent Jonathan Scanlan, who is being held on charges of attacking a federal officer."

"Those charges have been dropped. Mr. Scanlan is in the process of being released."

"I would like to see the recordings of the interrogation."

"Since Mr. Scanlan is no longer under arrest, the recordings are no longer relevant."

"I have visited Mr. Scanlan and it's clear he was beaten. I want the recordings."

"No. Since they no longer relate to a pending case, we will not be releasing them."

"I will be seeking a court order for them and, I don't want to hear they were lost in the system." Constantine stood up and left the office.

When she stepped out of the building she called her office. "Alice, Jonathan Scanlan is being released from the federal lockup. Have one of our people meet him and take him to one of the doctors we work with. I want photos and the doctor's evaluation of his injuries." Satisfied with a job well done, Constantine decided to do a little shopping before heading back to her office.

Agent Cain sat at his desk and thought about the repercussions that might flow from his meeting with Hollingshead. He picked up his phone and dialed an extension in the building. "Hi, Billy. It's Gregory. I need a copy of the recordings from the interrogation we did yesterday with Jonathan Scanlan." When Billy Stoll asked if he needed them immediately, Cain said, "Yeah, right away would be great."

Gregory Cain leaned back in his chair and let some of the tension ease. A little insurance is a great thing.

CHAPTER 35

Despite the handler's dislike for John Owen, he had to make the call. "Scanlan was just released from federal custody. Also, the feds figured out where Hulse was hiding, but by the time they got there, he was gone."

"Are the feds keeping Scanlan under surveillance?'

"I don't know. This just happened."

"Find out and have a crew ready."

"They're already there."

Owen looked out the window of his office as he thought through his situation. If they could grab Scanlan and force him to tell them where Hulse had gone, his problem was solved. But, so far, that plan has not worked out, and Scanlan was not an idiot. He had to have a plan B if the shit hit the fan.

He had some money, but not enough. His home a good portion of his net worth, and there was no way to sell it quickly if he had to run. He thought he could figure out how to obtain false identity papers, but where to go, and how to get enough money?

He had heard about the dark web, but had never looked into it. Maybe a place to start.

———

A young man in a suit was waiting for Jonathan when he was released from custody. He told Jonathan that he worked at Constantine Weiland's law firm and had been told to take Jonathan to a doctor's office on Sutter Street.

Not in a trusting mood, Jonathan called Weiland's office to confirm the man's story. Satisfied, he went to the doctor's office at 450 Sutter and patiently allowed the woman to examine his face and to take photos.

That accomplished, he was not sure what he should do next. He tried calling Cal only to have it go to voicemail. Hie next tried Cory, who answered immediately.

"Jonathan, how are you?"

"I'm fine. They dropped the charges and cut me loose. I'm in the city, but I don't know what I should be doing."

"We're at a motel in Cupertino while Cal is trying to line up a new place."

"I don't think it would be smart for me to go to my apartment. Could Myron come and pick me up?"

"I'm sure he could but let me ask." A moment's pause, and she was back. "Sure, where will you be?"

Jonathan gave it a moment's thought. "How about on the Embarcadero at the end of Market, on the bay side of the street."

"I'll tell him. It will probably take him an hour to get there. At this time of day, maybe a little more."

"Thanks, I'll be waiting."

It was a warm, sunny day and Jonathan took his time walking down to where he would be picked up. He stopped at a Starbucks for coffee and a Danish on the way, enjoying the day. His battered face did get a few looks.

Myron arrived in a Ford SUV, a new rental. When Jonathan slipped into the passenger seat, Myron took one look and said, "Man, you got whacked. How'd that happen?"

"The head of the local FBI office got a little aggressive."

Myron shook his head and pulled away from the curb. As they were making their way out of the city, Myron said, "Yesterday afternoon I did a quick drive by past Cory's place. Two guy s were sitting in a car across from her building."

"FBI?"

"I don't think so."

Jonathan was sure Myron could tell the difference between FBI agents and thugs. "If they're watching her place, they'll be on my apartment and Cal's condo."

When they reached their new motel, they gathered in Cal's room. Cory gasped when she saw Jonathan's face. She raced across the room and hugged him. He smiled and said, "It looks worse than it is."

Cal stood up and moved closer to his friend. "How did this happen?"

Jonathan related his last two days, starting with being taken into custody. When he mentioned Constantine Weiland, Cory interrupted. "Who's Constantine Weiland?"

"The lawyer who had them drop the charges and release me." Cory's features relaxed.

Cal asked, "Tell us again about how that happened," as he pointed to Jonathan's face.

"We were in an interrogation room at the FBI office. The head of the bureau in San Francisco was questioning me, and I made a comment that pissed him off, and he hit me."

"Was anyone else in the room?"

"Yes, there were two other agents in the room."

"And I assume this was all being recorded."

"I believe it was."

"Jon, you could sue them over this."

"I think that's why Constantine sent me to a doctor's office when I was released. I'm not sure I want to get involved in another legal battle. I will say I wasn't happy when he claimed I attacked him and arrested me."

Cory was visibly upset as she stared at Jonathan. "Jonathan, I know you don't need more money, but people in positions of authority shouldn't do something like this."

Jonathan thought about it and nodded. "I'd be satisfied if the man was fired. Let me call Constantine."

Cal turned to his computer. After a few minutes search, he said, "How about Alexander's Steakhouse?"

Jonathan and Myron's hands went up, and Cory said, "I guess they'll have something on the menu besides steak."

Jonathan, Cory, and Myron went to their rooms as Cal called for reservations.

The restaurant was conveniently located on Stevens Creek. The three men dug into the steaks and prime rib while Cory found an acceptable chicken dish.

The following day, Cal's realtor called about a three-bedroom rental in Burlingame. They agreed to take it under Myron's name and sent him off to the realtor's office with a check for a month's rent.

The home turned out to be a one-story rancher on Larkspur Drive. It lacked the charm of the house in Los Gatos, but no one complained as they did not plan to be long-term tenants. Once in the door, everyone went to their respective bedrooms to unpack.

In less than an hour, Cal was on his computer, searching for a crack in Independence's firewall. Jonathan and Cory went off grocery shopping while Myron hunkered down in the family room with a David Baldacci book.

As Jonathan and Cory were leaving the house, he wondered how long this cat-and-mouse game would go on.

CHAPTER 36

While Carmen and Gregory's relationship was progressing nicely, everything was not so copacetic at the San Francisco FBI office. Richard Hollingshead clearly viewed Agent Cain, and to a lesser extent, Agent Costello, as unacceptable employees, lacking loyalty, and made no attempt to disguise his feelings. While Cain had been his golden boy, he now assigned Cain and Carmen to any unappealing investigation that popped up.

Carmen had talked to Suzanne Kroeber, the woman she reported to in Los Angeles, about returning to LA. She really did not want to be separated from Gregory, but the situation was becoming untenable.

Jonathan had a long conversation with Constantine Weiland about the beating and the fraudulent arrest. Constantine recommended filing suit and asking for monetary damages, but Jonathan did not want to go through everything that would be involved with a trial. He told Constantine he would be satisfied if the attack and phony arrest cost Hollingshead his job.

Constantine smiled. "I just processed a court order requiring the bureau to produce a copy of your recorded interview. I think we should file suit just to get their attention. They can't deny the court order if it's tied to the suit. We can always dismiss the suit."

"All right, I just want the man reprimanded."

Two days later, Cory told the group that she had to attend another mandatory meeting at Lockheed. Myron said he would drive her and pick her up when it was over.

————

John Owen's daily phone calls were driving the handler crazy. When the call came, he would answer, then put the phone down until Owen was no longer shouting, then tell the frantic man that he would call when he had news.

He had people watching the Hulse, Scanlan and Bishop residences as well as the Lockheed facility. Surveillance at Lockheed was the most problematic. The watcher had to park a good distance from the main building's entrance to avoid attention from security, and a fairly high volume of people came and left the facility. It would be quite easy to miss the woman.

The man watching Lockheed arrived at 4:30, parked in the visitor's lot, and settled in with a Diet Coke and a sandwich. He positioned himself far enough away from the entrance to avoid interest from security but still be able to observe the people leaving the building. He had a pair of binoculars and used them whenever a tall, blonde woman appeared.

Unfortunately, there were a number of tall, blonde women who left at the end of the workday. Several times, he was about to call the handler, only to decide the woman was not Cory Bishop. The last thing he wanted to do was identify the wrong woman.

Cory left the building threw a side exit, walked to Myron's rental, and slid into the passenger seat. Myron drove around the building to the main driveway leading to the street. The handler's man caught a momentary glimpse of the woman in the SUV. He immediately called his handler.

"There's a woman leaving Lockheed in a silver SUV. It could be her."

"You're not sure?"

"No. She didn't leave the building through the main entrance. If it's her, she's in the passenger seat and a man's driving."

"Follow them."

The man started his car and drove across the parking lot. The silver SUV was behind another car, waiting for the signal to change. The man, driving a two-year-old beige Honda, was behind several vehicles stopped at the exit. He was worried that, now blocked by several cars, he might lose the SUV. He was also worried that the woman in the vehicle was not the one they wanted.

His phone rang through the Honda's speakers. He picked up the call, knowing it would be the handler. "Where are you?"

"I'm in a line of cars waiting for the signal at the exit."

"I have others moving toward you, but it'll take some time for them to get there. Stay on the phone and keep telling me what's happening."

The signal finally changed, and the cars began streaming out of the parking lot. When he was clear of the facility, the man had four cars between him and the SUV. The street was two lanes in each direction, and as drivers moved to different lanes, he now only had two cars between his Honda and the SUV.

The SUV stayed in the right lane and took an abrupt right turn. The man knew the SUV driver was checking for tails but had no choice but to follow. Fortunately, the car in front of him also turned right.

The man knew that if the driver took one more turn and he followed, they'd know they had a tail. He thought for a moment, and when the SUV took a left, he pulled to the curb and waited. After a short pause, he pulled back on the road and made the turn. The SUV was almost a block ahead of him. He hoped the driver ahead would now think he was clear and not make any more evasive moves. He told the handler what he had done.

"Good. Stay with them."

———

Cory turned to Myron. "Jonathan asked me to pick up a few things at the market for dinner. There's a Safeway a few blocks from the house."

Myron simply nodded as he turned toward the freeway.

When they reached the market, Myron stayed in the car as Cory grabbed her purse and stepped out of the vehicle. Given his profession and his nature, Myron tended to remain aware of his surroundings. He noticed two vehicles pull into the parking area and park next to a beige Honda. What caught his attention was that the two cars, a late-model Ford and a slightly older GMC, both contained two men. The Honda had a single male driver, and none of the men stepped out of their vehicles to shop. Definitely a red flag.

He pulled out his burner and called Jonathan. When Jonathan answered, Myron said, "I think we have a problem."

"What's happening?" He could hear the tension in Jonathan's voice.

"Apparently, we picked up a tail, and we now have three cars on us."

"Where are you?"

"At the Safeway near our place. Cory's inside the store."

Jonathan thought for a long moment. He finally said, "All right, go into the store and stay with Cory. I'll come with the other rental and pick you and Cory up. Leave by a back door."

Myron left the keys on the floor, got out of the SUV, and walked into the store. He found Cory near the dairy cases. When he explained what was happening, Cory tensed up and was visibly shaken. Myron assured her that everything was going to be fine.

"Do you have everything you need?"

When Cory nodded, he took the milk from her hand, placed it in the cart, and said, "Let's get checked out. We'll leave through the back when Jonathan gets here."

A somewhat dazed Cory followed Myron to the check stand, where he paid for the groceries. He called Jonathan while they were being checked out and was told he was waiting behind the store. Myron picked up the bags and led Cory across the store. He pushed open the swinging door to the storage area. When one of the employees gave him a questioning look, he said, "Boyfriend problem. We're going out the back."

The man took in Myron's huge body and nodded, pointing to the door by the loading dock doors.

They left the store and piled into Jonathan's rental. Jonathan smiled and asked, "Everyone okay?"

Myron smiled and nodded and said, "I left the keys to the rental in the car. Can we have someone return it to the agency?"

Jonathan nodded. "I can take care of that."

CHAPTER 37

Owen listened in silence as the handler related the evening's events. Surprisingly, Owen did not rant; instead, he remained silent. The handler had no idea what was happening, as he had anticipated the usual screaming and insults. He finally asked, "Are you all right?"

"Of course, I'm not happy that we didn't get the girl, but we've made some progress."

"I don't understand."

"We now know the general area where they're hiding."

When the handler remained silent, Owen continued in a tone that might be used when speaking to a rather dense child. "People shop at stores near their homes. They're near the supermarket."

"I understand."

"Find out all the homes that can be rented for a short term within a radius of, say, three miles of the market."

As much as he disliked the man, the handler had to admit Owen had a point. "All right, it might take a couple of days."

"Do it quickly, they may not stay there long."

———

Cory, Myron and Jonathan displayed a wide range of emotions when they walked into the Burlingame home. Jonathan was relieved that Myron and Cory were safe. Cory was nervous and agitated, and Myron felt he had failed his friends by not losing the tail.

Jonathan's first reaction was to hug Cory and attempt to reassure her that she was safe and that everything would work out, while hoping what he was saying was true. When he felt some of the tension diminish, he sat her down and brought her a glass of wine. Jonathan then went to Myron, who was leaning against the wall, believing he was responsible for their near miss.

When Jonathan patted him on his back, he said, "This wouldn't have happened if I had lost the tail."

Jonathan looked up at the big man. "Myron, nobody's perfect. If you hadn't noticed the men in the parking lot, we wouldn't all be here. Try to get over it, we need you."

Jonathan went into the kitchen, retrieved a beer from the refrigerator, and took a seat in the living room. After a few moments, he glanced around the room at his friends. "We do have a problem. I'm sure they've gotten into the rental at the market. They'll trace the rental, and they'll have your name." He waved a hand toward Myron. "I don't have a clue how this stuff works, but they may be able to use the GPS to find out everywhere the car went." He let the thought hang in the air.

Cory was the first to speak. "Do we have to move again?"

"I think that would be wise." He looked over at Cal. "When your realtor lined up this place and the one in Los Gatos, you gave her Myron's name. If she can find us another rental, can we give her someone else's name for the lease?"

Cal nodded, "Sure, she doesn't ask for an ID."

"Give her a call. Just tell her this place isn't working out."

Cal picked up his phone and left the room. Jonathan said, "We do have another problem. The cars all have navigation systems that could track us. We need to either rent cars in someone else's name or obtain cars without GPS systems, like my Jeep."

Myron said, "Why don't we buy a couple of older cars, pay cash, and take our time registering them?"

Jonathan smiled. "I knew there was a reason to have you around."

The group turned to Cal as he walked back into the room. Jonathan asked, "What did your realtor say?"

"She was pissed that we kept jumping around, but she was fine when I agreed to a five-thousand-dollar bonus. She'll have a new place for us within two days."

Jonathan said, "I think we should bail out of here now. Maybe go back to the place on Lombard until we have the new rental."

No one argued with him, but no one was happy to be on the move again.

————

The handler called John Owen the following day. "We have a location."

It took a moment for Owen to respond. "Where?"

"Burlingame, about six blocks from the market."

"Take them all out." The CEO had leaped out of his chair.

"They're on the way."

"How did you locate the place?"

"We have a tech guy we use now and then. He got into the navigation system in the rental they left at the market. It showed everywhere the car had gone."

"Call me when it's done." Owen could barely believe the nightmare was almost over.

CHAPTER 38

Jonathan, Cory, Cal, and Myron were passing the San Francisco airport in their remaining rental car when six heavily-armed men kicked in the door at the rental in Burlingame.

The handler stalled for a few minutes before calling Owen. "They left the house just before we got there."

Owen almost dropped the phone. His voice was barely above a whisper when he asked, "How could this have happened?"

"I have to assume they figured out what we could learn from the rental's GPS system."

"I can't believe this is happening."

"We do know the name of the man who was with Bishop at the market." When Owen did not respond, he continued. "His name is Myron Rossi. He's hired muscle out of Los Angeles."

The handler could hear the desperation in Owen's voice when he said, "I don't see how that helps us."

"Maybe so, maybe not. It appears his name was used to rent the cars and lease the houses. He is probably the one who shot my men at INA."

A little more control in Owen's voice when he asked, "Any way we can locate Hulse and Scanlan through this man, Rossi?"

"Possibly. Rossi works for some loan sharks in LA. We're going to put pressure on them. They have to be able to reach him when he's needed."

Owen hung up and slumped back in his chair.

———

The same clerk was on the desk when they arrived at the Chelsea Inn in the city. The rooms were again rented by Lincoln Fenton as cash changed hands. Cory, who had not been happy with the move, perked up when she saw the new accommodations. "This isn't bad."

"I don't expect that we'll be here very long," Jonathan said as he began unpacking his bag.

Cory glanced at herself in the bathroom mirror. "You wouldn't happen to know where a gal could go to get her hair done?"

Jonathan laughed, "Not in my database. Go on the internet and I'll tell you which ones are nearby. I think the first thing we have to do is line up dinner."

After a brief internet search, Jonathan got the group together in Cal's room. "I'm sure everyone's hungry. Remember, no credit cards. Two people paying with cash wouldn't be noticed, but if we eat together and use cash, it might look strange. I suggest we split up. This is my neighborhood, so let me make a few recommendations."

After a little back and forth, Jonathan and Cory decided on the Balboa Café while Cal and Myron picked the Chestnut Street Bar and Grill. Thirty minutes later, they were on their way.

Cory and Jonathan found seats at the bar as they waited for a table. She glanced around at the busy café. "I've heard the name, but I haven't been here before."

"This place and Perry's are probably the best-known restaurants in the Marina. I understood at one time that one of the Getty family owned it and that Newsom had a piece of the action. I have no idea if that's true or still the case."

When they were finally led to a table, Jonathan ordered a cheeseburger and fries while Cory went with a salad with chicken.

Cory glanced up from her plate and said, "Do you have any idea when this will end?"

"I don't. Having to move around like this isn't helping Cal. The only way it will end is when he figures out what is going on at Independence."

Jonathan could see hopelessness in Cory's expression. "I know it's taken much longer than we thought, but I believe Cal will find the answer."

Cory offered a weak smile, but Jonathan could tell she was not convinced.

————

Using his private computer at home, John Owen began researching how to obtain false identification documents. He knew of the dark web, but had never tried to access it before, and was becoming frustrated with the process.

He was certain that obtaining false papers would be no problem for someone like the handler, but he knew he could not trust the man. He also worried that, should he locate such a source, it might be a trap set up by law enforcement.

Later that evening, Owen decided what he needed was a criminal he could trust, if such an animal existed. He gave thought to the black man he had met with over his grenade launcher plan. The man worked for the handler, but could he be bought? Perhaps the risk was too great.

The handler was also frustrated. There were too many failures, and the people he reported to were running out of patience. While Owen was clearly at fault for the botched attempt at the Ferry Building and the stupid plan to use a grenade launcher, he had been running the show at INA and not succeeding when they tried to take Scanlan at his garage. He had not even told them about the Woodside and Burlingame attempts.

Hulse's inability to get back into the Independence systems was buying him some time, but he knew what the outcome would be if they lost this race.

———

Jonathan and Cal made stops at their banks the following morning. When they returned to the Chelsea Inn, they provided Myron with all the cash he would need to buy two dependable used cars. Myron would focus only on private parties, knowing dealers would require too much paperwork. Cory tagged along to drive their remaining rental when Myron completed the transactions.

By 3:00, the rental was returned, and they were the proud owners of a six-year-old Lincoln Continental and a seven-year-old black Chevy Tahoe.

When Cal and Jonathan went out to the parking lot to examine their new wheels, Jonathan said, "A Lincoln Continental?"

Myron laughed. "I'm a big guy, so that'll be my ride."

Later that evening, Cal received a call from his realtor. He listened for a few minutes before putting down the phone. "We have a new rental. It's in Cupertino. Tomorrow, Myron will deliver two months' rent and the deposit. Why don't we stick with Lincoln Fenton as the renter?"

———

The San Francisco FBI office was a hotbed of speculation when Constantine filed suit on behalf of Jonathan. The suit, seeking significant damages, named both Senior Agent in Charge Richard Hollingshead and the bureau. Publicly, Hollingshead was angry and dismissive, while privately, he feared the possible outcome.

Shortly after the suit was filed, Hollingshead met with Ruben Silverstein, the FBI attorney who would handle the case. Silverstein was a small man with sharp features and intelligent eyes. Hollingshead tried to take control of the situation.

"Surely, you can have this suit dismissed."

Silverstein gave the senior agent a long look before responding. "I was brought into this about two hours ago, so I don't know what action we're going to take."

Hollingshead was belligerent as he waved his arms. "There is no merit to the charges."

Again, a long pause as the attorney studied his client. "Constantine Weiland does not have a history of filing frivolous lawsuits."

"A horrible woman."

Silverstein ignored Hollingshead's comment. "I need time to look into it. We'll meet next week."

Richard was not pleased with the initial meeting.

Carmen had looked over at Gregory as the brief meeting ended and Silverstein left the office. He shrugged and pretended to turn back to the report he had been preparing as he considered the ramifications of the suit on his career.

Carmen had decided that, should this go to court, she would tell the truth, regardless of the outcome.

When Jonathan had met with Constantine prior to the suit being filed, he stressed that he was not doing this for the money.

Constantine had offered a grim smile. "If we don't seek damages, there's no reason to file a suit and nothing at the bureau's office will change."

Jonathan had slumped back in his chair. "I don't want to give a deposition and go to trial."

Constantine leaned forward aggressively. "Trust me, you won't have to go to trial. This is the most slam dunk case I've ever handled. Hollingshead can't be allowed to beat up people he's interrogating. There are only two things the bureau fears: losing money and bad press. If this went to trial, they'd lose, and the media would kill them."

Jonathan had reluctantly signed the papers.

CHAPTER 39

The following day, Ruben Silverstein met, separately, with Special Agents Cain and Costello. The meetings were held in the bureau's conference room. In each case, Silverstein preceded the meeting by informing the agents that the meeting would be recorded.

Agent Cain waited until Silverstein began the recording before he asked, "Should I have a lawyer here?"

Silverstein shrugged. "You can if you wish, but I view you and Agent Costello as witnesses, not a target of the investigation."

Gregory thought for a moment, then said, "Okay, let's go ahead."

"I understand you were in the interrogation room with Senior Agent in Charge Richard Hollingshead, Special Agent Costello, and Jonathan Scanlan on May sixth."

"Yes."

"Tell me, in your own words, what happened."

"Senior agent Hollingshead conducted the interrogation. When Scanlan asked for a lawyer, Hollingshead told him he couldn't have one as he had not been charged. Scanlan asked why he was being held, and Hollingshead told him he was being held as a material witness. Scanlan asked what he was a witness to. There was a little back and forth, and Hollingshead hit him."

"Senior Agent Hollingshead claims Scanlan attacked him."

Gregory Cain took a moment before responding. "I'm sure you've seen the recording. Jonathan Scanlan made a sarcastic comment. Hollingshead lost it and hit him. Scanlan was seated in his chair at the time."

"And then?"

"Senior Agent Hollingshead arrested Scanlan for attacking a federal officer, and Scanlan was taken to lockup."

"I understand that charges were dropped, and Jonathan Scanlan was released the following day."

"Yes."

"A statement of our conversation will be prepared. You'll be asked to sign it."

"Fine, can I go?"

"Of course."

The meeting with Special Agent Carmen Costello solicited a nearly identical description of the events.

The workday was over in DC, but Silverstein knew the woman he reported to rarely left the office at 5:30. Kathleen Wolf picked up on the second ring.

"Evening, Kathleen. We have a problem."

"Give me the short version."

"Richard Hollingshead issued a BOLO on a man named Jonathan Scanlan for no justifiable reason. When a police officer spotted Scanlan, Hollingshead ordered him held. Agents from the San Francisco office arrived and took Scanlan into custody. During the interrogation that followed, Hollingshead beat Scanlan up, accused the man of attacking him, and booked him, only to drop the charge the following day."

"This has all been verified?"

"Yep, the interrogation was recorded, and two agents who were in the room described what happened."

"Know anything about the lawyer Scanlan is using?"

"A woman named Constantine Weiland, who is extremely successful and a world-class ball-buster."

"It just keeps getting better. From what you've told me, they have us. We'll lose if this goes to court and the media won't be kind."

"No question about it."

"Offer a generous settlement and agree that there'll be no record of the arrest."

"What about Hollingshead?"

"I'll handle that. He voluntarily resigns or he's fired."

"I'll call Scanlan's lawyer as soon as I'm off the phone."

Silverstein was able to set up a meeting at Weiland's office the next day. He spent some time thinking of a settlement offer that would not break the bank but would also not be rejected. His time had been spent researching what had been done to Jonathan Scanlan. In preparation for the upcoming meeting, he needed to know more about the man.

His research was informative but hardly encouraging. He had hoped the man would be fairly stupid, desperately in need of money, and a man with a criminal record. He found a college professor, a bestselling, rich writer with an unblemished record. His hope to find some form of negotiating leverage did not pop up.

Upon arrival at Weiland's office, Silverstein was led to a conference room. Jonathan and Constantine were already seated. When offered water or coffee, Silverstein declined. Constantine offered a professional smile as she addressed the FBI's attorney. "I assume you're here to make a settlement offer."

Ruben Silverstein cleared his throat and nodded. "Yes, I am. We would like to offer Mr. Scanlan three million dollars. Also, there will be no record of his arrest."

Jonathan offered no response. Constantine said, "I'm afraid that's inadequate. If we go to trial, I'm confident we will be awarded considerably more than three million."

"I believe the amount is fair, given the minor injury Mr. Scanlan sustained."

"Would you like to see photos of the minor injury? There is also the humiliation he endured when he was booked and spent the night in a cell.

Mr. Silverstein, should we not reach an agreement, my next telephone call will be to Harry Wixson at the *San Francisco Chronicle*. I believe Harry will love to write a feature piece about how the senior agent in charge beat up an innocent man in the bureau's interrogation room."

Ruben Silverstein's face was flushed as he sputtered, "This is extortion."

Constantine shook her head. "I'm sure you know the difference between negotiation and extortion."

Silverstein was waving his hands in the air. "What amount are you asking for?"

"Ten million and Harry doesn't get a call. Oh, we also want Richard Hollingshead fired."

The FBI attorney stared at Constantine for a long moment. His voice was barely able to be heard as he said, "I have to make a call." He then stood up and walked out of the room.

When Silverstein returned, he glanced at Jonathan and Constantine before speaking. "All right, ten million. You will both have to sign an agreement not to discuss the amount of the settlement or any details about Mr. Scanlan's injury or arrest."

"Agreed. What about Hollingshead?"

"Today is his last day at the bureau. I'll have the agreement prepared and delivered to your office later today." There were no handshakes before Ruben Silverstein left the room.

Jonathan, who had not spoken a word during the meeting, looked across the table at Constantine and said, "Remind me to never play poker with you."

CHAPTER 40

There were few tears shed at the bureau office. Decorum demanded solemn expressions and a thin veneer of sympathy for the departed senior agent in charge. The reality was that nearly everyone in the office wanted to pop the bubbly. Speculation was rampant over who would be named to the senior post.

The matter was quickly settled when Gregory Cain was named acting senior agent. While there were a few who felt disappointed that they were not given the position, the majority considered it an excellent decision and congratulated the man.

While Carmen was happy for Gregory, she wondered how the promotion would impact their relationship. When the dust settled and personnel drifted back to their workstations, Gregory buzzed Carmen and asked her to come to his new office.

Carmen assumed this was going to be a 'we have to stop seeing each other' conference. She closed the door and took a seat across the desk from the new senior agent.

Gregory smiled and asked, "Where do you want to go to dinner to celebrate?"

Carmen was stunned. "Can we do that?"

Gregory grinned. "Sure, technically, I'm not your boss. You're on loan from LA. So, we don't have a conflict. And keep in mind, I'm a lawyer."

Carmen returned his smile. "There's a nice Italian restaurant a block from my hotel."

"Make a reservation for seven. I'll call you when I'm on my way."

The rest of Carmen's day flew by in a flash. When she glanced in her hotel closet, she was pleased to see the product of the prior week's shopping. After a quick shower, she dressed and studied herself in the full-length mirror. The form-fitting, knee-length skirt and blouse accented her figure well. Two-inch heels matched the color of her black skirt.

Carmen went down to the lobby when Gregory called. She smiled to herself when she noticed she had the attention of several men. Gregory had changed from the standard office suit and tie to slacks, an open collar white shirt and a blue blazer.

They held hands as they walked to the nearby restaurant, both smiling at the start of their evening. The conversation over dinner was about family and friends, what they might do over the coming weekend. Issues at work were avoided. Predinner cocktails and a bottle of Brunello di Montalcino provided a pleasant glow.

After dinner, they walked back to Carmen's hotel, holding hands as they took the elevator to Carmen's floor. Once in the room, they kissed passionately, which led to discarding their clothing as rapidly as could be done without tearing their garments apart.

The balance of the evening exceeded all expectations.

———

Jonathan and Cory were together in the Chevy Tahoe with Myron and Cal following in the Lincoln. They took the 280, shifting to the 85 as they closed in on Cupertino. Cory used the GPS on her phone when they got close. The house was a two-story rancher somewhere in the seventies vintage. There was minimal landscaping in front, but it did appear to be well-maintained. The interior was functional in a rental unit way. As advertised, it had three bedrooms, two baths, and an open floor plan. The one unexpected feature was a decent-sized pool in the backyard.

Cal immediately began setting up his computer as the others unpacked. That accomplished, Jonathan and Cory went in search of the nearest supermarket, which turned out to be another Safeway. When they returned and finished putting away the groceries, all but Cal relaxed in the family room.

Myron shook his head and said to Jonathan, "You don't look like a man that just came into millions."

Jonathan stared at the floor for a moment before responding. "I really wasn't after the money. Constantine pushed for it. I wanted Hollingshead out, but she said it wouldn't happen if we didn't go for a big payday. She was probably right, but I'm sure she was also motivated by the big slice she would get."

Cory said, "Well, I'm happy the asshole is out. People like him shouldn't be in positions of authority. And you needed to be compensated for what he put you through."

Jonathan glanced at his friends. "Frankly, I think the settlement amount is ridiculous."

Myron smiled. "Maybe you can now afford a new Jeep."

———

The thought came to the handler like an electric shock. Who would know where Hulse and his friends were hiding? The realtor. He cursed himself for not realizing this simple fact sooner. Of course, there were about a million realtors in the area. There had to be a way to discover which realtor they were using. His understanding was that Scanlan was renting and probably had no relationship with a realtor. It could be through the woman, Cory Bishop, but he thought it would more likely be someone Hulse had used in the past.

He picked up the phone and made a call. He was told it would probably take two or three days to have the information. He was not in the mood for a three-day delay. "You will have two days," and hung up.

Thirty-six hours later, he had the name, address, and telephone number of the realtor: Jean Royce. Ms. Royce lived in a condo on Green Street, between Taylor and Jones Streets, in the city. The handler's next call was to Robert Curtis Allen.

Within hours, the short, muscular black man parked across the street from the address he had been given. He had googled the woman and printed out a picture of her from her website. He did not know the city well, but he realized the Russian Hill area was very affluent, and a lingering black man might gain some attention. He drove away, thinking about the best way to take the woman.

He sat at the bar at his hotel, sipping a California Pinot as he considered his options. Going after her at her condominium was a nonstarter. An upscale building such as hers would have effective security systems and cameras. He assumed she would be screaming, which is another factor, wherever he grabbed her. A lot to think about.

Another piece of information he had been given concerned Jean Royce's automobile. She drove a silver, late-model Mercedes sedan. His earlier visit to her building showed it to have underground parking. The following morning, he parked halfway down the street from Royce's building.

At 8:30, a silver Mercedes drove out of the garage and down Green toward the financial district. Allen followed, staying well back from the Mercedes. He was able to catch the license plate as it turned into the garage at the Transamerica building. It was not Jean Royce's car.

Damn, he thought. How many silver, late model Mercedes are at the condo on Green?

CHAPTER 41

At Cal's suggestion, Jonathan signed up with a new money manager to handle the funds from the FBI settlement, not wanting to keep all his eggs in one basket. He tried to avoid going back to the city to sign up with the investment firm but found the face-to-face unavoidable. When a meeting was set, he and Myron made the drive.

The meeting took less time than the drive, and they were back to their rental on Maple Street in time for lunch.

Jonathan looked over at Cal and asked, "Any progress?"

"Not much, this is a really tough nut to crack."

Jonathan knew Cal was working on it every waking hour. He looked around the house. Cory was working on her Lockheed contracts, Cal was on his computer, and Myron was reading a book. He did not feel like watching television or exercising and decided to jump into the pool. Of course, he had not thought to throw in a swimsuit when he left his apartment.

He went online and decided the closest store was a TJ Max on Steven's Creek. He turned to his friends and said, "I'm going to go buy swimming trunks. Anyone want to join me?"

Cal shook his head, and Myron smiled and said no. Cory looked up from her work and nodded. Jonathan gave her the address, and they took off in the Chevy. Cory used the GPS on her phone to lead them to the store. Jonathan turned to Cory and said, "I'll pay for whatever we buy in cash."

"You think they could trace us if we used credit cards?"

"I don't know, it's not worth gambling on it."

An hour and a half later, they were in the pool.

After splashing around for a while, Jonathan sat on the edge of the pool, enjoying the sun, when he glanced over at Cory. Her features showed her tension. "What's wrong?"

"What happens if Cal can't find the magic bullet we need?"

Jonathan knew the answer was that sooner or later their luck would run out, but instead he said, "Cal's probably the best in the world at what he does. He'll find the bullet."

———

Robert Allen was again waiting outside Jean Royce's condominium on Green. He'd parked closer to the garage exit so that he could see the license plates of the cars leaving the building. The first silver Mercedes to drive out was, again, not Jean Royce's vehicle.

The next silver Mercedes to drive out was, in fact, owned by Ms. Royce.

He followed as Royce drove east on Green, down toward the Embarcadero. She turned into a garage for a large office building on Greenwich. The man had limited experience with realtors but assumed the woman might be in and out for meetings with clients. This created a problem, but also an opportunity. There was no opportunity to take her if she just drove from her home to her office and back. If she left for client meetings, there might be an opening. He also knew a man sitting by himself in his car for long periods could raise someone's interest.

He decided the slight risk was worth it and settled in. He also regretted his second cup of coffee as he could see no convenient restrooms. He watched Royce walking out of the building at noon, accompanied by two other women, obviously going to lunch.

He left his car and scurried over to the Embarcadero, where he was able to relieve himself at one of the public buildings. He returned to his car as he waited for the woman to return. The three women walked back into the building shortly before one. The silver Mercedes did not leave the garage until the end of the workday. He followed Royce home, hoping she might stop on the way. That did not happen, and when she turned into her garage, he peeled off and returned to his hotel.

Not a successful day, but he now knew where she worked, and he was sure it would not be long before he would have the opportunity to grab her.

The second day, Allen went directly to the office on Greenwich to wait for Royce's arrival. He saw her pull into the garage and hoped today would be a meeting day. At 9:30, his wait was rewarded when the Mercedes drove out of the building.

He followed, leaving a three-car gap between his car and the Mercedes. It was a clear, fine day, allowing perfect visibility. Royce drove into the Richmond District, ending up in the Sea Cliff area at the end of 25th Avenue. The homes in the area were large, tasteful, and expensive.

He parked almost a block away from the home Royce had entered and wondered how long a black man could sit in his car before the police were called.

Royce left the home a little over an hour later and drove back to her office.

This time, when Royce left work, she drove to the Marina Safeway. Allen followed but saw no opportunity at the busy supermarket. He drove back to his hotel, knowing sooner or later there would be an opening.

Allen was waiting in his car on Greenwich when the silver Mercedes arrived. The morning passed uneventfully as he again watched Royce leave for lunch. He thought about following her, but quickly discarded the thought. There would be no way to take her at noon in the middle of the busy business district.

Later that afternoon, he watched the Mercedes leave the garage, heading south. He followed as Royce crossed the city, finally taking an on-ramp to the Bay Bridge. He stayed well back as she crossed the bay and followed the highway toward Emeryville and Berkeley. She took the Ashby exit, staying on the street as she drove into the Berkeley hills. After a few lefts and rights, she parked in front of a large Tudor-style home. The street was bordered by rows of eucalyptus trees on both sides of the road.

Sensing that this was the time, Allen parked a few yards behind the Mercedes, stepped out of his car, and moved behind one of the trees. The wait was not long. When Jean Royce crossed in front of him toward her car, he moved quickly behind her and hit her with a sap.

He dragged her unconscious body into the trees and taped her wrists and legs together. He placed a strip of tape over her mouth and half-carried, half-dragged her to his car and dumped her in the trunk.

He glanced around after the attack but saw no one. He drove away, looking for an isolated area to work on Royce. After a short drive, he found a road off Grizzly Peak that he thought would work.

Allen waited patiently for Royce to come around. He finally heard her stirring, and after a few minutes of wildly thrashing around, he moved out of the car and opened the trunk.

He stripped off the tape covering her mouth, leaned over her, and asked, "Where is Cal Hulse?"

Jean Royce blinked several times, as if trying to understand where she was.

Allen produced a knife and waved it in front of Royce's eyes. "Tell me or I'll start cutting."

Royce shook with fear. In a raspy voice, she whispered, "Cupertino."

"Where in Cupertino?"

Jean Royce realized she was about to die. She knew there was no way she would be leaving this vehicle alive. "Maple Street, 224 Maple."

Allen pulled her from the car, took out his handgun, and shot the realtor in the head.

He did not make the call until he was winding his way out of the hills and toward Highway 80.

The handler picked up on the first ring. "Hulse is at 224 Maple in Cupertino."

The handler hung up, not bothering to inquire about Jean Royce.

CHAPTER 42

The handler pulled up a Google map of the address and studied the satellite view of the property, then did a view of the entire street. He had enough men to easily storm the house. He knew at least one man, no doubt Myron Rossi, was armed, and a shootout would bring the police, which would not be in their best interest.

He decided on a night attack, using Allen and three others. The area appeared to be a quiet, residential one. There would be no way to avoid gunshots, and the noise would certainly bring the police. His team needed to use silencers and be in and out quickly.

Given past performances, he also decided not to inform his superiors until after the attack. He picked up the phone and called Allen. They agreed to stage the attack after 1:00 am.

They approached the house in a dark blue Honda with stolen plates. A streetlight down the block offered some illumination but mainly cast the street in shadows. Allen had disconnected the interior lights inside the Honda, so no light escaped as they slipped out of the car.

One man carried a battering ram, as they were not skilled at picking the lock, and the front doors of the homes appeared quite sturdy. They donned ski masks as they quietly walked to the house. Allen was holding a silenced Ruger as he motioned for the man with the battering ram to hit the door. As many times as he had done attacks such as this, his stomach still tightened with tension.

The man hit the door just below the lock, and the door flew open. The noise was significant, and he glanced outside to see if lights were going on. His attention immediately shifted to a large man at the top of the stairs yelling at them. Allen raised his pistol and shot the man in the heart, thinking he had just killed Myron Rossi, as the man was certainly not Cal Hulse or Jonathan Scanlan.

A woman stepped out of a bedroom and screamed. Allen shot her before she could turn and run. Within seconds he realized something was terribly wrong. These people were not the targets.

He yelled at his men and motioned them out of the house. They ran to their car, jumped in and drove away. Allen called the handler when they were several blocks away. The man answered instantly.

"We broke in and killed the couple inside, but they were not Hulse and his friends."

There was silence for a moment before the man asked, "How could this be?"

"The realtor gave me the wrong address."

The line went dead. As frustrated as he was, Allen had to admire what the woman had done.

————

Jonathan woke to the sounds of sirens, as he and the others threw on their clothes and rushed to the front windows, the street was bright with the flashing lights of several police cars. For a moment, he thought the police were coming for them, until he realized they were entering a home across the street.

Neighbors were leaving their homes and gathering in groups on the street, which was now blocked off by the police. No one had any idea what had happened. Everyone was pushed back as officers strung yellow tape around the property.

A middle-aged woman in a robe asked one of the officers what was going on. He simply said, "There's been a crime."

She pressed. "Are the Dugans all right?"

When he did not answer, they all knew the Dugans were not all right.

After standing around for a while and learning nothing more, Jonathan and his friends returned to the house. Jonathan slumped into a chair and looked at Cal. "What do you think?"

Cal stretched out on the sofa and shook his head. "I have no idea."

"I guess it could be unrelated to us."

"It could be." Cal said with very little conviction.

Cory, who was leaning against the wall, asked, "Do we have to move again?"

Nobody had an answer. Finally, Cal said, "Let's wait. This will be making the news by tomorrow."

Everyone went back to bed, but sleep did not come easily.

As soon as they were up, they turned on the television to a local channel. It was not long before the story broke. A woman with puffy hair and teeth that were too white stood in front of the Dugan home.

"We're at the scene of a double murder on this peaceful street, apparently the result of a home invasion. The police are not releasing the names of the victims, pending notification of the victim's family."

The reporter went on for another ten minutes with nothing of substance to offer.

Jonathan shook his head. "Nothing we didn't already know."

Myron said, "The police will probably be offering a statement sometime today. This doesn't appear to be a high crime area, so I expect it's going to get a good deal of attention."

When they looked out the window, they saw several police cars in front of the house, including a couple that were unmarked. A white crime scene van was parked in the driveway. They also saw officers going door to door along the street.

Jonathan said, "They're going to be here pretty soon. Cal, why don't you and Myron go into your bedrooms? Cory and I'll talk to them. They might find it odd if they realize there are four of us staying here without a good reason."

Myron and Cal had barely made it into their rooms when the

doorbell rang. Jonathan opened it to find a uniformed officer on the porch.

"Sorry to bother you, Mister?"

"Lincoln Fenton."

"As I'm sure you're aware, there was a shooting at 224 Maple last night." He looked over Jonathan's shoulder and saw Cory. "Did you or your wife hear or see anything?"

Jonathan shook his head. "Not until we woke up because of the sirens. Can you tell us what happened?"

"Sorry, no. There will be a police statement at some point." He handed Jonathan a card. "If you think of anything, please give us a call." He turned and walked back to the street.

Jonathan closed the door and offered Cory a weak smile. "Academy award quality?"

"Where did you come up with the name, Fenton?"

"He's the head of detectives in San Francisco, and he interrogated me after the Embarcadero shooting."

The memory of the event chased the smile from Cory's lips.

Myron and Cal came into the living room as they settled in for another day.

CHAPTER 43

They kept the local news station on the television, hoping for additional information. Jonathan went out and purchased the and the *Mercury News*, but he knew the story would not be covered that quickly. He was sitting in one of the living room's overstuffed chairs, skimming through the paper, when an article caught his attention.

A woman's body had been discovered in the Berkeley Hills, apparently killed execution style. While murder in the Bay Area was not uncommon, the manner of the death was rare. The woman's name had not been released.

He put the paper aside and began thinking about dinner. He thumbed through one of his cookbooks and came across a recipe he had not tried before, fresh chili puttanesca. He thought it sounded interesting. When he glanced at the ingredients, he realized virtually none of the items he would need were in the house, and several might not even be at Safeway.

Jonathan went online and found a specialty market in town that might have what he would need. He copied down the address and made a list of the ingredients he wanted. He went over to Cory, who was studying a contract online.

"Want to go shopping?"

Cory hesitated. "I really need to finish this."

Jonathan turned to Myron. "Come on, big guy."

They found the Cupertino Market quite easily, grabbed a basket, and began hunting for the items on the list. Some of the ingredients were easy to find, including spaghetti, tomatoes, olive oil, olives, and crushed red peppers. It took a little longer to locate the capers and garlic. The cookbook had specified fresh anchovies and Fresno chili. Jonathan had to go with canned anchovies and jalapeño.

Myron was staring at the now full basket. "You really know about all this stuff?"

"Not really. I've never tried to put something like this together. We'll see had it turns out. If it's a dud, I'll spring for pizza."

Dinner turned out to be a raving success, even though Jonathan thought he might have gone a little heavy on the jalapeño.

At dinner, Cory mentioned she needed to be at Lockheed the next day. Myron, of course, offered to drive her there and pick her up. They decided to use the, arrive early and leave by the side exit, technique.

The following morning, Cory and Myron left early in the Lincoln, which Myron referred to as his big boat. After he cleaned up and had his coffee and juice, Jonathan went out to pick up the day's newspapers. Both papers had articles covering the murders on Maple Street. While the Dugans were identified, there was little other information available. The police apparently had no idea what the motive had been. The Dugans were described as a loving couple nearing retirement. The husband, Ronald, was employed by the city of San Jose, and Margaret Ann worked at a nearby bank. The article did not mention whether anything was stolen during the attack.

As Jonathan was skimming through the *Chronicle*, he saw a brief article that identified the woman found in the Berkeley Hills as Jean Royce. It took a moment to register. He turned to Cal, who was working on his computer with intensity.

"Cal."

" Not now, I'm in the middle of something."

"Cal, now."

Cal looked up, irritated. "What?"

"What is the name of your realtor?"

"Jean Royce, why?"

"Her body was found two days ago in the Berkeley Hills. She'd been executed."

Cal's entire body went numb. He stared blankly at Jonathan. "Are you sure?"

Jonathan passed over the newspaper.

"What do you think?"

It took a moment for Cal to organize a response. "I don't know what to think."

Both men were silent for several minutes. Jonathan felt a chill as he realized what had happened. "Cal, your realtor knew where we are. They killed her to get the address."

Cal felt like somebody had just hit him. "Oh my god, she was a really nice person, and they killed her because of us."

"The attack across the street was meant for us."

Cal became very pale as the realization hit. "What do you think we should do?'

"I don't know. They obviously don't know where we are, but they might cruise around the area, thinking she might have said the right street, just not the right number."

When Cal did not say anything, Jonathan studied his friend. "I don't think we need to tell Cory. She's already uptight, and telling her wouldn't help."

Call simply nodded.

Jonathan decided to go for a run to clear his head. Thinking about the possibility of bad guys possibly cruising the neighborhood made him pause. He decided to drive to a different area for his exercise.

Later that evening, when they were all in the living room, Jonathan looked at his friends and said, "I have an idea. We've been playing cat and mouse with the people looking for us, and we're the mouse. Why don't we contact the FBI?"

His friends looked at him strangely. Cory blinked with confusion. "But they think we're the bad guys.'

"Maybe so, maybe not. Agent Cain asked me to trust him and Costello didn't believe we're trying to steal Independence's secrets."

Cal smiled and said, "It probably doesn't help that you got Hollingshead fired and they had to pay out a ton of money."

"I'm not sure Cain and Costello were big fans of Hollingshead. I admit, the payout might be burning their asses."

Cal said, "There's also the belief that I'm the hacker."

"I know. I just think we need to do something to change the picture. Tell you what, let's just think about it."

The following morning, over coffee, Cory turned to Jonathan and asked, "How do you think it would work? I mean, meeting with Cain."

"Well, it would have to be at some public place."

"What do you think you can accomplish?"

"I'm not sure. Cain's not stupid. He has to wonder why people are after us."

"I don't believe the FBI protects people."

"No, but the I in FBI stands for investigation. Maybe they could start looking at Independence."

Cory was doubtful but let it pass.

Cal and Myron joined them at the breakfast table. Cal gave Jonathan an inquisitive look.

"We were talking about whether I should get together with Agent Cain."

"Any conclusion?"

"Not really."

Cal studied his friends. "I've thought about it. You're right, I don't know if I can get what we want in the Independence systems or how long it might take. Perhaps, involving the FBI could buy us time."

Cory looked at Cal. "You think so?"

"If the bureau starts looking at Independence it might take some heat off us."

Cory sighed. "Give it a try but be really careful what you tell them."

Jonathan thought for a moment. "I will."

Myron was obviously uncomfortable. "I have a well-developed aversion to working with law enforcement."

Later that morning, Jonathan used his burner to call Special Agent Gregory Cain.

CHAPTER 44

When Jonathan placed the call, a woman answered, noting the caller had reached the Federal Bureau of Investigation. Jonathan did not know if the woman was answering all incoming calls or was Cain's gatekeeper.

"Special Agent Cain please."

"Can I ask what this is regarding?" Definitely the gatekeeper.

"No, you cannot. Please tell him Jonathan Scanlan is on the line."

The call was put through without further questions.

"Senior Special Agent in Charge Cain."

"Congratulations."

"Jonathan, thanks, but the assignment is temporary."

"Well, I hope it sticks. I'd like to get together with you."

"You know you're not all that popular around here."

"That's all right, I have enough friends. Are you interested in meeting with me?"

A slight pause. "I'll meet with you; do you want to come in?"

"No. Let's meet somewhere neutral."

"I can get loose this afternoon."

"How about the Japanese Tea Garden? I haven't been there for quite a while."

"All right three o'clock. Carmen Costello will be with me."

Jonathan wondered if Carmen had moved up the ranks, now that Cain had been promoted. "See you at three."

Jonathan arrived a half hour early. He was not concerned about them trying something. He believed that lesson had been learned. He just wanted to study the environment before the meeting. He sat on a bench near the Arched Drum Bridge, enjoying the afternoon sun as he watched the entrance.

Cain and Carmen walked in right on time. Senior Agent Crain was wearing a charcoal gray suit, white shirt and a muted red tie. Carmen was in a beige pant suit and low-heeled tan shoes. The two were in stark contrast to the casually dressed tourists touring the garden.

Gregory Cain stopped in front of Jonathan and stared down at the man. "All right, we're here. Why did you want the meeting?" His voice was neither hostile nor friendly.

"I know you're aware of the attempts on Cal Hulse at the Ferry Building and at INA. There were several other attempts on Cal and myself."

"Care to elaborate?"

Jonathan dropped his head for a moment, finally lifting it and meeting Agent Crain gaze. "A carload of thugs followed Cal when he left a Warrior game. They were stopped and arrested by the Woodside police and two men tried to grab me at my garage."

"How did you not get grabbed?" Jonathan caught a note of disbelief in Crain's question.

"I had help. We used a realtor to line up short-term rentals in order to avoid these people. Three days ago, she was murdered in the Berkeley hills. Her name was Jean Royce. This whole thing started when I was approached by a man named Thomas Scheer. He worked for the Department of Defense and believed there was corruption at one or more government contractors. The day after I met with the man he was run down by a hit and run driver while he was crossing the Embarcadero. He died."

"Why did Scheer go to you and not the FBI?"

"He did, and they blew him off. I was his Hail Mary."

Cain sat down and stared blankly around the garden as he

absorbed what he had just heard. He finally said, "So you think Independence is behind all this?"

"Yes."

"Mr. Hulse is a threat because he's hacking into their systems." Said as a statement, not as a question.

"No comment."

Cain thought for a moment. "I don't see how I can open an investigation into Independence based on what you just told me."

"I didn't think you could."

Carmen spoke for the first time. "I've spent some time looking at Independence, and I have to say, something's not right."

Gregory Cain smiled at Carmen and nodded. "I know."

Jonathan came to the realization that there was something going on between the two agents. His feelings were mixed, but overall, he was happy for Carmen.

Cain studied Jonathan for a moment. "I'm not sure what we accomplished here."

"Maybe a little clarity on who the good guys are and who the bad guys are."

"Maybe. Call me if you turn up anything I can use."

Jonathan sat, enjoying the sun as he watched the two agents leave the garden.

———

The handler was relieved that he had not told Owen or his superiors about the attack on Maple Street. He knew the people that directed his actions were wearing thin in the tolerance department. Owen would have again gone ballistic and probably use the failure against him.

He considered having his men break into the realtor's office to try to obtain Hulse and Scanlan's current address, but discarded the idea as too much risk for the possible reward.

He still assumed Hulse, Scanlan or Bishop would have to surface at some time. He had been assured by Owen that the additional safeguards that had been installed made hacking the system virtually impossible. If nothing else, they were buying more time to locate and eliminate Hulse and his friends.

The handler had talked to his superiors about John Owen's increasing instability. They had listened, but had not authorized any action. He wondered how long that would last.

He also considered that the realtor may have provided the correct street, just not the correct address. Unfortunately, Maple Street was several blocks long and he knew it was impractical to place surveillance on all the homes on Maple. The more he thought about it he realized he only had to consider homes that were rentals on the street. He began doing his research. Of course, the realtor could have provided the wrong street or even the wrong town.

His contacts quickly came back with the number of properties that were rentals on Mable. The number was six. None were rented by Hulse, Scanlan, or Bishop, which meant little. They could have easily signed someone else's name on the lease.

Surveillance of the properties would be difficult. Strange men sitting in cars for long periods of time on a quiet residential street was problematic, especially in the area of a recent violent crime. No simple solution came to mind. The handler knew when they had left the rental in Burlingame. That meant the new rental had to have been arranged shortly after they bailed out of the Burlingame house.

He wondered if he could find out which rentals occurred within this tight time frame. He began making calls.

CHAPTER 45

Cal and Cory anxiously awaited Jonathan's return from the meeting with the . Myron had less interest, not trusting anything the agents had to say. When Jonathan walked in the door, he waved his friends back in their seats. "The meeting went well, but I can't say we accomplished much."

He sat down heavily on the sofa. "They seem to agree that something is going on at Independence, but they don't have enough to start an investigation."

Cory's face was flushed with indignation. "How do they explain the fact that people are trying to kill us?"

"They understand and agree, but they don't see proof that the company is behind it."

Cal said, with heavy sarcasm, "Maybe we should carry notes that say, Independence did it, when they find our bodies."

Jonathan could see Cory's reaction. "Come on, calm down. You're going to find out what they're hiding, and we'll be fine." He hoped he was speaking the truth.

No one spoke for a long time.

After a while, Jonathan got up and went into the kitchen. He pulled a bottle of Heineken from the fridge, popped the cap, and took a long drink. His mind wandered to thoughts of Gregory Cain and

Carmen. Back in what he thought of as the *Culprit* days, he and Carmen had been close. Even then, he had been ambivalent over where he wanted the relationship to go. The parallel to his relationship with Cory was troublesome.

He mentally pushed those thoughts away and began considering what he wanted to prepare for dinner. Jonathan began thumbing through one of his newly acquired cookbooks. Braised chicken and poblano chilies caught his attention. He made a shopping list of the ingredients he would need and headed out to the Cupertino Market. No one was interested in tagging along.

Shopping took little time as he already had several of the items he would need. He picked up chicken thighs, poblano chiles, yellow onions, and coriander and was out the door. As he prepared dinner, he realized one of the reasons he had grown fond of cooking was that it took his mind off his other pressing problems.

Dinner and wine helped lift the mood in the room. Cal bitched, good naturally, that he was going to have to buy new pants, and Cory was ecstatic over Jonathan's newfound cooking skills. Myron simply asked for seconds.

After dinner, the group settled into its usual pattern. Cal huddled over his computer while Jonathan and Cory watched the news and then a movie on Turner Classics. Myron occupied himself with a Robert Crais novel.

———

The handler had not been able to determine when the rental agreements had been signed on the six homes on Maple. He knew from Allen's earlier comments that street-based surveillance was not possible, but perhaps there was another solution. His inquiries found that one of the homes was vacant and available for rent.

He had one of his people contact the realtor handling the property. After a cursory inspection, payment was made to secure the rental. His next problem was deciding who to place in the rental. This was a middle-class, middle-income neighborhood. Ideally, a young or middle-aged couple would be the best fit. Since most of his people were killers, no one came to mind.

After two days of unproductive thinking, he decided he had to bring someone in from the outside. He called a man he knew who organized high-end burglaries.

When the man answered, the handler said, "No names. Meet me at the Half Day Café in two hours."

The handler arrived early, took a table away from the other diners and studied the menu. Several minutes later, a short, overweight man came through the door. The man, who used the name Jasper, was singularly unappealing. His bloated features gave him an overfed piglike appearance, but the handler had no interest in the man's looks.

"I need a man and a woman for a surveillance job. They need to fit into a middle-class neighborhood."

"For how long?" The New York accent was grating.

"I'm not sure. I'll pay for two weeks. It could go longer."

"Four thousand a day."

The handler knew the price was unreasonable, but then it was not his money. "All right." He passed the man pictures of Cal Hulse and Jonathan Scanlan. "I'm looking for these people. I want to know where they're staying. I believe they're in the area of the rental your people will be using. It's possible they're renting a house on Maple Street in Cupertino. There are five rental properties on Maple, not counting the unit your people will be using. Here are the five addresses." He gave Jasper the list.

He gave the man the rental address and keys to the unit.

Jasper left, wondering if he should have asked for more. The handler decided on a BLT.

———

The tall, thin man, born Leo Zesiger, woke as morning sunlight streamed in from his hotel window. When he left San Francisco, he had bounced around Europe and the Caribbean for several weeks before settling in the Dominican Republic. At each stop, he had used different identities, none known to John Owen or any of his associates. He had no idea if Owen still wanted him eliminated or if the man had moved on to other priorities.

He found the problem somewhere between worrisome and annoying. It was like a pebble in his shoe that never went away. He also found his new existence extremely boring. While many would find lounging at luxury hotels the ultimate reward, the tall man was not wired that way. He felt a driving need to return to his former life.

As a parentless child in Eastern Europe, he had survived by his wits and whatever force he found necessary. Later, when he migrated to America, he worked to refine those talents. He never took pleasure in killing; it was always just business.

He knew Owen was connected, but he had no idea to whom the man was connected. If he took out John Owen, would his problem go away, or would the people Owen reported to come after him? Owen's decision to try to eliminate him was irrational, which was not a personality characteristic valued in criminal enterprises. He rolled out of bed, stretched, and decided on a run on the beach to clear his mind.

CHAPTER 46

It would be a stretch to describe the couple that moved into 110 Maple Street as working-class, average-looking citizens. The man, calling himself Forrest Mayock, was in his midthirties, sharp-featured, and in possession of a rock-hard physique. His personality tended to be over the top aggressive. The woman playing his wife was calling herself Linda Mayock, and also did not fit comfortably into the middle-class housewife model. Like her so-called husband, she was in her thirties and had the body of an Olympic triathlon competitor.

Not the best match for the neighborhood, but the best Jasper could come up with.

They had worked together on some of Jasper's burglaries, but neither liked the other. Each was hoping this surveillance gig would not last more than a few days.

The five rental properties were, unfortunately, scattered over three blocks. There was no way they could watch all five homes. They decided to focus on one at a time. If the people at the house did not fit the description of the two men they had been given, they would eliminate it and move to the next property.

Assuming most of the people in the area had jobs and would be going to work in the morning, they would take photos of them as they left their homes. None of the rental properties were close to their unit, so they bickered over the best way they could position themselves during the morning commute period.

It did not help that neither the man nor the woman had any surveillance experience. They were intelligent enough to realize they could not stand outside the target home with a camera, waiting for someone to go to work. Even sitting in a car across from the home for an extended period of time was problematic.

It was decided that the woman, sitting in her car, was less likely to draw attention than the man. They assumed most people needed to be at work between eight or nine o'clock. Adding driving time during commute hours meant watching the house from seven to eight-thirty.

The following morning, the woman parked across the street from the first home, lowered the car window, and focused her small camera on the driveway. She had barely set up when a man opened the front door, stepped out of the house, and retrieved his newspaper.

She adjusted the camera and clicked away, capturing the man before he reentered the house. Satisfied, the woman started the car and drove back to her rental.

A quick comparison of the man to the photos of Cal Hulse and Jonathan Scanlan ruled the man out. One house down, four to go.

The second day followed the same routine. The woman parked across from the target rental and set up her camera. A blonde woman drove a two-year-old Honda out of the garage. The woman in the car clicked away, but knew what she was doing was meaningless. They had no photos of a woman for comparison. An hour later, a man in his early forties drove a Ford F-150 out of the garage and down the street. She took her photos, but knew the man was not Hulse or Scanlan. The man who'd been sent by Jasper was growing increasingly angry. Other than going to the store for groceries, he had nothing to do. He did not like being idle, and he did not like the woman who was playing his wife.

That evening, he began hitting the Scotch. Always wanting to stay under control, he occasionally had a beer, but rarely anything stronger. It did not take long for the alcohol to hit him. He began bitching about the job, soon followed by what he thought of the woman.

The woman, whose first name was Olga, was no fading violet. The man, now slurring his words, was about to offer a new crude comment when she hit him with everything she had. The blow was to his abdomen, doubling him over. He dropped to his knees and threw up on the living room floor.

Olga bent down and hissed in his ear, "Leave or I will kill you."

When he recovered enough to stand, he stumbled into his bedroom, threw his clothes in a bag and left the house.

On the third day the woman set up across the street from the house rented by Cal and his friends. Unlike the prior two houses, no one left for work. Olga was not sure what to make of that. It could be a retired couple or people working from home. She decided to move on to the other two rentals.

The next two days followed the earlier pattern: people leaving for work that did not match the photos of Cal Hulse or Jonathan Scanlan. She called Jasper and gave her observations. Four of the rental properties were not occupied by the men in the photos. She had no idea who was in the one home, since no one was seen leaving for work.

Jasper relayed the information to the handler. The handler sat back and thought about the one home that was the exception. Like Olga, he could think of several reasons why no one had left for work. He also thought that Hulse and Scanlan would not be leaving for work. It was also possible that the people renting the home were away and the house was vacant. Too many unknowns.

He called Jasper and asked him to keep his people in place. He wanted them to focus on the one house.

Jasper called the handler after giving Olga the new instructions. "What you want will not be easy. The house you rented for my people isn't on the same block as the house you're talking about. They can't sit outside the place all day." He did not mention that his team now consisted of one woman, thinking the handler might want a discounted price.

The handler paused as he thought about the problem. "Keep them in place. I'll get back to you."

The odds were long that Hulse and Scanlan were not in the house, but the possibility did exist. He considered having one of his people, dressed in a PG&E uniform, knock on the door, checking on a gas leak. He immediately dismissed the idea. He had no access to a PG&E truck and who reported the gas leak? Certainly not someone in the house.

He called Jasper. "Is there any way your people can figure out who is in the target rental?"

Jasper considered the question for a minute. "Let me talk to them. I'll call you back."

Olga picked up on the first ring. When Jasper relayed the handler's question, she thought for a minute before answering. "I could do a sneak and peek, but to do that, I want more money."

"How much?"

"Ten thousand."

"I'll call you back."

He called the handler. "We can do a sneak and peek, but it'll cost fifteen grand more."

"Do it."

Jasper gave the green light to Olga."

Later that evening, Olga took a walk through the neighborhood. It was after eleven, and the lights were off at the rental. She strolled back to her place and prepared for the night. She dressed in all black, slipped on a lightweight mask, and gathered her gear.

At three o'clock, she slipped out of her house and drove to the target rental. Olga parked three doors down and moved silently to the house, staying in the shadows. There was a quarter moon and light clouds, perfect conditions, and there was no movement on the street.

She circled the house and examined the back door. It had a simple lock. Her electric lock pick took seconds. She slipped in and moved silently through the kitchen.

Olga noted an extensive computer system had been set up in the living room, but that told her nothing. The house was larger than the rental she was using, with the master bedroom downstairs and two bedrooms on the second floor.

Olga's night vision was excellent, but she knew it would be a challenge to identify Hulse and Scanlan in a pitch-dark house. When she moved across the living room toward the master bedroom, her hip bumped into one of the coffee tables, and a coaster fell to the floor. She stood still, waiting to see if anyone heard the noise. She heard nothing.

Myron, who was the lightest of sleepers, woke. He was not sure what had caused him to wake up, but instinct and experience told him to quietly make sure there was no problem. He slipped out of bed, picked up his Glock, and slowly made his way out of his bedroom and down the stairs to the ground floor. He was on the second-to-last stair when his weight caused a slight creaking noise.

As he reached the bottom of the staircase, a figure appeared and launched a spinning kick to his head. Olga misjudged the man's height, and the kick hit Myron squarely in the chest. He grunted, dropped his gun, but did not go down.

She was halfway into a follow-up kick when Myron hit her in the chest with his forearm. The blow took her off her feet and over the back of a sofa. Lights were being turned on and people were appearing out of their bedrooms. Things were definitely not going as planned.

Olga sprinted through the kitchen and out the back door. She raced to her car and laid rubber as she screeched away.

Everyone in the room stood still for a moment, as if in a fresco. Jonathan was the first to recover. "Pack up, we're out of here."

No one spoke as they rushed to their rooms and began shoving their things into their bags. Cal was hastily disassembling his computer. Myron helped him carry his equipment to the Lincoln. They were out of the house in twenty minutes.

They gathered in the garage, unsure where they would go. Jonathan said, "Let's go back to the Chelsea Inn."

Jonathan and Cory piled into the Tahoe with Cal and Myron following in the Lincoln. No one spoke in either of the cars as they thought through what had just happened.

CHAPTER 47

Olga drove several blocks before turning onto a side road and pulling to the curb. She knew there was no pursuit, but she did not want to be the only vehicle returning to Maple Street at three in the morning. She was mainly concerned with what she would tell Jasper and what, therefore, he would report to the person paying the bills.

At six o'clock, she drove back to her rental. She did not know if the police would be involved, but out of caution, she wiped down as much of the house as she could. She was not in the system, so DNA results would lead nowhere. Besides, the place was a rental with probably samples from a hundred different prior tenants. That done, she packed up and left the property.

She called Jasper as she was driving home. Olga decided on almost telling the truth. "I got into the house, but a man was awake and saw me."

This was not what Jasper wanted to hear. "So, what happened?"

"I had to get out."

"Was the man you saw one of the two men in the photos?"

"It was dark, but the man I saw was huge."

Jasper did not believe Cal Hulse or Jonathan Scanlan could be described as huge. "Was he alone?"

"No. There were others in the house, but I didn't see them."

Jasper was silent so long, Olga was not sure he was still on the line. He finally said, "All right, that's what I'll report."

Given the circumstances, Olga decided not to ask if she would still be getting the ten thousand.

Jasper stalled for another hour before calling the handler. He relayed what Olga had told him and waited for a response. He knew the handler did not like bad news.

The handler simply hung up. There was no question Hulse, Scanlan and their friends had been at the house, and were now in the wind. With their realtor dead where would they go? They might be able to use another realtor to line up a new place to hide or they might be forced to go to a motel. Hulse and Scanlan had been careful and had not been using their credit cards. Perhaps this time they will make a mistake.

———

There was a different clerk at the desk when Jonathan and his friends approached. After a brief bout of arguing about the policies at the Chelsea Inn, the offer to pay full fare plus a three-hundred-dollar bonus made the rules more flexible, and Lincoln Fenton received keys to three rooms.

After putting their things in their respective rooms, they gathered in Cal's room. Cal and Jonathan sat on the bed while Cory took the only chair, and Myron leaned against the wall.

Cory asked, "How do you think they found us?" Her voice was a little high-pitched, reflecting her anxiety.

No one had an answer.

Jonathan asked Cal, "Do you know another realtor that we could use?"

When Cal shook his head, Cory said, "I could talk to the realtor that I used to buy my condo."

Jonathan smiled. "That would be great. Give him a call tomorrow."

"It's a woman. I wouldn't want to put her at risk. Do we know how they figured we were using Jean Royce?"

Cal shook his head. "No, we were careful. We paid in cash. We used Myron's name at first, then the famous Lincoln Fenton, and we didn't actually meet with her. I don't know."

Myron asked, "Could they have gotten the rental records? Found out she set up the leases?"

Cal thought about it. "Maybe."

Cory said, "If that was h how they got to Royce, they could do the same with my realtor. I can't agree to put her in danger."

No one argued the point.

Jonathan glanced at his friends, "Well, we can stay here for a while. There's no way they can trace us to this place. Look, let's get some sleep. We can talk about what we want to do tomorrow."

Thoughts of the evening's events made a restful sleep difficult for all but Myron, who seemed unaffected by the Cupertino intruder. In the morning, they gathered at a table away from the other guests as they drank coffee.

Cal glanced nervously around the table. "Do you think we could set up some type of a sting with Cain. Maybe have Jon or me go to our places, and when they come for us, the FBI swoops in?"

Myron smiled and shook his head. "Even if we could pull it off, all you're going to have are a bunch of low-level thugs. They wouldn't have a clue who's running the show."

Cal was about to argue, then dropped his gaze to the table. "Yeah, you're probably right."

Jonathan said, "The only way out of this is for Cal to get in their system and figure out what they're hiding."

No one was happy with Jonathan's comment, but no one disagreed.

Jonathan had a thought. "Cory, wouldn't government auditors have access to the Independence system?"

She thought for a moment. "Yes and no. They'd have access to areas of the system dealing with things like production. Other areas would be partitioned off, like HR and finance."

Jonathan looked at his friend. "Does that give you any ideas?"

Cal's expression went blank as he considered Cory's comments. "Maybe. I have to think about what Cory just said."

Jonathan, Cory and Myron left Cal's room with a slight uptick in optimism.

———

Most of the FBI specialists had left Independence. While not admitting failure, they had not been able to tie the system's intrusion to Cal Hulse or anyone else. Their conclusion was that it appeared to have come from China.

John Owen was sure Hulse was the hacker, but his opinion carried no weight with the . The handler had provided an edited version of what had happened in Cupertino. Owen had simply hung up on the man.

Owen held no religious beliefs, nor was he superstitious, but he had a premonition that the walls were

closing in on Independence and on himself. He had been able to obtain a set of false identification

documents. The odious little man who supplied them had greatly overpriced the set, but when it's

something that might save your life, it's worth every penny.

One of his daily thoughts was, if I run, where would I run to. Places, like Brazil, that did not have extradition treaties with the United States, were high on the list, but would he be safe in those countries from the powers behind Independence? They had very long memories and no forgiveness.

One way or another, Owen decided to disappear at the first sign that authorities were moving in.

CHAPTER 48

I t had been some time since Cal and Cory had been back to their condominiums and Jonathan to his apartment. While they paid most bills online or charged them to their credit cards, there were some that arrived via snail mail. They asked Myron to stop by each of their homes and collect their mail. He agreed to make the circuit the following day.

It was a bright, clear day as he drove out of the city in the morning. Myron had decided to start at Cory's condo in San Carlos. She had given him the remote that would allow him to enter through the garage as well as the key to her mailbox.

As he drove into the building, Myron noticed that Jonathan's Jeep was no longer parked on the street. He also noticed two men in a car parked across the street. He was in and out in a matter of minutes.

The process was repeated when he reached Cal's condominium in Pacific Heights. He again noticed two men parked near the building. Picking up Jonathan's mail was more of a challenge. He would have to park on the street and enter through the front door. If Cal and Cory's places were being watched there was no question the same would be true for Jonathan's apartment.

Myron decided he needed a distraction and thought about what Cal had done at Woodside.

He made one pass down Green and saw two men in a dark green Honda Accord parked across the street from Jonathan's building. Using his burner, Myron called 911, and in a voice as hysterical as he could muster, he said two men had tried to get in his building and they were now in a green Honda across the street. He gave the dispatcher Jonathan's address and hung up when the woman asked for his name.

He parked the Lincoln a half block away and waited. When a black and white pulled next to the Honda, blocking it from leaving, Myron stepped out of his car and walked quickly up the street to the apartment building. He let himself in using Jonathan's key, gathered the mail, shoving it into his box, and left the building.

Myron knew the men in the car would be armed and he smiled as he watched the two officers, now with guns drawn, pull the men from the Honda and shove them against the side of the vehicle. He thought, this is fun.

———

The tall, thin man who had once been employed by John Owen arrived in Austin in the late afternoon. He was using the name William Ross for this trip, a name unknown to John Owen or anyone else at Independence. He had selected a hotel and a rental car agency that he had never used before.

After checking into his hotel, he drove toward John Owen's home. He had never been to the man's house and found the area, known as West Lake Hills, a maze of twisting roads. Even using the car's GPS, he took several wrong turns.

The homes in the area were large and expensive, many set well back from the street. Owen's address was on Sweet Sky Road, a short street only two blocks long. He assumed the area might very well have private security, as well as coverage by the Austin police.

Surveillance would be extremely difficult. The home was set back from the street and barely visible through the extensive landscaping. Another problem was getting out of the area quickly. He thought it would take at least ten minutes to wind his way through the neighborhood.

Perhaps hitting the man at his home was not the best plan.

He decided to drive to the Independence complex and follow Owen when he left work. He did not want to park in the visitor's parking area. He noticed a parking lot across the street from Independence's main entrance. It appeared to serve an office complex housing several firms. He pulled in and parked facing the street with an open view of Independence.

He had done a bit of research before making his trip and knew Owen owned a black Mercedes B and a silver Porsche Panamera. He took out his twenty-power binoculars and began watching cars exit the Independence facility.

At six o'clock, a black Mercedes B rolled out of the Independence driveway. The thin man started his car, pulled onto the street, and began following. The windows of the Mercedes were tinted, and he could not see the driver, but he doubted many of the Independence employees drove a hundred-and fifty-thousand-dollar car.

The Mercedes drove at a sedate pace, apparently in no hurry to get to its destination. The thin man, in an Audi, remained three cars behind. Independence was located in an industrial area on the east edge of Austin. If Owen was on his way home, it was going to take a while.

The Mercedes turned into the parking lot of Whole Foods on North Lamar Boulevard. The lot was crowded, and the thin man had to park three rows away from the Mercedes. He watched Owen leave his car and walk into the market. Since the market was not that far from the West Lake Hills district, he assumed the man would head home after shopping.

The thin man was in no hurry. He planned to observe Owen for several days before he would make his move. He knew at some point the opportunity would present itself.

The second day was uneventful as John Owen drove directly home from Independence. The thin man wanted to see if Owen might be leaving home that evening, but there was nowhere he could park near Owen's home that would not raise suspicion.

He knew Owen was not married and had no children, but that did not necessarily mean he lived alone. No doubt there would probably be a housekeeper, but housekeepers worked normal daytime hours. On the third day he drove to Owen's home, arriving at five in the evening. The thin man called Owen's home number, hanging up when it went to voicemail. There was no guarantee that the house was unoccupied, but he felt the odds were good.

He parked in the lot of a grammar school that was a mile from Owen's house. The school had ended classes hours earlier, and the lot was empty. He was wearing shorts, a T-shirt, and running shoes as he jogged to the house. He was also wearing sunglasses and had a baseball cap with the visor pulled down to obscure his features.

When he reached Owen's driveway, he moved quickly up to the vaguely Spanish-style home. The driveway split at the front of the house, with one branch curving around the structure to the garage and the other branch, circling around a massive fountain at the front of the house.

He walked around the house, studied the area, and moved into the shrubbery opposite the garage doors. He glanced at his watch, noting if Owen came directly home from work, he had well over an hour's wait, but the thin man was quite used to waiting. He unzipped his fanny pack, removed his Glock and suppressor. He screwed on the suppressor and jacked a round into the chamber.

The sun was fading, leaving long shadows across the driveway, when he heard the sound of a car coming toward the house. When it pulled around the house, a remote was activated, and one of the garage doors began to rise.

The thin man waited until the Mercedes was inside before moving toward the house. John Owen stepped out of the car carrying a briefcase. The thin man was six feet from Owen when he said, "Good evening, John."

Owen spun around with a confused expression on his face. He started to say something when the thin man shot him in the heart.

Owen was slammed back against the car door before sliding to the floor. While suppressed, the shot still made considerable noise. The thin man stood still, listening for sounds of movement from the house. Hearing none, he retrieved his shell casing and reached inside the Mercedes for the remote. Once outside he closed the garage door and walked down the driveway to the street.

He jogged back to his car. He had wiped his prints off the remote before throwing it into heavy shrubs. As he drove back to his hotel, he realized he had worked up quite an appetite. He decided to treat himself to dinner at Perry's Steakhouse and Grille on 7th street.

CHAPTER 49

News of John Owen's untimely demise was well covered by the media in Austin, but the coverage did not extend beyond the Texas border. When the initial police report occurred, the FBI agents struggling to pin down the hacker at Independence immediately notified the Austin office. Like a quickly spreading virus, news was passed on to bureau headquarters in DC and the San Francisco office.

A team was sent out from Washington to determine whether national security interests were at stake.

As soon as he heard the news, Gregory Cain called Carmen into his office. Carmen was stunned. The temporary senior agent in charge gave Carmen a questioning look. "Do you think Hulse or his friends could be involved?"

Carmen gave her boss and lover a look of incredulity. "Are you nuts?"

"Carmen, we know Scanlan and Hulse have a thing about Independence."

"So do I. You want to know where I was yesterday?"

Gregory Cain's face flushed. He waved his hands defensively. "Of course not. Take it easy." He motioned to the visitor's chairs, but Carmen remained standing. "All right, any ideas?"

"No, of course not. I never met the man. The report indicated it wasn't robbery. Who knows?"

"The is uptight. The man was president of a significant defense contracting firm. I know you've been digging around Independence. Any idea who would gain by killing this guy?"

Carmen shrugged. "Other than the person who will be taking John Owen's place, I have no clue."

Gregory was staring at his desk as if it might provide an answer. "Do you know anything about Owen?"

Carmen shook her head. "I've heard he's a major league asshole, but beyond that, no."

Gregory looked up. "Okay, now you know as much as I do. Dinner tonight?"

Carmen made him wait, as she appeared to be considering the question. She finally said, "Sure, but I have a lot going on tomorrow. I'll have to get to bed early."

Gregory smiled as he said, "I have no problem with that."

———

The news brought a smile to the lips of the handler. If he knew who shot Owen, he would have sent him flowers. He had no idea who would replace the man, but whoever it will be could not be worse than the dead man. For a moment, he wondered if the people he reported to might think he was behind the killing. He dismissed the thought; they knew he would not have acted without their permission.

The handler's moment of euphoria faded as the Hulse/Scanlan problem came to mind. They were still out there, representing a major threat. He thought about the two men who had been picked up outside Scanlan's apartment. Had the man returned to his unit? Unlikely, but possible.

His thoughts strayed to the woman, Cory Bishop. She was still employed by Lockheed. He did not have anyone at Lockheed that he could use to track her down, but there had to be a way to use the connection.

Cal Hulse and his friends learned about the killing several days later. Cal had taken a break from his efforts to break into the Independence systems. He was browsing through articles related to the company when he read about the murder. He called up articles in the *Austin American-Statesman* and the *Austin Chronicle*. The articles were long, but short on useful information. Basically, John Owen was shot to death in his garage, and there were no known suspects.

Cal brought the group together in his room and told them what he had learned. Everyone was silent as they absorbed the news.

Jonathan said, "I don't see how this relates to us."

Myron nodded, "Yeah, I don't see a connection, but from what Cal described, it looks like the work of a pro."

Everyone stared at Myron. Cory asked, "Why do you say that?"

"A single shot to the heart. No suspects. No mention of finding the casing. This was cold, not a shooter emotionally jacked up."

Cory looked around the room. "Do you think this changes things? I mean coming after us?"

Jonathan shook his head. "I'd like to say yes, but I don't think so. Whatever they're hiding is still there, and we're still a threat to them."

His statement did little to perk up the group.

———

Five days after the murder, John Owen's successor was announced. A man named Jordy Edward Chapel became the new president and CEO at Independence. The handler had never heard of the man and had no interest in finding out his background. The CEO position at the company was somewhat of a figurehead. He hoped the man would be easier to work with than Owen, but then, that was a very low bar to clear.

His focus was entirely on finding Cal Hulse and Jonathan Scanlan. He had to acknowledge that the men were intelligent, resourceful, and lucky. He had read Scanlan's two books and wondered if the people described as the Pacific Avenue Irregulars were helping their friends. Of course, since their actual names were not provided in the book, the point led nowhere.

He came back to Cory Bishop. His people would have seen her if she were commuting to Lockheed every day. While many companies allowed a portion of their employees to telecommute, they almost all required some on-site attendance. How was it that she had not been seen? Perhaps they were missing something.

He decided to expand the hours of surveillance at Lockheed.

CHAPTER 50

The group was growing restless at the Chelsea Inn. Basically, living in a hotel room was getting old. Jonathan stepped outside the Inn and noted it was a picture-perfect day; sunny skies and only a slight breeze off the bay. He went back to his room and changed into his running gear.

He worked his way down to the Marina Green, passing the yacht harbor, and entered the Presidio. He continued as far as Crissy Field before turning back. He had always enjoyed running. He was not sure he had ever experienced the runner's high, but it cleared his mind and allowed his thoughts to roam freely.

He was halfway back to Lombard when an idea appeared with stark clarity. He began thinking about how to put it all together.

After showering and putting a few notes together, Jonathan called Jessie Roberts. When Jessie's wife answered, he asked to speak to his former attorney. While both had benefited from the lawsuit against San Francisco State, Roberts had been uneasy about some of the methods Jonathan had employed.

Jonathan could hear the hesitation in Jessie's voice. "Hi Jonathan, in need of an attorney again?"

"Yes, Jessie. You do wills and trusts, don't you?"

In a far more relaxed tone, Jessie said, "Of course."

"I'd like to have them prepared."

"Sure, how about getting together tomorrow at three?"

"I'll be there."

Jonathan began making notes that he was sure his attorney would need to prepare the documents, such as who should be named executor and who would be inheriting. The executor decision was easy, but the decision on inheritance wasn't.

When his meeting with Jessie Roberts approached, Jonathan organized his notes and other documents he thought Roberts would need and headed across town to Jessie's office.

Lyn Roberts smiled and greeted Jonathan warmly. "Go right in."

Jessie rose and walked around his desk to shake Jonathan's hand. "I'm surprised you don't already have a will."

Jonathan returned Jessie's smile. "Until recently, I barely had enough money to pay the rent."

"Let's go over here to what I like to call our conference room." A long table had been set up in what Jonathan assumed had once been a dining room.

Once they were settled in, Jessie began asking questions. Jonathan named Cal Hulse as executor. When it came to the beneficiaries of the estate, Jonathan stalled.

"I'm not sure. Cal doesn't need the money. I guess my parents. I definitely want it clear that my brother Rick gets nothing. Can I change who gets what later?" He thought about Cory and even Myron.

"Yes, you just have to let me know."

"What about the trust?"

"A trust is designed to have beneficiaries avoid probate. It would be smart to have one."

"Okay, let's create a trust. How do I place my investments in it?"

"Once the trust is set up, you call whoever is handling your investments and tell them to put everything in the trust."

"How long will it take you to finish the will and trust?"

"It's all pretty much boilerplate. Give me two days."

Jonathan left Jessie's office and headed back to the Chelsea Inn.

Later that evening, when they were gathered in Cal's room,

Jonathan did not bother to mention his visit to Jessie Roberts or setting up a will and trust.

Cal appeared tired and a bit discouraged. "You know, if someone at Independence is selling sensitive information, I'm not going to uncover that in their systems."

Jonathan shook his head. "Selling secrets doesn't pass the smell test for me. I also don't see how someone stealing secrets would have the resources they've employed against us."

Cal countered, "Not the person stealing the secrets, but how about the people he's selling them to. Think, China, Russia, or Iran."

Jonathan nodded. "You could be right, but we don't know that. You have to keep digging."

On that note, everyone went to bed.

CHAPTER 51

Cory was again summoned by her boss at Lockheed for a mandatory staff meeting. Following their usual pattern, Myron drove her to work in the predawn hours. At six, the parking lot was nearly empty. A man sat in a dusty blue Honda in the far corner of the visitor's lot. He had arrived two hours earlier and had twice had to drive out of the lot to avoid a cruising security vehicle.

He was having trouble staying awake when an older Lincoln Continental drove into the lot. He dismissed the vehicle as an unlikely ride that Cory Bishop would use. He was pouring coffee from a thermos when a blond-haired woman stepped out of the Lincoln and entered the building.

The man was a long way from the building entrance, and he had not used his binoculars on the arriving car. He thought the woman might have been Bishop, or it could easily have been another blond-haired woman. He thought about following the Lincoln, but what if he left and Cory Bishop showed up when he was gone?

He was still debating the issue with himself when the Lincoln left the parking area the drove away. He decided it would be prudent to call the handler. The man picked up on the first ring.

"Sir, this is Egipto. A blond-haired woman arrived at Lockheed, but I couldn't get a good look. It could have been the Bishop woman."

"What type of car was she driving?"

"She was dropped off."

"Did you see who was driving?"

"No, it had tinted windows."

"What type of car?"

"An older Lincoln Continental."

This made the handler pause. The man's description of the woman was next to useless, and they had never seen her in a Lincoln. The odds were not high that the woman his man had seen was Bishop.

"Stay where you are and keep watch. You'll be relieved in three hours."

When two of his men arrived to relieve Egipto, the handler told them to watch for a Lincoln Continental. While the odds were long, at the moment, it was all he had.

At five, the Lincoln pulled into the lot and drove around to the side of the main building. The new watcher called and reported seeing the car.

The handler barked into the phone, "See if the Bishop woman gets in the car."

The two men were parked at the back of the visitor's lot, facing the building's main entrance. By the time they drove to the west side of the building, the Lincoln was pulling away.

When they reported this to the handler, he told them to follow the vehicle.

Myron had noticed the silver Toyota Highlander when it drove to the west side of the building, and his suspicion was confirmed when it followed him out of the parking lot.

The Toyota was three cars behind when Myron turned south on Lockheed Martin Way. He turned to Cory, "We have company."

Now somewhat used to the problem, Cory did not turn to look for the tail. "Can you lose them?"

"Yes, but they can't be sure you're in the car."

Cory gave Myron a puzzled look. He said, "The windows are tinted so they can't see who's in the car, and they've never seen the Lincoln before."

"But there has to be a reason they're following us."

Myron did not respond because he had no answer.

Myron called Jonathan. "We have a problem. We picked up a tail when we left Lockheed. I don't think they're sure Cory's in the car, but if I try to lose them, they'll know. Any ideas?"

"Look, I'm an hour away, so we can't do the supermarket trick." Jonathan paused as he thought for a minute. "There's an enormous mall in Palo Alto called the Stanford Shopping Center. See if you can lose them there. If that doesn't work, drop Cory off and park. We don't think they know you."

"All right."

Cory quickly used her phone to bring the mall up on her GPS. It took almost thirty minutes in heavy traffic to reach the shopping center. When they turned into the parking lot the Highlander was three cars behind. Myron drove as quickly as possible away from the main entrance. A slow-moving car, trying to leave the complex, blocked the Toyota as it turned into the exit lane. Myron was able to turn at the corner of the buildings and brake by one of the side entrances. Cory hopped out of the Lincoln and entered the building before the Highlander made the turn.

Myron continued driving around the complex before parking. He sat and watched the Toyota approach. He did not think they would try anything outside the crowded mall, but in case he was wrong, he placed his Glock in his lap.

The Toyota pulled into a parking spot two rows away from the Lincoln. Myron could see the driver on his phone. Myron decided to take a chance. He holstered his Glock, stepped out of the Lincoln, and calmly walked into the mall.

Once inside, he called Cory and told her where he was. He saw one of the men leave his SUV and walk over to the Lincoln. He did not have his gun out, but he had one hand in his jacket pocket. When the man realized the car was empty, he took out a piece of paper and copied down the license number.

The man walked back to the Toyota, got into the vehicle, and said something to the driver. Moments later, they drove away.

When Myron again called Cory and told her they could leave, she told him she was at Bloomingdale's and would join him in a little while.

When she finally arrived, she was holding two large shopping bags. Myron had an amused expression. She said, "I couldn't resist. I found two incredible blouses and two matching skirts."

CHAPTER 52

After coffee and Danishes Cory, Cal, Jonathan and Myron returned to their rooms. Cal whet back to his computer, Cory her contracts and Myron to a Daniel Silva thriller. No one noticed Jonathan as he left the Inn and drove away in the Chevy Tahoe.

The next several days repeated itself as Jonathan would periodically disappear. His friends assumed he was working out or playing golf. At the end of the week, he told the group at breakfast he had a surprise for them. Not sure what was going on, they bundled into the Chevy.

He drove west on Lombard, then turned left on Divisadero and right on Jackson. He pulled to the curb in front of a house on Jackson between Spruce and Maple. The Presidio was on the north side of the street.

Jonathan pointed to the stately two-story house. The path to the front door passed through a small, well-tended garden. "This is our new home."

Cal was totally bewildered and Cory alternated between staring at the house and at Jonathan. She finally asked, "What do you mean?"

Cal said, "This is unbelievable. What is the rent on it?"

"Nothing, I bought it."

Myron, crammed uncomfortably in the back seat, chuckled. Cal and Cory could not stop staring at Jonathan. He said, "Come on, check it out."

They stepped out of the Tahoe and Jonathan led them up the path to the front door. He used his key, opened the door and stepped aside. The ceiling on the ground floor was at least eleven feet high, giving the rooms a spacious feeling. Dark wood paneling rose five feet from the hardwood floors, intensifying a formal perception of the house.

The entry was large and open. The living room was to the right, dominated by a huge fireplace. Older, expensive, but somewhat dated, furnishings were scattered around the room, some facing a large screen television, and some forming conversation nooks.

The group moved through the living room to the dining room with a table capable of seating ten. When they came to the kitchen, formality gave way to modern appliances. A Viking cooktop was situated on a large, granite-topped island. The same granite appeared on the counters, which contrasted nicely with dark walnut cabinets.

Cory and Cal were stunned. Jonathan smiled at his friend's reaction. "Three bedrooms, two and a half baths." He turned to Cory, "You'll be pleased to know there's a wine room downstairs."

Cal, ever the pragmatist, asked, "How much did it cost?"

"I close friend once told me, if you have to ask, you can't afford it." Cal had to laugh, remembering his earlier comment, then turned serious. "Can they trace you through the purchase?"

"No, I bought it through a trust I set up. I didn't use my name on the trust."

"Smart."

Cory was having trouble understanding Jonathan's decision. "Why?"

Jonathan's tone lost its playfulness. "Several reasons. I love my apartment on Green, but I guess I've just outgrown it. Also, this gives us a safe place to stay while Cal does his magic. I like this location. I can go running in the Presidio, and I want to have a dog, and that couldn't happen at the apartment."

Myron broke out laughing so hard he started coughing.

Jonathan looked at Cory. "The couple I bought the house from is older and wanted to downsize. They took some of the furniture and art, but my offer included the furnishings you see. I want to upgrade the furnishings and art, and decorating isn't my thing. Do you think you could help?"

"Of course, but it needs to be the style you'd want, not like way I'd want it to look."

Cal was half smiling when he said, "I can line you up with my sports collectible guy."

Jonathan pointed upstairs. "The prior owners took the beds and most of the bedroom furniture. I've replaced the beds but haven't gotten around to the dressers and other stuff. Why don't you check the rooms out? We can move out of the Chelsea Inn today."

Later, when Jonathan and Cory were alone, she said, "The master bedroom and master bath are huge."

"Too big?"

"Are you kidding? I love them."

"When I bought the mattresses, the sales guy wanted to know whether I wanted soft or firm, and I wasn't sure, so I told him somewhere in the middle."

Cory winked and said, "Let's go see if you made the right decision."

―――――

The handler pushed back in his chair and thought about the Lincoln Continental and the blonde woman. A trace on the license plate yielded Miguel Soares as the owner. Information on Soares described a fifty-six-year-old man living in Daly City, working as a Lift driver. He dismissed Soares and the Lincoln as a connection to Bishop.

He thought about the money Hulse and Scanlan had to be using. They could not use their credit cards, knowing transactions could be used to trace their movements. Unfortunately, Hulse and Scanlan were well off and could stop at any branch of their banks to draw down cash. Not an avenue that could be pursued.

Research on Jonathan had produced information on his parents and his brother. His parents had moved out of state and probably would not know where their son was hiding. The brother was another matter. Rick Scanlan was living in Burbank, and his credit history was a disaster. The handler had no idea how close the relationship was between the brothers, but Rick Scanlan could be the weak link. He made a call to his contact in Southern California, telling the man to take a hard look at Jonathan's younger brother.

Information on Rick Scanlan came back surprisingly quickly. The handler's contact described the man as a total fuckup. Scanlan had an extensive history of investing in ventures doomed to failure. He was in deep with a loan shark and, as a result, had spent several days in a Burbank hospital. The contact had no idea about the relationship between the brothers.

The handler considered the fact that Rick Scanlan was heavily in debt, and his brother was quite wealthy. If they were close, why wouldn't Jonathan Scanlan bail out his brother? And if Rick Scanlan was such a lowlife, would he sell out his brother?

He thought about it for a few minutes and called back his contact.

CHAPTER 53

Three days later, the handler's contact called. "I met with Rick Scanlan earlier today. I believe he owes the shark and others about a hundred and fifty thousand. I offered three hundred thousand if he gives us his brother. He was drooling over the offer, but when I pressed him, all he knew was the apartment on Green Street in San Francisco."

"So, he doesn't have a problem selling out his brother?"

"No, he hates his brother. The guy had the balls to ask for twenty grand to go to San Francisco to look for his brother."

The handler thought for a moment. "Give him ten thousand and tell him the three hundred thousand offer still stands if he can find out where Jonathan Scanlan is."

The handler shook his head as he hung up the phone. What a piece of garbage, but he might know enough about his brother's habits to make this a good investment.

———

While Cal worked on his computer and Cory her contracts, Jonathan ran in the Presidio nearly every day. He was surprised, as a longtime resident of the city, that he had barely spent any time in the Presidio.

He found the Presidio, now a national park site, an ideal location for his workouts. Hiking trails laced through the expansive area and scattered hills offered an added degree of difficulty.

When Jonathan returned from one of his runs, Myron looked up from the Sunday edition of the *Chronicle*. "There's an article in the paper featuring local writers and artists who made good. You're one of the writers in the article."

Jonathan grabbed the Datebook section. "Shit!"

Myron was surprised by Jonathan's reaction. "Hey, it's a nice article."

"Not for someone who's hiding from people who want to kill us."

"Oh."

Cory and Cal had heard Myron and Jonathan's conversation and wanted to see the feature. "Cory said, "That's the photo on the back cover of your books."

Jonathan suddenly felt exposed and vulnerable. "I'm afraid someone's going to recognize me from this and we'll all be at risk."

Cal patted his friend on his shoulder. "I don't think there's much risk, Jon. Maybe stay out of the restaurants and supermarkets for a little while. By tomorrow, the paper will be in the recycling bins and the bottom of bird cages."

Jonathan was not convinced. "The *Chronicle* delivers a lot of papers in the city."

Cory hugged Jonathan. "Maybe we should leave the Bay Area for a week or so."

"Let me think about it. I'm going to take a shower."

The following morning, over coffee, Jonathan told his friends he was going to take a few precautions but did not think he needed to leave the city.

Cal looked at Jonathan and asked, "What precautions?"

"Myron can do the food shopping, and I'll stay out of the restaurants for a little while. When I go out, I'll wear a cap and sunglasses, and I'm thinking about growing a beard."

Cory laughed and poked Jonathan. "By the time you grow a beard, no one will have remembered the article."

Jonathan had to smile. "Yeah, you're probably right."

Jonathan continued to run in the Presidio, but now wearing a baseball cap pulled low and lightly tinted sunglasses. He occasionally came across other runners and hikers, but, if they acknowledged him at all, it was only a quick smile and wave.

When the prior owners left the house, they took almost all the small kitchen appliances, silverware, dishes, and cutlery. Myron purchased the basic kitchen items, but Jonathan ventured out to buy specialty items. Since he was paying with cash, he did not want to buy all his needs in one place. He divided his purchases between Sanko on Buchanan, Kamel on Chestnut, and Williams-Sonoma on Post.

With the kitchen finally shaping up, Jonathan announced, "No more pizza and Chinese, the Scanlan Café will be open tonight." His audience of three gave him a hearty applause.

Dinner consisted of a mango and avocado salad and cracker-crumbled fillet of salmon. Frank Family Chardonnay was liberally poured, and the dessert was a choice of three flavors of Häagen-Dazs ice creams.

Everyone gave rave reviews, even Myron, who was pretty much a meat-and-potatoes guy. Jonathan smiled as he glanced around the table. "I wanted our first dinner here to be special. Please don't expect every evening to be this elaborate."

Myron said, "If all our dinners were like this, I'd have to start running with Jonathan."

———

Carmen Costello continued to research Independence in her free time. She found their decision to bring in Jordy Edward Chapel as CEO an odd one. From what she could put together, the man had an unimpressive background. When she contacted his prior employer, a regional hardware store chain, they refused to comment on their prior COO.

Carmen had an out-of-the-box thought and ran a credit check on Mr. Chapel. The man's credit rating improved dramatically after he was hired by Independence. Carmen pushed back in her chair and considered why a successful defense contractor would hire Jordy Chapel as their Chief Executive Officer.

John Owen's murder also kept playing through Carmen's mind. She had used her contacts to follow the investigation, which appeared to be going nowhere. It was agreed that the hit was done by a professional. Owen had been carrying a good deal of cash, and none was taken. One theory being floated was that he was killed because of his position at Independence, perhaps by a foreign source. Carmen thought this was unlikely as his murder appeared to have no effect on the company's operations.

CHAPTER 54

The handler was under increasing pressure to bring, as the people who directed him termed, the Hulse/Scanlan matter, to a conclusion. Surveillance had produced a few close calls, but he knew the men he sought were highly intelligent and had learned from those close calls. Wherever they were, they had gone to ground.

He had little faith in Rick Scanlan's ability to ferret out his brother. Worth a try, but something more had to happen. He thought about hiring a private investigator, but there were a few problems with that idea. He did not want to provide his name as the client, and the investigator might have a problem if the people he found were killed.

However, the more he thought about the idea, the more he liked it. He could send one of his people in as the prospective client with a story. Perhaps a woman who would claim to be pregnant with Scanlan being the father. He's rich and hiding to avoid his financial responsibility.

When Hulse, Scanlan, and the Bishop woman were dead, the client would be nowhere to be found. He assumed the investigator would also cease to exist. He thought about the woman who had been used in the Maple Street surveillance. He had never met the woman. Hopefully, she was attractive. Scanlan was a rich, successful, good-looking man, unlikely to have an affair with an unattractive woman.

The handler called the man named Jasper. "I need an attractive woman for a plan I have. Is the woman who was used for the surveillance job we did in Cupertino attractive?"

Jasper paused before answering. "Somewhat. She's midthirties, and extremely athletic."

"What do you mean, somewhat attractive?"

"She has a few hard edges."

Not the answer he was hoping for. "Would a good-looking, successful man be attracted to her?"

Jasper was seeing a large payday slipping away. "Maybe, but there's another woman I use that would probably be a better fit."

"Before she joined my group, she was making good money conning rich men."

"If she was making, as you say, good money, why did she stop and go to work for you?"

"She was working in Dallas, and let's say, it got too hot down there."

"Send me her picture."

The handler studied the woman's picture when it appeared on his phone; blond hair worn long, blue eyes, and classic features. Definitely a believable match for Scanlan.

He called Jasper immediately. "She's perfect."

"What do you want her to do?"

"I want her to make an appointment with a private investigator in Los Angeles and employ him to find Jonathan Scanlan. Have her claim they had an affair and now she's pregnant. He's gone into hiding to avoid her financial demands, and she wants him found."

"That shouldn't be a problem."

The handler gave Jasper the name and phone number of the investigator he wanted them to use. The balance of the call was spent negotiating the price.

When Jasper asked where Scanlan might be, the handler told him somewhere in the San Francisco Bay Area. After he hung up, the handler sat back and wondered why he had not tried this before.

Two days later, the woman, identifying herself as Vivian Hughes, sat across the desk from Eric Bennett. The handler had selected Bennett for two reasons: he was a competent investigator and a man of limited ethics.

Unlike in the movies, the vast majority of Bennett's clients were neither attractive or pleasant people. The woman sitting across from him was a knockout. Beautiful face, unbelievable figure, and he couldn't care less if she had a pleasant personality. He had difficulty focusing on her story as he stared at her legs.

Forcing himself to make eye contact, he said, "So you want me to find this man, Jonathan Scanlan."

"Yes." She took an envelope from her purse and pushed it across the desk. "This is his home address and telephone number. Of course, he's not there. I do believe he's somewhere in the San Francisco Bay Area."

"Do you have a photo?"

"No, but go online. He's a bestselling author. Oh, he may be with his best friend, a man named Cal Hulse."

"I charge a thousand a day plus expenses."

She again dipped into her purse and handed him a thick envelope. "Here's ten thousand. You do accept cash, don't you?"

"Yes, cash is fine." Not only fine, he thought, but tax-free.

He was about to hit on her when Vivian said, "I'm flying back to San Francisco in three hours. The envelope I gave you has my cell number."

Bennett's eyes followed her as she left his office. Well, not today, but we'll both be in San Francisco, so maybe a few meetings over dinner to discuss the hunt for Mr. Scanlan and who knows where that might go.

He went online and started with Jonathan Scanlan's website. Good-looking guy, college professor with two successful books out. Bennett was not a big reader and had never heard of the author or his books. A Google search brought up several references to Scanlan, the most recent, a *San Francisco Chronicle* article that featured the author but contained no information he could use. Articles by critics seemed to cut across political lines. Conservatives praised him, and liberals disliked the man. Again, not useful.

Bennett then got busy making plane and hotel reservations and lining up a rental car. He fingered the thick envelope and called the Musso & Frank Grill for a reservation.

Vivian Hughes, who was actually Charlean Rando, called Jasper from her Uber ride to LAX. There was some apprehension in his voice when he asked how the meeting went.

"Everything went as scheduled. This guy is a piece of shit. He may be a good investigator, but he's certainly a world-class lech."

"Well, we can't all be classy people. When will he be up here?"

"He said tomorrow."

"Okay, keep me posted."

CHAPTER 55

Eric Bennett's cursory research had given him a feel for the man, but no lead to his location. His first stop on arriving in the city was Jonathan Scanlan's apartment on Green. The front door lock and the apartment door lock offered no challenge. What surprised him was that the apartment was empty. There was no question that the man would not be returning to Green Street.

There was a small collection of mail in Scanlan's mailbox, but all the junk mail of no importance. As he was leaving the building, he noticed two men sitting in a car across the street. They appeared to have settled in for a long wait. This piqued his curiosity.

It was nearing twelve, and Bennett decided to leave his car and walk down to Union for lunch. Over the years, he had spent a considerable amount of time in the city and knew Union Street was loaded with restaurants.

He picked Wildseed, ordered a hamburger and a beer, and thought about the two men in the car. When he finished lunch, he walked back to his rental and noticed the men were still there. He was quite sure the men were watching Scanlan's building. The odds were astronomical that they were also looking for Jonathan Scanlan, but why? It did not make sense that Vivian Hughes would hire him and also be paying these men to look for Scanlan. He began to wonder if there was more to the author's disappearance than what Hughes had told him.

He drove across town to the Hyatt Regency on Embarcadero Center, checked in, went to his room, and began working. A contact at AT&T confirmed that Jonathan Scanlan was a customer, but his cell phone showed no activity for the past several months.

He had earlier obtained Scanlan's parents' phone number. He dialed the number, planning to tell them he was an old friend trying to get in touch. His call went to voicemail. He was not deterred, knowing if finding the man was easy, he would not have been paid to locate him.

Bennett knew most people avoiding the authorities reverted to old habits and familiar surroundings. His research showed Scanlan to be an avid golfer and a runner. Unfortunately, you could run anywhere, and unless Scanlan was a member at a golf course, he could play at any public course.

He thought about Scanlan's background. He had taught contemporary American literature at San Francisco State and had written two successful books. One would think he would be a big reader, but Scanlan was not using his credit cards, so Amazon was out.

When he checked on the status of Scanlan's Jeep, he found it had been towed away and was sitting in an impoundment yard. No other vehicle was registered to Jonathan Scanlan in California. Another dead end.

Bennett began thinking it might be easier to find Scanlan by looking for Cal Hulse. Digging into Hulse's background was interesting, but not particularly rewarding. He decided a drive to Mr. Hulse's condo might yield something.

He knew from his research that Cal Hulse was a highly successful high-tech consultant and was therefore not surprised to find the man's condominium situated in an extremely expensive building in an extremely expensive neighborhood.

He was surprised to see two men sitting in a car opposite the condo. Bennett realized he was not the only person looking for

Scanlan and Hulse. Interesting. He also began wondering about Vivian Hughes and her story.

When he was back in his hotel, he used his laptop to learn more about Ms. Hughes. Hughes proved to be a common name, but no Vivian Hughes appeared. Bennett called a contact at the DMV, only to learn a license had been issued to a Vivian Huges. The licensed Vivian Hughes lived in Fresno and was sixty-one years of age.

Something definitely sketchy was happening, but ten thousand plus expenses was still ten thousand plus expenses. Bennett sat back at the small desk in his room and thought about who would be able to get in touch with Scanlan. His parents were not answering their phone or returning his call. Bennett knew almost nothing about writers, but he assumed successful authors would have an agent.

A Google search produced the names of two literary agents involved with Scanlan's books: Harvey Ballow and Mary Downs. He went to each of their websites and copied down their telephone numbers. His first call was to Ballow.

The man answered on the second ring. "Ballow and Associates."

"Harvey Ballow please."

"Speaking."

"Mr. Ballow, I'm trying to get in touch with one of your clients, Jonathan Scanlan. Do you have Mr. Scanlan's telephone number and current address?"

"I no longer represent Jonathan Scanlan, and I can't help you." Ballow hung up, leaving Bennett with the impression that the parting of the ways had not been amicable.

He dialed the number for Mary Downs. A woman with a pleasant voice answered.

"Mary Downs, please."

"This is Mary."

"Hi, my name is Eric Bennett, and I've been trying to reach Jonathan Scanlan. I understand you're his agent and thought you might be able to help me."

"Yes, I represent Jonathan. Can I ask what this is about?"

Bennett had anticipated this question and said, "I line up

celebrities and other well-known figures for public speaking engagements."

He could hear the woman's laughter. When the laughter died down, she said, "I don't believe Jonathan would be interested."

"Public speaking engagements are quite lucrative."

"Trust me, that isn't something Jonathan would want to do."

"I might be able to persuade him. Could you give me his number?" He knew he was pressing too hard, but he had to try.

"We don't release that type of client information. Goodbye, Mr. Bennett."

The investigator sat back and tried to think of his next move. He assumed Scanlan had put in a change of address with the post office, but he had no contact that would help him there. His thoughts turned to Cal Hulse. The woman thought Hulse might be with Scanlan.

Bennett thought Hulse might be easier to find than Scanlan. He was a big-time high-tech consultant, so there had to be a way for his clients to reach him. Bennett did not know which firms employed Hulse, but that was something he could find out.

Finding out proved more difficult than Bennett had originally believed. While Hulse's website stated that the man had worked for many of the Silicon Valley firms, it did not mention any of those firms by name.

Several years earlier, Bennett had been employed by a client named Leo Lipinski. Lipinski was the head of marketing at Salesforce and in the middle of a messy divorce. Lipinski's soon-to-be ex-wife was challenging their prenup agreement, which, if successful, would involve several million dollars.

Through several somewhat illegal procedures, Eric Bennett was able to produce photographs of Laurel Lipinski performing a variety of enthusiastic sexual acts with her divorce attorney. Leo was a happy former client.

Bennett called Leo and asked for help getting in touch with Cal Hulse. Lipinski said he would talk to the head of IT and get back to him.

Three hours later, Lipinski called Bennett's cell. "I got a number for Hulse. Hope this helps."

When Bennett called the number, it immediately went to voicemail. The message said that Hulse was traveling and could only be reached by email. Bennett sat back for a moment and thought about what he could put in an email that would draw Hulse out.

Bennett called Lipinski back. "Sorry to bother you again, Leo, but could you ask your IT guy the names of some of Hulse's clients?"

There was a pause. "I'll ask him, but I don't believe Hulse ever worked for us, and he may not know Hulse's clients."

"Thanks. Let me know."

Lipinski called the following day. "My guy believes Hulse has been doing quite a bit of work for INA."

"Thanks, Leo. I appreciate the help."

Bennett went online and researched INA. He made a note of the man's name that was the head of their information technology department. He then sat back and thought about how he could use the information to draw Hulse out.

CHAPTER 56

J ordy Edward Chapel's initial reaction to being recruited and hired as Independence's CEO was that he had fallen into a bed of roses. His salary was triple what he had been making at the hardware chain, with great benefits and a large corner office. The timing of the offer could not have been better. An unfortunate financial audit at the hardware firm had uncovered missing funds and he had felt the hot breath of the legal system breathing down his neck.

Chapel was intelligent enough to wonder why he had been selected by the defense contractor when he did not know a missile from a Honda. He assumed his brilliant interviewing skills had carried the day. After a day of congratulations, he was enjoying the comfort of his two-thousand-dollar Maitland Smith executive chair when his office phone rang.

A man's voice, that he did not recognize, said in a calm tone, "Mr. Chapel. We are aware that you are totally unqualified for your new position."

Chapel shouted into the phone. "Who is this?"

The man ignored the CEO's question. "You have been hired as a figurehead, nothing more. Please be aware that we know all about your financial misdeeds at your prior company."

Jordy Chapel's voice was shaking when he shouted, "I don't know what you're talking about. Who is this?"

"If you wish, I can provide you with a copy of the financial audit."

Chapel was suddenly sweating heavily. "What do you want?"

"We want you to go to work each day, pretending you're running the company. When I call you, you will do whatever I tell you to do. Do you understand?"

When Chapel failed to answer, the caller repeated his question.

It was barely a whisper when Chapel said, "Yes."

The caller hung up. Chapel felt so drained that he did not think he could stand. He also remembered reading that the prior CEO had been shot to death.

The handler was pleased with the call and Chapel's reaction. The man sat back and considered how he would need to manage Chapel so that the man's incompetence did not become too obvious. He also realized running the company through Chapel was going to take a good deal of his time. He hoped one of his efforts to eliminate the Hulse/Scanlan problem would bear fruit, allowing him to concentrate on Chapel.

———

Bennett was far from being a computer guy, but he did know the basics. Hulse would not be fooled by an email that did not come from Joseph Thompson, the head of IT at INA. That meant he had to learn the man's email address. A search on the INA website was unproductive. There was no question that a long list of people and companies would have this information, but it was not information they would release without a good reason.

He assumed a man in Joseph Thompson's position would be involved in one or more information technology professional organizations. A Google search produced a list of several organizations that the man might belong to.

Bennett made a list of the organizations and their telephone numbers. He understood they would probably not confirm that

Thompson was one of their members or provide his email address. A more indirect approach would be required. He went online and made notes about a high-tech company in Lexington, Kentucky, assuming no one he would be talking to would have ever heard of the organization.

He called one of the associations on his list, the Society for Information Management or SIM. A woman with a heavy Asian accent answered.

"SIM, how can I help you?"

"Hi, my name is Eric Bennett. I'm the IT Director at CABEM Technologies. I'm interested in joining your organization."

"That would be wonderful. Where is CABEM located?"

"Lexington, Kentucky. I'm in San Francisco for a conference. Could you send me the membership application to my hotel? I'm staying at the Hyatt Regency at five Embarcadero, San Francisco, 94111, and my name is spelled as it sounds, Eric Bennett."

"I can do that."

"Will the information you're sending me include a list of your members?"

"No. That will be provided after you've become a member."

Disappointing, but not surprising. "Thank you for your help."

Bennett called two other associations, the Association of Information Technology Professionals and the Information Systems Security Association, which yielded similar results, applications, but no membership list.

Bennett assumed the cost for the memberships would not be excessive and, anyway, it would be included in his expenses. He also knew Joseph Thompson might not be a member of any of the three organizations. There were other associations, but he believed the three he had talked to were the most promising. If this avenue did not work out, he would have to think of a different approach.

Jonathan left the house late Tuesday morning, not bothering to tell his friends where he was going. He took the Tahoe and drove across town and into the heart of the Mission District. He parked in front of a large glass-fronted building on Florida Street.

An older black woman sat at the reception desk in the entry. She smiled in greeting and asked how she could help him. The San Francisco SPCA Adoption Center occupied the building.

"I would like to adopt a dog."

Her smile widened. "You came to the right place. Can I ask you a few questions?"

"Of course."

"Have you owned or adopted a dog in the past?"

"No. Until recently, I lived in an apartment and could not have a pet. I now have a house in the city."

"You know, people who have not had a pet often don't understand the responsibilities that are involved."

"I understand."

"Can I ask why you would like to have a dog?"

Jonathan thought for a moment before answering. "Companionship."

"You know, taking proper care of a dog is a financial responsibility."

"That isn't a problem."

She again smiled and handed Jonathan a form. "Please fill this out. When you're finished, I'll have one of our people take you back where we have our adoptees."

When he handed the woman the completed form, she hit a button on her desk, and a young woman came into the lobby.

"This is Jana. She'll take you to see the dogs we have for adoption."

Jana gave Jonathan a shy smile and led him into the rest of the building. She glanced over to him as they began seeing a variety of dogs in large cages. "Are you looking for a particular breed? Not many of our dogs are purebred." The strong odor of disinfection assailed Jonathan as he walked past the cages.

"That's not important to me."

"Large dog, small dog?"

"Probably on the larger size."

A good number of the cages housed bull terriers, commonly known as pit bulls. While some wagged their tails, others seemed less friendly. Jonathan smiled to himself as he thought about Cal's reaction if he walked in the door with a pit bull.

They were halfway through the kennel when Jonathan stopped at one of the cages. The dog inside appeared to be a black labrador. The young woman said, "This is Horris. He's three years old, and very friendly. I don't know the whole story, but I heard a couple was getting a divorce and neither was willing to take Horris."

"Can you open the cage?"

Jana opened the door, and the dog came out and sat beside Jonathan. She smiled and said, "I think you found your dog."

Jonathan looked down as the labrador stared up at him with trusting eyes. He turned to Jana, "Horris?"

She laughed. "Give him two milk bones and tell him his new name."

Jonathan returned to the lobby, signed off on the adoption papers, and paid for the privilege of being Hossa's parent. The dog rode in the front seat of the Tahoe as Jonathan turned toward home. He used his phone to google pet supply stores and ended up at a Petco, where he bought everything his adopted child would need.

CHAPTER 57

Eric Bennett hated having to wait, but he had not been able to think of another avenue of inquiry other than obtaining Joseph Thompson's email address through one of the professional associations. The applications arrived on the third day, and he quickly filled them out and returned them, using an express delivery service. Then another wait.

He called his client, hoping he could get lucky after dinner and drinks, but the call went to voicemail, and the woman did not return the call. He thought about going to the racetrack, but found Golden Gate Fields had closed.

The membership information finally arrived. The membership list for the Society for Information Management did not include Thompson's name. He hit paydirt with the membership list for the Association of Information Technology Professionals. Joseph Thompson was a member, and contact information was provided.

The information included the man's position at INA and the company's telephone number. Bennett called the corporate number and asked to speak to Thompson. He was routed to Joseph Thompson's gatekeeper.

"Hello, this is Arnold Smith at AITP. We're updating our member information to include email addresses. Could you give me Mr. Thompson's address?"

"AITP?"

"The Association of Information Technology Professionals. Mr. Thompson is a member."

"One moment, please." The woman was, no doubt, checking with Thompson.

She was back after a brief delay. "Mr. Thompson's email is Joseph Thompson, one-two-three, at AOL dot com."

"Thank you so much."

Bennett began drafting an email to Cal Hulse that would bring him to INA. He knew when Hulse arrived at INA, there would be confusion, followed by suspicion. He did not care. He assumed that when Hulse left the facility, he would return to wherever he and Scanlan were hiding, and his task was over.

The reactions were varied when Jonathan and his Labrador arrived home. Cory and Myron smiled as Jonathan walked into the living room with his new roommate by his side. When Jonathan stopped, the dog sat, first staring up at Jonathan, then at Jonathan's friends.

Cory said, "He's beautiful."

Cal, who never had a pet, and his parents never had a pet, frowned. "You did it."

"Yes, I did it."

Myron, who seemed pleased with the new addition, asked, "What's his name?"

"The previous owners named him Horris, but that's going to change."

Myron asked, "Can you do that?"

Cory stood up and answered. "Of course you can. One of my parents' dogs came to us with the name Rodger. Within a day, he became Rusty."

Jonathan nodded. "That's what the woman at the SPCA told me."

Myron looked at the labrador. "So, what's his new name?'

"Bo."

Cal immediately perked up. "Great name. Bo Jackson was a superstar playing baseball, mostly for the Royals, and one of the best running backs in the NFL."

Jonathan just smiled at his friend. "I just like the name Bo."

Myron shook his head at Cal's conversion. "Where's all his stuff?"

"Out in the car."

"I'll bring it in."

It took two trips to bring in everything. The pile in the living room included two dog beds, a huge bag of dog food, boxes of treats, a water bowl, and a food bowl.

Cory looked at Bo's new possessions and said, "Where are his toys?"

Jonathan gave her a blank stare. She smiled and said, "Puppies need their toys. Come on, Myron. We need to do a toy run."

An hour later, Bo had a dozen toys. He looked at Jonathan and then at the toys, as if he was unsure what he was supposed to do.

Jonathan studied the dog for a moment. "Maybe he never had any toys."

Cory laughed and said, "He'll figure it out."

Jonathan handed Bo a rubber bone, and Bo was soon running around the room with his new toy.

Cal glanced at his computer for a moment, then looked up. "I have to be at INA tomorrow at ten."

Myron nodded. "I'll drive you."

Jonathan said, "Take the Tahoe, they've seen the Lincoln."

Later, as they were ready to go to bed, Jonathan grabbed one of the dog beds and headed for the master bedroom with Bo by his side.

Cory held up her hand. "Whoa. Bo is going to be sleeping with us?"

"In his dog bed."

"No, no, no."

The argument moved to the bedroom, with Bo following the back-

and-forth exchange. Eventually, a compromise was reached. Bo could sleep in the room unless intimate happenings were going to occur.

Cory was not happy but decided to press the issue later.

CHAPTER 58

The following morning, after breakfast, Jonathan left for a run in the Presidio, this time accompanied by Bo. Cal and Myron took off at eight-thirty. Traffic was heavy but moved along at a decent pace. They arrived at the INA ten minutes early.

Myron pulled to a stop in front of the main entrance, and Cal slipped out of the Tahoe with his briefcase and entered the building. Myron, assuming Cal's meeting would last two or three hours, drove away in search of a coffeehouse.

Eric Bennett watched Cal Hulse's arrival from the visitor's area of the parking lot. He knew Hulse was not going to be in a meeting.

Cal badged his way through security and took the elevator to the fourth floor. Joseph Thompson's secretary, Dorthy, gave Cal a puzzled look as he approached her desk.

"I'm here for the meeting. Is it going to be on this floor?"

"What meeting is that?"

"I received an email from Joseph yesterday telling me to be here for a ten o'clock meeting."

"Just a minute, Cal."

She knocked on Thompson's door and slipped into his office. A few minutes later, she was back. "There isn't any meeting, Cal. There has to be some mix-up."

Cal took his laptop out of his briefcase, entered his password, and went to his emails. He turned the screen toward Dorthy.

She glanced at the email and shook her head. "I don't know what to say. It's from Joseph's email, but there's no meeting scheduled."

Cal immediately sensed another trap. He took out his cell, called Myron, and told him what was happening. Myron told him to wait inside the main entrance and that he would be there in twenty minutes.

Cal called Jonathan while he was waiting. When Cal filled Jonathan in, his friend told him to expect another tail. "Have Myron try to lose them and, if that doesn't work, tell him to go to the Stanford Shopping Center."

When Myron pulled up in front of the building, a man walked by the Tahoe and dropped some papers as he was passing. He bent down to pick up the papers and continued on toward the entrance.

Cal slid into the Tahoe, and Myron sped out of the parking lot. He kept his eye on his rearview mirror as he wove through city blocks. He could not see anyone following, which bothered him.

He started back toward the city when he thought about the man who had bent down near the rear of the Tahoe.

Bennett walked back to his car and activated the monitor for his tracking device. He drove out of the parking area and turned in the direction taken by the Chevy Tahoe. He remained a mile behind the SUV with no need to keep it in sight.

He smiled to himself, thinking how well his plan had come together.

Myron exited the 101 when they reached Millbrae and drove into the town until he found a convenience store. He pulled to the rear of the parking area, parked, and stepped out of the vehicle.

Cal asked, "What are you doing?"

Myron did not answer, but got down on his hands and knees and began probing around the rear fender. It only took a minute to find the tracking device, magnetically attached to the underside of the fender. He detached it and came back to the driver's seat.

Cal looked at it. "What is it?"

"A tracking device. They don't have to follow us; they follow this." He placed it on the dash. "Call Jonathan and ask him what he wants us to do."

Jonathan listened as Cal told him about the tracking device. He considered telling them to destroy it, then thought of a better idea. He told them to stay online while he went to his computer. When he came back, he told them to drive back to the city and pitch the device into some plants at 189 Santa Ana Avenue.

Myron looked at Cal, and they both shrugged as Myron returned to the freeway and motored on to the city. Cal used the GPS on his phone to direct Myron across town to St Francis Wood. The address was on the corner of Santa Ana and St Francis with a large fountain dominating the intersection. Following Jonathan's instructions, after wiping his prints off the device, Myron pitched it into the shrubs bordering the walkway to the building's front door. Like most of the homes in the area, the building was a two-story, Mediterranean-style home with a white stucco exterior and rust colored tile roof.

Myron turned to Cal. "Nice neighborhood."

Cal nodded. "A lot of the city's politicos live here."

When they were home, Cal looked at Jonathan, who was smiling. "Dropped it off like I asked you?"

Both Cal and Myron nodded. Jonathan glanced at the telephone number he had written down, picked up his burner, and made the call. "An armed home invasion crew is going to hit the home at 189 Santa Ana Avenue in the city, probably tonight."

He hung up as the person on the other end was shouting questions. Myron asked, "Who lives at one eighty-nine Santa Ana?"

"Lincoln Fenton."

Bennett followed the electronic trail toward San Francisco. When the Tahoe left the freeway at Millbrae, he assumed they were just stopping for gas, or some other inconsequential reason, such as a bathroom stop. When he reached St Francis Wood, he cruised by 189 Santa Ana. He was not surprised that Hulse and Scanlan would be in an expensive house. They were both quite wealthy. He passed the address a second time to ensure his electronic reading was correct.

He called the number Vivian Hughes had provided, again going to voicemail. This time, he left a message telling her he had located Jonathan Scanlan. The woman called him back almost immediately.

"Your message said you found Jonanthan Scanlan."

"Well, I followed Cal Hulse to the address. I assume he and Scanlan are together."

"What is the location?"

"One eighty-nine Santa Ana in San Francisco."

"That's great. Let me know your expenses, and there will also be a nice bonus."

"I will. Say, why don't we get together tonight to celebrate?"

"I'm sorry, I have other plans."

"Well, maybe the next time you're in Los Angeles."

"Sure." After she hung up, she immediately called Jasper with the address for Hulse and possibly Scanlan. He, in turn, wasted no time calling the handler.

Within minutes, the handler had organized the troops.

CHAPTER 59

E ric Bennett checked out of his hotel and caught an early evening flight to Los Angeles. The following day, he was in his office in Century City, paying bills, when a man knocked on his office door. The man at the door was a middle-aged white man of average height with thinning brown hair and fleshy features. He was dressed in an inexpensive blue suit.

Bennett gestured with a wave for the man to come in. The man closed the door behind him and offered an innocuous smile as he took one of the visitor's chairs.

"Mr. Bennett, I presume?"

"Yes, Eric Bennett. How can I help you?"

"Actually, I'm here on behalf of Vivian Hughes. She wanted me to give you this." He reached inside his briefcase, drew out a nine-millimeter Sig Sauer P938 with an attached suppressor, and shot Eric Bennett in the forehead. The force initially rocked the investigator back before his upper body fell across his desk. The suppressor muffled much of the sound, but the weapon's discharge was still somewhat loud.

The man in the visitor's chair listened for any sound of alarm. Hearing none, he stood and left the office, again closing the door behind him after wiping his prints off the doorknob.

———

The morning after his call to the police, Jonathan and his friends turned to the local news station. There was no news regarding a home invasion attempt at the house on Santa Ana Avenue. Jonathan was not surprised. He thought it might take more than half a day to put together such an attack.

Jonathan decided to hit some balls at the driving range at the Harding Park Golf Course. Bo followed him to the door only to be left with an expression of abandonment. He finally stopped staring at the door when Cory offered a couple of treats.

At two in the morning, two large sedans pulled up in front of 189 Santa Ana. The lights that normally would go on when the sedan's doors were opened had been disconnected. The seven men who stepped out of the vehicles silently closed the car doors.

All but one man drew silenced pistols as they made their way to the front door. The other man carried a heavy battering ram. The house was silent and dark. The lead man motioned to the man with the battering ram. The man swung the ram with force, hitting the door just below the lock.

Knowing the noise could alert someone in the neighborhood, the men stormed into the house, planning to kill its occupants and be out in minutes. Suddenly, the entry lights went on, and police in tactical gear swarmed the entry, pointing their weapons at the intruders.

The police were shouting for the seven men to drop their weapons and get down on the floor. One man raised his Glock and was immediately hit by a dozen bullets. The remaining six dropped their pistols and got down on their knees.

The weapons were kicked aside, and the six men's hands were cuffed behind their backs. The entire episode took less than ninety seconds.

One of the officers in SWAT gear bent down by one of the intruders and said, "How fucking stupid can you be to hit our chief detective's house?"

A woman from the prosecutor's office stepped forward and told the officer to back off. "These guys haven't been Mirandized. I don't want this screwed up." It was not lost on the woman that, unlike every other home invasion she knew of, these guys came to kill, not steal.

The police had filmed the event, and the press was now screaming for it, but a police statement explained that it would be made available at a later time. They were happy to release the mug shots. When questioned, the spokesperson for the department was vague when questioned about how the police had prior knowledge of the attack.

Jonathan, Cory, Cal, and Myron were totally engrossed with the local news coverage. Jonathan thought that being the home of SFPD's chief detective, it might also appear on the cable networks.

——————

While the handler was also following the news intensely, his attitude was not as upbeat as those at Jackson Street. By nature, he was not one to overreact, but at the moment, he wanted to throw something against the wall.

He also did not believe in karma, but there were way too many botched attempts. He accepted that Hulse and Scanlan were highly intelligent, perhaps even clever, but this was over the top. He knew the investigator had followed Hulse into the city using an electronic tracking device. Obviously, the device had been discovered.

He was also running out of soldiers. He had no concern about any of the intruders giving the authorities information that would lead back to him. They had no idea who hired them. His biggest problem was that he was running out of ideas.

He considered hiring another private investigator, since Mr. Bennett was no longer available. He knew Bennett had drawn Hulse out with a false email from INA. That would not work twice. Perhaps a literary award for Scanlan? After INA, the validity of such an award would certainly to checked out. He went back to thinking Cory Bishop was the weak link with her continued employment at Lockheed.

His people had hacked into Lockheed's employment files, but her residence was still shown as the condominium in San Carlos, which was, of course, vacant.

The handler wondered how much longer the people he reported to would wait before they began shopping for a new handler. He had been told that they had nothing to do with John Owen's demise, but he had doubts.

CHAPTER 60

The foursome was sitting around the breakfast table, still discussing the Santa Ana debacle, when Cory turned to Jonathan. "Will this change anything?"

Jonathan's smile evaporated. "Not really. Until we can expose Independence's secrets, whatever they are, we're still a threat."

He turned to Cal. "Any progress?"

"Not really. I'm thinking about attacking from a different angle."

"Which is?"

"Follow the money."

Cal was greeted with three blank stares. "The money that was used to set up the company."

Myron asked, "Can you do that?"

"We'll see."

Later that morning, the doorbell rang. Since they were neither expecting a guest or a delivery, everyone momentarily froze. Myron drew a gun as Jonathan approached the door. He peered through the glass surrounding the door before opening it.

Carmen Costello smiled at Jonathan. "Morning, Jonathan."

"Carmen." Jonathan stood stunned in the doorway.

"Can I come in?'

"Of course." Jonathan stood aside as Carmen walked into the entry.

"My Jonathan, quite an upgrade from Green Street."

When Jonathan did not respond, Carmen made her way into the living room, carefully stepping around Bo's toys. Cory was staring at her from a sofa while Myron was leaning against the wall by the fireplace. The fact that Myron was holding a Glock G19 by his side was not lost on Carmen.

"Beautiful home, Jonathan. And this must be Cory Bishop. Is Cal around?"

As if on cue, Cal walked into the room. She looked at Myron. "I don't believe I've had the pleasure."

In response, Myron left the room.

Jonathan moved next to the FBI agent. "How did you find us?"

Carmen paused, as if deciding whether she wished to answer the question. She finally shrugged and smiled. "Your change of address at the post office."

Jonathan stepped back, realizing this simple act had exposed his friends.

"Calm down, Jonathan. It was easy for me as an agent. It wouldn't be so easy for the people at Independence."

Cory studied Carmen Costello. She had to admit the woman was quite attractive and dressed well to enhance her figure. She also thought her mannerisms with Jonathan seemed to suggest familiarity. While perhaps unfounded, she did not like Agent Costello.

Jonathan's expression was not warm and friendly. "So, why are you here?"

"I'm aware of the attacks on you and on Cal, and I have no doubt that someone at Independence is behind them." She glanced across the room at Cal. "I'm also sure Cal is trying to uncover what Independence is trying to protect. I want in on it when he has the answer."

"Ah, career enhancement."

"Yes, but you might find it useful to have a friend at the bureau."

"What does Senior Agent in Charge Cain think about all this?"

"He agrees there's something fishy going on, but at the moment, he's staying on the sidelines."

Jonathan stared at Carmen. "Does he know about this visit or where we are?"

Carmen shook her head. "No."

"Is the bureau looking at Independence?"

"No. Their only involvement was trying to track down the hacker who got into the company's systems." She glanced at Cal. "They have no idea who the hacker is."

Cal's face flushed with anger. "I was questioned."

"Yes, I know. An anonymous phone call claimed it was you."

"Anonymous, my ass."

"I agree. Independence believed it was you and set up the call."

Jonathan wanted a little more. "How far is this friend at the bureau willing to go?"

Carmen handed him a slip of paper. "This is the number of a burner phone I just bought. I'm not willing to put my career on the line, but I'll give you whatever help I can. I have to get back to the office." She took Jonathan's arm, gave it a squeeze as she walked out of the room. Jonathan followed and opened the door for her. She gave him a kiss on the cheek as she whispered, "She's very beautiful."

Obviously, this was not lost on Cory. When Jonathan returned to the room, she said, "I don't like that woman. Do you think we can trust her?"

"Up to a point. If we figure out the big secret at Independence, she'll want a piece of the credit. Look, she isn't interested in us, and maybe she can prove helpful."

From her expression, in was obvious Cory was not sold on Carmen Costello. She could barely wait until they were alone when she could drill Jonathan on his history with the agent.

CHAPTER 61

Rick Scanlan had no investigative experience and, therefore, no plan for how to find his brother. After checking into the Marker at Union Square, Rick drove to Jonathan's apartment on Green Street. There was no answer when he buzzed Jonathan's unit, so he tried other apartments in the building.

One apartment buzzed him into the entry. A middle-aged woman in jeans and a sweatshirt opened the door of her ground-level unit.

Rick had prepared a bullshit story that he thought would fly. "Hi, I'm Rick Scanlan, Jonathan's brother. I'm trying to get a hold of him. Our father just had a heart attack, and I haven't been able to reach Jonathan. I know he moved, but I don't have his new address. Can you help me?"

"No, I'm sorry. I've only been here a few months and barely knew him."

"Do you think anyone else in the building might know where he is?"

"I have no idea."

Realizing he was getting nowhere, he thanked the woman and left the building. He did not know the city well, but he did know that Union Street was an active area, and his brother was a single guy who did not cook.

He walked down to Union and began checking out the bars and restaurants. It was past the lunch hour and too early for the dinner crowd, but Perry's was open. The hostess greeted him when he walked in with a nice smile.

"Would you like a table?"

"Not right now, thanks. Do you know Jonathan Scanlan?"

Her smile faded as she took a serious look at Rick. "Yes, I know Jon. Why?"

Rick thought he might be getting somewhere. "I'm his brother, and I'm trying to get in touch with him. Our father had a heart attack, and I can't find Jonathan. He moved out of his place on Green, and I thought, if he was a regular here, someone might know where he is."

The hostess was young and pretty, but not stupid. "I have no idea."

"Would anyone else know, like the bartender?"

"No. Jon never hung out at the bar. I'm sorry, but I can't help you." She turned and walked back into the restaurant.

Rick was not discouraged as he walked back to his car. He had not expected to hit paydirt the first afternoon.

While Rick and Jonathan were far from being close, Rick was familiar with Jonathan's habits and interests. He knew Jonathan had been a highly ranked amateur golfer. Rick had no interest in golf and had never played the game, but he did know the basics.

He knew avid golfers spent time at driving ranges and putting greens to work on their game. He purchased a map of San Francisco and the Bay Area. If Jonathan were still in the city, he assumed he would practice at a local course. He also knew Jonathan was, by nature, not a joiner, so he thought it unlikely his brother would be a member at a private golf course.

The map also provided an index that listed organizations and facilities by categories, such as libraries, hospitals, and cemeteries, and noted the location of each facility on the map. Eight golf courses were listed. Rick went online and wrote down the phone number of each course.

He eliminated Sharps Park and Cypress because of their locations and began calling the other six. He asked two questions: are you a public course, and do you have a driving range? The Olympic was private, and the Golden Gate Park course was only nine holes, dropping the list to four courses.

Rick had purchased Jonathan's first book and cut his brother's picture out of the back cover. He noted the locations of the four eighteen-hole courses, all of which had driving ranges. His plan was to visit each the following day.

Feeling good about his game plan, Rick went downstairs to happy hour at Tratto.

The following morning, Rick rolled out of bed with a slight hangover. A Bloody Mary with breakfast helped stabilize things. Rick did not consider himself an alcoholic, just a social drinker, a conclusion some might dispute.

Rick's first stop was the Presidio Golf Course in the Richmond District. He went to the driving range and tried to find the manager. Eventually, he found a man of about fifty with the weathered face of someone who spent a great deal of time outdoors.

Rick showed him Jonathan's picture, and the man shrugged. "A lot of people come here to hit a few balls. I don't recognize him."

"If he comes here, he'd probably be a regular."

"I don't know what to tell you. Like I said, I don't recognize him."

"Thanks."

Rick went back to his car and drove across the park to the Lincoln Golf Course at 34th Avenue. The manager at the range also did not remember Jonathan coming to the course. A woman at the Lake Merced course also did not recognize Jonathan from the picture. She added, "Good-looking guy like that; if he were here, I'd remember him."

Harding Park Golf Course at Lake Merced was a different story. Harding was a championship course with a history of hosting major pro tournaments. The manager at the driving range, David Sato, smiled when he saw Jonathan's picture.

"Sure, that's Jon. He's here pretty often. Man, he has a sweet swing."

"Does he come on a particular day, like Wednesdays?"

"Not really. What's this about?"

Rick could sense Sato was becoming suspicious. "I'm doing an article on him, because of his books, and I'm having trouble locating him."

David Sato was having a bad feeling about the man and now regretted telling him anything.

Realizing he had pushed it as far as it would go, Rick thanked the man and left.

He sat in his car in the parking lot, trying to think of his next move. He had found a place frequented by his brother. Of course, it could be weeks before Jonathan returned to the course. Sato was already suspicious and sitting in his car in the parking lot day after day would probably have the man contacting Jonathan or the police.

He thought about contacting the man who had made the offer and fronted the ten thousand. Rick assumed the man was as unethical as he was, and as soon as he mentioned Jonathan's connection to Harding, Rick would no longer be needed.

The driving range hours were from 6:30 to forty-five minutes before sunset, six days a week. Mondays, it opened at 7:30. Rick did not know exactly when sunset occurred, but if he had to watch the range on a constant basis, he would be in for twelve-hour days. Not a task he would be looking forward to.

If the driving range were in Southern California, Rick had people he could use, but he did not have any contacts in the Bay Area. He thought about setting up a camera to cover the parking lot, but technology was not his thing, and he had no idea what his brother was driving.

He knew Jonathan was not a crack-of-dawn type of guy, and he could not see his brother showing up to hit balls in the early morning, so he was probably looking at 9:00 to 4:00, a little more manageable.

As he drove out of the parking lot, he looked for a place where he could park and observe the golfers as they drove into the facility. He found a spot just outside Harding Road.

Rick decided to start his surveillance the following morning.

CHAPTER 62

The daily routine resumed at Jackson Street. Jonathan and Bo would go for their run around ten, Cory worked on her contracts, and Myron went for long walks, exploring the Presidio. Cal had found new energy as he attempted to track down the source of the original investment money at Independence.

When spending money started to dwindle, Cal and Jonathan would make their way to one of their banks. They never used the same branch twice and would frequently leave the city so as not to create a pattern.

It had been several days since Jonathan had hit balls at the range, and even longer since he had played a round. The short courses like Golden Gate and the Presidio held no appeal, and he did not find Lincoln or Lake Merced adequately challenging. He gave Harding a call, but all the tee times were booked.

He sighed and decided to at least go out and hit some balls. It was early afternoon when he threw his bag in the back of the Tahoe and headed out to the Harding range.

Rick was bored to tears after five days of sitting in his rented Nissan Murano and was beginning to doubt his game plan when Jonathan drove past in his Chevy Tahoe. It took a minute for Rick to figure out that he had just scored. His thoughts raced to the money that would bail him out when he told the man in LA where Jonathan was staying.

His nerves were tight as he waited for his brother to leave the golf course. For a moment, he thought Jonathan might be playing a round, which meant at least a four-hour wait. That thought was dispelled when the Tahoe drove out of the facility in a little over an hour.

He gave Jonathan a minute's headstart before he pulled away from the curb. Rick did not want to give his brother too much of a lead, as he was afraid of losing him at a stoplight. He pulled his Lakers cap down, hoping it would keep his brother from recognizing him. As it turned out, Jonathan seemed to pay no attention to the car behind him as he drove across the city. Rick fell back when he sensed Jonathan was close to his destination.

Rick was taken aback when Jonathan pulled into the driveway of a large, impressive home on Jackson Street. He watched his brother take his golf bag out of the Tahoe and walked into the house.

Rick could not wait. He dug the phone number of the man in Los Angeles out of his wallet and dialed.

The man answered on the second ring.

"I found him."

"Who is this?"

"Rick Scanlan. I found my brother."

"Where is he?"

"In San Francisco."

"Wonderful, where in San Francisco?"

Rick smiled and said, "I'll tell you when I have my money." Rick had a long history of dealing with people with promises.

"We'll give you your money, just tell me where he is."

Rick pulled out his checkbook. "My account at Wells Fargo is 284115048. I'll tell you when I can confirm the money is in my account."

"Come on, Rick."

"How long will it take you to make the deposit?"

There was a pause on the other end. Then, "Maybe two hours."

"Call me when it's done. I'll check with the bank, and if it's there, I'll give you the address."

Rick ended the call and sat back in his car, impressed with how he had handled the call."

The man in Los Angeles immediately called the handler. The handler listened without comment as the man related the conversation. When he finished, the handler asked, "Do you believe him?"

The man thought for a moment. "I'd give it fifty-fifty. He's a hustler, but he might have found Scanlan."

The handler took so long, the man wondered if he had lost the connection. "Finally, the handler said, "All right, give me the account number."

Two hours later, Rick's phone rang. "Check with your bank."

"I'll be back to you in two minutes."

It was more like ten minutes. "Okay, he's at 2710 Jackson Street."

"I hope for your sake he is."

The man's last statement bothered Rick as he put down his phone.

As soon as he had the address, he called the handler. Within minutes, the handler contacted the man who replaced Robert Allen, who had been part of the Santa Ana fiasco. "Put together five or six men to hit twenty-seven ten Jackson in San Francisco. I want it done tonight, and I don't want anyone in the building walking away."

A few hours later, the man called the handler. "I was only able to bring in two guys. After Woodside and Santa Ana, we don't have many men left in the Bay Area."

The handler was not happy, but he had to acknowledge the problem. "Three should be enough."

CHAPTER 63

Jonathan, Cory, and Myron were watching a Hitchcock movie on Turner Classics when Cal rushed into the room.

"I have it," He shouted.

Jonathan hit pause as the three turned to him. Jonathan looked at his friend. "What?"

"I have Independence's big secret!" Cal's face was flushed with excitement.

"Like the old saying, I followed the money. The initial capital bounced around the world before landing at Capital One in New York. Before that, it was at Deutsche Bank and Barclays."

"So?"

"The money started its journey in Beijing." His three friends stared at him in silence.

"Independence is wholly owned by the Chinese, which means the CCP."

"Holy shit!" Was Cory's contribution.

Jonathan stood up and stared at Cal. "Are you sure?"

"Absolutely."

Jonathan picked up his phone. "I'm calling Carmen."

Carmen's phone rang three times before she picked up. "Carmen, you need to get over here right now."

"Jonathan, I was just about to go to bed."

"Cal figured out what Independence has been hiding."

"What is it?"

"Not over the phone."

"All right. I'm on my way."

Rear Window was forgotten as they sat in silence, absorbing the implications of Cal's discovery. Only Bo seemed unaffected by the news.

A half hour later, Jonathan answered the door and led Carmen into the room. Carmen's expression seemed to be a combination of hope and skepticism.

Jonathan said, "You might want to sit down."

Carmen ignored him and looked at Cal. "What did you find?"

"The capital that was used to start Independence came from Beijing."

It took a moment for Cal's statement to sink in. "Tell me what you know."

Cal repeated what he had told his friends. Carmen let Cal finish before she began asking questions. It was past midnight when Carmen accepted the validity of the discovery. She sat down as she thought through who she needed to call and what her next steps would be.

As the four stared at Carmen, waiting for what she would say, a black Mercedes rolled to a stop in front of the house. Three men left the car, one carrying a battering ram. They walked quietly up the path to the front door. The two men with weapons drawn stepped aside, allowing the man with the battering ram to approach the door.

He swung the heavy ram as hard as he could, hitting the door just below the lock. The noise was tremendous, followed by the heavy door crashing open. Everyone in the room spun around as the three men rushed into the entry with pistols drawn.

The width of the doorway made them enter the house in single file. The lead man was raising his pistol when Myron shot him in the chest. As he fell, the second man shot Myron. He then leveled his gun at Jonathan. Before he could fire, Carmen placed two shots in the man.

The third man, who had used the battering ram, was about to fire when Bo lunged forward. The impact of the seventy-pound dog knocked the man backward, and in doing so, he stepped on Bo's rubber bone. Before he could recover his balance, Carmen shot him.

Jonathan rushed to where Myron was kneeling on the floor. He picked up a sweater that had been draped on the back of a chair and pressed it against the wound that was bleeding heavily. He called out, "Call 911. Tell them we need an ambulance, that a man has been shot."

The police were the first to arrive. When they saw the three men on the floor, they immediately drew their weapons. Carmen shouted, "FBI," and stepped forward with her credentials in her hand. The lead patrol officer examined her creds before holstering his gun. He immediately called it in, explaining the situation and asking for support.

Minutes later, the ambulance arrived. Paramedics rushed in and, after confirming the three men on the floor were dead, they began treating Myron. As soon as they stopped the bleeding, they rolled him onto a gurney and hustled him to the ambulance.

Jonathan followed them as they loaded Myron into the ambulance. When he asked, they told him they were going to San Francisco General.

The large house quickly became crowded. When the SFPD detectives arrived, they herded Cal, Jonathan, and Cory into the kitchen. Gregory Cain showed up with two other agents in tow. A minor pissing match ensued between Lincoln Fenton and Gregory Cain over who would be running the show.

A tentative détente was reached with Cain having overall control while the SFPD technicians would work the scene. Fenton wanted access to Cal, as he recalled his earlier exchange with the man, but his demands were denied by Cain, who claimed Cal Hulse was part of a highly classified FBI investigation.

Lincoln Fenton was an unhappy man when he stormed out of the house.

Senior Agent in Charge Gregory Cain led Cal out of the kitchen while motioning for Carmen to join him. Once separated from the others, he asked Cal to repeat what he had told Carmen.

Cal walked the agent through the series of transactions that moved the money from the Bank of China to Capital One. When he finished, he said, "I can provide account numbers and transaction dates."

Cain leaned back against the wall, his mind churning with the implications of the discovery. After several moments, he said, "This is way over my head. I have to call DC."

Carmen asked, "Are you going to call the director?"

Gregory Cain shook his head. "He has to be told, but I have to go through channels. How many people know about this?"

Cal got a very bad feeling. He visualized being taken to a dark and lonely place while the government dealt with a major security disaster. Before he could answer, Carmen said, "Just Cal Hulse, Jonathan Scanlan, the woman, Cory something, and the man who was shot."

As if reading Cal's thoughts, Cain said, "Don't worry, you're not going to disappear, but we can't let word get out before we move on to Independence."

"So, we can just stay here until the dust settles?"

The senior agent thought about it for a moment before responding. "You and your friends are going to have to move out for a day or two while the forensic people do their thing. Is there somewhere you can go until they're done?"

Cal was thinking about it when Cain said, "We have a safe house in North Beach. Why don't we use that?"

Cal was not sure how safe the safe house would be when Cain turned to Carmen.

"Can you stay with them until they can move back here?"

"Of course."

"When the techs finish, you can move back, but I'll have security covering the house until this whole thing is over."

Cain turned away and began making calls on his phone. Carmen led Cal back to the kitchen and explained the new program.

When Jonathan was told they were about to be moved to North

Beach for a couple of days, he turned to Cory. "Pack up my stuff and take whatever Bo will need. I'm going to the hospital."

Carmen tried to explain that they were all going to the safe house. When Jonathan shook his head, she called Cain back into the room. He tried to convince Jonathan that it was safer if they stayed together."

Jonathan's expression was uncompromising as he looked at the senior agent. "I'm going to be there for Myron."

Cain stared at Jonathan for a moment, finally breaking eye contact. "All right, but one of my agents will accompany you."

———

The handler stared out the window of his office and thought about what had just happened and what his future would be. He was confident his connection to Independence was untraceable. The new CEO they had installed only knew him as a voice on a burner phone.

He was not confident that the people in Beijing would be understanding. He had always had an exit strategy, and he began organizing what he would need to disappear.

The attack on Scanlan's home had to have been a setup. An armed FBI agent at the house could not have been a coincidence. Besides himself, his man in Los Angeles and the men he sent, there was only one person who knew where Hulse and Scanlan were hiding.

He picked up his phone and called his man in LA. "Rick Scanlan told his brother we would be coming."

"Are you sure?"

"Yes. Take care of Rick Scanlan."

CHAPTER 64

When Jonathan and his FBI companion arrived at San Francisco General Hospital on Potrero, he was directed to the waiting room outside of surgery. An elderly man and a distraught couple in their forties were in the waiting room. Neither paid any attention to Jonathan or Agent James Siguenza when they settled onto their plastic chairs.

Jonathan had been told that Myron was in surgery, but no information was available concerning the extent of his injury. Siguenza was a pleasant man, somewhere in his forties. He attempted to make conversation with Jonathan, only to find the man unresponsive.

After a few hours, a doctor came into the waiting room and talked with the man and woman. He spoke in a hushed voice, but Jonathan understood their son had been in an accident. Whatever he said seemed to bring relief to the couple,

It was nearly four in the morning when a woman in scrubs came into the room and approached Jonathan and Siguenza.

"I understand you're here for Myron Rossi."

Jonathan stood while the agent remained seated. "Yes, I am."

"Are you a relative of Mr. Rossi?"

"No, a close friend."

"I see. Well, the surgery went well. He lost quite a bit of blood and sustained a good deal of muscle damage, but we expect he'll be able to make a full recovery."

"Great news."

"He'll be in intensive care for a day or two and then transferred to a private room. He's going to need a bit of physical therapy when he's released."

"Okay."

"I have to say, I've performed surgery on a good number of people, but never one quite like Mr. Rossi."

"I don't understand."

"The reason the damage was not worse is because the man's muscular development is incredible."

Jonathan had to smile. "I'll tell him that when I'm able to see him."

Jonathan was in a better place on the ride to the safe house. The house was a one-story building with little to say for itself as to style. An FBI agent sat in a chair in the small living room. When Jonathan asked, the man directed him to Cory's bedroom. He stripped off his clothes and slid into bed, careful not to wake Cory. He was asleep before his head hit the pillow.

Jonathan woke up to an empty bed. When he glanced at his watch, he realized he had slept late into the morning. He staggered into the bathroom, still only half awake, showered until the water began running cold, shaved, and threw on jeans and a T-shirt.

When he stepped into the living room, he found the small room crowded with Cal, Cory, Carmen, Gregory Cain, and Bo. Cory smiled. "I wanted to let you sleep in. I hear Myron is going to be all right."

Jonathan nodded. "It'll take some time and physical therapy, but they told us he'll fully recover." He turned to Gregory Cain. "So, what's the story on Independence?"

"We went in early this morning. All the senior management had cleared out except Jordy Chapel, the newly installed CEO. He had no idea what was going on."

"What's the word out of DC?"

Cain looked away for a moment before turning back to Jonathan.

"A lot of red faces at the DOD. I think they want to bury the whole thing."

Jonathan's face became clouded with anger. "Not going to happen. These people have been trying to kill us for months. Myron was shot, and let's not forget about the Uber driver, killed at the Ferry Building, and the husband and wife on Maple Street. What about Jean Royce, the realtor, and all the dead guys that were trying to kill us? How the hell can they bury all that?"

Gregory shrugged. "They're pretty good at it." He gave Jonathan a weak smile. "You didn't hear it from me, but the senior senator on the armed services committee just resigned. Rumor is, he was influential in pushing through the approvals when Independence came on the scene, not that you'll be writing about all this in your next book."

"I assume there aren't going to be any charges about Myron using an unlicensed gun."

"Of course not."

"I want him to be licensed as a private investigator in California by the end of the day."

"I can't do that. California has control over that process, and I know there's a long list of requirements, and I doubt Mr. Rossi could meet any of them."

"Myron will be a licensed investigator by tomorrow, or Constantine Weiland and I will be holding a press conference."

Jonathan's rage had been replaced by a smile. "Guess what. I have an idea for my next book." He turned to Cal and Cory. "Let's go home."

ACKNOWLEDGMENTS

Thank you to Amanda and Kate for your love and support.

I am thankful for my late wife, Linda. She was the original editor of my work and without her encouragement I may never have published.

Thanks to Stacey at Edits by Stacey for helping with the formatting and pubishing.

Finally, thank you, reader. Without you the story will just be in my head. Thanks for supporting indie authors.

ABOUT THE AUTHOR

Barry Solloway was born and raised in San Francisco. He has also lived in Los Gatos and Marin. He now lives in Napa with Champ, his chocolate lab, where he's close to his two daughters, Amanda and Kate.

To his mother's great discomfort, Barry as a teenager worked four summers as an ordinary seaman in the merchant marine, and two summers at casinos in Nevada. He took a year off between achieving his bachelors and masters degrees and hitchhiked throughout Europe.

After doing his service in the Army, he managed businesses in Silicon Valley. He now writes and enjoys all that Napa Valley has to offer.

IN BOOKSTORES EVERYWHERE

BARRY SOLLOWAY

www.ingramcontent.com/pod-product-compliance
Lightning Source LLC
Chambersburg PA
CBHW020656110726
47901CB00001B/203